FORGOTTEN BETROTHAL

A PRIDE & PREJUDICE VARIATION

L.M. ROMANO

Edited by Debbie Styne and Katie Jackson

Cover Design by Cloudcat Design

On the cover: *The Gallant Suitor*, Edmund Blair Leighton

ISBN 978-1-951033-83-5 (ebook) and 978-1-951033-84-2 (paperback)

To my husband, Brandon, who, despite his aversion to all things Jane Austen, was the first audience for every chapter that was written and an unwavering champion of his wife's literary ambitions.

TABLE OF CONTENTS

PROLOGUE

Staffordshire
December 1, 1791

A fire crackled merrily behind the grate, casting long shadows on the walls of the earl's study, the movements of the flames the only sign of activity in the otherwise still space. Two gentlemen sat quietly, one still fixed upon the missive in his hand as the other silently contemplated the look of disgust and defeat that had settled upon his friend's visage.

"Can you believe this drivel, Matlock?" the gentleman scoffed with considerable affront.

"I still believe you are giving this matter far too much weight. We both know Lord Pendley is a bothersome old fool. Do not let his presumption ruin the celebration that this visit is supposed to acknowledge!"

"I cannot simply set this aside! It is happening again. Everything I endured with my wife, all of those rakes who pursued her…and now it will happen to my little girl!"

"Your daughter is only a few months old. If you are

already worried about her presentation, I shudder to think what your anxieties will be once she is grown!"

"Did you not just read the same pandering rubbish I did? Pendley and his ilk are already after my child, and she is still in her cradle! How can I possibly protect her?"

In a fit of agitation, the master of the house stood and began to pace across the room. His restless movements were tracked by his concerned companion, but he could not stop. He needed an outlet to vent his frustrations and feelings of helplessness. He likely would have continued in this vein for some time, had his friend not risen and gripped his shoulders.

"Do you truly wish to protect her?"

"With my life, Matlock."

"Your life should not be necessary, my friend. I was thinking of a formal agreement. A contract. For my son and your daughter."

"A betrothal?" *A good family, a certain future.* The proposed solution settled over his fraught mind like the sudden calming of a turbulent sea. "Yes, I—I think that could work."

Matlock held out his hand, smiling as he said, "We can discuss the particulars during our stay, but I think this will resolve your troubles. After all, with her future secure, what harm could possibly come her way?"

CHAPTER ONE

London
April 1812

Sunlight filtered through the misty haze blanketing the southern end of Hyde Park, the fragrant perfumes of spring blossoms announcing to all the arrival of a new season, replete with new possibilities. Despite her immersion in the glories of nature, Elizabeth Bennet could find no peace in her beautiful surroundings. A new season was merely a reminder of her pressing need for reflection, for a new understanding, for anything that could help her divine the reason for the turmoil plaguing her mind following her disastrous visit to her cousin's parsonage in Kent. A visit that had ended rather surprisingly with the absolute worst proposal of marriage Elizabeth had ever received, which was a rather impressive feat.

Marriage. *The last man in the world I could ever be prevailed upon to marry*. Had she really uttered such cold and unfeeling words? Granted the monumental shock that Mr Darcy, a man Elizabeth believed had only ever looked upon her to find fault, a man who had professed her to be merely *tolerable*, had instead avowed an ardent love and admiration for her, was enough to excuse some lack of delicacy on her part in her reply. Even now, over a week later, Elizabeth could no more understand the genesis of his affections than she could his determination to offer for her. What was as baffling as his declarations was the outright consternation he displayed upon receiving her refusal. Was he really so arrogant as to believe she simply returned his regard because he wished it? Perhaps she ought not to dwell on the faults in his character any further, for while her momentary anger at his presumption provided temporary relief for her troubled conscience, ultimately her anger only fed her feelings of guilt. For while Elizabeth had excelled in extolling Mr Darcy's failings, she had also completely disregarded his virtues. Despite his lack of manners, his criticisms of her family, and his interference in the matter of Mr Bingley and her lovelorn sister Jane, Elizabeth was forced to acknowledge that he was, at heart, a good man. This revelation had come to her through a rather shocking and well-written letter following her virulent rejection of his hand, in which he disclosed the true nature of his dealings with Mr Wickham.

The thought of *that* gentleman brought Elizabeth back to her surroundings. After briefly checking to ensure she had not lost sight of her uncle's maid, who had proven to be a rather reluctant walking companion, Elizabeth allowed the gentle breeze to soothe her agitated spirits. She had arrived on the southeast edge of the Serpentine and promptly settled her gaze on the gently winding waterway, watching as the waters ebbed and flowed, slithering lines in the sunlight appearing across the shallow river.

Snake-like. How appropriate! Handsomely outfitted in his dashing regimentals, Mr Wickham had arrived in her world like a snake in the grass, perfectly poised to unleash his poisoned tongue into an all too willing ear. How had she been so thoroughly deceived? More importantly, how had she allowed herself to form so swift a judgment based on the tales of such a new and altogether unknown acquaintance? Painful thoughts intruded upon her reflections as Elizabeth was forced to concede that vanity had been her downfall. Mr Wickham had flattered her where Mr Darcy had only shown her disdain, or so she had thought. What a silly fool she was!

Delving ever further into self-recrimination, Elizabeth reached into her reticule and extracted the life-changing missive that had so wholly devastated her spirits. As if it were an act of penance, she read Mr Darcy's words once again, and the pain of his recollections seeped from the very pages in her hand. Not only had he disclosed Mr Wickham's dissolute habits during their years at university, but he had also thoroughly refuted the charges laid against him regarding the provisions made in his father's will for his wayward godson.

If only such reckless spending was the worst of his crimes, for the tale that followed was so shocking, so utterly contemptible, Elizabeth could barely credit its veracity were it not for the ultimately damning nature of its contents. Mr Darcy would never—could never—jeopardise the reputation of his most-beloved sister without cause, and so Elizabeth was forced to acknowledge the truthfulness of the tale, a tale so heart-rending that Elizabeth felt keenly for a young woman she had never met. Poor Miss Darcy would no doubt struggle in the years to come as she entered the marriage mart with a thirty-thousand-pound weight about her shoulders. At least her brother would be there to defend her from the Mr Wickhams of this world. Her brother…her *honourable* brother.

Whatever his faults, Elizabeth could not forgive herself for so viciously attacking Mr Darcy that fateful day in Kent. How it must have injured him to hear her defend a rogue whose actions had proven so injurious to his family!

Turning from the peaceful prospect in front of her, so at odds with the disquiet in her mind, Elizabeth began her journey back to Stanhope Gate where her uncle's carriage would surely arrive soon to bear her back to Gracechurch Street. As she walked, she determined her feelings of guilt could only be assuaged by the opportunity to seek forgiveness for her intemperate words. But would Mr Darcy ever wish to see her again? Surely, no man would desire to seek the company of such a seemingly hateful young woman, despite his earlier professions of regard—a regard that certainly had not survived her unrestrained criticism. Not that Elizabeth regretted the inevitable loss of his affections. No, she simply needed some way to atone for her serious lapse in judgment, some way to restore her composure, and move beyond this unexpectedly trying season.

"Pardon, miss. I believe you dropped this."

Elizabeth was startled from her thoughts by the appearance of a distinguished-looking gentleman at her side. To her embarrassment, he appeared to be holding one of the pages of Mr Darcy's letter that had apparently slipped from her grasp as she rambled along the path. That a stranger might have glimpsed her missive caused a pang of unease which Elizabeth quickly endeavoured to suppress.

"Thank you, sir. I fear I have been rather inattentive this morning, which is somewhat unpardonable considering my delightful location."

"Ah, a fellow lover of nature. It is as I suspected, for not many ladies take to the paths so early on a spring morning."

Unsure how to proceed in this somewhat improper conversation without an introduction, Elizabeth took a moment to carefully study the affable man in front of her. His clothing was finely made, his Hessian boots were expertly polished, his cravat was elegantly tied, and by all appearances, he seemed to be a typical example of the wealthy sort of gentleman who populated the surrounding neighbourhoods. Wary of appearing too bold, Elizabeth thanked him once again and moved towards the nearby gate, espying her uncle's carriage waiting in the distance.

Had she glanced behind her, she might have found her puzzlement over her morning's reflections paled in comparison to the confusion and shock that had spread over the stranger's earnest face.

CHAPTER TWO

Click…click…click… Insensible of all sights, sounds, and thoughts save the sharp rap of his boots upon the pavement, Lord Nicholas Grey, Baron Grey de Rotherfield, journeyed home from Hyde Park with one goal in mind. His morning had not gone to plan, not even in the slightest way possible. After enduring a rather trying evening in one of the fashionable parlours of one of London's many wealthy and titled hostesses, Grey had hoped an early morning stroll would restore his spirits before his next inevitable foray into one of the many events of the Season. Instead, a seemingly innocuous meeting with a pleasant young woman had thrown his mind into disarray, as the potential ramifications of this casual encounter were, at the moment, too terrifying to contemplate.

Could it even be possible? He must be fit for Bedlam even to be considering the likeliness of such an unfathomable development. That he would meet *her*, of all people, by pure chance was surely too great an accident to occur, barring the work of Divine Providence.

"Good morning, Lord Grey!"

Startled from his thoughts as he approached the stairs to his London home, Grey looked up to find his predictably cheerful, elderly neighbour, Mr Townsend, descending from his abode, undoubtedly setting off on his daily constitutional. Unequal to company or any form of idle conversation, Grey tipped his hat, muttered a brief greeting in reply, and entered the vestibule of Tamworth House.

After divesting himself of his greatcoat, hat, and gloves, and informing the butler, Mr Tewes, that he was not home to callers, Grey hastened to his father's study, his mind set on the one alarming image he could not erase from his consciousness since his glimpse of the young woman earlier that morning. Convinced he was merely imagining such an improbability, he was sure the proof he needed was within his grasp. Searching the shelves that bordered the warm, masculine space, his eyes eventually alighted upon the miniature portrait he had so desperately sought.

It was an older picture, a replica made of a larger portrait that hung in the gallery at the family seat in Staffordshire. His father, the Earl of Tamworth, had commissioned its creation, and it had since occupied this small space in their London home, a treasured memento of a time now long past. Though slightly faded with age, the image was still as beautiful as the day on which it was composed. Whatever solace Grey hoped to find as he gazed upon the painted figure quickly evaporated, and in its place, wonder, trepidation, and unalloyed astonishment took root in his heart. Had he finally found the means to restore his fractured family? To bring life and joy back to his dear mother, who had for so long merely existed as a shade of her former self?

Lost in reflection, Grey's thoughts turned to the painful events of twenty years past, events that had forever changed his home and family, leaving naught but a trail of devastation in their wake. In the winter of 1791, a savage fever had gripped the countryside surrounding Heatherton Hall, the

Grey family estate in Staffordshire. It seemed that few were to be spared from the raging illness, as the epidemic spread amongst the family and serving staff alike. One of the afflicted was his own nanny, Sarah Summers, who had served the Grey family faithfully since his birth eight years prior. While firm with her young charge, Sarah possessed a gentle soul and was naturally beloved by the young heir. Even now, despite his confusion and consternation at the events which followed, Grey still remembered her with fondness, recalling the many times she comforted him with fanciful stories and sang sweet melodies as he drifted off to sleep.

At first, it seemed as though the nanny had escaped the worst effects of the illness, save several crazed fits that manifested at the height of her fevers. When the sickness finally passed, all were hopeful Sarah would make a full recovery and return to her duties in the newly occupied nursery. It was only as the weeks passed that doubts began to surface regarding the sombre and restrained demeanour of the usually serene and jovial young woman.

Grief was a perfectly natural response to her recent experience, as many were lost to the epidemic on the estate and in the nearby village, including a housemaid of whom Sarah had been particularly fond. Her melancholy, however, had slowly been accompanied by a pervading derangement. Dangers lurked in shadowed halls, unseen by all except the increasingly mistrustful servant. Grey's night-time stories lost their whimsical nature, and the comfort Sarah once brought to his youthful heart was tainted by a growing feeling of unease in her presence. His parents had hoped the changes they perceived in her temperament would pass, and once Sarah had fully recovered from her ordeal, she would return to the poised and peaceful woman who had diligently served their family for so many years. Unfortunately, his parents' misguided hope would bring unforeseen and wholly unexpected consequences.

As Sarah returned to her duties, the principal part of her day was spent attending to the youngest Grey child, a daughter, who had been born in the late summer to the unparalleled joy of Grey's mother who had remained hopelessly barren since his birth. Though he had only been eight years old at the time, Grey could recall his infant sister with perfect clarity. She had been such a happy babe, forever giggling at his boyish antics and easily pacified following the slightest moment of distress. Grey's mother, the countess, had hoped that her merry daughter would prove a balm to the distressed nanny, for who could contemplate sadness in the company of such pure and innocent joy?

Indeed, it seemed as though Sarah clung to the hopefulness that radiated from the young child, as she rarely released the tiny girl from her sight and assumed a fierce level of protectiveness concerning her welfare. Perhaps such possessiveness should have given his parents pause, but their own vigilance regarding the well-being of their treasured and long-awaited child had apparently blinded them to the unanticipated threat of an increasingly troubled mind. For one morning, on a bleak and frigid day in early December, Sarah Summers had simply disappeared.

Unaware of the significance of the day ahead, a young Nicholas Grey had bounded into the nursery apartments, eager to greet his little sister before shuffling off to his lessons with his many tutors. Accustomed to encountering the usual scene of a babbling child on her faithful nurse's knee, he was instead met with an empty, silent room devoid of any life whatsoever. Confused by the image before him, Grey had run to his parents to enquire after his sister, convinced his mother must have arranged alternate plans for her day. The worry that had promptly spread over his mother's countenance haunted him still, as a subsequent search of the estate had confirmed Sarah had unaccountably vanished, and harder still to comprehend, she had not disappeared alone.

"My lord?"

A swift knock on the study door preceded the entrance of his butler and pulled Grey from his troubled recollections.

"Yes, Tewes, what is it? I would prefer not to be disturbed at present."

"Of course, my lord, but I thought you would like to know Peters has returned from his earlier errand. He said you were anticipating a full report."

"Ah yes. Thank you. Please send him in."

Grey took a moment to settle his nerves as his manservant entered the room. The fool's errand he had rashly set him upon this morning now seemed less and less foolish in the light of his subsequent discovery.

"My lord, I followed the carriage you identified this morning to its destination. The young woman, a maid, and a middle-aged man travelled to a modest town home on Gracechurch Street," Peters explained after a swiftly executed bow.

"Gracechurch Street?"

"Yes, my lord. To the home of a Mr Edward Gardiner of Gardiner Imports in London."

A tradesman. Grey was unsure whether this revelation would make his next move easier or more challenging, assuming he still knew what move he intended to make. After thanking Peters for his service and dismissing him to return to his other duties, Grey moved to the side table that held a small decanter of brandy and poured himself a generous glass. While it was normally far too early in the day to consider such libations, the events of the morning seemed to justify his need for fortification.

Never in his life had he been so unsure of his responsibilities. He was accustomed to managing the family affairs, particularly those in London, as his parents preferred the solitude of the country to the bustle of the capital. Yet, he was presented with the rather frightening prospect of opening old wounds, wounds that had never fully healed, and he knew not how to bring any of it about. What if his burgeoning hopes were entirely misplaced? Should he risk the future happiness of his family on such an unfounded whim?

Shifting in his chair, Grey's attention was once again returned to the miniature in his hand, the subject gazing back at him with dark, sparkling eyes. His mother had been a beauty when she first graced the London scene with her dazzling presence. By all accounts, his father had fallen in love with her within moments of first making her acquaintance, proposing marriage before the end of her first Season. On the occasion of their marriage, when his mother had been but twenty years old, his father had commissioned a portrait to immortalise his stunning young bride, producing the miniature that Grey currently clutched in his hand.

It was that image that strengthened his resolve, for it was not his mother who stared up at him from the gilded frame, but instead, the identical visage of the young woman he had met by chance earlier that morning, strolling aimlessly in the verdant park.

CHAPTER THREE

Darcy House, London
April 1812

In a similar posture, staring into a likewise full glass of brandy, sitting only a stone's throw away in Berkeley Square, Fitzwilliam Darcy was meditating on that same pair of dark eyes. Even in the fantastical portrait conjured by his slightly addled mind, he still could not help but be drawn to the laughter he saw in her gaze. Unfortunately for Darcy, even in his imagination, the object of her merriment was undoubtedly himself.

Had it come to this? For months he had struggled in vain to escape the siren call of Elizabeth Bennet and the hold she possessed over his heart. And for what? To be rejected out of hand! No, not just rejected—*humiliated*, *chastised*, *downright flogged* for even daring to offer her the coveted position of Mrs Darcy. He had never once considered that *any* woman would reject his proposal should he decide to offer it, let alone a young woman with no fortune and no prospects, the one and only woman he could ever—

The glass tumbler slipped in his hand slightly, recalling Darcy to his current occupation. He was seated before the great desk in his study, staring at the veritable mountain of correspondence that had accumulated during his visit to his aunt's estate in Kent, letters that had still, more than a week after his return, remained unanswered. Lost to his inner turmoil, Darcy had rejected all invitations, declined all calls, and secreted himself away in his personal sanctuary, claiming the need to attend to pressing matters of business without the threat of disruption. However, instead of engaging in the various matters and dealings before him, Darcy had spent the last week nursing his wounds, sipping brandy, and staring aimlessly into the crackling fire as he endeavoured to discover how everything had gone so utterly and horribly wrong.

Normally fastidious in all things, Darcy's current state of indifference was entirely out of character for such an ordinarily self-possessed and competent young gentleman. In all his eight and twenty years of living, the last five as the master of a considerably large and profitable estate, Darcy had never once let his sensibility override his sense of duty. His responsibilities were numerous, and he considered it a privilege to carry out his many obligations to his tenants, servants, and most importantly, his family. Never before, though, had he felt the weight of such burdens as keenly as he did now. For what was the advantage of wealth and consequence if he was meant to continue on alone?

Setting down his glass, Darcy shuffled through a recently delivered batch of missives until the deplorably ink-blotted penmanship of his dear friend caught his eye. *Bingley*. While usually any reference to his buoyant, young friend brought cheer to Darcy's typically solemn disposition, now any thoughts of his gleeful companion plunged Darcy back into his tainted memories of his doomed sojourn in Hertfordshire. His stay at Bingley's leased estate of Netherfield Park was not meant to be anything more than an opportunity to assist a friend as he began his foray into the world of the landed class.

Charles Bingley had inherited a fortune from his family's long and successful years in trade, and when they met at Cambridge, the two young men had found an affinity for one another despite their exceedingly different temperaments. Darcy had been pleased to guide him in such an important new venture, and by all accounts, the estate at Netherfield was a perfect prospect to begin Bingley's rudimentary instruction. There had been nothing particularly remarkable about the small town of Meryton and its environs. The area was populated by modest estates belonging to equally insignificant squires and their sheltered families. If only Darcy had known what awaited him at the deceptively benign country manor!

It had been at their second meeting in Hertfordshire that Darcy had realised the potential dangers involved in paying too much attention to Miss Elizabeth Bennet. During what was otherwise a fairly unremarkable evening spent in local society at Lucas Lodge, Darcy's attention had been unexplainably drawn to her fine eyes as she chattered away with friends and new acquaintances, breathing life into even the most mundane conversations.

At first glance, she was not classically beautiful like her blonde and willowy elder sister; nevertheless, once he spied that irresistible gleam of humour upon her countenance, Darcy could not bring himself to look away. Charles' sister had teased him that evening for his distraction, but he found he could not repine the time spent gazing at Elizabeth from across the room, even if he had to endure Miss Bingley's snide remarks. Darcy swiftly discovered Elizabeth's smile somehow possessed the ability to brighten her entire aspect, and the delicate way she arched her brow when exercising her clever wit only served to ensnare him further. By the time the two eldest Miss Bennets were installed at Netherfield for their brief and uncomfortable stay, Darcy knew he was in considerable peril of losing himself entirely to the lively young woman, but only if he allowed his fascination with her to press on unchecked. And so, he had tried to distance himself, even to the point of spending half an hour alone in her company in the Netherfield library without uttering a single word. Such a struggle and for what?

Struggle. Darcy's brows pinched in agitation as he reluctantly recalled having revealed the extent of his struggles during the course of his proposal. What had he been thinking? Surely, that was not the best way to recommend his suit. Despite the value he placed on honesty, a sentiment he felt she would appreciate, Darcy could now acknowledge telling Elizabeth he loved her in spite of his better judgment had not been the best way to secure her acceptance.

While he was still fully convinced he had been right when he told her that she wilfully misunderstood him during their teasing banter in Bingley's sitting room, Darcy could now acknowledge he had also wilfully misunderstood *her.* Where he thought she had been flirting with him through her intelligent and often impertinent comments, as he thought back on their engaging discourse, all he could see was her antipathy. Elizabeth's willingness to challenge him was a fundamental part of her allure, and he admitted he often provoked her for no other reason than to light a spark in her expression and see her eyebrow archly raised in defiance. Their confrontational dance during the ball at Netherfield was a torturous experience, as he was by turns excessively pleased with the ability to hold her gloved hand and admire her light figure, yet exceedingly exasperated by her probing questions regarding that miserable scoundrel, Wickham.

Desperate to avoid all thoughts of *him*, Darcy took another swig of brandy as he gazed across the room. He doubted he could recall the number of evenings he had spent in this very chair trying to forget the woman who plagued his thoughts. His retreat to London after the ball became an exercise in futility, as he visited countless sitting rooms and attended numerous events of the *ton*, all with the hopeless intention of finding a suitable rival for the enchanting country lady. Despite the many introductions he made, and all to women with the right pedigree and acceptable fortunes, he had ended each evening in his present location, staring into the same fireplace, incurably focused on an enchanting pair of dark eyes. Eventually he had given over any thought of discovering a replacement for his annoyingly persistent affections, and instead threw himself into other pursuits, visiting White's with more frequency and engaging his fencing master so regularly that he would not have been surprised had others at Angelo's placed bets on the likelihood of his participation in a duel in the near future.

Darcy's own inability to conquer his unsuitable fascination had undoubtedly given force to his desire to save Bingley from a similar fate. When Miss Bingley and Mrs Hurst had pleaded for his assistance in convincing their brother to remain in London and abandon Netherfield altogether, Darcy had not hesitated.

Your selfish disdain for the feelings of others. Elizabeth's angry words pierced his mind at that moment in a way they had previously failed to do. Had he been right to interfere in Bingley's affairs? Darcy realised now that he obviously knew little regarding the feelings of women—and Bennet women in particular. Elizabeth would not have been so angry about Bingley's apparent abandonment of her sister if Miss Bennet had not truly cared for his friend. Yet how could he have known what lay behind Jane Bennet's serene countenance and endless smiles?

She was such a contrast to her sister, as Elizabeth radiated life and energy with every expression, while in his mind Miss Bennet simply existed as a pretty ornament in the background. Perhaps that thought was ungenerous. He had not taken the time to become acquainted with the lady, as his focus had been repeatedly drawn in her sister's direction, and therein he supposed was his mistake. He had officiously interfered in Bingley's life without taking the time to consider the situation. Bingley was prone to falling in love quickly with a pretty face, and his infatuation with Miss Bennet seemed to be of that variety, at least until the expectations of the local neighbourhood had been voiced, vociferously and repeatedly, the night of the Netherfield ball. Not wanting his friend to make an unsuitable match, not only in regard to the lady's family who had displayed a rather shocking lack of manners that evening, but also in regard to affection, Darcy had strongly felt that removing his friend from the neighbourhood was best for all parties involved. Now though, before Darcy left for Kent, Bingley's rather subdued demeanour while in his company weighed on his conscience. According to Elizabeth, Miss Bennet was suffering…and so was Bingley…and it was all his fault.

"Fitzwilliam, is anything amiss?"

His sister's voice pulled Darcy from his thoughts as he hastily sought to conceal his glass behind a stack of correspondence on the desk.

"Of course not, Georgiana. Is there something you require?"

"No, but Mrs Woods thought you might like a tea tray sent up. She seemed to think you did not eat much from your breakfast tray this morning," his sister replied, the hesitancy in her tone displaying her concern.

"That would be much appreciated." Darcy paused, searching for the right words to dispel the uneasy expression that flitted across his sister's face. "I appear to be neglectful of late. I apologise if I have given you reason to worry, but you know how matters can accumulate in my absence. The time spent at Lady Catherine's this year seems to have resulted in an inordinate number of tasks to accomplish now that I have returned." *If one can consider self-flagellation and self-pity a task.*

"I understand. I do not mean to pry. I will let Mrs Woods know about the tea service before I depart."

"Depart, dearest?"

"Yes, Lady Matlock has invited me for tea this afternoon. Mrs Annesley will accompany me, so you need not be worried. Our aunt told me she did not expect any other callers, but Richard may return from his barracks today. Would you like me to send him to see you if he arrives?"

Darcy knew he was in no state to see the colonel, as his cousin would easily discern his flagging spirits and proceed to interrogate him with his usual military precision. No, better to put off the encounter until he had regained some measure of equanimity.

"I am afraid I have far too much work to conclude this afternoon. I can always see Richard at the club later if he remains in town."

"I shall let him know. Will you join me for dinner this evening?"

Her hopeful expression immediately filled Darcy with guilt as he realised how neglectful he had been since he had returned home. To ignore his business matters was one issue, but to disregard his sister's feelings…*selfish disdain for the feelings of others.*

"I would like that. Please feel free to arrange the menus with Cook. I am sure whatever you decide upon will be delightful."

With a small smile, his sister closed the door to his study, the sound of her footsteps fading as she retreated down the hall. Left alone again to his thoughts, Darcy allowed his feelings of guilt to consume him. Georgiana had barely started to recover from her ordeal of the prior summer when he had left for his yearly visit to Rosings. He had been dreading the visit, convinced that his aunt would once again take up her relentless campaign to see him wed to his cousin Anne. Resignation transformed into astonishment when Darcy arrived in Kent only to discover that *she* was there as well, only separated from him by a lane, visiting her ridiculous cousin at the parsonage.

Even Mr Collins's effusions were not enough to keep Darcy from calling on Miss Elizabeth almost immediately after his arrival. When she had sauntered into the parlour, flushed from her morning walk, her windswept curls framing her beautiful face, he knew in an instant that all of his efforts to forget her had utterly failed. Every moment spent in her company lured him further under her spell, and one by one, all of his previous objections to her suitability as a marriage partner paled in comparison to a life lived without her.

Anger filled Darcy once again as he thought of Elizabeth's rejection, particularly her stalwart defence of Wickham. She believed *him*, wholly and without reservation, and what was worse, she had challenged Darcy's honour. As he was about to give in to the desire to allow his indignation full rein, a knock on the study door brought him back to the present.

"Your tea tray, sir." A footman set it on the side table.

Darcy noticed his sly glance at the half-empty decanter as he set out the food and refreshments. In a decidedly cool voice, Darcy quickly dismissed him.

After the footman bowed and exited the study, Darcy's chagrin at his clipped tone effectively doused his remaining anger. It was not his servant's fault that he was suffering from misery of the acutest kind. He had failed to win Elizabeth, and he had failed to forget her. He could not even stay angry with her. Not even over Wickham. His own father never discovered the depth of Wickham's depravity, so how could he expect her to see through the rake's lies after mere weeks of acquaintance? Wickham always laced his stories with just enough truth to render it impossible for one to discern all the particulars without personal knowledge of the event itself. Had Darcy answered even one of her many queries regarding Wickham's tale of woe, he might have shielded her from his influence, but instead, he had left her vulnerable, and she had fallen into his honeyed trap. No, he could not blame her. He could only blame himself.

Downing the last of his brandy, Darcy set the glass down, propped his elbows on the desk, and cradled his face in his hands, longing to shut out the world. He knew he should wish to return to his life before ever meeting Miss Elizabeth Bennet, yet, the thought of living without her, even if she only existed in his fantasies, was too painful to contemplate.

Resting his head on the desk, Darcy was grateful his morning of intemperate drinking succeeded in pulling him back into the realm of dreams and into her presence once more.

CHAPTER FOUR

"I do not believe I have ever seen a sight that was so excessively diverting, Georgiana! She walked into Lady Castlereagh's salon wearing the most ridiculous set of dyed ostrich feathers. I cannot begin to imagine who advised her as to the colour. Such a garish shade of yellow I have never seen in all my life! My dear Amelia would have laughed about it for days had she witnessed..."

Georgiana Darcy sighed as her aunt continued to regale her with the latest gossip from the fashionable drawing rooms of London. Lady Eleanor Fitzwilliam, the Countess of Matlock, was one of her closest relations and could even be considered her surrogate mother, as she had taken the young girl under her wing following the death of Lady Anne Darcy when Georgiana was but two years of age. Usually, a visit to her aunt's home was anticipated with much pleasure, but today Georgiana could not summon any interest in her aunt's stories, as her thoughts continued to stray to the image of her brother, alone in his study at Darcy House.

His attempt to hide his glass of brandy had not escaped her notice, although she was fairly certain he had believed himself to be successful in his subterfuge. Something was horribly wrong—it must be for her brother to behave so out of character.

He had returned from Rosings a little over a week ago, and she had barely seen him for two hours complete. Day in and day out he had remained holed away in his study, rejecting all company and hardly eating anything at all. She prayed he was sincere about his agreement to join her at dinner, if only to ensure he consumed at least one full meal during the course of the day.

Before he left for Kent, she believed their relationship had been improving. Ashamed for having failed him so greatly during the disaster with Mr Wickham at Ramsgate the prior summer, Georgiana had pushed her brother away, unable to witness his disappointment in her behaviour, firmly convincing herself that he desired to be anywhere but in her presence. Her sorrow had flowed freely through her fingertips, as she spent countless days lost in the melancholy tunes emanating from her pianoforte. It was easier to lose herself in her playing, to give her troubled emotions a voice, even if it meant closing herself off to those around her. When the invitation came from Mr Bingley for her brother to join him in Hertfordshire, Georgiana had encouraged—nay, pleaded—for her brother to attend, if only to escape the guilt she had felt after having so utterly failed him.

But she had been wrong. While her actions had pained him deeply, Georgiana had been startled to discover Fitzwilliam had blamed himself for the whole affair and had been filled with guilt for failing *her*. Her ridiculous, noble brother! He had saved her from ruin, that much was certain, and she had repaid him by pushing him away.

When he returned from Hertfordshire, he had been distracted, throwing himself into the events of the little Season with more frequency than she had ever witnessed. Bolstered by the encouragement from her new companion, Mrs Annesley, Georgiana had reached out to her brother, inviting him to listen to her play and encouraging him in more frequent conversation during meals. His relief at her desire for his company had been palpable, and she had felt ashamed at her attempts to place distance between them.

After a few honest conversations, during which he confessed his feelings of guilt over her sorry indiscretion, they had finally come to a better understanding and a new resolve to share more confidences and heal the breach that had developed. Everything seemed to be setting itself to rights until he had been called away to his annual obligations at her aunt's forbidding estate.

"...and I cannot understand why Miss Grantley maintains the acquaintance. Perhaps they have more in common than I originally supposed. What do you think, Georgiana?"

A light touch on her hand startled Georgiana from her thoughts, and she perceived a look of concern on her aunt's visage.

"You were not attending. Are you well, my dear?"

"My apologies, Aunt. I am afraid I was distracted. Who were we speaking of?" Georgiana attempted to display an amused smile, hoping to alleviate the worry that had wrinkled her aunt's brow.

"Of Miss Bingley."

"Miss Bingley? Why would you be in company with her? I thought you did not approve of my brother's acquaintance with that family."

"I have nothing against your brother's friend, excepting his lack of control over his unmarried sister. That woman will be the death of him if he ever plans to establish himself in society. She talked of you incessantly as though you were the dearest friends! If I had to listen to one more utterance of *dear Georgiana* this or *dear Georgiana* that, I should have knocked those ridiculous feathers from her head!"

"Oh Aunt," Georgiana giggled, "you really should not allow her to upset you so. I know perfectly well the only reason she praises me to the skies is to forward her interest with my brother. Fortunately, Fitzwilliam has assured me that he has never once given any thought to Miss Bingley beyond maintaining his friendship with her brother. I believe he would cut her acquaintance if he could, but he would never do anything that might cause Mr Bingley harm in society."

"I am relieved to hear it. Not that I ever imagined he would pursue such a simpering creature. Miss Grantley may regret her decision to include Miss Bingley in her social calls, although I cannot remember a time I was so amused by such gaudy finery. I simply have to include a detailed description in my next letter to Amelia."

"Who is Amelia, Aunt? I know I have heard you mention her name before, but I cannot remember ever meeting her."

"Amelia, Lady Tamworth, is a dear friend. I do not believe you have been in her company since you were a babe. She prefers to stay at her estate, Heatherton Hall in Staffordshire, but I am hoping to lure her back to town. Your uncle and I usually visit the Tamworths on our journey back to Matlock every year, and I know your cousin James visits her family with some regularity. Amelia is his godmother, and he is exceptionally close to her son, Lord Grey."

"Is not Lord Grey your godson? I think Fitzwilliam has mentioned him to me before."

"Yes, Nicholas is the same age as your brother, although I do not believe they are particularly close. Lord Grey attended Oxford, but I believe he knew your brother as boys when they were at Eton."

The sound of heavy boots echoed down the hall until a soft creak at the parlour door signalled the entry of a newcomer into their feminine refuge. The smiling face of her guardian and favourite cousin drew Georgiana from her chair as she launched herself into his arms.

"It is good to see you too, little one!" he chuckled, spinning her around in a most undignified fashion before the quelling glare of his mother forced him to cease his actions.

"I cannot tell you how happy I am to see you! Are you staying in town for long?"

Colonel Richard Fitzwilliam, by nature a jovial sort of man, had re-joined his troops at the barracks for a week, determined to see how his regiment was handling their new training exercises before he returned to finish his leave with his family. Training troops was a welcome respite from dealing with Lady Catherine, but now Richard was determined to enjoy his remaining time with his infinitely more enjoyable relations.

"Yes, my dear. I have been given leave for at least another week, and I am determined to spend as much of the time as I can with my charming ward and her dour brother!"

"Has your batman brought your things, or are you planning to stay at Darcy House?" Though she never begrudged the time he spent with Darcy and Georgiana, the anxious expression on her face made it clear to Georgiana that Lady Matlock missed her son dearly.

"I plan to stay here, Mother. I am sure Darcy could use a rest from staring at my ugly mug all day after our trip to Kent." He wiggled his eyebrows at Georgiana in an attempt to make her laugh.

"Then I shall speak to the staff about preparing your rooms. Pray excuse me for a moment, my dears." Lady Matlock gracefully rose from her chair and exited the parlour.

Richard's reference to Kent brought Georgiana's thoughts back to the recent behaviour of her brother. If she wanted answers as to why he was so altered, the only person who could provide them would have to be Richard. Unused to prying into her brother's personal affairs, Georgiana gathered her courage.

"Richard, have you seen Fitzwilliam since you returned from Kent?"

"No, I have not. I left for camp almost immediately following our return," he replied with ease, displaying little concern. "Why? Is something the matter? I have to admit Darcy seemed more than usually annoyed upon our departure."

"Did something happen at Rosings?"

"Beyond Lady Catherine's usual behaviour? No, although I admit she harped on your poor brother a bit more than her typical wont regarding the match with Anne. Poor beleaguered Darcy!" he chuckled.

Georgiana was certain her brother's recent despondency had to stem from more than their aunt's unrelenting marital designs. Lady Catherine had boasted about the supposed betrothal for years, and her brother had never given any indication he was remotely close to capitulating to her desires. Lost in thought, her cousin's next observation startled her.

"In fact, the company at Rosings was significantly improved this year."

"Indeed? In what way?"

"Our aunt's parson, Mr Collins, had some guests staying at the parsonage—his wife's sister, a Miss Lucas, and Mrs Collins's dearest friend, Miss Elizabeth Bennet."

"Miss Bennet?" Georgiana queried, "the same Miss Bennet that Fitzwilliam met in Hertfordshire?"

"Have you met the lady, Georgiana?"

"No, no I have not, 'tis only that Fitzwilliam mentioned her in his letters while he stayed with Mr Bingley. Such a strange coincidence that she should be in Kent during your stay and so close to Rosings." A thought began to form in Georgiana's mind, but she needed more information before she could give it any credence. "Did you enjoy her company?"

"Yes, I certainly did. She is a fine woman, witty and

engaging, and rather comely if I do say so myself," Richard winked.

"Did Fitzwilliam enjoy renewing their acquaintance? From his letters he seemed to approve of her."

RICHARD EYED HIS YOUNG COUSIN WITH SUSPICION AND A fair amount of amusement. After all, it was most uncommon for little Georgie to concern herself with her brother's affairs, particularly those related to his rather limited female acquaintances.

"I believe he did, but you know your brother's ways—ever disposed to staring out of windows and avoiding conversation with those he does not know well." Richard refrained from adding he had noticed his cousin's gaze often had lingered on Miss Bennet. "She, however, did not appear to appreciate his taciturn behaviour. I do not believe I have ever seen a woman tease Darcy as much as Miss Bennet, yet he seemed to tolerate her delightful little quips quite well." He watched as a rather pensive expression covered the face of his young cousin. "Georgiana, is anything the matter?"

"I believe something has happened to my brother. Ever since he returned from Rosings, he has not been himself."

"You know how taxing it can be to cope with Lady Catherine's demands. I am sure Darcy will regain his spirits soon."

"No, Richard, you do not understand," Georgiana insisted, her pleading expression begging him to take her concerns seriously. "Fitzwilliam has locked himself away in his study for more than a week."

"Hardly strange behaviour for Darcy."

"'Tis not only the seclusion!" She sighed in evident frustration. "He barely eats, he barely even speaks to me, and this morning—this *morning*—well, I found him drinking brandy before I left the house."

This last piece of information caught Richard's attention. Darcy rarely indulged beyond a single glass after dinner. If he was drinking before noon, then Georgiana's concerns held more weight than he previously supposed. "Perhaps I should call on him before dinner."

"I already asked him if you should visit and he declined. He said he would see you at the club if you remained in town."

Her statement only confirmed Richard's previous thoughts, as Darcy rarely rejected his company. If Darcy truly wished to avoid him, it could only mean he desired to escape the inevitable interrogation Richard was bound to initiate. Well, he was not about to oblige Darcy's wishes if his actions upset Georgiana. It appeared he had a call to make, and he was not altogether sure of what he would find when he arrived.

"Do not worry, little one. I will take care of this. Your fractious elder brother is no match for His Majesty's finest."

CHAPTER FIVE

"And then what happened, Lizzy?"

Little Meg Gardiner looked up from her perch on her cousin's knee with a rapt expression on her angelic face, delighting Elizabeth with her enthusiasm for the story.

"Well, the dashing knight had no other choice but to mount his fearsome steed and race after the evil hag who had taken his beloved, for she had used her magic to kidnap the young princess and transported her to the world of the fairies."

"But how could the knight follow her there?" A sceptical look covered her cousin Matthew's visage. He was already a practical young man, less disposed to whims of fancy and more inclined to devote his time to his studies than the average eight-year-old. After offering a brief explanation regarding a previous adventure involving the brave knight and a helpful fairy friend, Elizabeth's doubtful cousin was suitably contented with the remainder of her fanciful tale.

Their younger brother, Edwin, sat nearby on his blanket playing with his wooden blocks, having lost interest in her story rather quickly. At only two years of age, she understood his disinterest.

As Elizabeth finished reciting her improvised narrative, little Meg sighed in delight, clearly pleased with the fate of the daring knight and his beautiful princess. A moment later, the door to the nursery opened as the lady of the house entered in search of her favourite niece.

"There you are, Lizzy! I had wondered where you had disappeared after luncheon."

"My apologies. I simply could not resist spending the afternoon with my darling cousins, for they always know how to lift my spirits."

"Well, I see you have all enjoyed what I am sure was another fascinating story, but I believe it is time to return to your lessons and time for young Master Edwin to take his nap," Aunt Gardiner replied, turning to her children and directing them to their different pursuits.

"Do you know where I might find Jane, Aunt?"

"I believe she went to her room to rest, but I am sure she would not mind your company."

"I think I will join her for a while before dinner."

"Very well, my dear."

As Elizabeth left the nursery, her thoughts returned to her walk that morning. Although she was grateful for the opportunity to ruminate on recent events in private, she had returned to her uncle's residence in decidedly low spirits. Spending time with her young cousins always succeeded in cheering her, and so her afternoon in their company had greatly helped to restore her.

If only she could bring such consolation to Jane. Having arrived at the door to her sister's room, Elizabeth lightly knocked. "Jane, may I come in?"

"Yes, Lizzy."

Her sister's listless tone increased Elizabeth's worry, and she opened the door to see Jane sitting by the window, staring out on the busy street below with a vacant expression. It was a sight Elizabeth had seen many times since her return to London, and as always, it continued to frighten her in the belief that Jane might never fully recover from Charles Bingley's cowardly abandonment.

"Dearest, is there nothing I can do to bring you comfort? You should have joined me with the children. It would have done you good to see their excitement today."

"I feel so foolish!" Jane softly cried, startling her sister as tears began to flow down her cheeks. In but a moment, Elizabeth gathered her weeping sister into her arms, gently rocking her back and forth in an attempt to soothe her.

"Foolish? What do you mean?"

"How many months have I wasted on a man who did not care for me at all?"

"You have nothing to feel foolish about, Jane! This was not your fault. Everyone could see how clearly Mr Bingley loved you."

"But did he really? I know now that I was wrong to trust his sister—her visit while you were in Kent clearly showed her desire to end our friendship, but is it possible I also misinterpreted his regard as well?"

"The entire county was convinced Mr Bingley would offer for you. You cannot think I would give you hope and encouragement where there is none."

"Of course not. As a rule, I would defend my belief that every man has the capacity for goodness, but I have never been hurt in such a way before. I would rather believe I was simply mistaken concerning his affections than the alternative—that he abandoned me without even saying goodbye."

As they were meant to leave for Longbourn in only a few days, Elizabeth had hoped to wait until they were home before she related anything of the events at Hunsford. Faced with the sight of Jane's tears, Elizabeth felt her hesitancy slip away, replaced by the need to bring her sister any solace she could provide.

"I know not how to begin, but I believe you should know I saw Mr Darcy while I was visiting Charlotte."

"Mr Darcy? Why ever would he be present at our cousin's home?" Jane's brows narrowed in confusion.

"I am sure you remember Mr Collins's many words of adulation regarding his patroness, Lady Catherine de Bourgh. Well, that lady is Mr Darcy's aunt, and he was there visiting her with a cousin during my stay in the area."

"Oh Lizzy, I am so sorry you had to endure the presence of one you dislike so during your trip."

Jane's comment brought a fresh wave of shame over Elizabeth as she once again lamented how vocal she had been in her dislike of the gentleman.

"It is not as though spending time with Mr Darcy required Herculean effort. I can admit now that perhaps I have been a bit too harsh on the gentleman, and he does improve on further acquaintance."

"I am glad to hear it. I, for one, never believed he was quite so bad as you described. But what brought about such a change in your opinion?"

Alarm filled Elizabeth's chest at the thought of revealing all that had happened between herself and Mr Darcy; however, one look at the understanding face of her closest friend and confidant convinced Elizabeth that she could not dissemble. All at once, the emotions she had been struggling to conceal since her return were released as she began her account of all the events and conversations that had occurred at Rosings, on the paths between the parsonage and that great estate, and most memorably at Hunsford.

"I was so shocked, and you will not be at all proud of how I reacted. I quickly informed Mr Darcy of my refusal with the barest trace of civility, and I will never forget how startled he looked. His face went so pale. He clearly had expected me to accept his offer without hesitation."

"I suppose that is not an altogether unreasonable assumption. I doubt he ever considered that *any* woman would refuse him, given all he can provide as a marriage partner. You must remember, Lizzy, not everyone is like us. There are plenty of people who do not require the deepest love to induce them into matrimony."

Jane's words tempered some of Elizabeth's lingering resentment against the man, and while she would have preferred some time to slip back into her thoughts on the particulars of Mr Darcy's proposal, she still had the most humiliating portion of her tale to relate.

"I realise now that my reaction was unsuitably severe, and you may disapprove of what I said next. When he asked for an explanation regarding my refusal, I accused him of separating you and Mr Bingley and of ruining the prospects of Mr Wickham. I was harsh and cruel in my retaliation and informed him that he could not have made his proposal in any way that would have tempted me to accept it."

"Oh Lizzy!"

"I cannot think of that night without regret. Not for my refusal, mind you, but for my behaviour. The whole affair was badly done. In any case, the following day he found me in the glen and gave me this."

Elizabeth passed Mr Darcy's letter to her sister, motioning for her to read it. While Jane perused the revealing epistle, Elizabeth watched as a variety of emotions played across her sister's face. Once she had finished the account, Jane looked to Elizabeth with sadness.

"Poor Mr Darcy! Poor *Miss* Darcy! I cannot believe one man can be so evil! How horrified you must have been to read this!"

"I have been chastising myself ever since for how blind I was regarding Mr Wickham. But let us not speak of *that* man. What I must know is what you feel regarding the portion of the letter concerning you and Mr Bingley."

For a moment, Jane was silent and thoughtful. Her voice when she did speak was hesitant, as though she could not quite find the words to communicate her feelings. "I am not sure how I should respond."

"But surely now you can see Mr Bingley did love you? If not for the interference of his sisters and his friend, he would have returned to Netherfield."

"That in no way proves his regard. To be fair, I can admit he did harbour admiration for me, but love? Consider Mr Darcy's rather unfortunate proposal. He knew there would be objections to his decision to marry you, yet he still made his offer. Do you think he would be swayed by others to abandon his designs simply because they could see no evidence of your regard?"

Jane stood and began to pace about the room, as traces of anger overcame her usually placid features. "He abandoned me based on the observations of his friend who barely spoke two words to me throughout the whole of our acquaintance. Is Mr Bingley so reliant on Mr Darcy's judgment that he cannot make a decision for himself? Is he the type of man to be forever ruled by others? Should I even *want* such a man?"

Elizabeth was forced to acknowledge the truth in Jane's words. Why had she been so insistent on blaming Mr Bingley's lack of resolution on Mr Darcy? Would she want her sister to be tied to a man who could be convinced to give her up so easily? When Elizabeth thought on Mr Darcy and the sentiments he professed during his doomed proposal, she had to admit that Jane was right. She could not see him giving in to the persuasion of a friend in such matters.

"When I marry, I want to know my spouse will value me above all others. We have daily proof of what happens between a husband and wife when that value is lost. I cannot imagine living such a life with a man who lacks sufficient resolve. I have been sitting here—for months—questioning my feelings for a man who could not be bothered to discover my own for himself."

"Oh Jane, was I wrong to share this with you?"

"No. In fact, I thank you for allowing me the opportunity to freely admit what I have long been thinking. Mr Bingley and I were not in love. At least, *he* was not. It was an infatuation at best—an infatuation that has been tested and found wanting. With my incessant doubts finally put to rest, I have only to conquer my own lingering feelings of regard, feelings that have certainly diminished after your revelations. My resolve will be firm, and hopefully in the future I will consider him to be nothing more than a charming and pleasant acquaintance."

Later that evening, as Elizabeth lay in her bed, her mind once again drifted to the complicated gentleman from Derbyshire. Her conversation with Jane had absolved Mr Darcy of yet another fault. For surely, even though his conclusions about Jane's feelings were wrong, his motives had stemmed from a desire to protect his friend, something Elizabeth herself would have done for Jane if she had felt Mr Bingley's affections were not sincere. Mr Bingley could have, at any time, decided to pursue Jane of his own volition. *She* would never desire a suitor with so little determination.

Somewhat startled by the turn in her thoughts, Elizabeth finally felt the full compliment of Mr Darcy's offer. She still did not regret refusing him, for she did not love him and still could not excuse his proud manners, but she could admit that perhaps she would like the chance to know him better—to discover who he truly was behind the mask he presented in public. He was intelligent, honourable, and mindful of his responsibilities, and perhaps they might be well-suited after all.

CHAPTER SIX

The following day sitting alone at his preferred corner table, Nicholas Grey casually observed the other gentlemen roaming around White's in the early afternoon. The bow window was currently unoccupied, as the Beau Brummell set had yet to arrive, sparing Grey the sight of London's dandified peacocks as they clucked about the various passers-by while drawing their snuff handkerchiefs from their coat pockets with alarming frequency. Thoughts of the Prince Regent's fast set in town always brought a frown to Grey's usually blithe face. He detested the debaucheries of his class, and in many ways, he was grateful for his family's preference for life in the country. Absent-mindedly swirling the drink in his hand, Grey's musings returned to the information he had learned the previous evening.

After deciding to pursue his desire to discover more about the young lady from the park, Grey had dispatched Peters once again to investigate the only link he currently possessed to the pretty, petite woman—the name of a tradesman, Mr Edward Gardiner. Peters had returned to his study well after the dinner hour, and the news he had to impart had reassured and confused Grey in equal measure.

"The man appears to be well-respected and is moderately prosperous in his business. His company, Gardiner Imports, was established in 1795 when his partner and mentor died and left his holdings to Mr Gardiner who had apprenticed with him since 1791."

"So, this was not a family business?" Grey enquired, the year of 1791 piquing his interest.

"No, my lord. Mr Gardiner hails from a small town called Meryton in Hertfordshire. His father was the local solicitor, a second son of a minor country gentleman from Surrey. Mr Gardiner's uncle, a Mr David Gardiner, appears to have been a rather dissolute gentleman, as he lost the family estate only ten years after he became its master. He died without issue, and it appears no other Gardiner relations currently reside in Surrey."

"What of Mr Gardiner's other relations? Does he have siblings?"

"Yes, my lord, two sisters who are both older in age. The eldest sister is married to a Mr Philips, who inherited the late Mr Gardiner's practice after clerking with him for several years. They have no children and currently reside in the small town. The younger sister married a local gentleman, a Mr Thomas Bennet of Longbourn. The estate is located on the outskirts of Meryton, and they have several daughters but no sons."

"And Mr Gardiner? Does he have a family?" Lord Grey waited with bated breath, hoping to hear something of the young lady he had met that morning.

"Mr Gardiner is married to a Mrs Madeline Gardiner, and they appear to have three children. Mr Gardiner is currently eight and thirty, and his wife is two and thirty. They have been married for ten years."

Mr Gardiner's age brought a swift halt to Grey's speculation, as he realised the man was far too young to have claimed to be a father at a mere eighteen years of age. No, perhaps the young lady was a relation.

"Were you able to enquire after the family of Mrs Gardiner?"

"I have only preliminary information. Mrs Gardiner hails from the town of Lambton in Derbyshire, but that is all I know at present. The close proximity of Meryton to London enabled the quick report on Mr Gardiner's family, but I am afraid it will take several days to obtain any response to my enquiries regarding the lady's kinfolk. Would you still like to proceed with the inquest, my lord?"

Grey paused to consider the request. If he waited to obtain more information on Mrs Gardiner's family, it would necessitate a delay in applying to the man himself for answers. For a reason he could not identify, Grey experienced a profound sense of unease with the thought of delaying the task, as though his hesitancy could provide the chance for the young lady to slip beyond his grasp.

"That will not be necessary. Thank you for your diligence and discretion."

At his master's dismissal, Peters gave a curt bow and exited the study, leaving Grey to his thoughts.

His sleep that night had been troubled, and so he resolved to apply to the tradesman the following afternoon, hoping to receive the answers he so greatly needed. Thinking again on the details presented by Peters, Grey surmised the young lady's connexion to Mrs Gardiner was most likely. Perhaps she was a younger sister. Derbyshire, as the neighbouring county, was much closer to Staffordshire than the home of Mr Gardiner's relations. How he wished he could discuss this with his father, but Grey was hesitant to bring any word of his discovery to his parents before he could be sure of at least the young lady's name and status. He would not raise his parents' hopes without just cause, so for the present, he was determined to carry this burden alone.

"Grey, old chap! So glad I found you here today!"

Startled from his ruminations, Lord Grey looked up to see the smiling face of his oldest friend sauntering across the room to join him at his table. He had known Lord James Fitzwilliam, Viscount Lisle, since his birth, as their mothers had been friends from the time of their days at school. The Fitzwilliam family had many ties to Derbyshire, and so visits between Matlock and Heatherton Hall had been a frequent occurrence throughout Grey's youth, owing to the relatively easy distance to the Grey family's home county.

"Lisle! I had no idea you were in town. The last I heard you had been called back to Matlock."

"Yes, Hayes wrote to Father with some crisis about the drainage system in the lower fields. Normally, I would not bother, as he has always been such a competent steward, but I believe the birth of his first child has left Hayes a bit bone-weary. Father thought it best to send me to oversee the repairs," Lisle replied, requesting a drink from the passing servant and settling in at the table opposite his friend.

"Be thankful your father has not required you to take up his seat in the House as of yet. If I could be spared the bickering of posturing old men for just one season, I would be eternally grateful."

"So, the earl still has no plans to return to town this spring?"

"Not at present, but perhaps I may be able to change his mind."

Grey hesitated to mention that if his parents *did* return to town this season, it would likely have nothing to do with the agenda in Parliament. Even though Lisle was a most valued confidant, he could not consider sharing any of his current plans when matters were still so speculative.

"You know, I broke the first night of my journey back to town at your estate. I thought I owed my godmother a visit after such a long absence."

"Ah, ever the dutiful godson!" Grey jested. "And how did

you find my mother?" He noted a look of concern flash across Lisle's face before he spoke.

"To be frank, her spirits seemed decidedly low. Though she no doubt took pleasure in my company, her mood was positively melancholy at times. Has something happened recently of which I am not aware?"

"Recently? No," Lord Grey replied, "I believe the cause occurred over twenty years past."

The veiled reference to the lost Grey child cast a sombre pall over the conversation. Grey had known for some time that the year of 1812 would be a difficult one for his family. As the months passed, the day his sister would reach her majority drew ever near. For his mother, that day marked the end of a stolen childhood, one which she would never be able to reclaim.

"Indeed," remarked Lisle. "Well, I believe you owe *your* godmother a visit. I was planning to call at your home if I could not find you here. Mother would like you to come to dinner this evening. She worries you spend too much time alone."

Grey appreciated his friend's efforts to lighten the air and eagerly seized the new topic of conversation. "I believe I should be able to manage it. How is your family faring? I admit I have not called as often as I should, though I do see your father on occasion in the House."

"Mother is perfectly well. Entertaining ladies day in and day out, and all the usual activities with the set at Almack's. Richard is in town, arrived just yesterday, in fact."

"How is the old rascal? Still leaving toads in ladies' pockets? I will forever have trouble seeing your brother as a respectable colonel after all the mischief he caused in our youth."

Lisle chuckled. "Oh, he still causes mischief. Just before he visited his regiment, he spent several weeks with the formidable Kentish Dragon."

Grey let loose a stream of mirth at the old invective they

had created for Lisle's dominating aunt, Lady Catherine. Having visited the lady's estate in Kent as a boy, Grey had been suitably cowed by the woman's petrifying gaze. The fear of becoming the object of her ire had driven the boys to her carefully manicured gardens for as much of the visit as possible.

"Did he take any shears to her topiaries? I will never forget the look on her face when Lady Catherine found her favourite cherub with a missing wing and a sizeable dent in its halo."

Lisle sniggered. "No, I believe Richard was forced to play peacemaker between her and our cousin Darcy for the majority of his stay, the poor sod."

"Ah, still harping on Darcy to marry your cousin, I take it?"

"Yes, and it drives the rest of the family positively mad—my mother, in particular! Of course, she wants the credit of arranging Darcy's marriage herself, and she would never want anything that would make Lady Catherine happy to succeed. Darcy is also in town, by the way. I believe Richard plans to bring him to dinner tonight, or at least he promised Mother he would try when he visited Darcy House yesterday."

"Darcy is in town for the Season? I thought he spent most years ensconced at that great estate of his rather than subjecting himself to the rigours of society. In fact, I do not believe I have been in company with him for several years. Is he endeavouring to improve his sociability?"

"Hardly likely. My cousin still detests idle gossip and repartee as much as he ever has. It is more likely that Darcy is simply succumbing to the pressure of my mother to finally settle down. I, myself, had to escape her parlour this afternoon and the never-ending parade of insipid debutantes she insists on admitting to our home. She says her need for grandchildren ought to outweigh our fondness for the bachelor state."

"So, are you finally considering getting caught in the parson's mousetrap, Lisle?" Lord Grey goaded his friend.

"No! At least, not immediately, well—oh, sod it! To be truthful, Grey, I think my father is starting to hint at his desire that I settle down and produce an heir. If I am honest, I cannot say whether I would absolutely refuse should he broker an alliance with some family or other that he trusts."

"A slave to duty, I see?"

With a hearty laugh, Lisle quipped, "You must have me confused with Darcy. No, it is only that I have always valued my parents' insights and my father's leadership in particular. I wonder whether I would have it in me to go against him in such a matter were he to ever press the issue. If only there was a simple solution! All I desire is to meet a suitably attractive woman who is also witty and engaging and whose family would not be a trial to endure. If my father could find such a woman, I would happily quit the marriage mart and defer to his judgment."

"I understand. I value my father's guidance as well, but for now, I still plan to marry with some regard for affection. After observing my parents, I believe it is the only way to build a marriage that endures the trials life will inevitably bring. I hope you are equally successful in finding such a wife."

"As long as she comes with the appropriate connexions and dowry?" Lisle queried with a sarcastic edge to his voice.

"Indubitably," Grey responded in kind.

Withdrawing his pocket watch from his coat, Grey noted the time and concluded if he planned to follow through with his call on Mr Gardiner, he needed to depart, lest he lose the opportunity to find relief for his restless spirit.

"I need to make a call this afternoon, but please tell your mother I will be happy to join you all for dinner."

"Oh, is there something pressing?"

"Merely a matter of business. I plan to see a man about some investments I am considering in the near future."

"Well, if you find anything of interest, let me know. It can never do any harm to increase the Matlock coffers."

"Of course, Lisle. I have a feeling this meeting may bring about great changes for the Grey family."

With that enigmatic statement, Lord Grey bid his friend goodbye and left the club, filled with both hope and trepidation that his next conversation might alter the course of his future happiness.

CHAPTER SEVEN

"I do not understand, Samuel. It was my belief the contract we negotiated had secured the appropriate ships, so why are the textiles still sitting at the port of Bengal?"

Edward Gardiner ran a hand through his thinning hair in frustration. His day had progressed from one vexing issue to the next as he encountered numerous obstacles in his warehouses since his arrival that morning. His poor clerk, Samuel Smith, looked equally distressed if the increasingly pinched look about his brow was any indication.

"My apologies, Mr Gardiner, but the shipping company claims several of their vessels needed to dock for unforeseen repairs. They insist it will take at least another week before the cargo can be moved."

"In that case, it is best that you contact the merchants on Bond Street about the setback. We had several orders for silks that will inevitably be delayed. I can only hope we will keep their custom after such a misstep," Mr Gardiner replied, mentally calculating the loss of income, should the previously agreed upon contracts fall through.

"Certainly, sir. I will do so at once."

As Smith left his office, Mr Gardiner lifted his hands to slowly massage his temples as he released a small groan. Reaching for his tea only to find it had gone cold during the previous interruption, he set aside the offending brew and pondered on the troubles that had so recently upset his life. For it was not only business matters that drew his concern.

No, for Edward Gardiner, the far more pressing issues that had occupied his thoughts centred on the two dear, young women currently installed in his home. His eldest nieces were especially cherished by him and his wife, and their visits were usually times of great joy and felicity in the Gardiner household. Never before had one of their stays been accompanied by such misery.

When he and his dear wife, Madeline, had noticed Jane's depressed spirits during the holiday season at Longbourn, he had hoped that their offer of escape to London would help his niece heal from her recent disappointment. He was saddened to see that even distance from Hertfordshire had not lessened the grief Jane felt, nor could he be sure that their company had provided the comfort she so obviously needed. Mr Gardiner's worry only increased at the recollection of her coming departure to Longbourn, as he doubted his sister Fanny's ever excitable nerves would have any positive effects on Jane's recovery. He had hoped Elizabeth's return from Kent would restore joy to Jane, only to be confronted with yet another niece who appeared to be in distress.

Elizabeth had always been possessed of an indomitable spirit, as she had often herself noted she was not fashioned for melancholy. And so, Mr Gardiner had anticipated the sight of his spirited niece, only to be met with a troubled Elizabeth, whose normally easy smiles seemed somehow tight and worn. Something had clearly happened in Kent, that much was certain, but neither he nor his wife would force her confidence. If Elizabeth chose to share her misfortunes, they would provide a ready ear.

His idea of a stroll through Hyde Park yesterday had appeared to be a welcomed distraction, yet Elizabeth seemed just as quietly pensive upon her return as she had when they set out that morning. He wondered if perhaps the stranger she encountered played any part in her continued woe.

Mr Gardiner had seen her brief conversation with the gentleman at Stanhope Gate. As they had only spoken for a moment, he had refrained from questioning his niece on her small lapse in propriety. Perhaps they had been acquainted with one another. Having grown up in the small town of Meryton, Mr Gardiner was painfully aware of the lack of suitable marriage partners for his sister's five daughters. Though he would never approve of her theatrical behaviour, Fanny's fear of starving in the hedgerows was not wholly unfounded, as her future security depended upon the successful marriages of her girls. With the entailment on Longbourn and little in the way of dowry, the Bennet daughters' prospects were never great. Mr Gardiner, however, knew his two eldest nieces were true jewels of the first order, and he had always been hopeful some young gentlemen would see their worth.

The arrival of Mr Bingley to the neighbourhood had been the fulfilment of his sister's wildest hope, convinced as she was that the gentleman had intended to offer for Jane. After witnessing Jane's sadness over the previous months, Mr Gardiner was not at all inclined to approve of his niece's erstwhile suitor. His opinion of Mr Bingley had also been materially damaged by the unforgivably rude behaviour of his sister when she called on Jane in February. His wife had wasted no time in informing him of the disastrous visit, and her account of Miss Bingley's condescending and disdainful tone and looks had left them both in no doubt of his family's disapprobation of Jane and her relations. If Edward

Gardiner had his way, then Mr Bingley would never again be permitted the privilege of his niece's acquaintance.

Although he knew his brother-in-law would insist upon Jane and Elizabeth's originally scheduled date of departure, Mr Gardiner wished he could somehow keep his dearest nieces in London until the end of the Season. Despite not moving in the highest circles of society, Mr Gardiner was convinced there were infinitely better marriage prospects in town than those in the vicinity of Longbourn. As much as he did not want to lose either Jane or Elizabeth to the married state, he knew it was past time they were introduced to a wider circle of gentlemen. Both young women needed the security that marriage would provide, should their father meet an untimely end, especially Elizabeth.

No, he could not allow himself to dwell upon uncertainties, for it had been many years, and beyond himself, only two souls had any knowledge of the event...and they were as unlikely as he to reveal such intelligence.

A rap on the door preceded the entrance of Smith, who still possessed a rather harried look about him. Dreading the revelation of yet another issue that would require his attention, Mr Gardiner was surprised when his young clerk passed him a calling card of exceptionally fine stationery.

"The gentleman does not claim an appointment with you, sir, but he asks if you have time to see him."

Looking down upon the dignified coat of arms, Mr Gardiner's curiosity was piqued as he read the name of his caller, carefully printed in elegant script.

Lord Nicholas Francis Grey
Baron Grey de Rotherfield
Tamworth House, London
Heatherton Hall, Staffordshire

While the number of his business associates and investors was vast, Mr Gardiner did not have many contacts that were members of the peerage. As far as he was aware, the Staffordshire Greys possessed a good reputation in town and were not known for the profligacies that seemed to plague the many families of the *ton*.

"I suppose it would not do to keep a baron waiting, Samuel. Please send in his lordship and have the tea service refreshed."

"Of course, sir," Smith replied, gathering the tea tray from the morning and quickly exiting his employer's office.

As the baron entered the room, Mr Gardiner worked quickly to mask his surprise as he stood to greet his guest, for standing before him in his fine and polished attire was the stranger who had spoken with his niece in the park the previous day. Perhaps his suspicion of a prior acquaintance had not been wholly unfounded after all.

"It is a pleasure to meet you, Lord Grey de Rotherfield," Mr Gardiner began.

"Lord Grey, if you will, sir."

"Very well. How can I be of service to you today, your lordship?"

Mr Gardiner bid his guest to take a seat while carefully scrutinising the young man before him. He looked to be in his late twenties, and despite his every effort to project an image of confidence, he seemed decidedly unsettled.

"I am afraid I am at a bit of a loss as to how to begin, Mr Gardiner. The request I have to make of you today is rather unusual and of a decidedly impertinent nature."

A teasing glint entered the stranger's eyes, startling Mr Gardiner with its familiarity, though he could not say where he had seen such an expression before.

"Well, if you will forgive *my* impertinence, I have always valued frankness in all of my dealings. You may be as open as you like, and I will try my best not to take offence to whatever it is you have to say."

A look of what Mr Gardiner believed to be respect settled over his visitor's features, followed by a calculating expression. After a moment of hesitation, Lord Grey reached into his pocket and produced a small object wrapped in cloth and placed it carefully on Mr Gardiner's desk.

Receiving a nod of consent from the baron, Mr Gardiner picked up the small package and removed the fine muslin, revealing a miniature portrait of stunning detail. A surge of fear and anger gripped his heart as he stared at the startling image before him, for there, clothed in beautiful finery, was the likeness of Elizabeth.

"I had thought to confront you about your rendezvous with my niece in the park yesterday, but I never imagined she would be taken in by such a rogue! Tell me, *your lordship*, how long have you been acquainted with my niece? For surely a portrait such as this requires an arrangement of long-standing."

Absolute fury flowed from Lord Grey in waves as he rose to his feet. "How dare you impugn my honour so easily, sir! And what of your niece? Is she the sort of woman to fall prey to such a libertine?"

Relief and reason penetrated the turbulent fog that had clouded Mr Gardiner's judgment. "Of course not! My Lizzy is the best of women. My apologies, my lord. I fear I spoke too quickly when I assured you of my objectivity earlier."

"Your niece Lizzy…her name is Elizabeth?"

Mr Gardiner was instantly caught by the hope that flitted across the baron's face. Bewildered and overcome by the sudden turn in their conversation, he bid his guest to return to his seat while he carefully considered his response.

"My second eldest niece, whom you saw in the park the other day, is Miss Elizabeth Anne Bennet of Longbourn, Hertfordshire. She is the daughter of my sister, Fanny, and her husband, Mr Thomas Bennet." He paused for a moment before continuing. "If you would, my lord, could you please explain *your* connexion to my niece?"

After a moment of contemplation, Lord Grey

responded. "I admit I had hoped you would be able to tell me."

Suitably alarmed by such an odd declaration, feelings of both dread and hope began to escalate in Mr Gardiner's mind, as the implication behind the baron's words nearly rendered him speechless with the potential possibilities of this astonishing meeting.

"Perhaps this conversation should begin with an explanation of the portrait I see in front of me. Who is the lady who bears such a startling resemblance to my Lizzy?"

"The woman before you is Lady Amelia Grey, the Countess of Tamworth, wife to Lord George Harry Grey, the Earl of Tamworth, and my mother. My father had that portrait commissioned when my mother was twenty years of age, shortly after their marriage."

Regarding his visitor once again, Mr Gardiner prodded, "I believe, Lord Grey, there is more to your tale than you have yet to reveal. If this is your mother, then how do you feel the painting is connected to my niece?"

"To answer your question, I would have to relate a rather personal tragedy that affected my family many years ago. When I was but eight years old, my infant sister was stolen from our estate by a servant who had been rendered unstable by a severe illness. In the winter of 1791, Lady Elizabeth Amelia Grey vanished, and my family has not seen her since, despite a lengthy search and a substantial reward for her return."

A heavy stillness settled over the room and its occupants, and after summoning his remaining courage, Lord Grey continued. "What I would like to know, sir—what I desperately hope you will be able to tell me is simply—your niece—is she, in fact, your niece *by blood*?"

Their conversation was interrupted by a knock on the door, as Smith returned with a fresh tea tray.

"Thank you, Samuel. Please set the tray on the side table."

After Smith left the room, Mr Gardiner prepared a cup of tea for himself and his guest, using the time to gather his thoughts before he began the exposition of a story he never thought to disclose to another living soul, let alone a peer of less than an hour's acquaintance.

"It seems the year of 1791 was an eventful one for both our families. I had just gained an apprenticeship here in London, and my mother, sister, and my sister's family had come to assist me in settling in to my new apartments during the late summer. My sister Fanny Bennet had insisted that I simply could not be trusted to set up house without her, as she always did like to coddle me.

"She was with child for the second time, and her family intended to stay for a few weeks before returning to Hertfordshire for her confinement. Despite the pleas of her husband to avoid overexerting herself, Fanny continued to bustle about the place, happy to be of use, until one day, tragedy struck. While carrying some items down the staircase, Fanny lost her footing and fell, landing on her back and prompting labour to commence. After many hours, she gave birth to a stillborn child, a daughter."

Stopping momentarily to regain his composure, Mr Gardiner looked at the man before him, recognising a similar feeling of loss, of shared grief, emotions that anyone who knew intimately the loss of a child would be able to comprehend.

"My sister was never the same. Despite her physical recovery, Fanny descended into a state of melancholy from which none could rouse her, not even her two-year-old daughter, Jane. She resisted all pleas from her husband that they return home to their estate and refused any correspondence with her neighbours near Meryton. She would not even write to our sister, who was visiting her husband's family near Bristol. She wanted no one to know of her loss, as though the mere act of writing in ink of the death of her child would crush whatever remained of her spirit. It was not until mid-December that Bennet eventually convinced her to return home, and, to my everlasting astonishment, the first missive I received from my sister was an announcement of the birth of their daughter, Elizabeth Anne.

"My brother Bennet wrote to me separately, explaining they had discovered a foundling on their journey back to Longbourn, and Fanny had desired the child so desperately they had resolved to keep her and lay claim to her as their own. I tried for many years to uncover the full tale behind Elizabeth's discovery, but Bennet was always quick to deflect any enquiries I made, insisting it was best that the knowledge be kept to him and Fanny alone. To this day, I am the only other person who knows Lizzy is not truly a Bennet, as I have not informed my wife of her uncertain parentage. You must understand, I would in no way harm Lizzy's reputation in the world. From the first moment I held her in my arms, I have loved her. Indeed, I believe no one who has had the privilege of making Elizabeth's acquaintance will not love her."

A wistful expression fell across Lord Grey's face. He was silent for a few moments before he remarked, "My sister, Elizabeth—I called her Bethy—was the same way. She was the happiest babe I have ever known, and she had the entire family and staff wrapped around her chubby fingers. How old was your niece when your sister and her husband found her?"

"Only a few months. That is why they were able to spread the story that Fanny had simply miscalculated the time until her confinement, and thus Elizabeth was born in London, necessitating a longer stay than the Bennets had originally anticipated."

"So, your niece is the right age, bears the right Christian name, and was discovered a mere week or two after my sister disappeared from Staffordshire. Considering her profound resemblance to my mother, I think we must consider the probability that my sister Elizabeth has been found at long last."

"What do you intend to do, my lord? Will you contact the earl and countess?"

"Not yet. With your permission, I would like to be properly introduced to Elizabeth first."

Mr Gardiner considered the request. It was not unreasonable, given the circumstances, but introducing Elizabeth meant telling her a painful truth at an already difficult time in her young life.

"Before I make any introductions, I would like to speak about this with my wife. Lizzy is very close to her aunt, and I believe we will need Mrs Gardiner's aid in order to make this disclosure with any delicacy."

"I understand," Grey replied. "The last thing I would want is to upset Elizabeth unduly."

"Might I also show the portrait to my wife? I believe she might need additional convincing before she will agree to such a meeting."

"Yes, of course. Would I be able to meet you both on the morrow? We could meet here to avoid raising suspicion in your household."

"I think that would be best, my lord."

"Very well then. I have a previous engagement this evening, so I am afraid I must depart. Thank you, Mr Gardiner, for your candour today and your discretion."

After shaking the baron's hand and giving similar assurances, Mr Gardiner was left alone again in his office, his mind reeling from the astounding conversation that had just taken place. How on earth was he going to recount all he had heard to his wife? How would they ever explain all to Elizabeth? Filled with a nervous apprehension, Edward Gardiner gathered his things and left the warehouse for his home, anticipating one of the most difficult discussions he would ever have in the course of his life.

CHAPTER EIGHT

As she surveyed the assembled gathering in the dining hall, a satisfied smile graced Lady Matlock's visage. It had been a long time since she had experienced the pleasure of her sons' company, for the lady considered each of the young gentlemen present as her children, whether by blood or by godly rite. Her eldest son James, Viscount Lisle, had grown into a fine, upstanding gentleman who was slowly assuming a portion of his father's responsibilities in preparation of his eventual inheritance. While she prayed that her husband, Hugh, had many years ahead of him as the family patriarch, Lady Matlock was confident that her firstborn would shoulder the weighty responsibilities of the earldom with the same fortitude as his father. If only she could see him successfully settled with an equally reputable wife.

Her youngest son's laughter redirected her gaze towards the opposite end of the dining table, as judging by the expressions on the other men's faces, he had just made an impertinent jest at his elder brother's expense. Richard had always been gifted with the ability to bring merriment to almost any situation. While this talent was much appreciated by the countess, she had endured many trials throughout his youth when her son's clever antics were directed to less appropriate ends, namely those involving Lady Catherine.

When Richard first declared his intention to join the army as his profession, Lady Matlock had begged him to reconsider, insisting his future would be far more assured by taking orders, allowing his father to gift him with a suitable living. Richard, however, had no wish to don a cleric's collar and had told her in no uncertain terms that life as a soldier was infinitely more palatable than spending his days making sermons. She ought to have expected it, considering his energetic temperament, but the looming threat of the Corsican tyrant did little to ease her disquiet concerning his continued safety.

Sitting immediately to her right was their guest for the evening, her godson Nicholas Grey, whose small smile and dark eyes brought to mind the cherished face of her oldest friend, his mother, Amelia. While usually more gregarious in the company of her sons, Lord Grey had been rather subdued since his arrival, preferring to watch and laugh at their childish banter rather than taking up his usually more active role in their discourse. Lady Matlock had thought often of the Greys this spring, as her recent letters from Amelia revealed a decline in her spirits. She was hoping to find an opportunity to speak to Nicholas alone after the meal finished, trusting she might be able to provide some motherly advice in her friend's absence.

The empty chair next to Richard drew her thoughts to her other godson, her nephew Darcy, who had declined to join them that evening. His sister, Georgiana, had seemed unusually distracted during her visit the previous day, and Lady Matlock wondered if all was well at Darcy House.

"Richard," Lady Matlock began, "will you explain again

the reason why Darcy declined the invitation for tonight? I hope nothing is amiss."

"Not at all, Mother. Darcy simply needed another day of recovery after the rigours of Kent."

Something in Richard's expression convinced Lady Matlock her son was dissembling, but as he was Darcy's closest confidant, she resolved to let his prevarication pass for the time being.

"Darcy must be going soft if a couple of weeks in Lady Catherine's company can do him in so thoroughly," Lisle quipped.

"On the contrary, Brother. We have plans to meet at Angelo's tomorrow morning if you are interested."

"There you have it, Lisle! A perfect opportunity to best your younger cousin and his near faultless record," Nicholas teased, lifting a brow.

"You will not goad me. I have no desire to be skewered on the end of Darcy's foil, or did you forget that his achievements at Cambridge far outstripped anything your pitiful Oxford fencing team could muster?"

"Not this again! Need I always be reminded of the Fitzwilliam family pride for their alma mater at every gathering?" Lord Grey sighed with an exaggerated pout.

"I have been labouring under the misapprehension that I would be enjoying the sophisticated company of my sons this evening, but they appear to be missing from our table," Lord Matlock said, sending a quick wink at his wife from across the table.

"Forgive me, Father," Lisle replied. "I was certain you could use a respite from the quibbling of your peers in the House chambers earlier today."

"No, no. I am not offended, I assure you." Turning to Lord Grey, the earl continued. "But, I had thought to canvass your opinion. What say you regarding the petition from those papists in Clare? Think you we ought to trust their declarations of fealty to the Crown?"

"Although I am in favour of relaxing some of the penal laws for recusants in England, there is something in me that baulks at trusting the Irish."

"I agree, although I had heard that Digby was far more vocal concerning the bill on whiskey than any member was concerning the plea from the Irish Catholics." Richard laughed. "I believe I overheard that his fondness for the barbarians' spirits far outweighs his distaste for their popery. I will wager the poor dolt will be amassing the vile swill before the ban goes into effect in December."

Lady Matlock fixed an exasperated stare at the men seated at her table. "No more politics this evening! Why do you torture your poor mother when she has no one else to keep her company? If only Georgiana were present, you all would have to keep to more acceptable topics of conversation. And you wonder why I am in such desperate need of a daughter!"

A chorus of groans was heard from all three young gentlemen at her reference to the topic of marriage.

"Perhaps you should focus your efforts on my unfortunate cousin. He is the only one who is currently his own master and in immediate need of an heir. The rest of us can bide our time quite well," Lisle replied.

"So is Darcy to be the sacrificial lamb due to his absence?" Lord Matlock questioned.

"Of course. 'Tis his punishment for not attending tonight. Besides, he has managed to make an appearance during the Season, and that has to count for something."

"Perhaps Mother ought to leave Darcy alone. After all, James, you are the eldest. Should you not prepare the way for us younger gentlemen? Brave the waters, so to speak?" Richard interjected, increasing Lady Matlock's suspicion that something was afoot with her reserved nephew.

"Richard has a point, James. Perchance I should include Lady Tamworth in my schemes as well. What say you, Nicholas? Do you think your mother would enjoy finding suitable ladies for her godson?" Lady Matlock queried, sending a sly glance at her eldest.

"I concede, Mother," Lisle surrendered with a conciliatory gesture in her direction. "Give full rein to your machinations, and I will do my best to remain in the selected lady's company for an entire ten minutes, at least."

Her son's sarcastic speech was interrupted by the arrival of the footmen to clear the final course from the table. Rising from her seat, Lady Matlock turned to Lord Grey.

"I know it is customary for you to join the other gentlemen, but would you mind keeping your godmother company while my menfolk down their brandy? It has been too long since we last spoke."

"Certainly, madam. I would greatly enjoy the chance for some private conversation." Rising from his chair, Lord Grey extended his arm towards Lady Matlock and escorted her to the parlour. Once she was comfortably installed on the fashionable settee, Grey moved towards the sideboard to pour her a small glass of sherry, while measuring out a dram of brandy for himself.

After he had taken a seat, Lady Matlock began her subtle inquest. "I could not help but notice you seemed rather distracted tonight, Nicholas. Is anything amiss with your family, or was it simply your distaste for the topic of matrimony that caused your reticence? Are you hiding a lady-love whom I have yet to meet?" his godmother quipped in an attempt to lighten the mood.

"No, my lady, nothing so serious as that," Lord Grey replied with a smile. "However, Lisle did mention my mother was in low spirits during his recent visit, and I have to admit the thought of her anguish troubles me, as I can do nothing to assist her from a distance."

"Yes, the impending date of your sister's majority weighs heavily upon your parents. I cannot imagine what I would feel were I in a similar situation. Amelia and Harry were so irrevocably altered by the events of that grievous winter. We all were."

Her words had a surprising effect upon her godson's countenance, and his expression became somewhat guarded, as though he were unsure how to continue the conversation. After a minute of silent reflection, something in his manner gave way to resolution, his look communicating his trust in her confidence.

"It was so unexpected, I cannot—that is—something rather remarkable has occurred over the course of the last few days. My parents have not been informed of any of my suspicions, but I would greatly appreciate your advice on how to proceed in a personal matter."

"You know that I will always provide assistance should you ever require it, but whatever has happened, my dear boy?"

"Lady Matlock, I-I believe I have found Elizabeth."

Overcome by shock, the countess sat rooted to the sofa as she attempted to absorb the wondrous intelligence.

"But how? When? Your parents—all of us—had searched for so long and *never* a trace of her was found! How on earth did you make a start?"

"It came about through pure happenstance. I was walking in Hyde Park when I retrieved a lost paper for a young lady who was wandering the paths."

As he related the details of his meeting with Elizabeth and his subsequent interview with Mr Gardiner in his place of business, Lady Matlock listened in utter silence.

Lord Grey paused for breath after he finished his account and took a sip from his glass. "Mr Gardiner was able to relate that his niece, whose Christian name is also Elizabeth, was not a blood relation, having been adopted by his sister and her husband as a babe.

"My lady, she is the right age and the timing of her discovery fits with all the particulars of my sister's disappearance. I have no doubt that further enquiries will prove that she is, in fact, my lost sister, Lady Elizabeth."

Lady Matlock was suspended in a state of consternation, as all of the implications of her dearest friend's lost daughter's recovery washed over her. After so many years had passed, it was not a possibility she had ever considered. Hope began to stir in her heart as she realised what this information would mean for Lord Tamworth and Amelia, what it would mean for *all* of them.

"I plan to meet Elizabeth's uncle, Mr Gardiner, and his wife tomorrow. Together we will decide when and how to bring our suspicions to Elizabeth. I would like your advice on how best to approach my mother. You know her better than anyone. I would not want to distress her in any way, yet I so desperately want to bring her hope that her most cherished desire has come to pass."

Lady Matlock gently patted the hand of her anxious godson. "Nicholas, I would advise caution before alerting your mother to the likelihood of Elizabeth's return. Meet the young lady first, and then hopefully you will have better insight on how to proceed. I would also counsel you to speak to your father. Remember, you were naught but a child when your sister vanished, and I believe there may be more to the tale of which you are not aware."

A puzzled expression crossed Lord Grey's face as he considered her advice. "I plan to summon my parents to town after I am able to meet the lady. Should this woman prove to be my sister, will you promise to be with me when I disclose the news to Mother?"

"You can depend upon my assistance. I would not leave Amelia to face this discovery without her family and loved ones. The Fitzwilliams will stand by you in this, of that you can be certain."

Later that evening while sitting before the mirror in her bedchamber, Lady Matlock slowly brushed her long, golden hair as she considered the jarring revelation she had received that evening. It had been so long since there had been any hope little Elizabeth would be returned to them. She had watched Amelia succumb to her grief as the years passed, her private suffering slowly chipping away at her naturally cheerful disposition. Her eyes had lost their famous sparkle, and the earl was left to watch her slow decline.

Her musings were interrupted by a knock on the adjoining door and the entrance of her husband in his heavy brocade dressing gown. Despite the arranged nature of their marriage, her regard for Hugh Fitzwilliam had grown over the many years they had spent together. He was a good man, and their alliance had resulted in two beautiful sons and a relationship that was marked by both affection and respect.

"I wanted to thank you, my dear, for such a lovely dinner this evening," the earl began. "I always appreciate the opportunity to spend time with our sons, and I was especially glad to see young Grey at our table. He has grown into such a fine young man. I am sure Tamworth and Amelia are very proud."

As he touched her shoulder in a light, affectionate squeeze, Lady Matlock raised her hand to his in thanks, gazing upon him with a wistful expression.

"Now, I know that there was a good amount of teasing at the table this evening, but were you serious about finally looking for a potential bride for James? Lord Randolph has been hinting he would welcome an alliance with our family. His eldest daughter is reputed to be quite a beauty, so perhaps James may be willing to consider her."

Lady Matlock observed her husband carefully as a veritable battle waged within her mind over whether she should share the astounding intelligence with her husband. He would be as affected by the news as the rest of her family, and he might be able to offer assistance to Lord Tamworth in the same way in which Nicholas desired her help with Amelia.

Her decision made, Lady Matlock began to reveal all to her husband. "Hugh, my darling, I have the most wondrous news. It appears Nicholas has found his lost sister."

As she recounted the full tale Grey had revealed in the parlour, Lord Matlock's face went ashen in shock, and he sat heavily down upon the bed. By the time she had finished imparting the news, Lord Matlock turned to his wife and voiced the one concern she had been reluctant to acknowledge for the entirety of the evening.

"But Eleanor, do you know what this means? I still have all of the papers in my study, signed and sealed as though they were composed yesterday. If this woman is truly their daughter, then I have no further need to speak to Lord Randolph, for our son James is already betrothed to Lady Elizabeth Grey."

CHAPTER NINE

After carefully mending his pen, Darcy turned once again to the many papers laid before him, determined to finish the letter on his desk and conclude his business for the day. It had been another long afternoon in his study, although he had managed to make a sizeable impact on the various piles of correspondence that had remained untouched for so long. Rolling his shoulders, Darcy felt all of the stiffness of his morning's activities.

He had agreed to meet Richard at Angelo's after spending the previous evening in his sister's company, carefully avoiding any intoxicating indulgences, lest he lose his resolve to move past the previous week's despondency. Embarrassed by his behaviour, Darcy had been even more humbled when Richard had landed several decisive hits during their sparring match at the academy. Clearly it was time to collect himself and become a man of action once more.

Thoughts of his cousin returned Darcy to their conversation two days prior, as Richard's alarm when he entered the study had shattered any hope Darcy possessed that his troubles might remain a private affair.

"Good God, Darcy! What the devil has happened to you?" Richard had exclaimed, rousing Darcy from his drunken stupor.

Lifting his head from the desk, Darcy had looked to Richard in confusion, shaking his head slightly to dismiss the faint ringing in his ears and wondering when his cousin had decided to invade his home.

"May I help you, Richard? I am not at all inclined to entertain guests at the moment."

"I imagine not, if the half-empty decanter of brandy is any indication." Richard crossed the room and poured himself a measure of the amber liquid. After taking a slow sip, he turned to Darcy with his usual biting humour. "You know, Cousin, this is a fine vintage. You *are* aware of the embargo in place at the moment, correct? If you continue on as you have been, the cellars of Darcy House may have to resort to the smuggler's ring to restock."

"Been pilfering through my stores again? Drink your glass and leave me. I am in no mood to endure your jokes."

"I am afraid I cannot oblige you there, Darcy. Your behaviour has Georgiana unsettled, and as her co-guardian, I do believe it is my responsibility to see to her concerns. If I did not know better, I would say you have the look of a man who has had his heart broken. But knowing you as I do, that would be unlikely, seeing as though you never bother to speak to a woman for more than two minutes complete."

Darcy tried and failed to keep the impact of Richard's words from showing on his features. To his humiliation, Richard seized upon his pained expression and began his interrogation in earnest.

"Oh ho! So there *is* a woman involved! Come now, man, you cannot escape my inquest now. Time to tell Richard all! So, who is this paragon who has captured the attentions of the elusive Fitzwilliam Darcy?"

Gritting his teeth, Darcy stared down his cousin from across the desk. Recognising the futility in persisting to deny his current plight, for Richard possessed a tenacity that few dogs displayed when chasing after a particularly juicy bone, Darcy succumbed to his cousin's request and replied in a quiet, yet clipped tone, "Miss Elizabeth Bennet."

"*Miss Bennet?*" Richard asked in shock. "Miss Bennet from the parsonage? Cousin to that ridiculous, bumbling oaf? *That* Miss Bennet?"

After receiving a short nod, Richard erupted in laughter. "So *that* is what this has all been about, then? I must admit you have an odd notion of courting! I believed you approved of her, for Miss Bennet is a fine woman, but I would never have discerned your interest. You barely spoke with her most days. Although, to be fair, you are perhaps not your most loquacious on evenings spent in Lady Catherine's company."

Richard's observation shamed Darcy as he came to the full realisation of how startling his proposal had likely appeared to Elizabeth. If Richard, who had known him all his life, could not detect his affection, then how on earth could she have anticipated his regard, let alone his request for her hand?

"Well, Darcy, I cannot say the family will be pleased by the lady's connexions, but if Miss Bennet means that much to you, which is clearly the case based on your rather alarming appearance, then you must know we will support you. Let go of that famous Darcy pride, and seize your happiness!"

"I am afraid that my situation is not as simple as you imply. I proposed to Miss Bennet before we left Kent, and I was refused."

"She declined your offer?" Richard interjected in disbelief.

"Unequivocally."

"How the blazes did that happen?"

"Perhaps it had something to do with the way I insulted her family, her low birth, and lamented on my struggles to repress my feelings for her that prompted her response. I believe I did, at one point, mention that I loved her, but it was clearly not enough to overcome her distaste for my other more vastly elucidated sentiments." As Darcy finished, a familiar feeling of remorse settled in his bones.

"Well, you certainly have made a muddle of—wait, do you mean to tell me that after the poor woman had to endure *our* overbearing aunt for weeks, you had the nerve to disparage *her* relations?"

"The irony is not lost on me. I have been torturing myself for over a week about my conduct and have come to the conclusion that Miss Bennet was perfectly right to refuse me. If only that had been the worst part of our exchange."

"Whatever do you mean? What could possibly be worse than your making a perfect fool of yourself in front of the woman you love?"

Darcy paused before continuing his tale, knowing Richard would not be pleased with a part of what he had to relate. Choosing to begin with the safer portion of Elizabeth's objections, Darcy proceeded to enlighten his cousin regarding her disapproval of his efforts to separate her sister Jane and Bingley.

"Now that I think on it, Richard," Darcy continued, "I cannot account for her knowledge of my role in the affair at all." An expression of both guilt and alarm spread across Richard's features, inciting Darcy's curiosity.

"I believe that is my fault. In my defence, I did not know the lady was sister to Miss Elizabeth. I merely wanted to raise her opinion of you by demonstrating how well you take care of your friends. She seemed displeased with you in some way, so I thought the story of your actions to assist Bingley would increase her esteem. Was your reluctance to pursue Miss Bennet the reason behind your actions with regard to Bingley's paramour?"

"Perhaps in part, but mainly I had convinced myself of her sister's indifference to Bingley and thought to save him from a match of unequal affections. The elder sister was so complying that I feared she would give in to their mother's more mercenary leanings."

"So, you ruined her sister's hopes. No wonder she was angry with you! While I can understand your dislike for Mrs Bennet's effusions, are we not all a little mercenary when it comes to marriage, Darcy? I myself have often admitted how I can only consider a bride with a healthy dowry if I want to maintain my current way of life as a married man."

"Yes, well, unfortunately that was not the only crime she laid at my door. I was treated to a rather rousing defence of George Wickham, as well as a thorough chastisement for my role in his current misfortunes."

"Wickham?" Richard's visage glowed with anger as he abruptly rose from his chair and pointed an accusatory finger at Darcy. "You never mentioned encountering the blackguard in Hertfordshire!"

"Sit down and calm yourself! I will explain all if you allow me a moment to collect my thoughts."

As his cousin took a long sip of his brandy, Darcy steeled himself for yet another discussion on the one man he would rather not acknowledge again.

"A few weeks after I arrived in the area, I came upon the Miss Bennets in the local village, speaking with an officer and a few other gentlemen. When I realised one of the men was Wickham, I left for Bingley's estate as fast as my horse could carry me. If I had stayed a moment longer in his presence, I would not have been able to control the impulse to run him through for all the harm he caused Georgiana.

"The next I heard of him, Wickham had purchased a lieutenancy in the local militia, and at subsequent gatherings where the officers were invited, he proceeded to divulge his usual lies concerning my father's will and the living he was denied in Kympton. Miss Elizabeth had no reason to believe him insincere, and I am sure he worked his considerable charm on her to poison any good opinion she had of me, though now that I look back, I see that I had never once done anything to earn her favourable opinion."

"An officer in the militia? I should have known Wickham would find his way into their dissolute ranks. 'Tis the perfect situation for him. Any unsavoury past can be carefully concealed behind a polished uniform and a charming smile." Richard paused before continuing. "I assume you informed the local gentlemen and shopkeepers of his habits, lest Wickham plague the neighbourhood's economy with his debts and compromise their young daughters."

Darcy's mortification was complete. If his outright neglect of the people of Meryton was not an example of a thoroughly selfish disdain for others, then he knew not what else could convince him of the rightness of Elizabeth's reproofs.

"To my everlasting shame, I did not. I could try and excuse my behaviour by claiming it was all done in the interest of protecting Georgiana's reputation, but in truth, it was simply that I thought it beneath me to expose my private dealings to people so wholly below my notice. Miss Elizabeth was right. I am an arrogant fool." Darcy ran his fingers through his dishevelled curls before turning to his cousin with a pleading expression. "What should I do? How is it that I love her all the more for her rebukes? She has forced me to see myself, and though I have come to the conclusion that I do not deserve her, I fear I cannot live without her."

"As far as I can see, there is nothing for it but to win her. You know what they say—*fortes Fortuna adiuvat*! So be bold, man! Go back to Hertfordshire, and court the lady properly this time."

Darcy responded in a decidedly dry tone. "While I am glad to see your education was not completely wasted, I believe that *boldness* did little to gain me her favour the last time we met."

"Perhaps you ought to focus on being practical. Can you not fix some of your misunderstandings? Prepare the way for a smoother path?"

"I plan to confess all to Bingley when he returns from Scarborough in a few days' time. If he is willing to forgive me for my interference, then perhaps he will permit me to accompany him back to Netherfield."

"Before you return to the area, I believe you have a letter to send to Wickham's superior officer. While I doubt the quality of most militia colonels, the least you can do is alert him to the presence of a more than usually adept villain amongst his ranks."

Standing to take his leave, Richard frowned as he looked to Darcy's desk. "You may also want to attend to that mountain of correspondence. I would rather not be forced to extricate you from the pending avalanche, should you disregard my advice and dive into your cups once more."

THE MISSIVE THAT RICHARD HAD CHARGED DARCY TO WRITE to Colonel Forster was currently lying on the polished surface of his desk. After Richard's departure, Darcy had seen to the tasks his cousin had recommended, finding comfort in the familiar habits of his life before his heart had been shattered. Only the precious gift of Elizabeth's love could mend those fractured pieces, but before he could earn that love, he needed to become a man worthy of her.

A knock on the door preceded the arrival of his butler, Mr Farley. "Lord Lisle to see you, sir."

Farley bowed and turned to leave the room just as Darcy rose to greet his cousin. It was not often that Lisle called at Darcy House, and judging by the viscount's agitated air, this was not to be a social call.

"Lisle, I had not thought to see you today. You look shaken. Is anything amiss?"

Without answering, Lisle took a seat before the fireplace while he fidgeted with his cravat, as though the offending article threatened to choke him.

"Perhaps you would like a drink? I can summon Farley and order a tea service?"

"Not tea. Brandy, if you will."

Reaching for the decanter, Darcy poured each of them a glass and returned to the chair across from Lisle, waiting in patient silence for his cousin to begin his account.

"I apologise, Darcy. I know I shall be poor company this afternoon, but I simply had to get out of the house. Richard would not understand, and God knows I cannot see Grey, not now."

"While I am more than willing to listen to your troubles, mayhap it might be best to start at the beginning? What has occurred that has unsettled you so?"

"I do not believe I would call it trouble, at least I think not. I did not mean to eavesdrop, but once I overheard what my parents were discussing, I knew I could not simply let the matter pass."

"Lisle…James, what are you speaking of?"

"I know I am not making sense." Lisle dragged his hand down the side of his face. "I overheard my parents debating in their sitting room whether or not they should relate some rather surprising news to me. Just as I was about to continue walking down the hall, my mother saw me and decided to reveal all."

Lisle paused and took a deep gulp of the drink he held, as Darcy began to mentally tally the various possibilities that would lead to such profound anxiety in his normally composed cousin.

"It appears Lord and Lady Tamworth's daughter has been found at long last."

Darcy's thoughts abruptly stalled as Lisle's declaration

was perhaps the last thing he had expected to hear. "They have found Grey's sister?"

"Apparently so. It was Grey himself who found her. He revealed everything to my mother last night after dinner."

"That is astonishing. I thought they had long given up hope of her recovery."

"Indeed they had. I visited my godmother earlier this week, and Lady Tamworth was more disheartened than I have ever seen her." Lisle seemed somewhat lost in the memory. "According to Grey, the young lady's resemblance to the countess is near perfect."

"I do not believe I have been in company with Lady Tamworth since I was a boy," Darcy declared. "From your mother, I was given to understand she rarely leaves their estate."

"Yes, she all but withdrew from society after the abduction. She has both good days and bad, but she simply has not been able to endure the stares of the *ton* with any composure in recent years."

"But I do not understand. Is this not good news? Why then do you seem so agitated?"

Lisle forcefully exhaled, stared down briefly at his hands, and then looked to Darcy in what appeared to be nervous excitement. "I am to marry her, Darcy. My father signed a betrothal contract the week before she was taken."

Lisle's statement was met with silence as Darcy gazed at his cousin in amazement. In an attempt to interject some levity, he uncharacteristically joked, "What is it about Lady Catherine's generation and their penchant for cradle engagements? You would think our parents had absolutely no faith in our abilities to find a suitable spouse."

Lisle replied smugly. "Need I remind you that your completely unappealing cradle arrangement is pure fabrication on our aunt's part? Mine comes with a marriage settlement, signed and sealed, to a beautiful woman whose family I would choose over our irascible aunt any day."

"Had you never any idea that you were intended for one another?"

"No, I was never told. It seems they never told Grey either, but as he was only eight at the time, I can understand their decision. Besides, it did not seem to matter, as all of their searches only led to dead ends and countless tears."

"They cannot force either of you to marry, should you not desire it," Darcy gently stated.

"Are you suggesting I should try and fight this? This could be the answer to my prayers! And though she is completely unknown to me, how could I ever go against the wishes of both my parents *and* my godmother in this matter? Not to mention that the lady's brother is my best friend. Could I insult them in such a way by denying their request? No, I could never attempt it, and furthermore, I do not think I would wish to. My godmother was a beauty in her youth, and so her daughter should be also. Beauty, connexions, fortune, and a family I already love as my own…I would be a fool not to agree."

Hoping to restore some calm and reason to his cousin's excited ramblings, Darcy gently gripped Lisle's forearm and fixed him with an earnest gaze. "You do realise, James, that the lady may not wish to marry *you*."

"What woman would choose to refuse the life of a future countess? I do not believe Grey's sister has reached her majority, and I very much doubt a newly recovered girl would possess the fortitude to go against her true family's wishes. I may not be quite so handsome as you, but I believe I am somewhat appealing to the fairer sex."

Rolling his eyes at his cousin's flippancy, Darcy responded, "Well, whatever happens, I will stand by you."

"I appreciate that, Darcy. Let us hope I can satisfy both the desires of the ones I love and my own in this instance."

After a few more moments, Lisle thanked him for his ready ear and left his cousin's home, baffling Darcy with his eagerness for such an arrangement. As the substance of his eldest cousin's situation washed over him, Darcy experienced a sincere flash of gratitude for his relative freedom, thankful that, despite the obstacles he had placed in his own path, he was at liberty to pursue his Elizabeth without such entanglements weighing him down.

Other than her feelings against me, of course.

CHAPTER TEN

Sitting quietly in the corner of the nursery, Madeline Gardiner rocked her sleeping son while slowly running her fingers through his flaxen locks. Poor Edwin had found little rest the previous evening due to complaints of a slight earache, and though his fever had all but subsided and the illness was clearly not of a serious nature, Mrs Gardiner was grateful for the opportunity to hold him close, if only for a short while.

Her two-year-old son usually enjoyed a boundless energy which had clearly been inherited from her husband's far more boisterous family. Liveliness was not the only Gardiner trait her son had received, for surely he possessed the same light blue eyes, pale complexion, and blond hair as his father, his aunt, and his eldest cousin. Indeed, the Gardiner features were so strong in her children that her five-year-old daughter, Meg, bore a remarkable resemblance to her cousin Jane. Only her eldest, Matthew, had inherited Mrs Gardiner's slightly auburn tresses and green eyes. Thoughts of her husband's family brought her back to the revelations that had so thoroughly shocked her the previous evening, and she unconsciously held her young son more firmly in her embrace as she reflected on the life-altering news she had received.

Dinner had been an unexpectedly awkward affair, as her normally jovial husband contributed little to the evening's conversation and appeared by turns to be both apprehensive and somehow pained in their company. Even though both of their nieces had been somewhat changed during their recent visit, Mr Gardiner still delighted in their society, and so his wife could not account for his strange behaviour, particularly the way he often gazed in Elizabeth's direction with a wistful, yet worried expression.

When they retired for the evening, Mrs Gardiner had intended to question her husband regarding his odd demeanour but was forestalled by a surprising start to their conversation.

"I had a rather unexpected meeting at the office earlier today. A baron, Lord Grey was his name, arrived unannounced and requested an interview."

"Oh? Did he come seeking an opportunity to invest? I am sure it would be a great boon for the business to involve a member of the peerage."

"No, my dear, his intent was to discuss a matter of a far more personal nature."

"I do not understand, Edward. What private dealings could you possibly have with a baron you have never met?"

Mrs Gardiner sat upright on the bed and turned to directly face her husband, noting his apparent nervousness. He reached out to grasp her hand in his, lowered his head, and inhaled deeply before once again raising his face to meet her gaze.

"I am afraid I have an important confession to make."

Mrs Gardiner's worry increased significantly at her husband's choice of words. They had never kept secrets from one another before.

"Pray understand, by the time we met, I rarely thought

on the incident. I did not deliberately keep this information from you, it was only that she was already ten years old at the time, and we all loved her so fiercely that I never gave any thought to her origins, as the circumstances of her birth did not matter to me in the—"

"Edward, stop! You are not making any sense. What on earth are you speaking of? *Whose* origins?"

"Forgive me, my dear." He paused, taking a steadying breath before giving his explanation. "What I am trying to relate is simply this—our niece, Elizabeth, is not in fact a true daughter to Thomas and Fanny. She was taken in as a foundling when she was only a few months old, as they had discovered her somewhere near Meryton on a journey home from London."

Mrs Gardiner silently listened as her husband revealed all he knew regarding Elizabeth's installation in the Bennet family, her heart breaking for the loss Fanny had endured, while yet concerned by the mysterious nature of Elizabeth's background.

"I always had trouble identifying any resemblance between Lizzy and the Gardiner family, but then, Thomas always insisted upon her resemblance to his late mother. Since both Mary and Kitty also possessed the Bennet brown hair, though not precisely the same shade, I always let the matter pass without further scrutiny."

"Bennet did not want anyone to question Lizzy's parentage, and seeing as his mother had passed on when he was but a lad, he knew there would be few who would question his assertion."

"I still do not quite understand. What has any of this to do with your caller this afternoon?"

At her question, Mr Gardiner left the bed and walked through the door to his adjoining chambers. When he returned, he held a small item in his hands that he passed to her carefully, motioning to her to unwrap the parcel. After she removed the cloth, Mrs Gardiner let out a startled gasp as she beheld an elegant miniature portrait of their niece—or at least, someone her niece greatly resembled.

She listened to her husband in surprised awe as he recounted the story of the baron's lost sister, Lady Elizabeth Grey. After finishing his tale, Mr Gardiner once again grasped her hand and fixed her with a beseeching expression.

"He wants to meet her. I have promised Lord Grey we will see him tomorrow at the warehouse, as I told him in no uncertain terms that your counsel would be vital in relating the news to Lizzy. She will need you, my dear, and so will Jane if the baron's suspicions are correct, and at this point, I have little reason to doubt them."

The nanny's entrance into the nursery pulled Mrs Gardiner from her recollections. She carefully passed her sleeping son into the woman's arms.

"I will be gone for most of the afternoon, Lucy, but Edwin appears to be recovering well. He only wants a bit of rest to be fully set to rights. If you have any trouble with him today, please call on Jane or Lizzy for assistance, as I am sure the presence of his cousins will serve to soothe him in my absence."

"Very good, ma'am," she replied, taking her charge to his crib while Mrs Gardiner left the room.

As she walked down the staircase, she heard the faint sounds of a light, soothing melody emanating from the front parlour. Walking into the room, she was unsurprised to discover Elizabeth at the pianoforte with Meg at her side, while Jane rested on a nearby chair attending to her needlework.

"I will be leaving shortly and anticipate being gone for quite some time. Your uncle left some important papers in his study, and so I plan to bring them by his office before seeing to another call. Would you mind looking in on Edwin if he becomes fretful before my return? I am afraid I do not know how long I shall be out."

"Of course, Aunt," Jane replied. "Is he very ill?"

"I suspect not, but Edwin can be rather challenging when he is forced to abandon his usual activities."

"Fear not, Aunt Gardiner," Elizabeth began, "I am sure Meg and I can provide ample entertainment until you come home. Can we not, Meg?"

"Of course! We will tell him the best stories, Mama!"

"Thank you, my dears. I shall see you before dinner."

Turning to leave, Mrs Gardiner felt a warmth in her heart at the obvious love her dear Jane and Elizabeth displayed for her children. That warmth, however, was promptly replaced by unease, as she had never before lied to them. She and her husband had prepared their relatively harmless deception to avoid arousing any suspicions, but the duplicity did not sit well with her. Mrs Gardiner supposed the coming meeting was only adding to her distress, so she called for the carriage that would take her to an introduction which was sure to produce rather far-reaching consequences.

During the brief carriage ride, Mrs Gardiner reflected on the slight changes she had noticed in her nieces the previous evening. After months of despondency, Jane finally seemed to have recovered some of her spirits, as her usual gentleness and slight smiles seemed more genuine than they had since before Elizabeth's return. Perhaps the comforting presence of her most beloved sister was helping to heal her broken heart. Elizabeth, however, had still not returned to her usual cheer, as her manner had been decidedly introspective. She had clearly not resolved whatever it was that had so bothered her in Kent. Mrs Gardiner only hoped the results of her coming meeting would not be too much for her young niece to bear.

Arriving at her husband's warehouse, Mrs Gardiner alighted from her carriage and entered the small front office. Young Samuel led the way to Edward's door, and when she entered the room, she noticed her husband was sitting quietly behind his desk, absently staring into his cup of tea. Upon her entrance, he rose to take her hand and led her to the small settee where they both sat to wait for the arrival of their guest, neither one speaking for fear of breaking the stillness that had settled over the space.

In but a moment, Samuel returned. "Lord Grey is here to see you both. Shall I show him in, sir?"

"Yes, Sam, thank you," Edward replied, rising from his chair.

As her husband gave the appropriate greetings and introduced her to Lord Nicholas Grey, Mrs Gardiner could do naught but stare in wonder at the young man before her. He was a handsome gentleman, with wavy, light brown hair and a bearing that suggested confidence in his place in the world. But what most held her attention were his startlingly deep brown eyes, the eyes of her dear Elizabeth, and she had no doubt that at the first trace of laughter, they would sparkle in the exact same way.

"Forgive me, my lord, but I cannot help but see your resemblance to my niece. This whole affair has me quite surprised, and I am still adjusting to the news."

"There is no need to apologise, Mrs Gardiner," Lord Grey replied gently. "I am pleased you see a likeness to Elizabeth in me."

As a small smile appeared on the baron's face, Mrs Gardiner noted yet another similarity in his features while her husband invited them all to sit so that their conversation could begin in earnest.

"I thank you both for meeting me. As I told your husband the other day, Mrs Gardiner, I am determined to go about this in the best possible way for Elizabeth's sake. I do not want to upset her with what I am sure will be rather surprising news. To that end, I would greatly appreciate any wisdom you have to impart."

"I think the first item that needs to be addressed will be the reactions of Thomas and Fanny Bennet," Mr Gardiner began. "You see, Lord Grey, you should become better acquainted with the situation in Elizabeth's home if this matter is to be handled with any delicacy. My sister Fanny, while a good-hearted woman, suffers from a nervous complaint and can behave quite improperly at times. After giving birth only to daughters, her worries for her future had an adverse effect on her behaviour. The Bennet estate, Longbourn, is entailed away from the female line, and a distant cousin, Mr Collins, is set to inherit upon Mr Bennet's death."

"Mr Collins is a parson in Kent," Mrs Gardiner interjected. "In fact, Lizzy has just come from a stay in his home, as her closest friend from Hertfordshire married Mr Collins shortly after the new year."

Continuing for her husband, Mrs Gardiner explained further. "The reason you need to know this, my lord, is that Fanny will most likely not take this news well—that is, she will not receive this news quietly. If you would like to keep Elizabeth's story from the ears of the entire county, then it would be best to leave Fanny uninformed for the time being. She would not be able to keep this information to herself."

"Moreover," Mr Gardiner continued, "I believe it would be best to keep this from Bennet as well. As I mentioned during our previous discourse, I was never able to extract the full tale of Lizzy's discovery from Bennet, despite my repeated enquiries. If he has no previous knowledge of your situation, his surprise may result in a more honest telling of Elizabeth's adoption. Lizzy is beyond doubt Bennet's favourite child, and he will be most reluctant to lose her." After a shared look with his wife, he admitted, "We should also discuss how to keep Elizabeth in London for the foreseeable future, which will not be an easy task. Lizzy and Jane serve as a calming presence at Longbourn, and since they have both been absent for several months, Bennet will desire their return, if only to bring order and sensible conversation to his household once more."

"If you sent the eldest Miss Bennet home, would that allow us any additional time with Elizabeth?"

"I think it best to keep Jane here for as long as possible," Mrs Gardiner replied. "Jane is Elizabeth's dearest friend. Elizabeth will need her when you deliver your news, and she will need Jane's assistance as she copes with such a change in her circumstances."

"I see. Perhaps a slight illness could be reported back to the Bennet home?" he asked.

Mr Gardiner concurred. "Jane took ill last fall. If her mother thought she was suffering from a recurrence, she would be more cautious about insisting upon their travel."

Lord Grey nodded. "After I meet Elizabeth, I plan to travel to see Mr Bennet and hopefully, my father will accompany me. My godmother mentioned the other evening that there was more to the story of my sister's disappearance than I was previously told, though I cannot imagine what it might be."

"In case Bennet insists upon their return, we should probably speak to Lizzy soon," Mr Gardiner recommended. "And Jane should be present as well."

"Would Miss Bennet keep this information from her parents?" Lord Grey looked doubtful as he voiced his concern.

"Jane will do what is best for Lizzy," Mrs Gardiner stated with confidence. "She is not unaware of her parents' faults, and in this instance, she will do all she can to see to the comfort of her sister."

After a moment's reflection, she decided it was best not to inform the young gentleman about the comfort her niece had needed of late. Whatever Elizabeth was struggling with, it was not her place to share it with this man, brother or no. She could see her words had assuaged his concerns regarding Jane, and so in the interest of moving the matter forward, Mrs Gardiner issued an invitation.

"You are welcome to join us for dinner this evening,

Lord Grey. I think my husband is right, and we should introduce you to Elizabeth as soon as may be."

A joyous smile, startling in its familiarity, spread across the young man's face. "Thank you, Mrs Gardiner, I would not miss this evening should Napoleon himself arrive to drag me away."

CHAPTER ELEVEN

Having bid her cousins goodnight, Elizabeth closed the nursery door and made her way back to her chambers to dress for dinner. She had been surprised when her aunt returned home from her calls, only to be informed they were expecting a guest for the evening. As her aunt seemed nervous, Elizabeth assumed the visitor must be an important business associate of her uncle's, for she knew he was currently taking on a few new investors in his latest shipping venture. The request that both she and Jane dress well for dinner seemed to confirm her suspicions, and Elizabeth wondered if perhaps her aunt was attempting to play matchmaker for Jane, as she had referred to the 'young gentleman' with a small smile upon her face.

Returning to her room, Elizabeth looked to the newly pressed gown that was laid across her bed. The beautiful green silk was one of her finest, and upon seeing it, she recollected the last time she had worn it in company.

Many of the evenings spent at Rosings were rather tedious, but on that singular evening, Elizabeth had been asked to demonstrate her proficiency on the pianoforte, ostensibly for the sole purpose of providing an object for Lady Catherine's criticisms. After stalking across the room, Mr Darcy had engaged her in one of their usual debates, the ultimate goal of which Elizabeth believed to be an effort to increase her mortification in the presence of his relations. She had teased him about his behaviour in Hertfordshire, admonishing him to practise his skills in the art of conversation in the same way she ought to attend to her deficiencies at the instrument. She had thought him to be mocking her when he seemed to compliment her skills. *No one admitted to the privilege of hearing you can think anything wanting. We neither of us perform to strangers.*

Now, with a better understanding regarding his feelings, their conversation took on new meaning. He had been trying to pay her a compliment, and his observation regarding his inability to converse with persons unknown was actually a reference to his shyness. *So many misunderstandings…so many missed opportunities.*

Jane entered the room, her blue silk gown swaying with her graceful movements, her hair perfectly coiffed and ready for the evening's entertainment. "Lizzy, why are you not dressed?"

"You have caught me wool-gathering."

"Well, it is no matter. Let me help you dress and then Betsy can finish pinning up your hair."

As the women bustled about Elizabeth's bedchamber, each offered her speculation about their surprise guest. After Elizabeth was deemed presentable, she left the room with Jane to descend the staircase and join their aunt and uncle in the parlour. They had just arrived when their visitor was shown into the room.

"Ah, there you are, my lord!" Mr Gardiner exclaimed. "Lord Grey, allow me to introduce my nieces, Miss Jane Bennet, and her sister, Miss Elizabeth. Ladies, Lord Nicholas Grey."

Rising from her curtsey, Elizabeth studied the young man before her, only to notice with a surprised start that he was the same man she had briefly encountered in the park a few days past.

"I am very pleased to meet you both, for your uncle has told me much about you. Especially you, Miss Elizabeth."

A slight pinch from Jane alerted Elizabeth that she had not responded to the young lord's acknowledgement.

With a slight nod of her head she replied in a somewhat shaky voice, "I thank you, my lord, but you appear to have the advantage, for my uncle has never mentioned you before this evening."

Their brief conversation was interrupted by the announcement for dinner, and as her uncle escorted her aunt into the next room, Lord Grey offered an arm to Jane and his other to Elizabeth. As he accompanied them to their seats, Elizabeth was surprised to note that the gentleman's focus remained on her, since usually men were instantly enthralled by Jane's beauty. Lost in thought and undecided as to whether she should mention his assistance in the park, Elizabeth left the others to make small talk.

"Does your family reside in London, Lord Grey?" Jane enquired.

"My family seat is in Staffordshire. Our estate, Heatherton Hall, is quite beautiful, and my parents prefer to keep to the country for most of the year."

"Will you be in town long?"

"I am here for the Season, as I currently attend Parliament in my father's stead. My mother has no great love for high society and my father prefers not to leave her side." Though Lord Grey replied to Jane, his gaze was consistently drawn across the table to Elizabeth.

"Do you enjoy your duties in the House, my lord?" Mr Gardiner asked.

"On some days, sir, but mainly I am subjected to constant bickering between my father's peers. I sometimes dread the day I will inherit the earldom, not only because my father is dear to me, but because it will inevitably entail more time spent amongst the society of those I rarely enjoy."

As her uncle continued to engage their guest in matters of politics, a topic Elizabeth would usually find intriguing, she found she could not cast aside her confusion regarding the man's presence in her uncle's home.

Did he recognise her from the park, and if so, how did he find her again? To what purpose? And why did his eyes seem so astonishingly familiar? She knew those eyes too well, for they were the same ones that stared back at her, day in and day out, in her bedroom mirror.

"You are awfully quiet, Lizzy," Jane declared, her voice rousing Elizabeth from her thoughts. "Indeed, I believe Mama would declare you to be 'quite dull' this evening."

The teasing expression on Jane's face removed any insult from her words, and Elizabeth sought to respond in kind.

"Ah, a capital offence! Particularly when in the company of a young gentleman who appears to be in want of a wife!"

With a lifted brow, Elizabeth directed an arch expression at her sister. She had only meant to tease, but the audible gasp Lord Grey uttered at her remark convinced her that she may have overstepped in mixed company, for it was not as though he had any experience with the ramblings of Fanny Bennet.

For the remainder of the dinner, Elizabeth stayed silent, observing the interactions between her family and their guest while continuing to struggle with the feeling of familiarity that had crept over her since she caught his gaze. After the last course was cleared, her aunt stood and Elizabeth and Jane followed, intending to leave Lord Grey and her uncle to both their after dinner spirits and to what she assumed were the business matters their visitor had come to discuss. She was surprised, therefore, when her uncle declared there was no need to separate and insisted that they join the ladies in the sitting room. Settling on the sofa with Jane, Elizabeth's curiosity increased as her aunt sat on her other side and gently reached for her hand. Before she could question her aunt, Mr Gardiner turned to her with a thoughtful expression upon his countenance.

"My dears, I apologise for any odd behaviour this evening and for what I assume will be an unusual topic of conversation." He paused briefly, as though what he dared to voice required an inordinate amount of courage. "Jane, Elizabeth, can either of you tell me what you were told regarding the story of Elizabeth's birth?"

The strangeness of this request brought an eerie silence to the room, as both young women were understandably puzzled by the question.

Finding her courage first, Jane replied, "Elizabeth was born in London. Mama, Papa, and I were visiting you and Grandmother Gardiner at your new apartments when Mama went into early labour. Papa said we stayed with you in London while Mama recovered, and only returned to Longbourn shortly before Christmas." Jane finished her statement with a hesitant tone that seemed to question the purpose of his enquiry.

"That is as I thought, Jane. Thank you, my dear, for obliging me in this rather strange request. The reason I asked is that I have a revelation to make to you both, for you see, your mother did go into early labour during her visit, but it was after a grievous fall and the child, your sister, was lost."

With this declaration Elizabeth's heart began to beat so loudly she thought all of the room's occupants would soon be able to hear it. She listened, caught between horror and shock, as her uncle explained that she had been found…*found*, not born, *found* by her parents on their return journey to Longbourn. She could feel Jane's hand squeezing her own tightly, but Elizabeth could not turn to look at her. She could do nothing but sit, mute and unmoving, until she recognised the voice of her aunt who pressed a cup of wine to her lips.

"Take a sip, Lizzy. You are extremely pale."

Numbly following her aunt's instructions, Elizabeth drank from the glass. She was not sure if she was expected to ask any questions about her uncle's revelation and was surprised to hear the gentle voice of their guest penetrating the fog that had clouded her mind.

"Miss Elizabeth, I know this is not easy to hear, but I would like to tell you a story I believe may shed some light. For you see, that very same winter, my family suffered a similar loss. After recovering from a severe illness, my family's nursemaid appeared to have lost some of her mental faculties. We were not aware of how far her illness had progressed, for if we had known, she would never have been allowed to return to her post. You see, her main responsibility at the time was tending to my sister, who was only a few months old. For some reason, the answer to which I have never learned, our nanny, Miss Summers, abducted my sister from our family's estate in early December, only a week or two before you were found by the Bennets in Hertfordshire."

Pausing in his tale, Lord Grey turned to Mr Gardiner and held out his hand. At his gesture, her uncle produced a small item that Elizabeth, in her distraction, had failed to notice. Unwrapping the item carefully, Lord Grey crossed the room, knelt before her, and placed a small portrait in the palm of her hand. Barely noticing her sister's astonished gasp over her shoulder, Elizabeth could do naught but stare at the image before her.

In an unsteady voice, she looked to the man on his knees and asked, "Who—who is she?"

"Her name is Lady Amelia Grey, and she is my mother—well, I believe she is *our* mother."

Elizabeth's gaze was resolutely fixed on the painting in her delicate grip as his statement settled over the tension and grief that had pervaded the room. After a moment, he continued.

"I have reviewed my family's story and your own with your uncle, and every piece of information I have gathered, including your astonishing appearance and familiar mannerisms, has only served to convince me of the truth... that you are...in fact...my lost sister, Lady Elizabeth Amelia Grey."

Elizabeth looked up in surprise at the connexion of her name and at the awareness of Jane's arms reaching around her in a tight embrace.

"When I saw you that day in the park, somehow I knew it was you—that at long last, God had chosen to smile down upon my family and return you to us. You do not know what your recovery will mean to everyone...to our parents."

"But sir," Elizabeth began, her voice small and unsure, "I do not believe you have definitive proof that I am your sister."

"I have no doubts, I assure you, but my next task is to summon my parents to town. It is my hope that my father and I will travel to your home in Hertfordshire as soon as we are able, for it is possible that Mr Bennet can provide the evidence we seek. Owing to your Christian name, it is likely he met Miss Summers, and if he retained any of your belongings from that day, we should be able to confirm all. You *will* be a part of our family once more."

Struggling with the weight of such a proclamation, Elizabeth lowered her gaze to the portrait once more, staring at the image of a woman who was so like her in every way. A strong masculine hand gently covered hers, bringing her out of her reverie.

"Elizabeth, do I have your permission to write to my parents?"

The hope in his voice convinced her to give a slight nod of acquiescence, though for the most part, she still felt remarkably numb in light of the evening's revelations.

With a small smile, Lord Grey stood and addressed the others.

"I shall take my leave now, but I would like your permission to see you again, Elizabeth, if I may?"

Unable to deny his request, Elizabeth again nodded as she leaned into Jane's embrace. With one last smile, their visitor took his leave.

When the door closed behind Lord Grey, Elizabeth faintly perceived the concerned voices of her relations as they discussed the events of the evening in hushed tones. The more they spoke, the more her unrest grew, until all at once she could bear their presence no longer. Desperately needing solitude and convinced that her chest was tightening about her, Elizabeth ran for the front door, insensible of the cries of her family behind her. Not bothering to grab a shawl, Elizabeth tore open the heavy aperture and dashed down the steps to the pavement below.

Making for a small copse of trees and a solitary bench in the modest park across the street, she failed to note the pounding hoof beats of an oncoming horse and its rider. A small cry of alarm escaped her lips as the rider quickly brought his mount to a stop, narrowly avoiding what could have been a rather disastrous collision. Tears streaming down her cheeks, Elizabeth looked up in thanks, only to see a familiar face looking down upon her in astonishment, his features slowly overshadowed with worry as he noted her obvious distress.

"Mr Darcy!"

CHAPTER TWELVE

A spirit of restlessness overcame Darcy following his cousin's visit that afternoon. The anticipated note of Bingley's arrival in town had been delivered to Darcy House shortly after Lisle's departure, bringing Darcy one step closer on his path to redemption. He had resolved to call on Bingley the next morning to make his long overdue disclosure, and he fervently prayed he would not lose such a valued friendship as a result. The suspense was agonising, knowing if Bingley chose to return to Hertfordshire, Darcy may have not only the means to correct his grievous error, but also the ability to see *her* again. He hoped that by restoring the happiness of her most beloved sister, Elizabeth's opinion of him might be improved and he would no longer remain the last man she would wish to marry.

His hopes rekindled, Darcy attacked the remaining business matters on his desk with vigour. After completing several letters for his solicitor, Darcy seized the opportunity to deliver the important articles in person, instead of following his usual practice of sending a trusted servant or waiting for his attorney to visit him at home. If he were to be completely honest, Darcy knew the prospect of riding through Cheapside, where he knew Elizabeth had stayed with her relations in the past, held too much promise for him. Despite his belief that the woman he loved had returned to Hertfordshire, the idea of riding down the lanes where she had previously walked felt somehow fitting as he contemplated the events the following day's interview might bring. The desk clerks at his solicitor's office had been suitably surprised by his arrival, impressing upon Darcy the relative incongruity of his behaviour, as his spontaneity was more akin to something Bingley might do in a fit of besottedness.

After completing his task, Darcy was reluctant to return to his home. Even with the knowledge that he would miss his evening meal with Georgiana, Darcy continued to ride aimlessly through the streets of London, his mind occupied with the countless possibilities the morrow could bring.

Some hours later, riding down Gracechurch Street in the cool, spring evening air, the ornate steeple of St Edmund's looming near, Darcy was so lost in thought that he almost failed to notice the figure of a young woman darting across the street. Pulling tightly on his horse's reins, Darcy was horrified to have almost injured the lady, even if she was rather foolish for running out into the street with only the soft glow from the windows of nearby dwellings to light her path.

Looking down to enquire after her well-being, he was startled to hear her gasp of surprise and his name upon her lips. For there, staring up at him, was the woman who had occupied his thoughts for the last seven months. At first, he was certain she was a vision conjured from his imaginings. The evidence of her tears, however, promptly convinced him of the truth of her presence and evoked his immediate concern. Quickly dismounting, Darcy moved to her side to steady her.

"Miss Bennet! Are you unharmed? I cannot apologise enough for startling you."

Her surprise at his sudden appearance had apparently rendered her speechless, as she continued to look upon him with an almost wild expression. Noticing she was trembling in naught but an evening gown, Darcy's concern increased. Removing his greatcoat, he draped the thick garment about her shoulders, rubbing her arms in an effort to erase the chill of the evening. Looking beyond her to what he thought was her intended destination, Darcy espied a small bench sheltered by two or three trees only a few feet away.

"Miss Bennet, may I escort you to that bench? I believe you should sit down. You do not look well."

Still unable to speak, Elizabeth regarded him in confusion before ultimately giving a small nod of assent. Wrapping her arm around his, Darcy led her to the small seat and quickly secured his horse's reins to a low-lying branch before settling in at her side. Her distress appeared to be profound, as a new wave of tears flowed down her lovely face.

"You are safe, Miss Bennet," he assured her. "Is there naught I can do to relieve your suffering?"

His sincere care seemed to rouse her from her state of shock, as all at once, her sobs began in earnest as she leaned into his side. Moving his arm around her, Elizabeth turned her tear-stained face into his jacket, clutching the lapel with a fierce hold as she poured out her grief into the stillness of the night.

Knowing her to be possessed of a nigh indestructible courage, Darcy knew her present affliction had to stem from more than just their chance meeting. Elizabeth was a rational creature, and her present attire and lack of a suitable companion suggested this was not an anticipated outing.

When her tears finally subsided, Elizabeth stiffened in his arms. With a face reddened in embarrassment, she slowly righted herself and accepted his offered handkerchief, wiping away the remaining tears on her cheeks.

"Forgive me, Mr Darcy," she began in a shaky voice. "I appear to have wrinkled your coat with my indecorous display."

"'Tis no matter. My valet may disagree with me, but he has had considerable cause to be irritated with me of late, so I doubt one more garment to attend to will lower me any further in his esteem," he replied, hoping to restore some of her humour. It seemed to work, for she gave him a small smile and fixed him with a curious expression.

"I am afraid I have trouble believing in the veracity of your statement, sir, as I have never seen you look in the least bit dishevelled. Are you truly that difficult to keep properly attired?"

Any mortification he might have felt was mollified by the humour he heard in her voice. "I assure you, madam, that what you see before you is the product of considerable time and effort. My hair, in particular, gives him ample grief. So much so, that at times I fear my valet will simply shave it all off one day."

Elizabeth giggled slightly. "Ah, well in that at least I can sympathise. Curly hair can be a bit of a curse to maintain. Mama has forever lamented how unruly my curls can become compared to the more manageable tresses of my sisters." At her seemingly innocent statement, a lost and anguished expression overwhelmed her features once more.

"Miss Bennet, are you sure you are well? I cannot help but notice your distress appears to be of a rather serious nature."

Looking down at his handkerchief that she held in her grip, Darcy could see her attempt to formulate a response as she slowly traced his initials embroidered in the corner of the cloth.

"I cannot…that is, sir—I do not know if I am at liberty to…"

Seeing her distress, Darcy quickly sought to reassure her. "Forgive me. I am fully aware I have no right to know your private concerns. I only wish to provide assistance if I may."

"No, no. I am not offended, I assure you. 'Tis only that I am so confused. I doubt I could explain my troubles even if I managed to make the attempt. Truly, I appreciate your solicitousness. It is far more than I deserve after the way I have treated you."

Darcy looked to her in bewilderment. "I do not understand. How have you ever treated me poorly? If anything, it is I that must make amends for my deplorable behaviour, not you, Miss Bennet."

"You are too kind, but surely you must remember how hateful I was at our last meeting. I cannot think on it without remorse, especially now that I know how thoroughly I misjudged you."

"Pray, do not dwell on that, for while your accusations were perhaps misguided and founded on false information, your reproofs were entirely justified. I have been a selfish being all my life, and my manners, both in Hertfordshire and in Kent, merited your ire. Your words convinced me that I know nothing of how to please a woman worthy of being pleased. For you are worthy, Miss Bennet, and I cannot express how sorry I am that I ever said anything to make you feel otherwise."

Elizabeth lowered her gaze once more to her lap, while Darcy hoped he had not been too forward with his apologies. When she raised her eyes to his again, he was relieved to see a slight smile on her face.

"Did my letter—did it improve your opinion of me?" he asked. "I fear I was too angry when I wrote it and that I achieved naught but to bring you more pain with my disclosures."

"Perhaps it was angry at the start, but I assure you it did not remain so. Indeed, by the end, you were quite charitable. I do not know how kind I would have been if forced to recount the deeds of one who had so injured me. Can you ever forgive me for believing Mr Wickham?"

"You do not need my forgiveness. If I had been more forthright when you first applied for information about that scoundrel, you would have never been taken in at all. He is a practiced deceiver, and I left you at his mercy simply because I would not expose my private dealings to the world. No, you do not need my forgiveness, but I fear I do need yours."

Darcy was shocked to see a rather determined expression settle across her tear-stained features.

"I will not allow you to take responsibility for this. It is not your fault that I abandoned all reason and propriety by giving merit to such a man, and worse still, one who chose to defame another to a person of less than one evening's acquaintance. I believed the worst of you, with what I now acknowledge to be little provocation. I would have your forgiveness, sir, if you are willing to grant it."

"In that case, of course, you are undoubtedly forgiven, but only if you will grant me that same absolution."

"We are a pretty pair, are we not?" she quipped with a laugh. "If you are as determined as I, then yes, sir, you have my forgiveness." All at once her humour changed to hesitancy. "Mr Darcy, if it is not too impertinent a request, may I ask, how does your sister fare?"

"She is—she is recovering. I admit that when I was in Hertfordshire, I was concerned Georgiana might be forever scarred by the events of that summer, but when I returned to London for the Christmas season, she seemed to improve once we were able to be honest with one another. In the same way I feel I failed you by not exposing Wickham's true nature, I also feel as though I failed her. Georgiana would not have behaved the way she did had I thought to inform her of his dissolute ways." He paused for a moment. "I believe, Miss Elizabeth, that you would find her words to me rather amusing, since they quite mirror your response as well. She was upset that I had placed so much blame upon my shoulders, but then again, she was but fifteen, and I was her guardian."

"Miss Darcy sounds quite wise for such a young woman. You cannot bear all of the responsibility for the affair, as I believe there is but one person to whom the majority of the blame must be rendered."

Her words comforted him as much as her absolution, and he could not help but smile at her for it.

With an answering smile that near took his breath away, Elizabeth continued. "Tell me, what is Miss Darcy like? Is she as reserved as you, or is she more boisterous like my younger sisters?"

"I wish she possessed some of your family's spirit, but Georgiana is painfully shy, and as I suffer from a similar disposition, I have often feared for her ability to make friends. I suppose that is why my father appointed Colonel Fitzwilliam as her co-guardian. He knew she would need a more buoyant influence than I could ever provide."

"Well, the colonel certainly is lively, but I am sure Miss Darcy appreciates your guidance all the same," she replied with a slight shiver.

Distracted as he had been by their conversation, Darcy had failed to note the dropping temperature.

"Forgive me, you must be nearly frozen by now. Please allow me to escort you home."

"I suppose I must return, for my relations will be worried by my absence," she concurred, raising his handkerchief once again to her face. "I must look an absolute fright."

"You are lovely as always, though perhaps a bit blue about your lips."

With a decidedly arch expression that set his heart to racing, Elizabeth enquired, "Oh? Is that so? I suppose lovely is a far sight better than *tolerable*."

At her emphasis on the word, Darcy was instantly

immersed in the mortifying recollection of that horrible evening in Meryton. His embarrassment must have shown upon his face, for she hastily sought to reassure him.

"I should not have said anything! It was unforgivably rude after the comfort and kindness you have shown to me this evening. I only thought to tease, but perhaps I should have held my tongue."

"Once again, it is not your fault. I was not sure you had heard me that evening. No wonder you held me in such poor regard! I truly do not merit your forgiveness for such uncivil and untruthful words." Pausing to direct his earnest gaze on her beautiful face, Darcy professed, "It has been some time since I have considered you to be the handsomest woman of my acquaintance."

In spite of the cold, his compliment rendered her such a becoming shade of pink that he had trouble recalling himself to the task at hand. Once again, her slight trembling alerted him to the need to seek shelter.

"Well, shall I escort you home? You are staying nearby, I take it?"

"Yes, with my aunt and uncle. Their home is just across the way."

She pointed to a modest but well-appointed town home, where Darcy swore he saw the closing of a curtain at her gesture. That would explain her lack of attendant, he thought, for someone must have been watching her from the window.

Extending his arm to her, he was relieved when she took it without hesitation, allowing him to convey her across the street and up the steps to her relations' home. As she reached for the handle, Darcy paused and looked to her with a questioning glance, his nerves somewhat unsettling him as he gathered his courage.

"Before we go inside, would it be too much to ask how long you plan to stay in London?"

"I cannot say—that is, I am not certain of my immediate plans. I expect I will be staying longer than I originally intended."

A far-off, troubled look covered her face, and his concern increased at the sight of it. Clearly, all was not well in her world, and he wished there was something he could do to alleviate her pain.

Pressing on, Darcy made the application he desired. "In that case, would you allow me to call on you tomorrow?"

He was encouraged by the happy, yet understandably cautious expression that brightened her face. "Yes, I believe I would like that very much."

Feeling far lighter than he had in weeks, Darcy opened the door to her uncle's home and ushered her inside. Upon their entrance, Elizabeth was immediately embraced by a rather distraught Jane while an elegant couple, Darcy assumed to be her aunt and uncle, watched on. Their anxiety for their niece was clearly displayed; however, it seemed to be tempered by their curiosity regarding his presence.

"Oh Lizzy, I was so worried when you ran from the house! You must be thoroughly chilled!"

"I will admit to being cold, but as you can see I am quite well," Elizabeth assured her sister, stroking her back as Jane continued to hold her tightly in her arms.

After a few more moments of soothing her sister's worries, Elizabeth pulled back and turned her gaze to Mr Darcy once more. Recognising the need to make introductions, Elizabeth looked to her aunt and uncle as she invited the gentleman forward.

"May I present Mr Fitzwilliam Darcy of Derbyshire. Mr Darcy, this is my uncle Mr Edward Gardiner, and his wife, Mrs Madeline Gardiner."

"I am pleased to make your acquaintance. I apologise for the unusual circumstance of our meeting, but I found your niece just outside and thought to offer my assistance."

"It is much appreciated, Mr Darcy," Mr Gardiner

replied. "I understand you have met my sister's family during a visit to Hertfordshire."

"Yes, indeed, sir." Recalling his manners, he turned to Elizabeth's sister and continued. "I am pleased to see you again as well, Miss Bennet."

With a polite curtsey, Jane replied, "I am most grateful for the services you rendered to my sister. I was quite worried for Elizabeth when she left without even a shawl for protection against the cold."

Her words prompted Elizabeth to look down at his greatcoat that still hung about her shoulders. Divesting herself of his garment, she handed the coat back to him, and he was delighted to note that her jasmine scent still clung to the fibres.

"Well, I shall leave you in the care of your family, Miss Elizabeth, as I am sure that my own is no doubt wondering where I am." Turning to her uncle he added, "With your permission, sir, I would like to call on Miss Elizabeth on the morrow. I wish to be sure she has suffered no ill-effects from being exposed to such a chilly evening."

"Certainly, Mr Darcy," Mr Gardiner replied, though Darcy swore he sensed a bit of unease in his tone as he looked back and forth between himself and his niece. "Again, please accept my gratitude for your care of Lizzy tonight."

"It was my pleasure, Mr Gardiner."

He made his bow to the ladies. Pausing to take Elizabeth's hand in his, Darcy looked directly into her eyes as he bowed over her delicate palm and said, "Until tomorrow."

"Until tomorrow, Mr Darcy."

By the time he returned to Berkeley Square, Darcy could neither recall precisely how he had arrived at home nor how long it had taken him to traverse the darkened city, for hope—unbridled and unfettered hope—had sprung to life in his chest. Though still concerned by her obvious distress, Darcy could not believe he had obtained Elizabeth's forgiveness for all he had said and done.

He supposed that was not *entirely* true. They had not canvassed the issue regarding Bingley and Miss Bennet, but at least that was one task he could see to before he visited her again. Retiring to his bed, Darcy knew his dreams would be filled with her, but this time, Elizabeth's smiles would not be imagined. No, this time he would meditate on the brilliance of a very real expression of delight, made all the more enchanting by the knowledge she did not in fact despise him any longer.

CHAPTER THIRTEEN

Staring at the imposing façade of the Hursts' Mayfair home, Darcy knew he would much rather be in Cheapside, anticipating an afternoon spent in Elizabeth's incomparable company. Instead, he was faced with the prospect of a decidedly awkward interview, one in which he was unsure he would receive the forgiveness Elizabeth had so undeservedly granted him the previous evening.

Elizabeth. Darcy still had to resist the constant urge to pinch himself to be positive that the prior night was not merely a figment of his imagination. He had seen her, spoken to her, and somehow she had agreed to allow him to visit her, but before he would allow himself to do that, he had a confession to make.

Gathering his courage, Darcy gripped beneath the ornately engraved brass lion's head and knocked upon the door, the sharp rap resonating in time with the pounding in his chest. When the butler answered, Darcy was pleased to discover the men were alone in Hurst's study, as he had no desire to see the ladies of the house. The idea of having to endure the thoughtless pandering of Miss Caroline Bingley was enough to make him wish he had simply summoned his friend to Darcy House. Chastising himself for harbouring such arrogant tendencies, Darcy returned his focus to the task at hand as the butler announced him to the gentlemen in the room.

"Darcy! So glad to see you, old chap! Though I do have to admit that when I sent my card 'round yesterday, I had no idea you would call so soon!"

Nearly bouncing with his usual light-hearted energy, Bingley quickly rose from his chair and crossed the room to shake Darcy's hand. For a moment, Darcy was at a loss as to how he should greet his cheerful friend, distracted as he was by the decided change in Bingley's spirits since he had last seen him. The genuine smile that stretched across his friend's face was not at all what Darcy had expected to encounter upon entering the study.

"I had been anticipating your return to town, and since I had no other demands on my time this morning, I thought I would call," Darcy prevaricated, unwilling at first to broach the topic that had brought him to Bingley's door. "Did you enjoy your trip to Scarborough? Your family is well, I take it?"

"They are now, I assure you," Hurst interjected. "We brought Caroline back with us."

"Oh come now, Hurst! It was not quite so bad as that," Bingley objected.

"Speak for yourself. You do not have to put up with Louisa when she is provoked by her sister's ill humours. The pair of them can create quite a stir when they put their minds to it."

Sensing Bingley's discomfort over Hurst's ruffled feathers, Darcy thought to redirect the conversation. "I believe you said you were visiting your uncle's family? Were you able to spend much time with them?"

"Yes, I quite enjoy their company, though I will concede that perhaps my sisters were less pleased with the arrangements than I. Deuced if I know why, though, for they are perfectly lovely people."

With a sarcastic edge to his tone that was more cutting than Darcy had ever heard before, Hurst levelled an incredulous look at his brother-in-law and replied, "I believe your sisters made it quite clear that they were far above spending time with relations who still possessed the 'stench of trade.' Not surprising, considering their relentless efforts to invade the higher circles of society." Hurst paused to down the contents of the glass tumbler he held. "If you will excuse me, Darcy. I fear I am poor company this morning, but please feel free to carry on in my absence."

Bingley turned to Darcy after Hurst left the room. "I am sorry, my friend. I think all of the recent travel has left my brother in a foul mood."

"It is no matter. I desired to speak to you privately."

"Oh? I do hope it is nothing serious," Bingley replied with a smile. However, upon seeing the sombre expression on Darcy's face, his expression grew puzzled.

"Yes, well—you know I value your friendship, but I fear perhaps I have not always acted in a manner befitting a friend. Rather, I believe my desire to provide you with assistance has sometimes led to my interference in your personal matters in a particularly presumptuous fashion."

"I am afraid I do not follow. What interference?"

"I suppose I should not cavil now, that is—you are aware of my dislike for any kind of deceit, and it was beneath me to behave in such a way, but the fact of the matter is that Miss Jane Bennet has been in town since January, and I knowingly hid that information from you."

Darcy awaited his friend's judgment as the room was enveloped in silence. He expected Bingley to immediately react in some way, whether in shock or anger, yet all he did was stare at him with a curious expression upon his face.

After what seemed much longer but was probably only a minute or two, Bingley replied in a rather hesitant tone. "I see…I will admit to being rather surprised by your interference, as you call it. I know you look out for my interests, as any good friend should, but I must tell you that I am already aware Miss Bennet is in town, or at least, she was several months ago."

Darcy was stunned. "How? That is—who informed you of her presence in London?"

"Caroline," Bingley replied, only confusing Darcy more, as he was sure Miss Bingley would have never revealed the intelligence willingly.

"I see. When did she tell you?"

"While we were up north. But I had no idea you were involved in the matter."

Bingley's calm demeanour only served to unsettle Darcy further. Did he no longer harbour any affection for Miss Bennet? Perhaps he still believed her to be indifferent.

"You should also know I have reason to suspect that my observations concerning Miss Bennet's regard may have been in error. In truth, I did not take pains to know the lady and should have never given you counsel one way or the other."

"Come now, Darcy. I have always valued your advice. I do not hold anything against you."

Unsure how to proceed, Darcy thought to alter the course of the discussion, hoping it might help him to discern Bingley's intentions regarding the eldest Bennet sister.

"Have you given any more thought to your plans for Netherfield? Will you return to Hertfordshire after the Season?"

"I believe I may give up the lease. As you well know, my sisters were hardly impressed with the place."

"So you do not intend to return to the neighbourhood? Do you no longer wish to pursue Miss Bennet?"

Bingley began to fidget in his chair, and Darcy could not

help but think that perhaps his friend was not quite as sanguine as he tried to appear.

"You must understand, Darcy. I know your opinion of the Bennets was no better than that of my sisters, and while I still consider Miss Bennet to be an angel and any man would surely be lucky to have such a wife, I have had several talks with Caroline over the course of our travels, and I simply cannot dismiss the risks involved in pressing forward my suit, even if Miss Bennet does return my affections."

Thoroughly ashamed by Bingley's reference to his overt disapproval of Elizabeth's family, Darcy pressed on. "Risks?"

"Well, yes. You see, while I was in Scarborough, Caroline reminded me of how far our family has come in society, and well, she made several valid arguments about how her prospects might be damaged if my wife's family were to prove an embarrassment. I know I said before that their conduct did not matter to me, but I had never considered that the impropriety displayed by Mrs Bennet and her younger daughters might affect Caroline's chances to secure a husband."

"Did you plan on bringing the entire family to London? I am sure you observed just as I that Mr Bennet does not seem to care for society. Besides, with proper guidance, the younger girls may improve their manners. Miss Lydia is but fifteen. Surely, her character is not yet fixed," Darcy argued, surprised by how easy it was to defend Elizabeth's relations.

"It is not only Miss Lydia, is it? According to Caroline, all of the younger sisters possess some degree of unsuitability. Even Miss Elizabeth saw fit to quarrel with you in company."

"There is absolutely nothing wrong with lively debate," Darcy argued, attempting to quell the indignation he felt rising on Elizabeth's behalf. "Simply because you dislike any sort of disagreement does not make Miss Elizabeth's manners improper. If anything, she was remarkably kind when handling the veiled insults Miss Bingley subjected her to during her stay."

"I did not mean to imply *I* disapprove of Miss Elizabeth. It is just—Caroline cannot seem to tolerate the Bennets. How could I expect her to live with them? Jane is all that is sweet and obliging, and I know she would be wounded eventually by Caroline's disdain. It would not be fair to either of them."

"So you are determined to be ruled by your sister in this matter?"

"I have a responsibility to Caroline. Louisa already married a gentleman, but Caroline's future is not yet secure. If I marry well, I may be able to further ease her way in society. Surely, you would not do anything to damage Miss Darcy's prospects?"

"Marrying a woman of good character who displayed both compassion and kindness would do far more for Georgiana than simply bringing loftier connexions and additional funds to the Darcy fortune."

"Yes, of course, and I want to marry an admirable woman, but could you live with Georgiana's open displeasure of your choice of a wife?"

Darcy was somewhat galled that Bingley would ever consider comparing his harpy of a sister to sweet Georgiana. "While I love my sister dearly, it is not Georgiana who will live with my wife for the remainder of her days. I am aware our circumstances are somewhat different, in that I am more father in some ways to my sister than brother, but ultimately I believe Georgiana would wish for my happiness. What of *your* happiness, Bingley?"

"Well…perhaps after Caroline marries, I could consider pursuing Miss Bennet again. I do love her, but I am still young, and it could prove foolish to settle down so quickly, especially since my choice seems to have such strife attached to it at present."

While he had always harboured suspicions that Bingley

lacked resolve in difficult matters, Darcy had never anticipated he would capitulate so fully to the machinations of his sisters. Bingley's concerns regarding the Bennet family had filled Darcy with guilt, as hearing his friend's open dismissal of their worthiness led Darcy to wonder if somehow *he* was at fault for Bingley's current understanding. His friend claimed to love Jane Bennet, yet he had set her aside not once, but twice, at the instigation of others.

Perhaps Bingley was right, and he was too young to contemplate marriage, for Darcy could not believe anyone would ever be able to dissuade *him* from pursuing his Elizabeth. But then again, Darcy knew himself to be steadfast where he chose to bestow his affections. He had never once claimed to love another woman before Elizabeth, and he was certain that he would never love another after her. Bingley on the other hand, had often claimed to be in love in the past, and clearly his infatuation with Miss Bennet was not serious if it could be so easily set aside.

Uncomfortable with his current musings, Darcy noticed the time and realised he needed to leave if he still planned to call at the Gardiners' residence. "If you are sure that this is what you want, I will not gainsay you, but I do hope you will ultimately be happy with your choice."

"You have always been a good friend, Darcy."

"Perhaps not always, but I thank you nevertheless," Darcy replied, feeling rather awkward. "In any case, I must be going, as I have another call I plan to make today."

"Of course, of course. Shall I see you at White's later this week?"

"I believe so, but I will be sure to inform you if my plans change."

"Very well, let me see you to the door."

As they entered the front hall, Darcy's progress was halted by the contrived, modulated tones of an approaching Caroline Bingley.

"Why, Mr Darcy! I had no idea you had stopped by for a

visit! It is always such a pleasure to have one's dear friends call."

Turning to give her a stiff bow of greeting, Darcy was vastly displeased when she attached herself to his arm, her possessive grip akin to that of a hawk that had subdued its prey.

"We simply must dine together again soon, as I am desirous of spending time with dear Georgiana. Indeed, I cannot tell you how glad I am to have returned to town, for there is nothing in the country that can compare to the more refined society we enjoy here."

As she continued to prattle away without any need for his response, Darcy could not help but compare her hollow speech with Elizabeth's unaffected interest and concern. Elizabeth never flattered him, did not defer to him in all things, and when she asked after his sister, her care was completely genuine. She never displayed the calculating expression that he so often caught in Miss Bingley's looks, something that had always made Darcy particularly wary when displayed by the so-called elegant females of the *ton*. Detaching her talons from his coat sleeve, Darcy interrupted her trivial speech to bid farewell to both Bingley siblings.

"I am afraid I have little time available at present, and I cannot guarantee any invitations to dine in the near future. Please accept my apologies." Turning to shake his friend's hand he continued, "It was good to see you, Bingley, and I will let you know about meeting at the club when I have the chance."

"Certainly! I hope to see you soon, my friend!"

Climbing into his carriage, Darcy had trouble reconciling how his interview with his friend had proceeded compared with what he had expected. While he no longer needed Bingley's assistance to be able to see Elizabeth, as for all intents and purposes she was to remain in London for the time being, he was still concerned his failure to right the wrong he had committed against her sister would hinder any progress he hoped to make in his attempts to court her properly. Would Elizabeth wish for her sister to have such an irresolute suitor? Frustrated by his morning's conversation, Darcy quietly groaned at the potential for yet another obstacle in obtaining his heart's desire.

CHAPTER FOURTEEN

The early afternoon sun glinted off the top of his polished walking stick as Nicholas Grey once again wandered the paths of Hyde Park. He had many reasons to be grateful for the recent spell of balmy weather, not the least of which was his ability to escape his study once again for more soothing pursuits. For indeed, London in the springtime was rarely so temperate, and Grey chose to interpret such favourable conditions as yet another sign of God's favour upon his current circumstances. Such warmth would ensure the presence of dry roads and expeditious travelling times, reassuring Grey that his urgent message would, in all probability, be delivered to his parents that very evening. Knowing his father would respond swiftly to his request, he could be reasonably assured his parents would depart for London on the morrow, and barring any complications, they could arrive at Tamworth House in as little as two or three days.

Thinking on their pending arrival had left Grey in a state of restiveness, particularly after the events of his early morning call. The business matters that awaited his attention at home could not hold his interest, and so Grey resolved upon walking the very path that had led him to his current felicity. The excited twitters of a pair of wrens drew his gaze to a nearby tree, their birdsong mirroring the lightness in his heart after a morning spent in Elizabeth's company. *Elizabeth. His sister.*

After longing for her recovery for so many years, Grey was delighted to find she exceeded his expectations in every way. Even though raised far from their home and in decidedly lesser circumstances, Elizabeth was like a breath of fresh air—an intelligent, witty young woman who in no way resembled the pretentious debutantes of his circle. Recalling the many stories he had been told by his father, he imagined Elizabeth was similar to what his mother must have been like when she first arrived in London. For truly, her very presence sparkled, even though she must have felt a tremendous upheaval in her previously uncomplicated existence.

Acutely aware of her distress the prior evening, Grey had hoped a night's rest would sufficiently calm her enough to afford him the opportunity to know Elizabeth better before his parents' arrival in town. He had called at the home of her aunt and uncle at precisely eleven o'clock, trusting his early visit would guarantee her sole attention for a half an hour at least. Upon entering the Gardiners' parlour, Grey was pleased to note Elizabeth appeared much more composed as she sat quietly with Miss Bennet, fiddling with an embroidery sampler that rested on her lap. Once alerted to his presence, the two young women rose and greeted him with small curtseys.

"Lord Grey," Miss Bennet began, "it is a pleasure to see you again so soon."

"Thank you, Miss Bennet. I trust that you are well, Miss Elizabeth?"

Elizabeth looked up at his question, and he was pleased to see a small, nervous smile in place of the appearance of shock and grief that had so dominated her countenance the previous evening.

"Yes, my lord. As you see, I am quite well."

Uncomfortable with the appellation of *my lord*, Grey wondered how he could convince her to use a less formal mode of address when Miss Bennet conveniently provided him with the opportunity for the private conference he desired.

"If you will excuse me, I have some matters I need to attend to on behalf of my aunt. I shall leave the door to the sitting room open."

"I thank you, Miss Bennet. You are very kind."

With a reassuring smile directed at her sister, Miss Bennet gathered her things and quit the parlour, leaving him alone with Elizabeth. Recognising her obvious discomfort, Grey took it upon himself to begin their conversation.

"I would like to begin with an apology, if I may, Miss Elizabeth. I realise in my elation last evening I took to addressing you quite informally without your permission."

"There is no need to apologise, my lord, for I did not take offence. I barely recall such an oversight, distracted as I was by your rather startling admission," she replied, appearing pained at the thought of the previous evening's revelations.

"I am relieved; however, I was wondering if perhaps we might consider using a more familial mode of address now. It is most disconcerting to hear one's sister refer to you as *my lord*," he stated with a smile.

"Ah, I see. So you seek the permission you had previously taken for granted? I must say I do not know if it would be wise to comply with your request. After all, I have yet to be claimed as your sister, and any lapse in etiquette could be perceived as rather presumptuous on my part."

"Perhaps, then, you would agree to such terms if we limited them to private discourse?"

"Again, I must remind you that there is yet no proof of your—"

"Please, Miss Elizabeth, I know it is hard for you to accept such news so quickly, but I beg of you to trust my assertions. I would not make such claims if I still harboured any doubt."

She regarded him carefully, and after a moment's pause, she tapped her chin as a teasing glint entered her eyes. "Well, in that case, I suppose I must relent. Tell me, are all elder brothers so demanding? Jane and I had always wished for one, but perhaps we overlooked the trials inherent in dealing with such determination."

Pleased by this glimpse of the wit he had only briefly experienced the night before, Grey replied, "As I have a few surrogate elder brothers myself, I am afraid I must disappoint you. We are, on the whole, a rather self-possessed lot —especially the heirs. It is difficult for young men not to develop an irrational penchant for impudence when raised with the knowledge that one day they will rule their corner of the world."

Her genuine laughter filled the room. "Oh yes, I believe I have encountered similar confidence before. When such pride is not under good regulation, I fear we poor country ladies are taken quite unawares by such bold declarations as these 'young heirs' are wont to express."

"Is that so, dear sister? And tell me, which young heir has acquainted you with our high-handed ways?" he queried, his eyebrow lifting in challenge.

A flash of embarrassment covered her face as she quickly sought to evade his teasing. "*Dear sister?* I suppose your words bring us back to the task at hand. How should you prefer that I address you, *my lord*? Mayhap you might once again tell me your full name, for I must admit I fail to remember anything beyond your surname."

Willing to overlook her subtle manoeuvring for the present, Grey replied, "You may as well hear everything, title and all, lest I confuse you further with the various names that our family possesses. My full name is Nicholas Francis Grey, and I am the current Baron Grey de Rotherfield, while our father, George Harry Grey, is the Earl of Tamworth. Amongst the family, I am called Nicholas, and our father is known as Harry. I would be pleased if you would call me Nicholas."

"Nicholas…yes, I suppose I can manage it, but again, only in private. As for myself, you are free to call me Elizabeth if you prefer. As you have no doubt noticed, my family refers to me as Lizzy, but I do have one friend, Charlotte, who calls me Eliza."

"Eliza?" he questioned with a look of slight distaste.

"Yes," she laughed, "and I have to admit it is not my favourite. I was once acquainted with a rather conceited young lady of some wealth who seemed to dislike me rather fervently. I believe she called me 'Miss Eliza' in an attempt to unsettle me whilst I was forced to endure her presence. If my friendship with Charlotte was not of such long-standing, I might request that she change her mode of address, yet when she uses the same name, I find it rarely bothers me at all."

"I would like to hear more of your life in Hertfordshire if you do not mind. I do not know much of the area beyond its relative proximity to London."

"Meryton is primarily known as a small stop near the Great North Road, so I would not imagine you would be familiar with the neighbourhood surrounding Longbourn if you had never before visited."

"Ah, Longbourn. 'Tis the Bennet estate?"

"Yes, I believe I have heard Papa state it has been in Bennet hands for more than seven generations. Such a pity that it will pass to Mr Collins in the future," she remarked. "In any case, the estate itself is not terribly grand, but I must own I adore the natural beauty of Hertfordshire. One spot in particular, Oakham Mount, provides the most glorious view of the surrounding countryside."

The wistful expression that appeared on her face displayed her open enjoyment of the outdoors, a preference Grey shared. A pained expression quickly followed, however, exposing her uncertainty about the treasured place she had always called home.

"You like taking walks, do you?" he enquired, hoping to distract her from her melancholy.

"Yes, I confess I often try Mama's nerves with my tendency to dirty my petticoats whenever I step outside. I suppose it is not terribly ladylike of me to prefer such undertakings," she quipped, almost daring him to disapprove of her habits.

"If it sets your mind at ease, I believe you can blame your desire to go wandering on your Grey heritage, for I myself have often struggled to remain indoors, particularly when the weather is fine. Do you always walk, or do you ride?"

"I prefer walking to riding. I can ride, but I have never derived much enjoyment from the exercise. Jane is a much better horsewoman than I."

"So your love of nature is shared by all of your siblings?"

"Definitely not! A more disparate group of sisters you will never find, I assure you. Well, excepting perhaps the two youngest, Kitty and Lydia."

"How many sisters do you have?"

"Four. Jane is the eldest, as you know, and you will never find a more perfect picture of goodness than she. Mary is one year younger than I, and she prefers to either play the pianoforte all day long or bury her nose in *Fordyce's Sermons*."

"Fordyce?" he queried, wrinkling his brow in amusement. "I had not thought his works to be enjoyed by a young female audience. He tends to be quite severe upon your sex."

"Aye, I am aware and have heard plenty of his opinions espoused across the dinner table. The two youngest, Kitty and Lydia, are already out in society, and I fear the presence of a militia regiment in the area has quite erased anything but officers, parties, and ribbons from their minds. They can be rather boisterous in company, but in essentials, they are good girls, if only a little silly."

"And Mr and Mrs Bennet?"

"Papa is a highly intelligent man, a true lover of books, but I fear he often prefers them to the company of others. He has always encouraged my efforts to improve my understanding, and I believe he appreciates my similar wit. I have come to observe recently, however, that he prefers the role of spectator to that of participant in the life of his family. He enjoys people's foibles and inconsistencies, but I wish when it came to his wife and daughters, he would exert himself more on our behalf. I love him dearly, but I am not blind to his faults." After a slight pause, she continued. "Mama and I sometimes have difficulty understanding one another, as our temperaments are quite different. I know she loves me, but sometimes I think she wishes I were a bit more like Jane and less prone to displaying impertinence, particularly in the company of single gentlemen."

"Well, you have my full permission to discourage as many suitors as you like, for I do not believe I wish to lose you to matrimony so soon after finding you again."

The brilliant shade of pink that overwhelmed her cheeks made Grey wonder if perhaps she had already rejected suitors. It would not surprise him if she had, but the thought did not bring him comfort. He hoped her embarrassment was due to a failed courtship, for he could not begin to contemplate the complications that might arise if she was currently the object of any gentleman's pursuit.

"Perhaps you could tell me more about your own family?" Elizabeth asked.

"I would be happy to tell you more of *our* family, as I

know our parents will be most eager to meet you once they arrive in town."

"Are they already on their way?" she enquired, with a slightly shocked look upon her face.

"At this moment, no, but as I sent the express last night, I believe they should have it by this evening at the latest. If they depart as soon as may be, then they should arrive by the end of the week."

"I suppose I did not realise it would be so soon."

Taking her hand in his, Grey squeezed her palm gently in an effort to reassure her. "You must understand, losing you nearly destroyed our family. Our mother had waited for you for so long. Your birth was practically miraculous in our parents' estimation, and we all doted upon you excessively. In fact, I see much of our mother's spirit in you, at least that is, before you were taken. Her liveliness and cheer near disappeared once you were gone, and our father's grief was compounded by not only the loss of his cherished daughter but that of his wife as well."

A tear rolled down Elizabeth's cheek, and she quickly brushed it aside, averting her eyes from his gaze.

"I do not say these things to upset you, but rather I would have you prepared for the reunion you will face. Our parents are good people, honourable and kind, but they have been living only half a life for the past twenty years. It is my hope that with your recovery, our family will finally be able to mend and flourish once more."

"I own it is difficult for me to understand what you have suffered, as I have barely had the time to adjust to the inconceivable revelation that my life—indeed my very identity—is not what I have so long claimed. I do hope something good can come of this, though you must forgive me for wishing it did not come at the expense of my security. It is difficult and excessively painful to fathom that I have been lied to my entire life."

The chime of a clock alerted them both to the time, and

Grey was curious to note how Elizabeth's gaze turned to the front window, as though she were expecting someone to appear. Reluctant to leave her side, yet not wishing to tax her further with such weighty topics, Grey hesitantly rose to take his leave.

"I fear the time has quite run away from me this morning. Perhaps I should leave you to rest for now."

"I would not wish to keep you from your duties, Nicholas," Elizabeth replied, smiling slightly as she uttered his name.

"May I return tomorrow? We have a lifetime's worth of information to impart."

"Ah, but quite possibly we will have a lifetime ahead in which to share such confidences," she replied. "And of course you may visit."

"Please give my compliments to the Gardiners and Miss Bennet," he replied, gripping her hand one final time before bowing slightly. "Until tomorrow, Elizabeth."

"Goodbye, Nicholas."

Her smile of farewell had stayed with him during his ride home, and the recollections of their meeting had filled his thoughts as Grey continued to stroll through the park. The gentle breeze and swaying yellow daffodils that surrounded the path reflected the warming hope that stirred within him, as the reality of her presence in his life sank in with every step he took. His desire to ride off to Hertfordshire to uncover undisputable proof of Elizabeth's parentage could barely be repressed. Only the knowledge it was his father's right to question Mr Bennet regarding the details of Elizabeth's discovery held him back. He was anxious to claim her as his sister before all the world, and God willing, such a declaration would be possible soon.

CHAPTER FIFTEEN

Unaware he had missed the previous caller by a mere ten minutes, Darcy climbed the steps to the Gardiners' home in nervous anticipation. He had hoped that Bingley would have accompanied him to renew his addresses to Miss Bennet, but now that he was faced with his friend's irresolution, Darcy was unsure how to proceed in his efforts to show Elizabeth that he had attended to her reproofs. Should he relate his disappointing interview with Bingley? Surely such a telling would lower his friend in Elizabeth's opinion, and Darcy was not at all comfortable with using another's failings to advance his own cause. Putting his thoughts on Bingley's recent display of puerility aside, Darcy focused on trying to settle his nerves, knowing Elizabeth would not take kindly to the reappearance of his aloof manners while amongst her relations. From what he had observed the previous evening, the Gardiners seemed to be fine people possessed of genteel comportment. It should not be difficult to converse with them during the span of a single social call.

Upon entering the parlour, Darcy was greeted with the

sight of Elizabeth, slightly tense, but still smiling in the presence of her aunt and sister. As the ladies rose to welcome him, Darcy was pleased to note that Elizabeth's smile did not diminish in his company, and she appeared to be at least somewhat recovered from the events of the previous evening.

Darcy bowed to the ladies. "Thank you for allowing me to visit today, Mrs Gardiner."

"Of course, Mr Darcy," she replied. "It is kind of you to call. Shall I ring for some tea?"

"That would be most welcome. Thank you."

As Elizabeth was seated on the sofa next to Miss Bennet, Darcy chose to take the chair closest to her side as he settled in, while once again encouraging himself to overcome his natural reserve. He need not have worried though, for Elizabeth's aunt was a seasoned hostess, and in many ways her easy conversation reminded him of Elizabeth.

"I cannot tell you how delighted I am to have a fellow Derbyshire native here, for you see, I have tried many times to convince my nieces of the superiority of that particular county, and as of yet I have had little success."

Pleasantly surprised by the topic, Darcy responded with a smile. "You are from Derbyshire, ma'am?"

"Yes. I spent my youth in Lambton."

"Lambton? Why, that is but five miles from Pemberley!"

"Indeed it is. I once had the opportunity to tour your estate when I was a girl, and I must say the grounds were an absolute marvel." She turned to Elizabeth. "I believe even your thirst for nature would be well satisfied by such an idyllic setting, Lizzy."

Grateful for the opportunity to speak of his much beloved home to the woman he hoped would one day share it, Darcy seized upon the opportunity to engage Elizabeth's interest.

"I recall your fondness for walking about Hertfordshire, and I can assure you that you would enjoy a stroll through

Pemberley's gardens and woods. I must concur with your aunt that I believe Derbyshire to be the finest of counties, but I suppose I will always be partial to my own home."

"A perfectly natural sentiment, sir," Elizabeth replied, "though I cannot help but wonder at your preferences in gardens, particularly after spending so much time wandering the meticulously ordered flower beds of Rosings."

At the mention of his aunt's estate, Darcy noticed a small twinkle brighten Elizabeth's face. Her look issued a challenge, almost daring him to agree with Lady Catherine's preference for ostentatious displays.

"I find I cannot agree with my aunt's desire for order in all things, including her gardens, but then again, Kent is a far more subdued landscape than my home. One of the great beauties of Derbyshire is its natural wildness—something my ancestors have long encouraged, rather than repressed. While there are some formal gardens near the house, including a hedge maze that Georgiana particularly loved to explore as a child, the majority of our park lands have been left to reflect creation's natural allure."

"It sounds perfectly lovely," Miss Bennet interjected, with a sly look at Elizabeth. "Your description seems ideally suited to my sister's preferences."

After sending a slight glare in her sister's direction, Elizabeth was saved from the need to respond by the sudden appearance of a small intruder.

"Mama, please tell Matthew that Cousin Lizzy *will* be joining me soon for our tea party, for he does not believe me!" exclaimed a young blonde girl in apparent exasperation.

As Mrs Gardiner was rising to escort her daughter from the room, they were interrupted again by the arrival of a panting young lad whose eyes shot daggers at his sister.

"I am so sorry, Mother. She ran out of the nursery while Miss Lucy was attending to Edwin."

"Mr Darcy, I do apologise for the behaviour of my children. They know better than to insinuate themselves upon our social calls."

At their mother's reprimanding look, both children quieted and displayed suitable expressions of chagrin.

Wanting to set Mrs Gardiner at ease, Darcy responded, "Do not trouble yourself, madam. In fact, I would very much appreciate an introduction if you will."

Darcy was gratified to see Elizabeth's small smile at his request.

"It would be my pleasure, Mr Darcy," Mrs Gardiner replied. "This is my eldest, Matthew, and his sister, Margaret, whom we call Meg. Children, this is Mr Darcy of Pemberley. He is a friend to your cousins."

As the children bowed and curtseyed, Darcy could not help but notice that young Miss Gardiner looked remarkably like Miss Bennet. It was soon apparent, however, that she shared more in disposition with Elizabeth, as she displayed a delightfully precocious nature. Striding across the room, the little girl approached her cousin and clasped her hands.

"Cousin Lizzy, have you decided which story you plan to tell at our tea party today? Miss Lucy helped me arrange my dolls while Edwin was napping. Are you coming soon?"

Elizabeth giggled, her delight in her young cousin apparent. "As you can very well see, we have a guest, and it would be rude to leave him all alone while we carry on with our party."

"Oh," Meg replied, her energy deflating somewhat. "Perhaps he could join us?"

At this request, Elizabeth's gaze moved to Darcy's face, and he was enchanted by the look of pure amusement in her expression.

"I doubt Mr Darcy would like to join your dolls for a tea party in the nursery."

"On the contrary, Miss Elizabeth, you seem to forget I

have a much younger sister. I have attended many such entertainments in my time."

"Do you consider yourself a true proficient in the art of little girls' tea parties?" Her raised eyebrow and arch expression thrilled him, while her less than subtle reference to his opinionated aunt nearly prompted his laughter.

"A true proficient? I regret I cannot make such a claim, as I merely possess the experience of a doting brother who was far too easily swayed by a pair of large blue eyes. I suspect young Miss Gardiner is as hard to deny as was Georgiana at such an age."

At that moment, Mrs Gardiner rose to collect her daughter and return her to the nursery. "Come along, Meg. Please bid Mr Darcy good day. It is time to return above stairs."

"But Mama, Mr Darcy could join our tea party!"

Seeing the slight vexation upon Mrs Gardiner's countenance at her child's recalcitrance, Darcy sought to intervene. "Perhaps another time, Miss Gardiner, with your mother's approval, of course."

"I suppose," Meg said, her displeasure at returning to her rooms crinkling her brow.

Taking her brother's hand, the little girl left the room as Elizabeth turned to him.

"Thank you for indulging my cousin."

"I assure you, I remember well that age with Georgiana. She was particularly relentless in her pursuit of my attention whenever I returned from school."

"Did she have playmates? Despite meeting several of your relations, I confess I know little about your family."

"I am nearly twelve years Georgiana's senior. Our cousin Anne is perhaps the closest in age to her, but she is only two years younger than I. We are a small family, and Georgiana and I are the last of the Darcy line. Apart from the women at Rosings, my uncle's family is all that remains of my mother's relations. You have already met Colonel

Fitzwilliam, and he has but one elder brother, Viscount Lisle."

"Goodness! That *is* a small family. Did your sister have much in the way of female companionship in her upbringing?"

"Georgiana is rather frightened of Lady Catherine, and so she has had little interaction with Anne, but fortunately our other aunt Lady Matlock has been able to provide some motherly guidance and affection in our mother's stead. Our aunt always wished for a daughter, a fact she never fails to mention to both of her sons."

"Ah, I see! Does the colonel face much pressure to marry?" she asked with no little amusement.

"Richard? Not as much as his brother. Lady Matlock's focus is Lisle, for he is three years older than I and, until recently, has been reluctant to consider any inducements towards matrimony."

It was at this point in their conversation that Darcy noticed the frequent glances Miss Bennet continued to make in her sister's direction. Her assessments appeared to be slightly protective and anxious, as though she would have no trouble intervening should her sister show the slightest distress.

"I must say how pleased I am that you are well after last night, Miss Elizabeth. I quite worried you would take a chill."

"Thank you, sir," she replied in a rather subdued voice. "I possess a hearty constitution, so you need not be concerned."

Darcy cursed himself as he noticed her withdrawal from the conversation. Looking for a way to recover their previous ease, Darcy scanned the room for a suitable distraction. Upon noticing the sunshine filtering in through the lacy curtains, he asked, "Perhaps you would like to take a stroll now, Miss Elizabeth, for the weather is undoubtedly fine."

"An excellent idea, Mr Darcy," Miss Bennet interjected as Mrs Gardiner returned to the parlour. "Aunt Gardiner and I shall join you. Come, Lizzy, let us gather our spencers and bonnets."

As the two young ladies removed themselves from the room, Darcy turned to their aunt. "I hope you do not object to such an outing. I apologise for not asking you directly."

"It is a fine idea. Nothing can quite guarantee the good spirits of my niece as a walk, though I must concede her preference for the country in such matters. London is not ideally suited to her tastes, as she rather chafes at the restrictions her uncle places on her morning rambles."

At his enquiring expression, Mrs Gardiner continued. "You see, Lizzy does not like to be accompanied by a servant or family member whenever she goes out. Oh, she understands the need for such precautions, I assure you, but it does not mean that she welcomes the intrusion."

"I understand, though I must say I am quite relieved at your husband's demands, for I would not wish to see her come to any harm."

Mrs Gardiner gave him an appraising look. "No, I do not believe you would."

Saved from further scrutiny by the arrival of Elizabeth and her sister, Darcy offered his arm to Elizabeth, and together they descended the steps of the Gardiner's residence. He was pleased to note Miss Bennet and Mrs Gardiner had fallen back a few paces, allowing him relative privacy in his conversation with Elizabeth.

With a clear effort to set her despondency aside, Elizabeth cheerfully enquired, "What shall we discuss, Mr Darcy? Books perhaps?"

"Oh no. I do not believe I could discuss books while walking, for indeed, it would almost be as difficult as discussing them while *dancing*, which I know you cannot abide."

Her delight at his reference to their less than congenial

dance at Netherfield was obvious, for she conceded with a laugh, "How correct you are, sir! My apologies. Well then, if not books, what about friends? Have you been able to visit many of your acquaintances during your stay in town?"

Her mention of friends brought his mind immediately to Bingley and their disappointing conference that very morning. He must have stiffened at her enquiry, for she quickly retracted her request.

"Of course you do not have to respond to anything so personal. Forgive me, I should not have asked."

"No, no. It is just—I made a call before I arrived here that did not end as I would have liked. You see, Mr Bingley has returned from Scarborough."

Clearly uncomfortable, she recovered quickly and queried, "But why should that distress you, for he is a dear friend, is he not?"

"He is, but in truth, I did not anticipate his pleasure in our meeting, for I had already resolved to confess my interference in the matter with your sister. So you see, I believed we would part ways with decidedly uncharitable feelings."

"But why would you do so, sir?" she asked with a puzzled look.

"As I have already admitted, my actions in concealing your sister's presence in town were beneath me. I should never have behaved in such a duplicitous manner, and I should not have interfered in their relationship at all. You were quite right. I had no knowledge of your sister's affections, and I should not have presumed to know after such a brief acquaintance."

She accepted his explanation with a small nod. Hesitantly, she enquired, "Was Mr Bingley angry with you?"

"I expected him to be, but to my surprise, he was not."

Her look of astonishment mirrored his own, and he felt he must give some explanation as to the contents of his morning's interview.

"I have often noted Bingley falls in and out of love

with relative ease, and at first I believed his infatuation with your sister was of a similar nature. His spirits, however, were somewhat depressed after we left Netherfield in the autumn, which led me to believe he had been serious in his interest towards her. However, it appears Miss Bingley was able to persuade him against any further pursuit of your sister whilst they were visiting their relations in the north."

A wry expression pinched her lovely brow. "I can well believe that, Mr Darcy. But you need not worry, for Jane and I have come to realise the true fault in the whole affair must rest with Mr Bingley. For even if you did offer misguided advice, it was not your decision to abandon Jane.

"My sister is recovering, sir, of that you may be certain. In fact, I believe her anger over Mr Bingley's lack of resolve has done much to improve her spirits of late. It is a wondrous thing to behold, for Jane is rarely angry about anything," she quipped.

"I am relieved to hear it. As you must know, I would never want anyone in your family to suffer harm on my account," he replied with an earnest expression, allowing his hand to grasp the one that lightly rested on his forearm with a reassuring squeeze.

"All is well, Mr Darcy. You see, I could never want such a suitor for my dearest sister. Jane and I have always desired a union of deep and abiding love were we ever to consider marriage, and a man who cannot defend her against a well-meaning friend and a scheming relation is not someone to inspire such love and devotion."

"I, too, cannot imagine giving in to such persuasions so readily. My affections when formed are quite steadfast, I assure you."

The look he bestowed upon her produced a rather pronounced blush. Casting about for another topic of discussion, she turned to him with a rather curious look. "You mentioned being displeased with your call this morning. Forgive me, but if Mr Bingley was not upset with you, then why should you have parted ways in distress?"

"At the time, I believed you would wish him to renew his addresses to your sister, if only to relieve her suffering. When confronted with his irresolution and his belief in Miss Bingley's assertions, I must own I was rather disappointed in my friend."

"It is natural, I suppose, to want to hold your friend to such a high standard, for I am beginning to realise you expect such honourable behaviour in others simply because you expect it of yourself."

Her open, unaffected air rendered her simple compliment so profound that his answering grin produced that familiar sparkle in her eyes.

"Your forgiveness of my earlier faults continues to astound me, for I know I am not so deserving as you imply."

"You must adopt some of my philosophy and think only on the past as its remembrance brings you pleasure. There is no need to wander further down the path of recrimination."

So absorbed in their conversation was he, that Darcy failed to note they had arrived back at the steps of her relations' home.

"I suppose it is time for me to depart, but before I go, I was wondering if I might make a request?"

"Certainly, Mr Darcy," she responded.

"I would very much like—that is, I was wondering if you would permit me to introduce you to my sister. Georgiana is currently visiting our aunt, Lady Matlock, but she will return home in a few days, and I should like to introduce you if you still plan to be in town."

"Of course, sir! I believe I would quite enjoy making her acquaintance. Perhaps she might tell me more about these charming tea parties you attended in your youth."

"I would never suspend any pleasure of yours, Miss Elizabeth, despite the cost to my dignity. Until she returns, however, do you believe you would be satisfied with merely my own presence? I should like to call on you again if I may."

Walking up the steps, Elizabeth turned to face him, her gaze alight with mischief. "I would enjoy that, for after all, how else am I to correct my hitherto erroneous sketch of your character? It is proving to be quite a rewarding endeavour, as I suspect such a complicated study will continue to confound me regularly with fairly gratifying results."

Bowing as he took his leave of Elizabeth and her relations, Darcy entered his carriage with more hope than he had previously allowed himself to feel. She had enjoyed his company and even expressed pleasure in his return, and for now, that was enough.

CHAPTER SIXTEEN

As the wheels of the carriage rattled down Curzon Street, Grey did his best to stare resolutely out the window as his father attempted to soothe his understandably distraught mother who had yet to quell the silent stream of tears that flowed down her cheeks. Once again raising her handkerchief to her pale face, Grey could not help but be touched by the reassuring grip with which his father held her hand or the way in which he whispered calm reassurances to his wife of thirty years. The anticipated interview had been as difficult as he had expected, as his parents had been by turns shocked, doubtful, overwhelmed, and cautiously hopeful regarding his discovery. He had known their anguish over their lost child would never be mollified by mere words. The wounds left by her abduction were simply too deep. And so, only a mere thirty minutes after their arrival in town, the family was bundled back into their carriage, quietly making their way towards Gracechurch Street.

The earl had sent a messenger ahead to Tamworth House once they reached the outskirts of the city on their journey from Staffordshire. This had allowed Grey enough time to summon the Matlocks from their town home as he had previously arranged with his godmother. Grateful for their assistance, Grey knew their meeting would have been far more difficult had he been forced to communicate his news alone. Thinking back on the scene that had just taken place in his family's sitting room, Grey was comforted by the lasting friendships that had supported his family through such a harrowing experience, not only during the events of 1791, but also as they moved forward together into a hopefully more joyful time.

His godmother had arrived soon after he had dispatched the important missive, and he had at first been surprised by the appearance of her husband as well.

"Lady Matlock, thank you for answering my summons so quickly. I believe my parents should arrive momentarily."

"We were already planning to depart our home when your message arrived. Our niece Georgiana has been staying with us for the past few days, and we were just leaving to return her to Darcy House."

"Then it seems that I caught you at an opportune time." Grey paused and turned to his other guest. "How kind of you to come. I take it you have been informed of the purpose of our meeting today, Lord Matlock?"

"Yes, Grey. Pray do not be upset with Eleanor, for she knew your father would need some encouragement today as well. This is truly a momentous day for your family."

"I agree it is, and I imagine it will be a difficult one also."

"Now Nicholas," Lady Matlock began, "there is no point in focusing on the challenges this day will bring. Instead, why not tell me what you have planned for after you relay your news?"

"You are right, of course," Grey replied. "I informed Elizabeth of my parents' likely arrival today and requested she not accept any callers this afternoon in case they want to see her as soon as may be."

"Does she usually have many callers?" Lord Matlock questioned.

"I am not sure. Towards the end of my visits each day, Elizabeth has often looked to the front parlour window, as though she anticipates another guest. I have yet to ask her directly about it, as we are still only just getting to know one another."

His godmother seemed curious. "Have you ever asked her if she has suitors? She is, after all, twenty years of age, so I would not be surprised if she has caught someone's interest, either now or in the past."

"I have teased her on occasion, and I have deduced that her adoptive mother has some rather pronounced match-making tendencies. Some of my remarks have caused her to blush quite furiously, but I have never asked for more information."

An uneasy look passed between Lord and Lady Matlock before the earl responded. " I suppose the subject will come up eventually with your parents. Besides, anyone who pursued her when she was naught but a country gentleman's daughter would probably not pass muster with your father, particularly if they have been calling at a tradesman's house. I doubt her aunt and uncle possess any lofty connexions."

Grey resisted the urge to roll his eyes at Lord Matlock's response. He was a good man, but a bit more conscious of his status than Grey ever cared to be, although to be fair, his views were common amongst his father's generation.

Seeking to redirect the conversation, he enquired, "Do you plan to join us and meet Elizabeth?"

"No, Nicholas," Lady Matlock replied. "Your parents should first see her alone, and we would not want to overwhelm Elizabeth while everything is still so new. I will speak to your mother soon about hosting a dinner," she continued, "as Elizabeth must be introduced to James and to Richard again as well."

"Naturally, although I declare I would rather keep my sister all to myself. She is quite beautiful, and I have warned her that I have no plans to approve of any suitors in the near future. I have only just gained a sibling, and I do not intend to lose her again so soon, considering I have almost two decades' worth of overprotective brotherly behaviour to redress. I believe Elizabeth's liveliness would enchant both of your sons, so perhaps their introduction should be postponed."

He had uttered his statement in jest; however Grey could not help but note both his guests seemed distinctly uncomfortable. He did not have time to contemplate their odd behaviour further, as at that moment, he heard the front door open and could discern the voices of his parents as they greeted Tewes. Turning towards the parlour door, Grey could not help but smile at the sight of his mother and father as they came to greet him.

"Nicholas, my darling, what on earth could be so important for you to summon us to town at the height of the Season?" his mother questioned as she leaned in to kiss his cheek. Though somewhat travel weary, he thought she looked remarkably well.

"Are you not pleased to see me then, Mother?"

"I am always pleased to see you, as you well know. Indeed, it has been far too long since you last visited Heatherton Hall."

"Nicholas has many responsibilities," his father interjected. "Nevertheless, though your request was unexpected, I was happy to have an excuse to join you here for at least a short while. It is good to see you, Son."

Grasping his father's hand in a firm shake, he turned to the other occupants in the room. "I realise you probably would prefer time to settle in and remove the dust from the road, but as you can see, we have guests."

"Eleanor, Hugh! Whatever are you doing here?" his mother enquired.

"My dear Amelia," Lady Matlock began, coming forward to take his mother's hands, "I cannot begin to tell you how happy I am to see you. Nicholas has asked us to be present for his news, and I could never refuse him anything."

As Lady Matlock embraced his mother, Lord Matlock reached out to shake hands with his father. "It is good to see you, Tamworth!"

"And you, Matlock, but I cannot begin to account for your presence here." Turning to his son, he asked, "Is this a serious matter? I knew your request was of an urgent nature, but I must say you have me quite baffled."

"Perhaps it would be best if we all sat down," Grey stated, guiding his mother to a nearby settee as he took the chair opposite, while his father sat at his mother's side. "I apologise for the secrecy in my actions, but I could not send word of this development through a letter. Not only is the information too important to entrust to the post, I also could not imagine any other way to tell you than in person."

"What is it, Nicholas?" his mother asked. "You are making me rather anxious."

"It is not my intent, Mother, but I fear there is no easy way to relay my news. You see, about a week ago I experienced the most extraordinary encounter while walking in Hyde Park. I met a young woman whose appearance startled me, so much so that I had to investigate who she was, and what I have found not only confirms my suspicions, but also my dearest hopes. Simply put, I believe I have found Elizabeth."

Silence settled over the room and its inhabitants. Grey could see the shock which covered the faces of both his father and mother as they struggled to grasp the startling news he had delivered.

"This is not amusing, Son." Disbelief clouded his

father's features with a healthy measure of scorn. "How can you think to torture your mother so?"

"Harry! You cannot believe that Nicholas would summon us to town in jest—not for this!"

Chastened, his father began expressing his doubts to the room. "But how can this be possible? It has been twenty years since your sister disappeared. We never learned anything of where she was taken or even if she was still alive."

"I know this is difficult to accept, but you must believe me when I say that I am sure it is Elizabeth."

Tears had already pooled in his mother's eyes, and they trickled unheeded down her face. "How—how can you be certain?" she asked.

"If you could only see her, you would feel as certain as I, for she is the mirror image of yourself at twenty." Turning to his father he continued. "I found the miniature of mother in your study, the one made after your wedding, and the likeness is so profound that you could assume Elizabeth is the subject."

"Her name—her name is truly Elizabeth? You have spoken with her?" his father asked, hope beginning to lighten his features.

"Yes, Elizabeth. She was taken in by a gentleman's family and has been known all of her life as Elizabeth Anne Bennet."

His mother began to cry in earnest, and Lady Matlock rose from her chair and knelt beside her friend.

"Amelia, dear, I have not yet met her, but I believe you should let Nicholas finish his tale, for there is more to know, and I feel you will have further reason to hope once he is finished." Turning to Grey she nodded to him.

"I knew I could not approach her directly, but I was able to meet her uncle, a Mr Gardiner who lives in Cheapside. He too, was startled by the likeness in the portrait, and it convinced him to reveal his niece's unusual history. For you see, she is not his niece by blood, as she was found by Mr Gardiner's sister and her husband on the road from London to Hertfordshire in December—*mid-December* 1791."

"She was found as a babe that same year?" his father queried, betraying a slight eagerness as the new information was revealed.

"I do not know the dates exactly, but it cannot be more than a week or two after Elizabeth disappeared from our home."

"Have you met her, Nicholas?" his mother asked, her voice shaky through her tears.

"Yes, Mother, and Elizabeth is everything we ever hoped she could be. Even raised apart from us, she still possesses some of the same family mannerisms. I cannot tell you how startled I was the first time she raised her eyebrow while teasing her sister, for it was the same look both you and I wear when we affectionately taunt Father. She is well read, loves the out of doors, dotes upon her young cousins, and above all, is kind, compassionate, and good-humoured. It has been but a week, yet her place in my heart is already secure."

"She was so easy to love as a babe. I do not think I was the only one she had wrapped around her finger," his father concurred in a quiet, awed tone.

His mother seized his hands. "I *must* see her, Nicholas. Pray, tell me you will take me to her now, for I must know. I must see with my own eyes."

"I have told her to expect us today, and she is waiting. I will take you there as soon as you are ready to depart."

A BUMP IN THE ROAD JARRED GREY FROM HIS THOUGHTS AS he looked across the carriage at his parents. Their anxiety was easy to discern, but the hope that had kindled in their hearts had yet to fade. Grey saw their destination rapidly approach, and in short order, he and his parents had descended their carriage and stood at the steps to the Gardiner's residence. Grey noticed his father give a brief nod, signalling they were ready for the coming introduction.

After being granted entry to the home and passing their coats and hats to a servant, Grey and his parents were announced to the small company seated in the front parlour. Mr and Mrs Gardiner sat to one side of the room, while Miss Bennet sat with Elizabeth on the sofa. The sisters appeared to display a restless nervousness, and Grey was slightly pained to note that Miss Bennet seemed most determined to remain at her sister's side.

Upon their entrance, all rose in greeting, but Grey was acutely aware of the astonishment which covered Elizabeth's face as she looked upon his mother. Intending to perform the introductions, Grey was halted by the sudden movement of his father who had quickly crossed the room to take Elizabeth's hands in his.

"If I did not know it impossible, I would believe I was somehow transported back to that same ballroom over thirty years ago where I met Amelia for the first time," he softly declared, tears running down his face in apparent wonder. "Can you be my Elizabeth, my little girl?"

"My lord?" Elizabeth uttered in a quavering voice, looking to Grey as she stood transfixed, caught by the emotion in the visage of the man before her.

"Elizabeth, this is our father, Lord Harry Grey, the Earl of Tamworth." He turned to his mother, who was still frozen in place beside him at the door. "And this-this is our mother, Amelia, Lady Tamworth."

Gently taking his mother's arm, Grey calmly led her across the room to join his father. Slowly, his father stepped aside as his mother approached her long-lost daughter. Raising her hands to cup Elizabeth's face, she lightly traced her features before looking intensely into the familiar pair of dark brown eyes. As a few tears began to fall down Elizabeth's face, their mother pulled her into a firm embrace, rocking her slightly as she cried alongside her daughter.

As Grey looked about the room, he noted the heightened emotion present on the countenances of the Gardiners and Miss Bennet, as they too, were moved by the sight of the reunion.

When his mother and Elizabeth began to quiet, Grey turned to the others in the room and said,

"Perhaps I should make the remaining introductions, and then we can all be seated."

"Of course, Lord Grey," Mrs Gardiner replied. "We would be delighted to be introduced to your family, and I will have refreshments served."

After the introductions were completed, Mr Gardiner began the conversation. "It is a pleasure to meet you, Lord and Lady Tamworth. We have been anticipating your arrival since we first met your son."

As his mother took a seat beside Elizabeth who again sat next to Miss Bennet on the sofa, Grey and his father took the nearest chairs. Grey noticed his father's gaze rarely left Elizabeth's face, even as he addressed her uncle.

"I understand you were the first to learn of my son's suspicions regarding Elizabeth?" Lord Tamworth asked.

"Yes, my lord. I was suitably shocked when I first saw the portrait, but his story allowed me to finally obtain some answers regarding Lizzy's birth, for I was never able to account for her discovery by Mr Bennet and my sister."

"Nicholas believes we may yet discover more about the circumstances that winter if we question Mr Bennet ourselves. Do you think your brother can help us confirm her identity?"

"I can make no guarantees, but I believe that Bennet will reveal all he knows if he can see that portrait and hear your story. He loves Lizzy dearly, and as much as he would never want to give her up, I believe he would be compelled to disclose the truth if only to protect her and her place in this world. There is no one who knows Lizzy is not actually a Bennet beyond Thomas, Fanny, and the people in this room."

Turning to Elizabeth, his mother clasped her hand. "This must have been such a shock for you, my dear. I cannot imagine what you have been through this past week."

"I believe I have yet to fathom all that has been revealed," Elizabeth began, looking down at their joined hands. "I always believed myself to possess fortitude, yet I cannot begin to count the number of times I have been reduced to weeping. I am not usually prone to such displays, but I have discovered more cause to doubt myself this spring than during the previous twenty years of my existence," she revealed. "I am sorry, it is not my intention to pain you with my distress. I should be rather disappointed with myself, having been reduced to such a maudlin creature," she quipped, allowing a slight smile to grace her features and a twinkle to shine in her eyes.

Caught by her expression, both his parents smiled as they gazed at her, and Grey understood they had seen what he had since his first evening in her presence.

Looking at his son, Lord Tamworth spoke with surety. "I believe we have a trip to Hertfordshire to make on the morrow, for I will not rest until I can claim my daughter, and we can be a family once more."

CHAPTER SEVENTEEN

Pacing at the foot of the polished mahogany staircase, Darcy resisted the urge to withdraw his pocket watch and check the time yet again. His sister was overcome by nerves in anticipation of finally meeting Elizabeth, to the point that she apparently needed to make changes to her wardrobe mere minutes before they were scheduled to depart. While finding some amusement in the situation, Darcy was all too eager to leave, as he had sorely missed Elizabeth's company in the two days they had spent apart. On his last visit, Elizabeth had informed him that family matters would keep her from receiving guests on Saturday, and as Sunday was reserved for church and family, he was forced to forgo her company for two entire days.

Darcy knew their short separation was not wholly bad, as it allowed him to spend some uninterrupted time with his sister since her return home on Saturday morning. Her visit with Lady Matlock had permitted Darcy the freedom to begin courting Elizabeth without alerting Georgiana to his movements until he was ready. On her return home, Darcy had finally felt ready to disclose his interest in Elizabeth and was suitably shocked by Georgiana's enthusiasm, as she assured him that she had already suspected his partiality towards the young lady.

Throughout the last two days, his sister had questioned him relentlessly, not only about Elizabeth's general disposition, her likes and dislikes, but also about the details of their rather tumultuous acquaintance. He had suffered no shortage of embarrassment as he related his less than gentlemanly behaviour prior to their recent meeting in London, and while Georgiana could not condone his actions in every respect, she was remarkably sympathetic towards his plight, comprehending better than others his reserve and awkwardness when establishing new connexions. Darcy took considerably greater pleasure in disclosing their recent meetings at the Gardiner's home, happy to reflect upon their easy conversation and improved understanding of one another.

For all of her jests regarding appropriate venues to discuss literature, Darcy was delighted to discover that once he and Elizabeth did share their mutual passion for the written word, they possessed singularly complementary preferences. Even in circumstances where they disagreed, their lively debate carried a playful tone, and it was clear they held mutual respect for the other's opinions.

What a difference from their antagonistic debates at Netherfield! There existed such a contrast between her looks and speech from the previous autumn that he was now acutely aware of when she took pleasure in his company. Her enthusiasm for their discussions filled him with anticipation that one day he might introduce her to his library at Pemberley, knowing she would fully appreciate the great collection of books his family had accumulated over generations of careful selection.

The sound of footsteps at the top of the stairs preceded the arrival of his sister, who appeared ready to depart. For all of her additional preparations, Darcy could not determine how her wardrobe differed, but he felt it best to ignore that fact in favour of encouraging her confidence for the coming meeting.

"You look lovely, dearest. Are you ready to leave for our visit?"

"Yes, Fitzwilliam. I apologise for keeping you waiting, 'tis only that I am so nervous! I very much want Miss Elizabeth to like me."

"She will, I promise. Come, let us be on our way."

As he ushered his sister out the door and into their carriage, he could see Georgiana still harboured some doubts regarding her reception, if the constant wringing of her handkerchief was any indication.

"You must try and calm yourself. I assure you, Miss Elizabeth could never find any reason to disapprove of you and has expressed her own eagerness to make your acquaintance."

"Truly, Fitzwilliam? But does she know of Ramsgate?" She cast her gaze towards her lap. "I would not blame her should she judge me for my folly."

"She knows, Georgiana, but believe me, she does not hold you at fault. The blame for that affair has been placed squarely on the shoulders of the man who deceived you. Besides, you must remember that Miss Elizabeth has several younger sisters, and some that are prone to less than proper displays of decorum. She knows all too well the indiscretions of youth, and she would never disparage you for something you have come to regret."

He could see his words helped to soothe her worries somewhat; however he anticipated she would not be fully at ease until Elizabeth herself confirmed his assurances. Darcy dearly hoped Elizabeth's friendship would inspire greater confidence in his sister, for he could think of no finer example for Georgiana to emulate than Elizabeth, a woman who could engage anyone in conversation and leave them enchanted by discussion's end. He was also convinced his sister would greatly enjoy the company of the Gardiners and Miss Bennet.

Over the last week, Darcy had developed a sincere appreciation for their company, crediting Mrs Gardiner's genteel manners and engaging conversation as the example that both Elizabeth and Miss Bennet followed. Mr Gardiner was also to be valued for his intelligent discourse and friendly demeanour. He was so different from his sister, that oftentimes, Darcy had trouble remembering he and Mrs Bennet were siblings.

The location of the Gardiners' home was also to Darcy's advantage, a fact which secretly amused him as he remembered Miss Bingley's distaste for Cheapside. For indeed, had Darcy been paying call to any woman in Mayfair so regularly, his movements would have no doubt been noted by the gossip sheets.

After what seemed like ages to Darcy, the carriage finally arrived at their destination. Escorting his sister up the steps, Darcy greeted the servant at the door before escorting Georgiana towards the parlour where he found the women of the house. Rising to greet them, Elizabeth displayed a dazzling smile that near took his breath away. Distracted by her presence, he was slightly embarrassed to discover that his abstraction was made apparent by the lapse in conversation in the room, owing to his need to introduce his sister. As Elizabeth directed a pointed look at him and then towards Georgiana, he finally remembered the task at hand.

"Ah, excuse me, ladies. May I introduce my sister, Miss Georgiana Darcy? Georgiana, this is Mrs Gardiner and her nieces, Miss Jane Bennet and Miss Elizabeth."

Rising from her curtsey, Georgiana's anxiety was plainly displayed on her features. "I-I am pleased to meet you all. My brother has told me how much he delights in visiting here," she quietly stated.

No doubt sensing Georgiana's distress, Elizabeth came forward to grasp his sister's hands in greeting.

"I cannot tell you how happy I am to make your acquaintance, Miss Darcy! Your family has nothing but the highest praise for you, and I am eager for the chance to know you better."

"My brother exaggerates, I assure you."

"But there are many people who speak well of you, not only your brother, though he is, I grant you, a very faithful champion. Colonel Fitzwilliam has spoken of you fondly to me, and your aunt Lady Catherine has assured me that you are quite accomplished on the pianoforte, which is high praise indeed," Elizabeth replied. "Why, even Miss Bingley has extolled your talents! A dazzling feat, for I confess, I do not believe I was ever able to accomplish anything that merited her approval," she quipped with a playful grin.

Darcy was pleased to hear Georgiana's quiet giggles in response to Elizabeth's merriment, as he once again marvelled at her ability to charm people out of their discomfort. As she led Georgiana to the sofa, Darcy sat in a chair by Miss Bennet as Elizabeth began to question his sister regarding her favourite composers.

"I have always loved Bach and Beethoven; however I simply adore Haydn. His Sonata no. 54 is a favourite of mine," his sister disclosed, her voice growing more confident as their conversation continued.

"See, you have revealed your talent! I have been working on a piece by Haydn recently, but I must concede I have trouble with the fingering. Mozart has always been my preference."

Glancing to the side, Darcy beheld the serene smile that graced Miss Bennet's face. In her expression, he could see the true satisfaction she enjoyed at witnessing the recovery of her sister's lively spirits.

His observation was interrupted by Mrs Gardiner as she excused herself briefly to attend to an issue with her children, and seeing that Georgiana was focused on her conversation with Elizabeth, Darcy reasoned it was probably the best opportunity he would have to seek a private discussion with her sister.

"Miss Bennet," Darcy began in a hushed tone, "I am well aware that Miss Elizabeth has informed you of my unseemly interference in your personal matters, but I would be remiss if I did not seize the occasion to ask for your pardon myself."

"There is no need to seek my forgiveness, for I feel as though you have done me a kindness. While I admit I still admire your friend, I have come to the conclusion that we would not have suited each other well after all," she explained, pausing briefly to gather her thoughts. "Lizzy and I have always longed for a true partnership when we eventually find the man we wish to wed. It is what makes a union successful. Uncle Gardiner has the highest opinion of my aunt, and he would never allow anyone to claim she was unworthy in any respect. I hope, one day, to inspire the same devotion."

"I am sure you deserve it, Miss Bennet. Truly, you and your sister are both worthy women."

"I find I must thank you for your devotion to my sister," Miss Bennet stated, appearing almost startled by her boldness. "Forgive my impertinence. I know it is not my place to comment on such things, but I must tell you how reassured I have been by the constancy of your affections for her."

Darcy coloured slightly. "As I have already informed Miss Elizabeth, when formed, my affections are steadfast. I could never leave her, and only her absolute refusal could ever send me away—well, her *second* refusal," he conceded.

"I believe you," she replied with an indulgent smile, "and again I thank you for your care of her." As she paused to observe Elizabeth, sadness clouded her visage, as though she were experiencing something profound. Quietly, Miss Bennet continued, "I believe she will need your loyalty in the days to come."

Puzzled by her cryptic declaration, Darcy's thoughts were interrupted by the return of Mrs Gardiner.

"Forgive me, Miss Darcy, but it seems my daughter has been plaguing her nanny all morning with requests to join us. Meg finds it hard to stay in the nursery when her cousins have visitors."

"I can sympathise with your daughter. I was always the only child in a room of adults, and I fear my brother was bothered quite frequently by my need for his attention."

"You could never be a bother, Georgiana," Darcy interjected. "I often prefer your company to that of most people, fully grown or otherwise."

"What did I tell you, Miss Darcy? A staunch defender, indeed!" Elizabeth teased. "I fear, Aunt, that Meg's distraction is my fault. I promised her earlier that I would teach her a simple folk song on the pianoforte after our guests have gone. I see now that I probably should have waited until later in the day to make such commitment."

"So you are teaching your cousin to play, Miss Elizabeth?" Georgiana enquired.

"Only simple tunes. Meg is but five, my talents are limited, and I am not an appropriate tutor."

"I remember Fitzwilliam teaching me simple songs when I was that age. But surely you are being too modest, Miss Elizabeth! My brother has told me how much he enjoys to listen to your playing, and he never exaggerates, I assure you!"

"You play the pianoforte, Mr Darcy?" Elizabeth asked, clearly surprised.

"I must defer to your superior skills, and Georgiana has long surpassed any efforts of mine."

"I would love to hear you play sometime, Miss Elizabeth," Georgiana affirmed. "Fitzwilliam has told me that he has rarely heard anything that brought him such pleasure."

Elizabeth was spared from answering his sister's request when a maid entered the room with refreshments. Standing to assist her aunt, Miss Bennet redirected the conversation towards Derbyshire, and soon Georgiana and Mrs Gardiner were happily sharing their stories of Lambton while Miss Bennet asked after their favourite haunts in the village. Bringing him his preferred cup of tea, Elizabeth joined Darcy on the other side of the room.

"You have been withholding information, sir. There I was, chained to the instrument at Rosings, when you could have rescued me from your aunt's scrutiny by displaying your undoubtedly superior talents."

Smiling in reply, Darcy acknowledged, "Perhaps I could have, Miss Elizabeth, but you are by far the superior player. In fact, I have not played before anyone outside my immediate family since I was a boy. I was in earnest when I told you that I do not perform to strangers."

"Do you have a reason for keeping such talents hidden?"

"Not particularly, it is only that my instruction came from my mother. She was a marvellous performer, but her music was always distinctly personal, a feeling my sister shares."

Elizabeth's genuine interest gave Darcy the courage to continue. "My mother was always rather delicate, you see, and during my youth, she spent many hours in the music room in place of more active pursuits. I was often drawn to her music, and some of my fondest memories of her are the moments she would give towards my instruction. It may not have been the most common of interests for a young boy, but I felt privileged to share her passion." He paused as his thoughts turned slightly mournful. "After Georgiana's birth, my mother's health never recovered and she rarely left Pemberley. On my holidays from Eton, we spent quite a lot of time in that music room, playing together with Georgiana in her basket at our feet. Georgiana suffered from colic, and nothing seemed to soothe her except for my mother's music. After Mother died, I continued to play for my sister in her stead."

A light hand on his forearm pulled him from his recollections, and as he turned to gaze upon Elizabeth, her kind sympathy radiated from her countenance.

"What was she like, your mother?"

"She was a gentle soul, much like your sister Miss Bennet. 'Tis not a common trait for a Fitzwilliam, I assure you. The more lively nature of my cousin Richard is more in tune with the rest of the family. I suppose with such a strong sister as Lady Catherine, it was easier for my mother to yield to her natural reserve, a trait she passed to both of her children. In looks, she was much like Georgiana—blonde curls, blue eyes, though a lighter shade, and a fair complexion. While I strongly resemble my father, I believe I inherited much of Mother's temperament, though perhaps not her innate gentleness," he finished with a faint smile.

"I would not be so sure of that, Mr Darcy, for you seem to possess hidden depths behind that mask you present to the world. Was your father also reserved?"

"No indeed. While not overly boisterous, my father tended to favour those of a livelier disposition. I felt he was sometimes disappointed by my reticence, as he often encouraged my association with those he felt would inspire me to overcome my shyness."

Darcy could see Elizabeth instantly understood his reference to Wickham, but she bravely pushed past the allusion.

"Well, you seemed to have developed a taste for liveliness if you prefer my company," she teased. "Though I must say that I enjoy learning more of your family. It is clear to me how much you care for them, and I believe in the importance of appreciating your blessings. You never know how fragile it can all become."

Her uncharacteristically solemn expression encouraged him to ask, "Are you sure you are well, Miss Elizabeth?"

"I hardly know, sir, but I have great hope I soon will be." As she looked into his eyes, she seemed to seek reassurance, and her smile grew. "Indeed, I believe I have every chance of happiness."

Darcy felt his own chances for felicity had increased tenfold since his arrival that afternoon. An irrepressible hope settled in his chest, convincing him that perhaps his greatest desire was not quite so far out of reach.

CHAPTER EIGHTEEN

It had been nearly twenty years since Lady Tamworth stood before this door in her London town home. Though her visits to town had been infrequent at best, she had always been careful to avoid this room, acutely aware of her own lack of fortitude to face what lay beyond the entrance. Deciding it was time to put old ghosts to rest, Amelia turned the knob and entered the long-abandoned space. Crisp, white sheets covered the furniture, but even so, she could still discern the outline of a crib in the corner and a rocking chair by the window. The room had been preserved, almost as a morbid shrine, for the child who would never occupy it.

Amelia recalled selecting the bedding, the curtains, and several other items on her last visit to London before Elizabeth's birth. The first and only time that Amelia had entered the nursery after Elizabeth's abduction, she had collapsed in a ball of tears on the floor, so lost to her misery that nothing could rouse her. There she had stayed until her husband had lifted her in his arms and carried her out the door, ordering the servants to close up the room as he took her back to her chambers, whispering soothing words of affection as her tears dried.

As she gazed over the dusty suite, Amelia could not help but imagine what life would have been like had Elizabeth never been taken. Perhaps she might have attempted her first steps or uttered her first words in this very room. In any case, it would serve no purpose to dwell on what could never be. The courage even to open the door was only made possible by new assurances of a much brighter future, and so, after one last look, Amelia turned and exited the nursery, closing up the room once more. Unless she could convince Nicholas to take a wife, it was unlikely the space would be needed again for many years. Wandering down the hall, Amelia pressed on to her next task, one which would serve as a suitable distraction until her husband and son returned later that evening.

The day after meeting Elizabeth, they had been adamant about journeying to Hertfordshire in haste. However, Amelia had convinced them to wait another day after pointing out that imposing upon the Bennets on a Sunday would not be entirely proper. Before departing with his father just after sunrise, Nicholas had encouraged Amelia to go in his stead at his usual time of calling upon Elizabeth and spend some uninterrupted time in her daughter's company.

Despite her apprehension that Elizabeth was not yet ready to welcome another mother into her life, her morning had gone infinitely better than she had ever anticipated. Upon her arrival at Gracechurch Street, Amelia's attention was caught by the light melody emanating from the direction of the front parlour. Before her presence could be announced, she dismissed the servant that attended her in favour of silently observing the beautiful vision of her daughter seated at the pianoforte. Elizabeth played the whimsical tune with great feeling, somehow filling the room with palpable cheer and bringing a sense of joy to Amelia's heart that had long been missing. As happy tears trailed down her face, she watched as Elizabeth finished the piece and began to rise from the bench. Amelia quickly removed her handkerchief to dab at her cheeks while alerting Elizabeth to her presence in the room.

"You play beautifully, my dear."

Elizabeth started, her surprise evident. "Lady Tamworth? I-I was not told to expect you."

"Nicholas said he usually calls on you at this hour, and since he and your father are currently on the road to Hertfordshire, I had hoped you would not object to my presence in his place this morning."

"You are most welcome, of course! I apologise, my aunt and sister are out this morning, but I expect their return in a half an hour. Would you care for some tea? Pray come in and be seated."

Amelia smiled at the nervous expression that flitted across Elizabeth's face. She clearly had not expected to be disturbed, and Amelia found her flustered appearance to be rather endearing.

"Tea sounds lovely, and I would be happy to sit with you for a time."

Settling in on the settee, Amelia watched as her daughter pulled the bell to summon a servant. Despite her noticeable nerves, she seemed more than capable of executing her responsibilities as hostess with a calm kindness and considerable poise. After ordering the tea service, Elizabeth joined her, a timid smile etched upon her countenance.

"I must admit," Amelia began, "that even though Nicholas had informed me of your rather strong resemblance to me, I could never have imagined how apt his description would be."

"You are not alone in your astonishment, I assure you. I believe a part of me, even after seeing your portrait, still doubted Nicholas's assurance of my parentage, but when I saw you the other day…"

Seeing her hesitation, Amelia gently took Elizabeth's hand. "I know this will be hard, dear, but matters will improve in time, you will see."

"I do not doubt it. However jarring and painful the events of the past few weeks have been for me, I have always noted a lack of familiar features in regard to the Bennet family. You see, Papa—that is, Mr Bennet—well, he had always insisted so strenuously on my likeness to his mother, and I simply assumed I was the only one who favoured my father's side. I never thought to question it."

"And why would you? It is not surprising that you should be so shocked by this discovery when you had never been told of your origins. "

Looking down at their joined hands, Elizabeth's expression grew pensive. Sensing her daughter was still struggling with the profound shock of recent revelations, Amelia hoped to provide her with some motherly comfort.

"Nicholas has told me little of what happened the evening that you first met, so perhaps you could tell me of your own experience? It might help you to settle your thoughts."

Elizabeth's expression seemed almost hopeful. "I have not been able to speak freely of all that has occurred yet to anyone. Usually I confide in Aunt Gardiner or to Jane, but I know how distressing this has been for them, and I have been concerned I may injure them somehow. My sister is quite fearful she will lose me, just as I cannot contemplate losing her. To learn that they are not my true family, yet they are the dearest people in the world to me—I do not want to burden them further."

Amelia noted Elizabeth turned to her aunt for counsel, rather than Mrs Bennet. "Elizabeth, I am in earnest. Your father and I would never separate you from those you love!" Gripping her palm in reassurance, Amelia continued. "My world was shattered the day you were taken, as I imagine yours was the day you discovered you were not the Bennets' child, so I feel I may understand your feelings somewhat. Do not be afraid that you may injure me, for I can assure you that I long to know your thoughts."

"Very well then…if you are sure."

Giving a slight nod, Elizabeth began to recount the events of the evening, prompting Amelia's laughter at her initial belief that her aunt had meant to introduce Nicholas as a potential suitor for Jane.

"Did Nicholas tell you of our meeting in the park?"

"Yes, he did. For it was what motivated him to seek out Mr Gardiner for answers."

"Of course. And once he was introduced, there was little else I could think of throughout dinner. When my aunt suggested we retire to the parlour, I was surprised that he and Uncle chose to join us, and when my uncle started asking questions about what Jane and I knew concerning the story of my birth, a horrible sense of dread came upon me. To learn that I had been *found* by my parents…it felt as if all I had ever known was a lie." After a slight pause, Elizabeth continued. "I did not *imagine* my family's love for me, nor mine for them, but my foundation had been shaken to a degree I had never anticipated, and believe me, my faith in myself has been rattled in the recent past."

A distant expression came over Elizabeth that was soon replaced with a subtle grin. "When Nicholas told me his own story, I began to realise I was a part of a tragedy worthy of something penned by Mrs Radcliffe! That I would be the lost daughter of an earl? I could barely credit it…until he showed me your portrait. From that point on, I believe I merely sat in a haze of confusion until his departure. I gave my sister quite a fright afterwards, as I ran outside for some desperately needed fresh air and then…"

"And then what, my dear?" Amelia enquired, noting with sudden awareness that Elizabeth seemed mildly frantic, as though she had not intended to mention that particular part of her tale. Suppressing her momentary disappointment, Amelia realised it would not be fair to expect Elizabeth's full confidence so soon.

"I believe I cried a bit on the bench across the street until my alarm subsided. When I returned, and once Jane could be assured of my well-being, physically at least, I retired for the evening. Ever since that night I have spent a good deal of time trying to come to terms with my new situation."

"I hope you have had some relief from your contemplations, for I know too well how disheartening it can be to reflect endlessly over circumstances you cannot change."

"I have been truly blessed by the support of my family… and friends. They have helped to wrest me from my gloomy thoughts and spark my courage once more. In fact, I have been reminded recently that I once declared that my courage would always rise at every attempt at intimidation. As difficult as this circumstance may be, I am determined to face it with optimism and an open heart."

"Nicholas was right. You are a wonder, my dear! He has told me of his visits, and how much he has come to care for you."

Blushing at such praise, Elizabeth looked to her lap. "And I have come to care for him. I always longed for a brother, which I suppose is not a surprise after being raised in a home with four sisters."

"Four sisters! My goodness!" Hesitantly, Amelia asked, "Would you tell me about your life in Hertfordshire? I should so very much like to know you better. Perhaps you could tell me of your interests? I would enjoy knowing how you spent your days there."

A nervous expression settled on her features as Elizabeth conceded, "I cannot say I have lived an exciting life thus far, until recently of course, but I would be happy to share what I can."

Elizabeth began to recount her routine while living on the Bennets' estate in Hertfordshire. While she had never doubted Nicholas's report that her daughter was suitably educated and an avid lover of nature, Amelia was nevertheless pleased to hear Elizabeth's account, enchanted by the animation she displayed when sharing her favourite pastimes. Though she appeared anxious that some of her tales might garner disapproval, once her recollections began to prompt Amelia's laughter, Elizabeth seemed more eager to share stories from her childhood, many of which involved her neighbours the Lucas family.

"I shall never forget the look on Hill's face when I arrived at the kitchens, covered in mud and clutching my makeshift sword." Elizabeth laughed. "Jane had warned me that playing pirates with Charlotte's brother, John, was not a good idea, but I simply could not resist the temptation to run about the woods in pursuit of adventure! Fortunately, Hill was sympathetic to my plight and managed to remove the mud before Mama found out."

"And how old were you when this little misadventure occurred?"

"Seven, I believe! Lydia was a rather rambunctious toddler, which made it quite easy for me to evade capture and escape the nursery when I grew restless. Jane always refused to join me, but even then the thrill of nature called to my little soul."

"I do not doubt it," Amelia replied with a fond smile, "for you seem to have much in common with your brother. Our housekeeper at Heatherton Hall, Mrs Steeley, could commiserate with your Mrs Hill over the amount of mud Nicholas managed to transport into the house during his youth. To this day, she still manages to corner him with the boot brush whenever he arrives, convinced that he will leave footprints all over the floors. I hope *you* managed to ease the burden of your housekeeper as you grew older."

"I suppose it would depend upon whom you were to ask,

for I was recently chastised for wearing petticoats that sported six inches' worth of mud. Though, to be fair, Miss Bingley tends to exaggerate. All I can say in my defence is that I would brave much worse to tend to Jane. She had fallen ill, you see, while visiting our neighbours, and knowing she would never admit to needing assistance for fear of burdening her host, I resolved to see to her comfort myself."

"My goodness, well, I cannot fault your reasoning. It gladdens my heart to know how deeply you care for others. Your compassionate nature is a credit to the family that raised you. I can only hope that your father and I would have done as well should you have remained with us."

Hesitantly, Elizabeth reached out and took Amelia's hand once more. In a rare show of complete vulnerability, at least to Amelia's discernment, Elizabeth made a sombre confession.

"I have often wondered over the past week or so if Elizabeth Grey would be the same person as Elizabeth Bennet. I —I cannot regret the life I have lived, yet a part of me has wondered if it is enough. Should proof be found of my birth and I live in your home, will I find a place in your world, or shall I be scorned for my upbringing? Will people expect me to become someone else, and if they do, who should that person be?"

Seeing her lost expression, Amelia gently patted Elizabeth's hand. "Elizabeth, your father and I would never want you to be anyone other than who you are. No matter where you were raised or what society you were raised in, you will *always* be enough for us. There is no reason for Elizabeth Grey to be anyone other than Elizabeth Bennet, for trading a surname and attaching a title can do little to change who you have always been. I shall be proud to claim you as my daughter, when the time comes."

Their poignant tête-à-tête was interrupted by the return of Mrs Gardiner and Miss Bennet, and Amelia had been pleased to further her acquaintance with the two women who were so dear to her daughter. Before she announced her departure, Amelia noted with curiosity Elizabeth's fleeting glances towards the front window. Had she been expecting someone else? Perhaps her son would be able to provide clarification when he returned from his trip, as Amelia did not want to pry into her daughter's affairs so soon.

Upon her return to Tamworth House, Amelia had resolved to first confront her fears, inspired by the courage her daughter had displayed that morning and to move forward with an altogether more satisfying task—the preparation of her daughter's new rooms. Convinced her husband would not fail to find the information he sought, Amelia wanted to prepare Elizabeth's apartments at their London home so she could welcome her there at the earliest opportunity. While the housekeeper and staff aired several chambers in the family wing, Amelia was instantly drawn to a spacious set of rooms decorated in cheerful spring colours of yellow and green, complete with a comfortable window seat with a charming view of the back gardens on which she could picture Elizabeth resting with a book perched in her hand. The sudden arrival of the butler pulled Amelia from her pleasant musings.

"What is it, Tewes?"

"Lady Matlock has arrived to see if you are available to callers."

"I will gladly see her. Will you direct her to this room?"

"Certainly, my lady." With a bow, her butler departed, and a short time later he returned to usher her closest friend into the freshly opened space.

"Eleanor! I had not expected you today. Pray come in and sit with me."

Crossing the room, her friend approached the window seat and after taking Amelia's hands and pressing a swift kiss to her cheek, Lady Matlock sat by her side.

"I had to come and see for myself how you were faring! 'Tis no small event that has brought you to town, and I would hope you know my family is ready to be of help to you in any way we can."

"Harry and I are truly grateful for your assistance. When the time comes, we will need you to help us face the scrutiny of the *ton*. I shudder to think what society will make of such an announcement."

"Then you are certain there will be one?"

"As certain as I can be. Nicholas was right, Eleanor. Judging by her appearance, Elizabeth could only be my daughter. I thought Harry might faint the first time he saw her, and I assure you I was in no better condition."

"What good news! I am so happy for you, and do not give a thought to what society may think! Your family is still highly respected, and with the backing of two earldoms, Lady Elizabeth Grey will be a force to be reckoned with, I am certain!"

"She would be an indomitable force regardless, my friend, of that I can attest. I do not know if I could praise her well enough, for she is a treasure. Thoughtful, intelligent, kind, and witty! I would speak of her beauty, but then I fear it would seem quite vain to remark upon her looks when they are so similar to mine."

Laughing, Lady Matlock replied, "She is fortunate to favour you, my dear, for I remember well how enraptured Lord Tamworth was when he first made your acquaintance. I have no doubt your daughter will delight a future suitor in a similar fashion if she is all that you claim." After a notable pause, Eleanor continued in a noticeably timid tone. "Speaking of suitors, have either you or Tamworth given any thought to the arrangements made at Elizabeth's birth?"

"The betrothal contract?" Amelia enquired, startled slightly by the memory. "To be frank, the thought had not crossed my mind, and I doubt Harry is thinking about giving his daughter away after so recently finding her again."

"Is it something you would wish for? To see Elizabeth married to James?"

"I love my godson dearly, you know that, Eleanor. However, I cannot help but fear that mentioning anything about the arrangement would only serve to unsettle Elizabeth. I do not want to give her any reason to reject us as her family, and I have already noted my daughter does not possess a timid spirit. I do not think she would accept such a plan so soon, not when she is still so apprehensive concerning her place in our society. Perhaps we can discuss it later, after she and James have been given time to come to know one another."

"I only mention it because Hugh seems to have his heart set on the matter, and James seems particularly eager at the possibility. I cannot deny I would greatly desire my son to marry, and who better than the daughter of my dearest friend? However, I would never do anything to upset either you or Elizabeth."

As their visit continued, Eleanor seemed thrilled to hear all that Amelia could relate about her morning visit with her daughter, but despite her enthusiasm for the topic, Amelia could not quell the rising fear that had settled over her at the mention of her daughter's betrothal. After Lady Matlock's departure, Amelia sat and stared out of the window in Elizabeth's newly appointed room, searching her heart for the reason why such a development should plague her with such doubt.

She loved James almost as dearly as her own son, so why should the thought of him courting Elizabeth unsettle her so? As she sorted through her feelings, Amelia began to remember the many small smiles that had adorned Elizabeth's face throughout their exchange, and the almost wistful glances she directed towards the front window at the end of their visit.

Could it be? A suspicion quickly formed in her mind that her daughter may already have a suitor. The thought quickly filled her with dread, as Amelia could not imagine how such a complication would unfold in the weeks to come, and what threats it would pose to Elizabeth's future happiness.

CHAPTER NINETEEN

As the carriage continued its journey past Meryton, Lord Grey was presented with his first glimpse of Longbourn Village, complete with quaint country homes and a small parish church. While his eager eyes absorbed the locale his sister had known almost her whole life, Grey could not help but notice his father's focus was not on his immediate surroundings.

At the start of their trip from London, the earl had questioned him relentlessly about Elizabeth and all of their prior meetings, longing for every bit of knowledge Nicholas could share regarding his daughter. After he had finished recounting what he could, Lord Tamworth had fallen silent, staring out of the carriage window with a rather lost expression. Grey could not imagine what it would be like to be introduced to the man your own daughter called father, and who might have had some role in keeping her from you for twenty years.

Soon, the carriage turned onto the drive that led to Longbourn House, revealing a modest two-storey country manor of grey stone in the distance. A simple, white portico framed the front door, but the building's real charm came from the vines of ivy that crawled across the front façade. The house was nothing to Heatherton Hall, with its Palladian architecture, rows of polished glass windows, and expansive grounds, but even so, Grey could easily perceive how Elizabeth could have spent a happy childhood in such a place.

Turning to his father, Grey commented, "It is comforting to find Longbourn exactly as Elizabeth described. I declare it makes me wonder how accurate her depictions will be of its inhabitants.

"Neither you nor mother have asked a great deal about Mr and Mrs Bennet, but I believe it will be to our advantage to trust Elizabeth's assessment of their characters."

At this statement his father became slightly alarmed. "Nothing unsavoury, I hope? Surely, you would not hide from me if my daughter has suffered under their roof!"

"That is not what I meant," Grey immediately replied in an effort to extinguish his father's rapidly rising ire. "'Tis only that Elizabeth has oft described Mr Bennet as rather flippant. He delights in the follies of others, and so it is my belief we would be best served in approaching him as directly as possible with both our story and Mother's portrait. We should consider that he may be fearful of losing Elizabeth, which would discourage him from taking our word seriously. We should give him no room to dismiss our assertions."

"Understood. Tell me, is there anything I should know about the mother? I would not care to be caught off guard today if at all possible."

"Elizabeth has frequently mentioned her younger sisters and Mrs Bennet can be quite voluble, and she is often forced to go on walks about the countryside to find some modicum of peace."

"She goes walking alone?" the earl asked with a horrified expression.

"In Hertfordshire, yes. I know it is not ideal, and we will have to speak to her about her safety, but I am sure that as a minor country gentleman's daughter with little to no dowry she felt reasonably protected. It is not as though this is a common location to find gypsies or highwaymen."

"Still, I cannot understand how Mr Bennet would allow her to walk about unattended! Did you not mention there is a militia regiment encamped close by?"

"Yes, indeed. Elizabeth has admitted she possesses a decidedly stubborn nature, so I am sure her reluctance to lose one of her daily pleasures allowed this lapse in her father's oversight. Mr Bennet can be fairly indolent regarding the correction of his children, something Elizabeth mourns in the case of her younger sisters."

"How he deals with his own children is his prerogative. I, however, take great offence at his negligence towards *mine*," his father retorted.

As soon as they arrived before the manor house, Grey stepped down onto the drive and breathed in the fresh, spring air, allowing the familiar scents of the country to soothe his nervous agitation over the coming meeting. As his father descended from the carriage, a young groom stepped forward to direct their polished equipage towards the stables with a look of slight wonder upon his face. Clearly, the Bennets did not entertain many peers, and their presence must have been fairly surprising, given that they had sent no notice of their arrival.

Gesturing to his father to take the lead, they turned and walked towards the front door which was promptly answered by a kindly looking woman whom Grey assumed was Longbourn's long-standing—and as Elizabeth had often quipped—*long-suffering* housekeeper, Mrs Hill. She greeted them warmly, but upon receiving their cards and their request to speak to the master of the house, her face showed a trace of alarm. She quickly recovered her calm demeanour, however, and after confirming Mr Bennet was presently available for company in his book room, she led them both through Elizabeth's childhood home.

Upon entering the small but cosy space, it was easy to determine how Elizabeth had developed an ardent love for the written word, as shelf upon shelf was packed with a fairly impressive collection of various tomes. This was the home of a well-read gentleman, Grey thought as he turned to gaze upon the man himself.

At their entrance, Mr Bennet stood to welcome his guests, and Grey detected an amused glint in his host's shrewd gaze, slightly hidden though it was by his wire frames. Mr Bennet was a man of average height, with tufts of white, curly hair that framed his face, and attired in the modest wardrobe of a country scholar, content with his lot in life.

"I know not how I have earned the pleasure of this introduction, my lords, but you are welcome to Longbourn all the same. I am Thomas Bennet. My housekeeper said you have some business with me today?" He gave a small bow before gesturing to the armchairs by the fireplace, inviting his guests to sit.

"Thank you, Mr Bennet. I am the Earl of Tamworth, and this is my son, Nicholas Grey, Baron Grey de Rotherfield. We have come on an important matter and were given your direction by your brother, Mr Edward Gardiner."

"Gardiner? I had no idea my brother kept such exalted company!" Mr Bennet quipped with a slightly sardonic grin.

Determining their previously agreed upon plan to approach the topic directly was best, Grey boldly entered the conversation.

"It was I who sought out Mr Gardiner after I made a rather shocking discovery in Hyde Park over a week ago, but before I elaborate further, I feel there is something you should see." Reaching towards his father, the miniature portrait was handed to him as he turned back to face Mr Bennet. "This portrait was created in 1781, and I believe its subject will be of interest to you."

Offering the piece for Mr Bennet's perusal, Grey was unsurprised to see the shock displayed upon the other man's face as he stared at the image before him, his complexion paling until Grey began to fear somewhat for his health.

"How—I do not understand. Who is this?"

The earl took up the tale. "The woman in the portrait is my wife, Lady Tamworth. I commissioned the painting on the occasion of our wedding. Ten years later, my wife and I lost something most precious to us. Our infant daughter was stolen from our family estate in Staffordshire by her nursemaid, a woman named Sarah Summers. Despite our searches, we never found any trace of her after her disappearance on the ninth of December 1791, what I have long considered to be the worst day of my life.

"I understand from your brother that you discovered a foundling child only weeks later on the road from London to Hertfordshire, and that you adopted the child, a baby girl named Elizabeth." His father paused as he took in the stricken expression on Mr Bennet's face. "I imagine you have determined the reason for our visit today, for you see, I have every reason to believe the child you have raised is in fact *my* daughter, Lady Elizabeth Grey."

In an effort to settle the man seated across from him, Grey calmly stated, "I know this is difficult for you, Mr Bennet, but we have met with Elizabeth, and she is now aware of how she came to your family. I ask now that you help me reclaim my sister, that you help my family by telling us what you know of her discovery that winter."

After setting the portrait down with a shaky hand, Mr Bennet abruptly stood and returned to his desk on the other side of the room. Swiftly producing a key, he unlocked a large bottom drawer and lifted another locked box from its depths. Returning to his chair at the fireplace, he took a deep breath as he unlocked the case on his lap and silently handed it to the earl. With a small wave of his trembling hand, Mr Bennet gave his permission to view its contents.

After looking to his son with a confused expression, the earl lifted the lid and gazed in awe upon what he found within. An infant's gown was removed from the box, and Grey's attention was drawn to the way his father lovingly stroked his hand across the delicate embroidery that encircled the hem of the garment. Upon closer inspection, Grey understood why his father's vision had clouded with tears, for there upon the dress was his mother's signature pattern, an intertwining ribbon of her favourite flower, the lily of the valley, and the heather that surrounded his father's estate.

"We had waited so long to be blessed again with a babe that Amelia spent weeks of her confinement adding adornments to every conceivable piece of cloth that would touch our child." Reaching into his inner coat pocket, his father produced his handkerchief and passed it to Mr Bennet. There upon the edge was the very same embroidery.

After a sharp exhale, Mr Bennet spoke for the first time since they related their tale. "Well, there can be no doubt. I suppose that settles the matter."

"Not so hasty, Mr Bennet," the earl began, "I believe I have the right to know how my daughter came into your care."

"And it was never my intent to deny you, my lord, forgive me. I fear my story will paint me in a rather poor light from your perspective, but perhaps I should feel the shame of my inaction, for once in my life at least."

A grim expression settled over the man's face. "Before I begin, I feel it my duty to assure you that I have always loved Elizabeth. In fact, I will even own to a certain level of favouritism in her case. She possesses so much wit and intelligence, traits that I have sought to encourage throughout her youth, but even these aspects of her character are surpassed by her loving nature. She is exceedingly precious to me."

Mr Bennet paused to regain his composure. "As you have probably surmised by the fact that I kept her garment, I had sincere doubts at first when we originally took Elizabeth into our care. If you have spoken with Mr Gardiner, I am sure you are aware of the family tragedy that took place earlier that year in London. After my wife lost the babe, I did not know if she would ever return to her spirited, exuberant self. When I finally convinced Fanny to return to Longbourn that December, we had a most unlikely encounter upon the road, just before reaching the coaching inn at Meryton.

"A post-chaise headed south had broken down on the side of the road, and since only myself, my wife, and our daughter Jane were in our coach, I deemed we would be able to provide assistance to someone who might desire to return to the inn. When I approached the disabled carriage, I saw a young woman holding a crying infant. She seemed agitated and nervous, so I introduced myself and offered to return her to the inn at Meryton, should she need shelter until the post arrived once more. She told me her name was Sarah Clifton and that she desperately needed to reach London."

The earl started at the name, clearly prompting Mr Bennet's curiosity.

"Does the name mean something to you, my lord?"

"Beyond the Christian name of Elizabeth's abductor, Clifton was the surname of a maid in our service, one who had died from the same illness that produced such a change in Miss Summers's mind. As I understood from my wife, the maid and Sarah were close friends before the former's death."

"An illness, you say? I should not be surprised, for from the first, Miss Clifton's overall demeanour bespoke of an unnatural distrust. She was not pleased to be deterred from her southern trip, and it took a fair amount of convincing to persuade her to enter the carriage. I appealed to the comfort of the child, assuming she would not want to expose the babe to such frigid air for an extended period of time. When she finally joined my family, she was notably distressed by Elizabeth's continued cries, and so my wife asked if she might soothe the babe. Fanny had such an intense look of longing on her face, and at first this seemed to discompose Miss Clifton further. I do not know exactly why she chose to relinquish Elizabeth, but my wife was able to calm her quickly, and soon enough she was sleeping comfortably with my little Jane looking upon her in delight. They made such a beautiful picture—my smiling wife and daughter with a precious bundle between them."

A wistful expression covered Mr Bennet's face before he cleared his throat and continued. "I began to ask Miss Clifton about her circumstances and that of the child, and she informed me that she was delivering the babe to its only living relatives in London. She claimed the child was born of a friend of hers, a servant, who had recently perished, and she was unsure whether the family in London would agree to take her in. Her story, told in a somewhat flustered manner, aroused my suspicions, as anyone could clearly see the child's clothing was finely made. When I asked after the babe's name, she instantly uttered Elizabeth, but I could not persuade her to share the child's surname, which only served to increase my misgivings. I resolved from that point to pay close attention to anything else I could convince the young woman to reveal, as I fully intended to make enquiries with the authorities should she provide further cause to doubt her story."

"Yet you did not," Lord Tamworth replied in an angry tone. "We searched for years for my daughter, and we never heard any reports of a foundling in Hertfordshire. Why did your plans change?"

"I am coming to that, my lord, and as I said before, I do not feel it reflects well on me. Once I knew the child was not her own, I enquired about her travels. She related that her travelling companion, a wet nurse, had left her to return north at the last coaching inn, as Miss Clifton had exhausted the majority of her funds and could no longer pay her to continue, thus her urgent need to reach London."

"Where would Miss Summers acquire enough money to travel from Staffordshire to Meryton and pay for the services of a wet nurse along the way?" Grey asked his father.

"After your sister disappeared, we searched the house for any trace we could find regarding Summers's plans. I discovered someone had entered my study and somehow gained entry to the hidden cast-iron chest in the bookshelf behind my desk. The key was missing as well, which only further confirmed that the abduction had been planned in advance. While a large portion of bank notes and coins were missing, most of the papers within had also been rifled through, though I do not believe Summers found what she had been looking for."

Puzzled by his father's words, Grey looked to him with a raised brow, silently inviting him to elaborate. The earl, however, merely shook his head, and turned back to Mr Bennet, encouraging him to continue his portion of the story.

"I assured the young lady that I had a recently widowed tenant who was willing to offer her services as a nurse if they were required. She had already planned to assist Mrs Bennet in nursing our lost child, so I was reasonably certain that she would agree to my request. When we reached the inn, I settled the women in a private parlour while I looked into arrangements for our guests for the night. As the inn was crowded, I returned to the parlour to wait until the innkeeper had time to provide assistance. Questioning the girl seemed the best use of my time, so I mentioned the babe looked to be only a few months old. Miss Clifton responded that the girl was not yet four months, having been born on the twenty-eighth of August."

Grey gasped. "She gave you Elizabeth's actual birthdate? I always assumed Miss Summers would have lied about any important information. I never thought to ask Elizabeth about her date of birth, as I felt reasonably assured she would not know the true day."

"It is not an easy thing to maintain a web of lies. Whenever I asked for specific information, like Elizabeth's family name, Miss Clifton either gave the information so readily it seemed almost unconsciously done, or she refused to respond. In any case, as we sat in the crowded inn, the noise level continued to rise, so much so that we could hear the voices from the public rooms in our private parlour. As the noise grew, the young woman became even more agitated, and at times she began to mutter to herself. I could not discern most of what she said, but she seemed focused on the babe in my wife's arms as she kept repeating some nonsense about refusing to sell the child."

At this statement, Grey's father blanched, which further confirmed there was something about this whole affair Grey had not been told. Not willing to broach the topic in front of Mr Bennet, Grey resolved to confront his father in the carriage ride home. Mr Bennet did not seem to notice the reactions of his guests as he continued to relate the events at the inn.

"A serving lad eventually came into the parlour and informed me that the innkeeper was ready to assist with procuring a room. After speaking to the man, I returned to the parlour, only to find my wife alone with the children. My wife told me that Miss Clifton had left to use the privy, and she would return shortly. So we sat and waited.

"By that time, Elizabeth was awake and alert, her natural curiosity shining through, and after one glance, I could see my wife was enchanted. She had been so despondent since the stillbirth that I feared she would never fully recover, yet her face at that moment was filled with a joy I had rarely seen her display. She set about introducing the babe to little Jane, who was thoroughly delighted with Elizabeth's incoherent babbling. At that moment, I could picture what our family would have been like, had our infant daughter survived. I know this means little to you in light of what you have suffered. I only wish to convey how happy we were to have met your daughter, and indeed, I had no thought of keeping her until Miss Clifton disappeared."

"Disappeared?"

"Aye, my lord. We waited for a full quarter of an hour for Miss Clifton to return to the parlour before I asked after her. Apparently, another post-chaise had arrived in the interim, and the innkeeper informed me that he had seen the young woman we were with board the coach with her belongings. For a reason we will never know, she left your daughter in our care. Originally, I intended to place a notice in the papers about Elizabeth's circumstances, but once my wife had learned Miss Clifton had gone, she begged me to allow her to keep the child. To my shame, I could not deny her—not after what she had so recently endured. We boarded our carriage and took Elizabeth back to Longbourn, telling one and all she was our new daughter, born in London at her uncle Gardiner's residence. Fanny and I agreed we would never share the details of her discovery with another living soul. We even refused to disclose all of the particulars to Gardiner and Fanny's mother."

"So you kept my child," the earl uttered in a soft, defeated tone.

"Yes, Lord Tamworth, we kept her, and all these years we have raised her as our own. I have no words to convey my sympathy for what you have lost, for I know better than anyone the true treasure that Elizabeth is. She has been my pride and joy for the past twenty years."

Mr Bennet bowed his head towards the hands folded in his lap. His posture was simultaneously remorseful and dejected. Grey looked to his father and could see he was fighting to keep his anger contained. As much as Grey could sympathise with his father's emotions, looking at Mr Bennet, he could feel naught but pity. He may have been at fault for failing to act on his suspicions, but it was not his actions that ultimately led to Elizabeth's abduction. No, it was the same reason they had always known—the product of a sadly unstable mind.

Turning to his father, Grey said, "I believe it is time for us to depart. You have our thanks for helping us today, Mr Bennet, and I would like to thank you for your care of Elizabeth as well. I am grateful that my sister was raised by people who obviously loved her."

Closing the case with Elizabeth's garments, his father stood and stared at the man who had reared his daughter in his stead.

"My son is right. I cannot pretend I do not feel some anger regarding your decision to keep my child, but even I can recognise your love for her. I have every intention of reclaiming my daughter, but if Elizabeth chooses to maintain the connexion, I will not deny her."

Mr Bennet's posture sagged in relief. "I thank you, Lord Tamworth. I would like the opportunity to explain our story to Lizzy in my own words, so I would request the opportunity to write to her. She knows I am a dreadful correspondent, but I feel I owe her the truth of my actions after keeping this from her for so long."

"I am sure Elizabeth will appreciate that, though I feel I must warn you that she has suffered a great disappointment. While she understands your desire to protect her reputation, she feels deceived. It may take some time for her to accept your account," Grey responded.

As they were turning to leave the book room, a great commotion was heard from the entry hall in the form of high-pitched, female voices. One in particular was decidedly shrill and loud. Dreading the coming introduction, Grey and his father stepped out of the library only to meet the mistress of the house and two of her younger daughters, both of whom dissolved into giggles upon seeing Grey.

"Oh Mr Bennet, you never mentioned we were having company!" the woman fluttered, waving her lace handkerchief about in nervous excitement. "You simply must stay for dinner, good sirs, and of course, enjoy the company of my lovely daughters!"

At this statement, Mrs Bennet looked specifically in Grey's direction, nearly prompting his laughter as he discovered how apt Elizabeth's descriptions of Mrs Bennet's efforts at matchmaking had been.

His father, he noticed, seemed rather appalled at Mrs Bennet's forward nature, though to be fair, he had not had enough time to recover from their conversation in the library before meeting Mrs Bennet. How difficult to be faced with the very woman whose melancholy had resulted in the loss of any hope to recover his child—the one who replaced his beloved wife as the mother to his most cherished daughter!

"I am afraid we have pressing business in London, madam. You will have to excuse us." Turning to Mr Bennet, Grey gave a small bow in farewell. "Thank you once again for your assistance today, sir. It has been invaluable."

After his father gave a similar nod, they turned and exited the house, leaving the shrill cries of the Bennet ladies behind as they boarded their carriage.

"I cannot believe *that* woman had a hand in raising my Elizabeth," his father huffed in indignation as they settled themselves.

"Elizabeth avows Mrs Bennet is truly a loving woman, but she has acknowledged her behaviour is often an embarrassment to both herself and Jane."

"That much is apparent."

Still bothered by the uncomfortable suspicions their interview with Mr Bennet had aroused, Grey fixed his father with an assessing look. Cautiously, he confessed, "I cannot help but feel you are still hiding something about this whole business. You mentioned Miss Summers searching through your papers."

"Nicholas, now is not the time to have this discussion," his father stated firmly.

"Respectfully, sir, I disagree. I am no longer an eight-year-old child. I feel I have the right to know the complete truth about my sister's disappearance."

Levelling a stern look at his father, Grey could see the moment his resolve crumbled.

"Before you respond, please allow me to tell you all. I strongly suspect you will disagree with my actions, but I assure you, I did not make these decisions lightly." After Grey nodded in agreement, his father continued. "You might not remember, but the week before Elizabeth was taken, Lord and Lady Matlock visited Heatherton Hall with James and Richard."

"I remember. It was the first time they met Elizabeth."

"Yes, well, Matlock was delighted that a girl had been born, as we had always imagined that our families could join through marriage one day. Matlock was eager to make a formal agreement of some kind, and so that week, we wrote a betrothal contract between your sister and James."

Grey was overtaken with disbelief. "I do not understand. You wrote—"

"Patience, I have more to relate. You must understand, your sister's dowry is considerable and could prove to be quite a temptation for the wrong sort of man. I know you detest the depravity of so many in our set. I could think of nothing better than to secure your sister's future with a family of good morals, who had long shared the bonds of friendship with both myself and your mother.

"Elizabeth was meant to be raised alongside James, and it was our hope that a true attachment would form. In any case, while Matlock and I were discussing matters, Miss

Summers entered the study unannounced, claiming she could not find your mother, and she had a pressing question about the baby. After that day, her manners towards me changed, and I have long suspected she overheard that portion of conversation. I am sure in her mind it seemed as though I had sold my child for purely self-serving aims, ensuring her life as a future countess."

"Thus you believe that she was searching for the contract?"

"Yes, but Matlock had taken it with him to his solicitor in London, so there was nothing for her to find beyond the coinage she needed to make her escape."

A momentary anger came over Grey as he fought to understand his father's actions. "So this was the reason—the *true* reason Sarah took Elizabeth?"

A wave of pain suffused his father's countenance as he replied, "Yes—yes, I believe it was."

"And now?" Grey asked. "Do you intend to hold Elizabeth to such an agreement now that she is found again?"

"Nicholas, please understand. The reasons for the contract's creation still exist. I do fully intend to speak of this to Matlock. I have no intention of forcing Elizabeth to do anything, but I believe a marriage to James is desirable. He has grown into a fine man, and he would be a good husband to her. He is your best friend. Can you not agree he could make your sister happy?" Noting his son's doubtful expression, he continued. "I have absolutely no intention of allowing Elizabeth to marry anyone before her majority and hopefully, not for several years after that. We have lost so much time with her, and I could not give her away to a suitor so soon. In fact, I doubt I will ever be prepared to let her go."

CHAPTER TWENTY

In a rare moment of quiet, Elizabeth seized the opportunity to relax on the window seat of her room. The book of poetry in her hand, however, was quite forgotten in favour of indulging in a few pleasant recollections which centred on one person in particular and served as a suitable distraction from the painful issue of her parentage. Elizabeth's preoccupation with Mr Darcy did not wholly surprise her, as she had never been so assiduously courted, having been completely unaware of her current suitor's previous regard, and of course anything was preferable to the bumbling, long-winded speeches of Mr Collins. She could not have been more thankful when that exceptionally short and ultimately doomed courtship came to a close last autumn.

Her current courtship, however, was another matter entirely. For the past two weeks, Mr Darcy had made every conceivable effort to display his continued interest in her, allowing Elizabeth to come to know him better and ultimately surprising her with how much she enjoyed his company.

While still somewhat reserved, Elizabeth owned she found his shyness rather endearing. In company, he was much more open and relaxed than she had seen him in the past, and he genuinely seemed to enjoy his time with her uncle's family. Elizabeth had always been proud of her London relations, but to see Mr Darcy's clear approbation of them gratified her exceedingly, especially when she considered they were connexions he had previously disdained. He also appeared to delight in her more playful manners, and she found herself consciously making an effort to elicit his smiles and laughter in all of their conversations. To be the object of those smiles was something to be desired, for Elizabeth could not deny that her suitor was an incredibly handsome man.

If she allowed herself to admit it, Elizabeth had to concede she had always found Mr Darcy handsome, even when she fervently disliked him. His dark, curly hair was a perfect contrast to his pale complexion and deep blue eyes. Elizabeth assumed this feature was a Darcy trait, as his sister, Georgiana, also possessed the same striking colour. Those eyes still followed her when they occupied the same room; however, instead of disconcerting her, Elizabeth found herself secretly thrilled by Mr Darcy's attention. Now that she had come to know him better, it was almost laughable to remember how she once assumed he looked at her only to find fault.

Reflecting on their conversation the previous day, Elizabeth owned that not only were Mr Darcy's manners and looks pleasing to her, but she sincerely valued his opinions and respected his good character. Whilst she had previously conceded he was a generally good sort of man after the revelations following their horrid misunderstanding in Kent, Elizabeth had not anticipated the depth of her admiration for his fine mind and honourable nature.

There were new revelations to be shared, but disclosing to him all she had learned about herself, her origins, and her true place in society, was too difficult to contemplate. His friendship and devotion was too dear to her to risk its loss or possible alteration, and so she remained silent.

When he arrived to call at Gracechurch Street the day before, Elizabeth had been waiting for him in the front parlour, perusing the same book of poetry she currently held in her hand. After greeting her sister and aunt who were seated on the sofa near the door to the entry hall, Mr Darcy crossed the room to take a seat at her side.

After they exchanged greetings, Elizabeth began their conversation. "I hope I am not detaining you from important matters, Mr Darcy, for you seem to be spending a fair amount of your time in my company of late."

"I believe you are well aware there is no place I would rather be than here with you," he professed with a slight smile. "Unless, of course, you desire my absence."

"Certainly not! I quite enjoy your visits, but I know great men such as yourself have so many demands on their time," she returned with an impish smile of her own.

"Great men? I declare I know not what to make of such a title. Perhaps you mean to make sport of me, and in that case, I ought not to encourage your impertinence."

Laughing, Elizabeth replied, "Well played, sir! You are too good to tolerate such wilful impudence on my part!"

"Tolerate it? No, I assure you, I revel in it. No one has ever dared to tease me the way you do, and 'tis a shame, for I find my life all the richer for your liveliness."

Acutely aware of the blush spreading across her cheeks, Elizabeth's gaze turned down to the book upon her lap.

"May I ask what you are reading today?" Mr Darcy enquired.

"I was drawn to an old favourite. I assume you have read *Songs of Experience*?"

"Naturally, although I must confess I had thought Blake's earlier work, *Songs of Innocence*, would be more appealing to you. That volume seems to better express the joy with which you approach life."

"And you would be right, sir. It is not often I choose this particular piece on which to meditate. I have found lately, however, that my mind has a more philosophical bent, perhaps owing to the many changes that have unsettled me so recently."

He regarded her with concern, and in that moment, Elizabeth had been thoroughly grateful Mr Darcy was not the prying sort. He valued his own privacy and seemed equally conscious of guarding hers, despite his clear desire to provide comfort where he was allowed.

"Is there a poem in particular that has caught your interest?"

"Before you arrived, I was reading '*The Clod and the Pebble*'," she answered, opening the volume on her lap and passing it to her suitor.

Mr Darcy took the offered book and began to read the short poem much to Elizabeth's delight, as his smooth baritone was ideally suited to such an endeavour.

"Love seeketh not itself to please,
Nor for itself hath any care,
But for another gives its ease,
And builds a Heaven in Hell's despair.

"So sung a little Clod of Clay
Trodden with the cattle's feet,
But a Pebble of the brook
Warbled out these metres meet:

"Love seeketh only self to please,
To bind another to its delight,
Joys in another's loss of ease,
And builds a Hell in Heaven's despite."

"So, Mr Darcy, shall we enter the realm of debate today? Do you believe love is inherently selfish or selfless? Does it merely exist to give, or is it truly meant to take? Is it Heaven or is it Hell?"

"Weighty matters indeed! Had I known I would be expected to expound upon the true nature of love during our discourse today, I might have prepared in advance," he remarked with a smirk.

"Come, sir! I know you enjoy a challenge as much as I, and I must own a certain curiosity regarding your thoughts on the subject."

"Is that so? Well, then, I shall be happy to oblige you. As I am sure you must have concluded, I do not believe Mr Blake is encouraging his reader to take either side of the argument as it is presented. Love should not be selfless to the point of losing one's true character like that of the clod, who is shaped through submission and literally trampled underfoot. Nor should love be so unyieldingly selfish as the pebble, who delights in discomfiting its object. Love should be an edifying experience for both parties, an emotion that challenges us to become our best selves in response to the care and devotion we both receive and seek to give to another. As for its being a Heaven or Hell, I can only determine from my own experience that a selfish love, a love that does not look to the well-being of another, can be a form of personal torment. Once redirected, however, and focused towards improving oneself to be worthy of the gift of another's love, I believe there is no greater joy to be found in achieving such a state."

His earnest expression caught Elizabeth off guard, as though he were willing her to see through his interpretation to his true meaning. For her part, Elizabeth could not help but be thrilled by his words, for in seeking to build a love that both supported and challenged its recipient, Mr Darcy was clearly expressing her value to him. Despite her awful rebukes, his love had not abated, but rather, he had taken on her critiques and sought to amend what she had perceived as flaws in his character.

"Can one truly be worthy of such love? I have begun to see my own failings all too clearly recently. I am not sure I should ever inspire such devotion."

"I cannot agree with that, Elizabeth. As I have said before, you are most certainly worthy in my estimation."

Thinking back on that conversation as she rested in her chambers, only now did it occur to Elizabeth that he had used her Christian name. It had been uttered so effortlessly that he did not seem to realise what he had done, and she wondered if he thought of her as *his* Elizabeth. She had always enjoyed the way he said her name, for despite the formality, for some unknown reason it seemed fitting, as though one or all of her shortened monikers somehow failed to express the depth of his feelings for her. To him she was simply *Elizabeth. Elizabeth Bennet.*

But she was Elizabeth Bennet no longer. On Monday evening, Nicholas had returned to the Gardiner's home to relate the outcome of his journey to Longbourn, offering the proof of her parentage in the form of a beautiful infant's gown, complete with her mother's delicate stitching.

She was Lady Elizabeth Grey, and tomorrow she would leave the only home she had ever known in London to take up her true apartments in her parents' luxurious town home on Curzon Street. Tomorrow she would leave the life of Elizabeth Bennet behind, so where did that leave Mr Darcy's *Elizabeth*?

Having her world so thoroughly shattered had brought about the unexpected result of opening Elizabeth's eyes to the truth of her feelings for the quiet gentleman from Derbyshire. Since the evening he had found her, distraught and alone, on the streets of London, he had somehow become the only tangible thing in her world—a reassuring, steadfast presence, that despite the tumult she endured, remained thoroughly convinced of her worthiness and eagerly sought to appreciate her simply for who she was.

It was a heady feeling to be the focus of such admiration, for had he not already declared such sentiments to her? *You must allow me to tell you how ardently I admire and love you.* Elizabeth found she could no longer deny that despite the relatively short period of their current courtship, she loved him in return. She was quite certain Fitzwilliam Darcy was the best man she had ever known.

"THERE YOU ARE, MY DEAR! HOW LONG HAVE YOU BEEN hiding away?"

Bustling into her room with one final trunk in her arms, Aunt Gardiner set the valise down upon the bed and came to sit by Elizabeth's side.

"You disappeared after breaking your fast. Have you been up here alone?"

"I have not had much time to myself lately, and I found I needed a brief reprieve from the general excitement this week has brought," Elizabeth answered with a slightly tired and forlorn expression.

"I know this has been trying, Lizzy, but I hope you are looking forward to this new adventure before you."

Elizabeth wiped a few errant tears aside, a common occurrence in recent days. "An adventure indeed! I nearly lost my way during the tour of Tamworth House a few days ago. They might as well leave bread crumbs to direct me from my chambers to the principal rooms in the house!"

"Oh dear!" Mrs Gardiner chuckled. "Well I suppose you must become accustomed to grander surroundings than you have inhabited in the past."

"Never fear. As always, I am sure my courage will rise to the occasion. And if I have to use my woeful drawing skills to conjure an adequate map, so be it."

"I am glad to see your resilience shine through. Take

heart, my dear niece, for no matter where you go or what you are called, your uncle and I will always be prodigiously proud of you. We love you very much, and you will always be part of our family."

Elizabeth leaned into her aunt's embrace, grateful for the care and direction she had received in this home over the years and over the past several weeks in particular.

"Now then, do you need any assistance to pack the last of your things? I realise there is not much here, but your uncle arranged to have your belongings from Longbourn delivered to your new home."

"Did he? I had not thought to enquire about it yet."

"Does that trouble you? Would you have liked to have done it yourself?"

"I-I do not know what I feel about Longbourn at the moment. It is probably best that I stay away from Hertfordshire for the time being, at least until I feel more settled in my new situation. While Papa's—I mean, Mr Bennet's letter did help to explain why they kept me in their care, and I am not such a simpleton as to discount their reasons for not making the story known, I still feel as though a part of my world has been stolen from me. I can no longer stroll the familiar country paths I have tread on all of my life, for I am not, on the outside at least, a simple country girl any longer."

"As I have said before, Lizzy, just because your name will change does not mean you must change along with it, and I believe Lady Tamworth has expressed such sentiments. Do not discount the value of a simple country girl, for you have the capacity to find endless joy in even the simplest of circumstances. While I know little of high society, it is quite possible you may be the breath of fresh air they so desperately need."

"Your confidence in my abilities humbles me, Aunt. I sincerely hope your trust is not misplaced."

"I assure you it is not! Besides, the rich can do as they

please. Should you prefer the country to town, I doubt anyone will mind. Just look at your parents and Mr Darcy! None of them spend much of the Season in town." She paused and gave her niece a sly look. "Speaking of which, should you not be preparing for your usual bevy of callers today?"

"Nicholas has already told me not to expect him. Apparently, he has some business to attend to today in the House of Lords with Lord Tam—my father. My mother is busy working on preparing my rooms, even though I have already told her my chambers are perfectly lovely. Surely, you have never seen such a charming space! The colours remind me of wildflowers, and the furniture, while very fine, is not so ostentatious as one might expect in the home of an earl. I can hardly believe such apartments will be mine alone come tomorrow, as I am sure not only Jane and my quarters in Longbourn, but Mary, Kitty, and Lydia's as well could fit inside! Do I need my own dressing room, sitting room, and private bath?"

"You are the daughter of an earl. It is time to accept that fact, no matter how strange it may be," Aunt Gardiner replied, gently patting her hand before fixing her with an earnest gaze. "And Mr Darcy? Does he still plan to call this afternoon?"

"I believe so, at least, he never said anything to make me expect otherwise."

Her aunt regarded her carefully as Elizabeth once again directed her gaze to her lap and fought to keep the blush from her cheeks at the mention of Mr Darcy's name.

"Lizzy, dear, I believe it is time to tell him. You have postponed the conversation long enough."

"Have I?"

With an exasperated huff, Mrs Gardiner replied, "Most certainly! You would not have him arrive to call on you only to find you have quit our house altogether. Do you not see how that would wound him? I do not understand why you did not tell him all on Tuesday, once you were certain of the truth. Instead, you have let him continue to call for the past week without any indication of the changes that are coming, changes that will surely affect him as well!"

"You are right. I know you are. 'Tis only that I could never find the words to tell him! How does one explain such a thing? And I suppose...I suppose a part of me did not *want* to tell him. He is the only person who sees me simply as Miss Elizabeth Bennet of Longbourn, and for some reason I can hardly fathom, for him it is enough. I used to think Mr Darcy proud and above his company, yet you can see for yourself how comfortable he is with our family—even the children. I could not bear for his opinions of me to change, or worse, for him to be somehow relieved to see that I possess much more exalted relations than he had previously supposed."

"My dear, you do that young man a great disservice if you think anything could change the way he feels about you. Anyone with eyes can see how much he loves you, and if I am not mistaken, I believe you return that love as well."

Nodding through her tears, Elizabeth clung to her aunt. "But that is the worst part! I have deceived him! I was so scared that somehow his feelings would change that I have kept this from him since the night we became reacquainted. Mr Darcy has been nothing but kind and solicitous of my feelings, and I have repaid his care with dishonesty. He once told me how much he abhors disguise of any kind. What will he think of me?"

"It cannot be so bad as you are imagining," her aunt replied in a soothing tone. "These are extraordinary circumstances. 'Tis not as though you have had any control over what has occurred. And I stand by my previous assertion. That young man would not abandon you for the world! You need to trust him, my dear."

"You are right, I know. I will tell him today. I promise."

"Very well, then. I will send Betsy to attend you. You

have at least another half an hour before he should arrive, so take your time. I will see that no one else disturbs you."

"Thank you, Aunt. I do not know how you can so easily subdue my stubborn nature. It must be your calm goodness, like Jane's."

"Oh, I believe that young man of yours has more than enough of his own stubbornness to challenge you on any given day. 'Tis a good thing, too, for I daresay Mr Darcy will need it."

Left alone to her thoughts once more, Elizabeth rose from her perch to stand before the washbasin and splashed cool water on her cheeks as she sought to regain her equanimity. She could not put off this conversation any longer, and she should have faith in the constancy of Mr Darcy's affections. After all, had he not already proven his regard was unshakeable? Just as her life plunged into chaos, he had arrived to lend her strength with such tenderness, even going so far as to thank her for the bitter words she had unjustly levelled at him. She needed to repay such devotion with the truth…and her trust.

After the maid set her hair to rights and fixed her attire, Elizabeth descended the steps and made her way towards the front parlour. Her aunt had arranged for Betsy to sit outside the parlour door, maintaining propriety, but allowing them a certain level of privacy for the delicate conversation that was needed. Sitting upon the sofa, Elizabeth could not help but fidget with the handkerchief in her hand as she waited for Mr Darcy to arrive. Only belatedly did she realise the cloth she was twisting between her fingers was embroidered with Mr Darcy's monogram. It was the one he had given to her the night she learned the truth of her birth. Distracted by this realisation, she failed to note Mr Darcy's entrance.

"Miss Elizabeth, why are you sitting alone? Should I call for your aunt or Miss Bennet?"

"I apologise, sir, for my distraction. And no…it will only

be the two of us for today. As you see, Betsy sits outside the open door."

"I do not understand. Is aught amiss?"

"No, no…at least—do come and sit, and I shall explain."

Mr Darcy crossed the room and hesitated before choosing his seat. In a show of encouragement, Elizabeth patted the spot on the sofa beside her, giving him permission to sit at her side. As soon as he settled, he turned to her with an apprehensive look.

"I believe you have often wondered what caused my distress the night we met in town, and I feel…no, I *know* the time is right for an explanation. You deserve to hear the truth from me."

"Miss Elizabeth, as much as I would like to support you, please do not feel that you owe me anything. Your private concerns are yours to disclose as you wish."

"I thank you for that, but I fear my troubles will not remain private for much longer, and I would not have you caught unawares by their revelation. I esteem you too highly for that."

Mr Darcy's eyes filled with hope. "I am more than willing to hear whatever it is you feel you must share."

"I suppose it would be easiest to begin with the rather shocking news that I received from my uncle after dinner that evening. I know this will sound outlandish to any person with a rational mind. In truth, I had trouble believing it myself."

Mr Darcy tentatively reached out his hand to grasp hers, giving it a reassuring squeeze.

"You see, my parents had hidden a rather important fact from me for all these years—that I was *not* actually their daughter, but a foundling child they discovered on the road from London to Hertfordshire when I was but a few months old. I am not, in fact, a Bennet at all," Elizabeth revealed in a quiet, trembling tone.

Mr Darcy's grip on her hand tightened, prompting her to raise her gaze and look upon his startled face. After staring upon her in astonishment for some moments, he finally found his voice.

"I know not what to say! I am only now impressed by how well you recovered from your shock that evening after such a disclosure. I-I do not understand, though, why would they choose to tell you now? And why would your uncle take on such a task instead of Mr and Mrs Bennet?"

"The Gardiners had a visitor that evening—a young man who had come for the express purpose of relating his own family's story of a lost child. He had met me earlier that week in the park and had recognised in my features something akin to his mother in looks. As it turns out, his suspicions were correct, and it has since been proven beyond doubt that the man who visited that night is actually my brother."

Darcy gasped. "Is it certain? Mr Gardiner—your family, are they convinced as well? 'Tis no small thing to entrust your care to strangers."

Seeing Darcy's concern, Elizabeth hastened to reassure him. "Yes, indeed. We are all quite satisfied. Papa—Mr Bennet—had kept my infant gown. The embroidery was stitched by my true mother's own hand."

"Then you have found your family? Can it be?"

"I would say I have found my family, but it would be more accurate to state they have found me."

"If you are certain, then this is good news, is it not?" he asked with a look of encouragement on his face.

"Of course! I am still having trouble adjusting to my situation, but I am afraid I will have little time to settle into my new circumstances, for you see, an announcement will be made shortly in the papers regarding my recovery. That is why I had to tell you before it became widely known."

"An announcement? A formal one? But why?"

"I am told it is customary when great events take place in the lives of those from certain levels of society."

"Certain levels of society? Elizabeth, will you tell me—may I ask *who* are your real parents? What is your true name?"

Taking a deep breath, Elizabeth looked into Mr Darcy's eyes. "My father is the Earl of Tamworth, and my mother is Lady Amelia, Countess of Tamworth. My name—my name is Lady Elizabeth Grey."

Elizabeth was alarmed to see how rapidly Mr Darcy's countenance paled. He stared at her for a moment in what could only be described as utter shock, until she saw, with heart-rending dismay, his long-discarded mask of reserve descend over his features. Standing abruptly, he moved to the window, keeping his back turned to her as she waited silently for him to say something—anything.

After a torturous wait, he turned to her and spoke in a calm but somewhat aloof tone. "I am pleased for you, Lady Elizabeth. I regret I have just recalled a meeting I must attend, and so I can stay no longer. I-I thank you for your trust in me, and I hope I shall see you again soon."

"You need not call here, Mr Darcy. I will be removing to Tamworth House tomorrow. Today is my last day on Gracechurch Street."

"Of course. In that case, I shall seek to call upon you there…in time."

Reaching for her hand, he bowed over it and seemed reluctant to let it go as he gazed upon her face. While the rest of his visage seemed calm, Elizabeth noted his eyes betrayed an extreme anxiety.

She watched in confusion as Mr Darcy quickly exited the parlour, only waiting until after she heard the front door close to succumb to the tears that had threatened to choke her. It was all she could do to sit there and wonder what exactly had gone so wrong.

CHAPTER TWENTY-ONE

With his composure hanging by a thread, Darcy left the Gardiners' residence and boarded his carriage. Once the door was closed, his face crumpled, and his hands rose to pull at his hair while he fought the urge to cry out in frustration and anguish. He knew he must have looked dreadful upon his return to Darcy House, as he had startled both his butler and Georgiana with his wild appearance. Unwilling to allow his sister to witness his total collapse, he had dismissed her cries of concern as he informed Farley he was not home to callers before proceeding to his study for some desperately needed solitude.

After closing the door behind him, Darcy wasted no time in approaching the sideboard, willing his shaky hands to pour two fingers of brandy before hastily downing the entire glass. Whether he hoped the spirits would rouse him from his shock or make him numb to the myriad emotions swirling in his mind, Darcy did not know. He moved to his usual chair before the fireplace, perilously close to capitulating to his desire to begin mourning the loss of an irreplaceable woman.

For he had lost her, had he not? That Elizabeth, *his* Elizabeth, should be the newly found Grey child, his cousin's own betrothed! Darcy avowed this must be a heretofore undiscovered circle of Dante's Hell, to have come so far in earning Elizabeth's approval only to have all of his hopes dashed by a mere circumstance of birth!

Looking to the chair across from him, he recalled the excited posture of his cousin Lisle the day he had found out about his betrothal. He was thoroughly convinced Lady Tamworth's daughter was the solution to his ongoing distaste for the marriage mart. Lisle was no fool. He would see Elizabeth's worth upon their first meeting and rejoice in it, whereas Darcy would suffer for the rest of his life for his failure to do the same.

How different his life would have been had he courted Elizabeth properly all those months ago in Hertfordshire! They could have been married for several months by now, and then no one, absolutely no one, would have been able to take her away. Instead of being forced into the role of a bystander as Elizabeth coped with the turbulent changes that had overtaken her life, he would have had the rights of a husband to comfort her as he had so long desired. By marrying him, he was certain Elizabeth would have been restored to her rightful family, particularly if the resemblance to Lady Tamworth was as marked as Lisle had claimed. Lady Matlock would have surely recognised her, but by then no faded documents of a cradle betrothal could have interfered with their happiness.

Why could she not simply be Elizabeth Bennet? An irrational anger momentarily filled him, but it was quenched quickly, for what outlet did he possess for directing his ire? It was not Elizabeth's fault that she had been stolen as a babe, nor could he blame the Bennets for giving her a home and family for the last twenty years.

Darcy let loose a grim chuckle at the irony of it all. He would have infinitely preferred for the Bennets to be Elizabeth's true family, he would have rather borne any number of embarrassing relations for the mere chance of obtaining Elizabeth's hand. Mr Bennet would not have denied him, that much he knew, but Lord Tamworth had no reason to accept Darcy's suit, considering he already had a more eligible, titled, and eager suitor—one he had long looked upon as a son.

But what about Elizabeth? Could he walk away from her now? Darcy had been certain that he had seen a change in her feelings towards him. He knew she now enjoyed his company, but it was more than that—there was a new tenderness in her captivating eyes as she spoke with him, laughed with him, teased him, and directed those bewitching smiles his way. She trusted him enough to share her life-altering news.

Only for me to abandon her without a word of explanation. Oh God! What have I done? What could I have done? Clearly she knew nothing about the contract, and it was not his place to enlighten her, as that could only bring about the sure displeasure of Lord Tamworth.

Darcy's wallowing was cut short by the sudden entrance of his cousin Richard, who had apparently ignored the warnings of his butler and forced his way into Darcy's private sanctuary.

"What the devil is going on? Georgiana sent the most alarming message to Matlock House with one of your footmen, claiming that you had taken leave of your senses!"

"As much as I would like to deny that statement, I admit I cannot," Darcy replied.

"And may I ask what has brought about such a change in your spirits? I was under the impression that all was going well of late."

"Until today, it was."

"Out with it, man! What on earth has happened? You know you cannot hide anything from me for long."

"I could not hide this even if I tried, for if I do not tell you, you will surely find out on your own soon enough."

"Quit speaking in riddles, and get on with it!"

"Very well, then. It appears Miss Elizabeth Bennet is in fact Lady Elizabeth Grey. Her true identity was confirmed only this week. She told me so herself when I called upon her this afternoon."

A heavy silence settled over the room, prompting Darcy to look upon the ashen face of his cousin. Apparently, Richard had the same inclination as Darcy for a stiff drink, for he quickly poured himself a glass of brandy before returning to sit with Darcy near the fire. Richard's struggle to marshal his thoughts was clearly displayed as he attempted to speak one moment, only to fall silent the next. After a minute or two of lingering indecision, he finally summoned his courage.

"I cannot believe it! *Your* Elizabeth is my brother's new betrothed?"

"She was never mine, and now she never will be."

"Darcy, you need to speak to my brother. Surely, there must be some solution!"

"And what would I say? Lisle knows nothing of my courtship, and he is already eager for the match!"

"You have spoken to him about this?" Richard asked in surprise.

"He visited the day he found out. He was shocked but ultimately pleased he would be connected to the Tamworth family. He had already heard her brother's description of her beauty. I believe he sees Elizabeth as a supremely desirable wife. *He* will not make the mistake of presuming her to be inferior! Good God, what have I done?"

Just as Darcy feared losing himself once again in bitter reflections, a firm grip on his forearm demanded his focus.

"Marriage settlement or not, *nothing* is yet written in stone, Darcy!"

Startled, he replied, "You believe I still have a chance?"

"Yes, and so would you if you could take a moment to pull your head out of the ground! I realise what a shock this must have been, for I myself can barely make sense of it! But you are facing down a twenty-year-old piece of paper, not the Minotaur! I love my brother, but I cannot see how this proposed marriage should go forward as you seem to be forgetting one essential component of this entire affair!"

"And that is?"

"Miss Elizabeth, you fool! I cannot believe the simple country miss who would not give way to our overbearing Aunt Catherine would somehow be cowed enough by her new circumstances to assent to an arranged marriage!"

For the first time since Darcy had learned the dreadful news, a spark of hope began to burn within his chest. Richard was right. His beautiful, stubborn, fierce Elizabeth would not simply follow society's dictates with no thought to her own happiness.

"Have you not spent the last two weeks courting this woman? Resolving your earlier misunderstandings and gaining her favour? For she does truly welcome your calls, does she not?"

"Yes, I believe she does. In fact, I felt today that I could detect a significant change in her regard for me. At one point, before she relayed her news, she even mentioned how highly she esteemed me. I almost wished I could have renewed my addresses at that very moment."

"Perhaps you should have done!" Richard huffed. "It could have saved us all this grief!"

"I doubt that. Not only would it have been completely unfeeling on my part to interrupt her disclosure of what had so lately troubled her, but I also would have found myself in the very same predicament I now face. I have unknowingly courted an earl's daughter without permission, something Lord Tamworth is unlikely to overlook."

"Surely the Gardiners knew your intent. I wonder they did not mention anything to you!"

"And what would they have said? 'Tis not as though they were at liberty to reveal anything to me, although I suppose it does explain the certain uneasiness I detected in Mr Gardiner when he first agreed to allow my calls."

"Well, in any case, I believe you have every reason to hope where the lady is concerned."

"Do you truly?"

With a roll of his eyes, Richard exclaimed, "Darcy, are you daft? Miss Elizabeth trusted you enough to divulge all before even a formal announcement was made! This is going to be the biggest news society has seen in a decade, yet she went out of her way to assure you of her trust by telling you to your face. She was under no obligation to make any such disclosure, and I do not believe she would have done so if she wished to cry off from your courtship!"

"And look at how I repaid such trust!"

"What do you mean?" Richard asked, a nervous look etched upon his countenance. "What did you do, Darcy?"

Unable to face his cousin, Darcy stood and leaned against the mantel, dragging his hand down the length of his face. "I left. Right after she told me her real name. I believe I uttered some nonsense about being happy for her and that I hoped to see her again at some point, but at the end of it all, I simply abandoned Elizabeth. I was too overcome by my own emotions to provide the comfort she needed. I am a cowardly fool!"

"You really are your own worst enemy, but I doubt all is lost. 'Twas not the best response, I grant you, but the shock of the situation should allow some concessions to be made for your lapse."

"But you do not understand. Only a week prior Miss Jane Bennet thanked me for my unswerving devotion to her sister, confessing Elizabeth would have need of my loyalty in time. I had thought her remark rather strange in the moment, but now it makes perfect sense! Elizabeth is being thrust into a new world with all new expectations, and instead of standing by her, at the first sign of trouble, I retreated. I do not deserve her."

"Why do we not let Miss Elizabeth make that decision? I may not understand why she would choose to tie herself to your dour mug for all eternity, but I shall not gainsay her if that is her choice," Richard quipped with a mocking grin.

In a decidedly dry tone, Darcy responded, "Your faith in me is inspired, Cousin. But the problem remains, what do I do now?"

Cracking his knuckles so sharply Darcy flinched at the sound, Richard straightened his cuffs and levelled Darcy with a determined look. "Well, now we are back on familiar ground, for you know there is nothing I love more than executing a well-crafted plan of attack!"

"This is not a battlefield, Richard," Darcy admonished. "Do I simply approach the earl and explain my previous acquaintance with his daughter?"

"I think we need to perform a little reconnaissance before making our first move."

"*Our* first move? And pray tell, how are *we* to go about gaining any new information?"

"I suppose that brings me to the first reason I intended to call this afternoon. You see, I was already on my way out the door when Georgiana's note arrived which is why I was able to come here so quickly. My mother's current mood is akin to that of an excited little whirlwind, for she has been pestering the staff day and night with new plans for a dinner party she is hosting in two days."

"That is not unusual. Your mother always hosts events throughout the Season."

"You are particularly slow-witted this afternoon, but I shall forgive you for the moment due to your current dilemma. My mother is not planning one of her usual entertainments. This is a very important dinner to reintroduce the long-lost daughter of Lord and Lady Tamworth to the Fitzwilliam family."

"Elizabeth will dine at Matlock House?"

"Yes, and mother has extended the invitation to you and Georgiana as well."

Darcy stopped to ponder the opportunity before him. He could see Elizabeth again in as little as two days, but would he be ready to face her with her new family? Could he watch the introduction of his cousin Lisle to his would-be bride? Lisle had always possessed an easy-going nature, much like Richard in many respects. What if Elizabeth preferred his effortless manners to Darcy's decided awkwardness?

And then there was her new family to consider. Her brother was Lisle's best friend, though Darcy had not seen much of him for many years. Grey's reputation in town was faultless, much like his father's, for both had never been known to engage in the sort of illicit behaviour so common amongst the *ton*. Indeed, now that he thought on it, Darcy was relieved that if Elizabeth was to be claimed by a family of the first circles, he could hardly have chosen a more honourable one to protect her.

Protection. How on earth had he not already considered this? The Tamworths were a wealthy family, and now Elizabeth would be a target for every scheming rake and greedy society matron who would attempt to exploit her lack of familiarity with high society to lure her. Not that Darcy doubted Elizabeth's intelligence, but the fact remained that she possessed an innocence, a precious innocence, that most in their world had long discarded.

Elizabeth's stubborn nature could present an additional problem. She chafed at the need for a servant to accompany her on her morning walks! London housed many criminals, and the lure of a newly reclaimed earl's daughter would surely be strong. Much as Georgiana's weighty fortune had almost destroyed her life, Darcy could not bear to think Elizabeth might be exposed to a similar fate. Perhaps this was the reason for an arranged marriage in the first place?

"Darcy? Are you attending? Come, man! Leave off your contemplations of your supposed Sisyphean task, and help me plan the next manoeuvre!"

Darcy's attention turned back to his cousin. "Tell me, has the army issued you a copy of Homer as required reading? I apologise if the events of the day have overcome my abilities for rational, ordered thought, but in this case, I believe my distraction is justified."

"My apologies, but we have matters we can address now if you are willing. First, will you come to dinner?"

"Yes. Yes, I believe I shall."

"Excellent! I think it will be a good opportunity to gauge not only your lady's feelings but her family's as well. I have not seen Lord and Lady Tamworth for several years, owing to the movements of my regiment, but I have spent a fair amount of time with Grey." A pensive look wrinkled Richard's brow as he paused to sip his brandy. "Now that I think on it, I can see some similarities between Miss Elizabeth, pardon—*Lady* Elizabeth—and her brother and not only in their features. Grey may not be quite as lively as she, but I suspect that is in part due to his family's unhappiness. He is a good man, and I daresay he will be a devoted brother. In fact, I highly doubt he would have approved of an arranged marriage for his sister, even to James, had he known of it. You never know. Grey may turn out to be an important ally."

"I suspect that would greatly depend upon his willingness to see his sister courted at all. Do you believe I would be remotely sanguine about anyone daring to approach Georgiana?"

"You have a valid point, I grant you. Still, I believe he

might be more encouraging to a man of her choosing rather than an arrangement made by their father."

"Perhaps," Darcy conceded. "What about *your* parents? Do you know their desires regarding the betrothal?"

"My mother would never encourage anything that would pain Lady Tamworth or her daughter. My father is another matter. You know him well, Darcy. The temptation to solidify an alliance with a house he has long respected and admired would be too great for him to ignore. However, I do not believe we should completely discount his affection for you, especially were he to know your true feelings about Miss Elizabeth.

"I highly doubt the earl is even contemplating his daughter's marriage at the moment," Richard continued. "You have not seen the Tamworths since you were a child, so you cannot know the pain they have lived with since they lost their daughter. I have always greatly admired Lord Tamworth for his devotion to his wife. He has placed her well-being above all others, regardless of society's censure. Instead of abandoning her, Lord Tamworth has seen assiduously to his duties in Staffordshire, while Grey has taken the reins of the family's interests in London. There is nothing the earl would not do for his family, and I have no doubt this care will extend doubly so towards Lady Elizabeth."

Darcy rubbed his face in frustration. "He may not want to give her away at all."

"'Tis a possibility we cannot overlook, to be sure."

Pausing to collect his thoughts, Darcy broached his next concern with his cousin. "I shall not bring Georgiana with me to dinner."

"Why ever not? Her presence may make Lady Elizabeth more comfortable, since they already share an acquaintance."

"You are right, but something might be said which Georgiana should not hear."

"You cannot possibly believe the betrothal contract would be addressed as a topic over dinner!" Richard scoffed.

"No, but Georgiana is *very* aware of my interest in Elizabeth and knows full well I have been courting her. I cannot have the earl find out about our courtship through some offhand comment made by my younger sister. If I find a way to move forward in all of this, he deserves to hear the truth of it from me directly."

Richard looked towards him with an amused gaze. "Of course. The nigh unflappable Darcy honour!"

Darcy finally gave in to his frustration. "Damn my honour, Richard, should it lose me the one woman I cannot live my life without!"

With a steely look, his cousin turned to him, gripped his arm, and said in a calm, yet determined voice, "Then do not let it."

After a moment's pause, Richard released his cousin and strode from the room, leaving the honourable Fitzwilliam Darcy alone with his thoughts once more.

CHAPTER TWENTY-TWO

"I do not know what set Mama's nerves on edge more, the fact that Lizzy broke her arm, or that she did so while wearing breeches in the presence of our neighbours!"

Nicholas laughed uproariously at Jane's tale, thoroughly pleased by her recollections of Elizabeth's less than ladylike childhood endeavours. For some reason Elizabeth could not fathom, Jane had felt that a recounting of her disastrous attempt to rescue a kitten in Longbourn's park was a perfectly suitable exploit to share with Nicholas. While not precisely sanguine about Jane's choice of story, Elizabeth smiled at the sight of her dearest sister and newfound brother's budding rapport. After learning the truth of her identity, it had been one of Elizabeth's sincerest hopes that she would not lose her sisters, particularly Jane, and that Nicholas would feel comfortable in his role as her brother.

The last few weeks had been difficult ones for Jane, as Elizabeth knew underneath her sister's brave serenity dwelled an undercurrent of dread that they might be irrevocably parted. While Elizabeth recognised it was highly unlikely the earl and countess would ever want a close connexion with the Bennets, she had been hopeful they at least would not feel threatened by her attachment to Jane. Though her parents were still somewhat cautious, Nicholas seemed to enjoy Jane's company and delighted in asking questions about their childhood.

Happy chatter filled Elizabeth's newly appointed sitting room, a delightful space decorated in calming greens and cheerful yellows, yet still grand enough to serve as a constant reminder of the inescapable alterations in her life. Elizabeth herself had considerable trouble engaging in the present conversation, for her thoughts were still occupied by the surprisingly abrupt departure of Mr Darcy the previous afternoon. Even though both her aunt and Jane had posed a rational theory for his desire to quit the room so suddenly after she had made her revelation, none of their assurances had succeeded in soothing her growing worries.

Elizabeth had been unaware of exactly how much time she had spent alone in her aunt's sitting room before Jane arrived. Only when she felt the reassuring and familiar embrace of her beloved confidant did she realise she was not alone.

"I cannot fathom what went wrong, Jane!"

"I gather Mr Darcy did not take your news well?" Jane gently stroked Elizabeth's hair, calming, if not quite quelling her distress.

"At first, everything went well. He was concerned and attentive, but when I told him my real name and that of my family, he went so pale! And then," Elizabeth paused and took a deep breath, "he told me he was pleased for me, but that he had to leave. His manners changed. I cannot describe it, but he was so cold, not at all like the man I have come to know over the past few weeks. He said he would try to call on me in time; however, he seemed so uncertain and hesitant, and then…"

Jane wiped a tear from her sister's face with a handkerchief.

"When he took my hand to take his leave—his eyes, Jane. While his countenance was decidedly calm, his eyes revealed how troubled he was. He was worried and fearful, and I cannot account for why he would feel that way at all! I am so confused."

"Oh dearest, I am sure there is a perfectly reasonable explanation."

"Then what could it be? Why would my true name unsettle him so?"

Drawn to the parlour by the distressed cry of her niece, Aunt Gardiner entered and rushed to Elizabeth's side. "My dear Lizzy, whatever is the matter?"

"It seems Mr Darcy did not react well to Lizzy's news," answered Jane, sparing Elizabeth from recounting her meeting with her suitor a second time. "He was not unkind in any way, but it appears that he was troubled upon learning of Lizzy's family."

"Well, I suppose that should not have been so wholly unexpected, my dear."

Startled by her aunt's response, Elizabeth turned from Jane's embrace to look upon her dear aunt. "Why would you say that?"

Her aunt fidgeted for a moment. "Perhaps I should have spoken of this with you earlier, Lizzy, but I see now that I did not aid you by concealing my concerns over how your new identity might affect your courtship. I think a part of me wished to believe you were aware of the possible complications, seeing as you refrained from mentioning Mr Darcy during your visits with your family."

"I wished to keep our courtship private, at least for a time. But I do not understand, Aunt. Is Mr Darcy not precisely the type of suitor of which my family would approve? I am aware he holds no title, but he is the grandson of an earl and considerably wealthy. None of that matters to me at all, and I do not honestly think those considerations will mean more to my family than our mutual affection. I still do not understand why he should be so troubled."

"Even though Mr Darcy may have had your uncle's permission to call upon you in our home, he does not have permission from Lord Tamworth to court you. He may well occupy the same social circles as your parents, but he cannot assume your father's approbation of his suit. I admit I believed Mr Darcy would speak of his concerns with you rather than leave so abruptly, but I should have considered how unexpected this news would be for him. Even though he was well aware you had some recent troubles, I highly doubt he expected anything as momentous as your news."

Jane appeared gratified by the explanation. "Mr Darcy is an honourable man. I am sure he will apply to your father soon for his consent."

"Of course he will, my dear! Your news will surprise a great many people, and you must give them time to recover from their shock," her aunt added in a calming tone. "And I stand by my previous assertion. Mr Darcy will not abandon you!"

Jane nodded earnestly. "He loves you. I am certain of it!"

"I know he does. If only I had been more open in showing my own regard! I do not doubt his affections or his resolve, but I still feel as though something is amiss. The worry in his expression went beyond mere shock. I simply cannot dismiss this notion—this feeling I possess—that something is terribly wrong."

Jane took her hands in her own and fixed a determined look upon her agitated sister. "Mr Darcy told me himself that he would only ever leave if you sent him away, and even if you did, I am not entirely sure he would comply. I have observed you both over the last few days in particular, and it is clear to me that you are very much in love. I know that your new family will see it too. Please do not despair, dearest."

"You are right, Jane. I am sure all will turn out well in the end."

DESPITE THE ASSURANCES SHE HAD OFFERED HER SISTER, Elizabeth remained in a state of protracted dread since that horrible afternoon. It would not do to continue to worry Jane and her aunt, so she had done her best to placate their concerns, all the while remaining doubtful that Mr Darcy's reaction was simply a result of his worry over gaining her father's approval.

After coming to know him better, Elizabeth had quickly realised his proud and aloof mask was simply that—a mask. He was not the sort of man who was comfortable sharing his emotions with the world, and it was clear to her now that he was capable of deep feeling. Once he was comfortable in familiar society, he was significantly less guarded, and she had been privileged to see his mask fall away, revealing the wonderful man beneath.

Mr Darcy had become so relaxed in her presence, so desirous of showing his regard, that the blow she had felt upon seeing his attempt to hide his emotions from her once more had taken Elizabeth by surprise. Yet, despite his efforts, he could not conceal his distress from her completely. The grip with which he had held her hand, and the fear that filled his deep blue eyes remained imprinted upon her mind, refusing to release her from her inner torment. Relief would remain out of reach until she could see him again…but when? His vague reference to meeting her 'in time' had left her puzzled.

Nicholas's voice startled her from her recollections, and as she looked between her brother and Jane, Elizabeth was quickly able to perceive their identical expressions of concern.

"Oh my, Nicholas! I apologise for not attending. I suppose I am a little distracted. What were you speaking of again?"

"Miss Bennet was enquiring about our plans for the remainder of the Season, but perhaps you may know more about this than I," Nicholas replied with a smirk.

"My brother takes far too much delight in vexing me over my coming social obligations and all of the shopping it will necessarily entail!"

Jane laughed at the exaggerated pout that Elizabeth sent in Nicholas's direction, replying with a mischievous grin, "I see you have become acquainted with Lizzy's distaste for trips to the dressmaker."

"How was I to know my sister so disliked shopping? It was always my belief that young ladies liked nothing more than acquiring new gowns and bonnets!"

"Yes, well *you* did not grow up in a house with six women," Elizabeth replied, "nor did you have a mother whose views on the quantity of lace provoked a new argument at every visit to the dressmaker."

"'Tis true, my lord," Jane concurred. "Lizzy and I have always preferred simpler styles than Mama, so little disagreements were not uncommon."

"What Jane is too polite to say is that our choices were often met with rather loud protests. Not to mention that Kitty and Lydia preferred to bicker over their choice of ribbons while Mary sat with a book in the corner, regarding us all with a decidedly severe expression."

Laughing, Nicholas replied, "You do paint quite a pretty picture; however, shopping with Mother will not even remotely resemble such chaos."

"That does not mean I will necessarily enjoy the experience, for despite my courage, I must own being seen on Bond Street with Mother rather frightens me. I have never been a topic of gossip before, and I fear Mother will not appreciate such notice."

"You may be right," Nicholas sighed. Looking to Jane, he continued. "You see, Miss Bennet, our mother has not moved in society in years, even at the behest of her closest friends. She has been in such high spirits since Elizabeth's identity was confirmed, I had not thought about how she would react to being the topic of such scrutiny again."

"Mayhap you might accompany us, Nicholas?" At his comically horrified expression, Elizabeth clarified. "Only to the shop! I do not expect you to wait while I am poked and prodded into all manner of fabrics. Surely, there must be another store close by that will hold your interest for a time, and perhaps Father might join you as well. I cannot help but think that Mother ought to be more at ease with all of her family around her."

He smiled in agreement. "'Tis a good plan. I will ask Father if he has the time to join us. His presence in town has sparked a fair amount of curiosity. We were positively overwhelmed at the club the other day. Once his peers learned the family would remain for the rest of the Season, the air was unmistakably rife with speculation. I am afraid the news that Mother is also in town only added fuel for the gossips, and make no mistake, the men at White's are just as likely to spread rumours as the ladies at Almack's."

"Well, 'tis not as though they will remain in doubt for long," Elizabeth sighed, her discomfort plainly visible across her features. "Father mentioned this morning that the announcement will be in the papers in three days."

"At least my godmother's dinner will remain a quiet affair. Although *quiet* is a relative term," Nicholas chuckled. "Whenever Lisle and Richard are together, you can depend upon a lively evening!"

"Lisle and Richard? Forgive me, but though you may have mentioned them before, I cannot quite place their names."

"How odd! I know I have told you some of my stories when we compared our childhoods, although I grant I have been far more interested in hearing of your upbringing than telling tales from mine."

"These are friends of yours?" Jane enquired.

"Yes, Miss Bennet. Lisle, or rather, James, has been my closest friend since birth. He is my godmother's eldest son, and together with his younger brother Richard, who is now a colonel in the regulars, they have been my playmates for as long as I can remember."

A feeling of unease settled over Elizabeth as she listened to Nicholas. "A colonel, you say?"

"Yes! Colonel Richard Fitzwilliam is highly respected, though I must admit I do tease him a bit with my doubts about others following his orders. He was such a rascal in our youth that I have trouble picturing him as a figure of authority."

"Mother mentioned your godmother was her dear friend, Eleanor, but I am afraid she has never mentioned much about their family," Elizabeth replied, hoping Nicholas did not detect the slightly shaky tone in her voice.

"My godmother is the Countess of Matlock. The earl is also good friends with Father, which is why Lady Matlock insisted she be the first to host you for dinner here in London. You will have a fine time, Elizabeth, for they are excellent company!"

Elizabeth glanced at Jane, and judging by her rather pale complexion, she too had recognised the names of Mr Darcy's relations. An idea quickly formed in her mind as she turned to her brother.

"Do you think that Mother and Father would allow Jane to join us? I must admit to being a little nervous about meeting such close family friends, and I believe her presence would help me to be more at ease."

Jane looked slightly startled by her request, but after Elizabeth sent a pleading look in her direction, she gave a small smile of support.

"They can deny you nothing, Elizabeth! I am sure they

would be happy to include Miss Bennet in our party. In fact, let me find Mother and seek her approval now. Excuse me."

Once Nicholas quit the room, Elizabeth's expression of good humour crumbled as the implications of her brother's words became clear. "Whatever can this mean? If Mr Darcy knows my family, why did he not say anything!"

"I confess I am just as mystified as you are, Lizzy. This is certainly an unexpected development."

Elizabeth reached for her sister's hands. "I am sorry for placing you in a difficult position, but I simply cannot bear to face this introduction without you by my side. The fact that I am already known to the colonel will make this dinner awkward enough, as I will have to tell my family at some point about our prior connexion."

"You know I would do anything for you, so please, do not worry on my behalf! Perhaps the colonel can give you some news of Mr Darcy. Do you think he knows of his cousin's regard for you?"

"From all he has said, I believe Mr Darcy looks upon the colonel as more of a brother than a cousin. It would not surprise me in the least if he knew."

"I know you are still anxious about your encounter yesterday, but please look upon this news with hope. Whatever answers you seek may come soon, and all you can do now is trust in Mr Darcy's affections and his devotion to you. I do not believe he will fail you now," Jane said with a quiet earnestness.

"You are right—of course you are! I should not return to the weepy fright I was yesterday, for it quite undermines Mr Darcy's faith in my courage. I *do* trust him, and I will endeavour to set my worries to rest before facing his family." After a few calming breaths, Elizabeth looked to her sister with a slight grin. "I suppose I should be grateful for the distraction that a day on Bond Street will bring now. Just imagine it! A whole world filled with the likes of Miss Bingley!"

CHAPTER TWENTY-THREE

It was with a heavy heart that Mr Bennet set aside his most recent letter from his eldest daughter. By her account, the plans for Elizabeth's move to the home of her true relations were proceeding apace, and soon his little Lizzy would be beyond his reach forever. His only hope of seeing his favourite child now rested on her desires for a reconciliation, and based on the reply he had received in response to his confessional missive, it would be some time before Elizabeth would be ready to face Longbourn again. Not that he could blame her in any way, for his concealment of her origins had upended her world in a manner few would experience.

As Jane desired to stay in town for at least another week to ensure that Elizabeth was comfortably settled, Thomas Bennet knew the time had come to confess all to his wife. The latest news from his brother Gardiner revealed he would be sending a few servants to collect Elizabeth's belongings from Longbourn, an act Mrs Bennet could not fail to notice.

Knowing how difficult the discussion would be, it had

been a challenge to summon the fortitude necessary to relate such astonishing and heart-breaking developments. They had lost their Elizabeth, and their lives would never be the same again. A feeling of overwhelming guilt gripped Mr Bennet as he considered all he had denied the earl and his family, for while he, his wife, and their daughters would grieve Elizabeth's loss, his inaction so many years ago had deprived a good family of a special young woman.

Mr Bennet was also pained to acknowledge the extent to which he had neglected his own wife and daughters, even Jane. Elizabeth had been his unquestioned favourite, and the space she now left in their family was akin to a gaping wound, raw and painful to behold. His failures as a husband and father appeared all the more evident in light of this recent change, and it was time to correct as much of the damage as he was able.

Gathering what little resolve he possessed, Mr Bennet pulled the bell for Mrs Hill and asked her to please find the mistress and send her to him. It was a well-established fact at Longbourn that the master shut himself away in his book room to *avoid* his family, and beyond Elizabeth, they were rarely invited to share his private space. After only a few moments, the door was opened once again and Mrs Bennet entered, clearly baffled by her husband's unprecedented request for her presence.

"Mr Bennet, you wished to see me?"

"Yes, my dear. Pray come and sit with me, for there are matters which we must discuss."

After taking her seat, she relaxed slightly as if suddenly struck by some idea. "I suppose Lydia has told you of her invitation to Brighton! What a lovely thing for our girl! Was it not kind of Mrs Forster to request her company? My dear Lydia is such a favourite amongst the officers that I am sure she must find a husband when surrounded by an entire camp full of soldiers!"

"Lydia, go to Brighton? My dear Mrs Bennet, I have not

heard a word of such plans, and I beg you not to encourage our daughter, for I fear she will suffer disappointment. Lydia is only fifteen. Far too young and silly to marry, if you ask me."

When it looked as though his wife would protest, Mr Bennet quickly silenced her. "I have not called you here to discuss Lydia, though I own that we should have a conversation regarding our younger girls soon. I received a letter from Jane, and I thought you should be aware of its contents."

"Oh my sweet Jane! Has her health improved? Will she and Lizzy come home soon? I heard the most *dreadful* rumour today that Mr Bingley is giving up the lease at Netherfield. Not that I care for such an odious man who would sport with my Jane! But I did think—well, 'tis no matter. The next tenant will surely be another single gentleman who would surely notice our daughter, for Jane cannot be so beautiful for nothing!"

"Calm yourself, Mrs Bennet! To answer at least one of your questions, I have it on good authority that Jane will return home in a week's time."

"Thank goodness, for I long to have my dear girl with me again! But what about Lizzy? I am sure you told me she was in London, for she must have left the Collinses weeks ago! Why she would want to visit those grasping creatures in the first place is beyond me! I am sure they spoke of nothing but how they would one day take possession of our home!"

"Your thoughts on my imminent demise are always such a comfort to me, my dear, but it is the matter with Lizzy I wished to speak of with you."

"Matter with Lizzy? Whatever do you mean?"

Pausing to take his wife's hand, Mr Bennet pressed forward with his disclosure. "Do you remember the two gentlemen who visited Longbourn last week?"

"Why, of course I do! Such a fine-looking carriage! Was the younger man here about our Lizzy?"

"Yes, my dear, but not as a potential suitor. I am afraid that would be quite impossible, and before you protest, I beg you would please allow me to tell you all before you ask any more questions."

Though he could see how much his request pained her, she ultimately acquiesced with a small, shaky nod.

"Mrs Bennet…Fanny…I know we have not spoken of this in years, but you do remember how Lizzy came to us, do you not?"

Fear filled the lady's eyes before she gave, yet again, another small nod.

"It seems, my dear, that our girl was not an orphan after all, but rather, she was stolen from her rightful family by the very woman who gave her into our care. Due to a rather remarkable resemblance to her true mother, Lizzy was recognised in town by her brother, the young man you saw at Longbourn. The older gentleman," Mr Bennet explained, pausing to swallow past the lump that had risen in his throat, "was Elizabeth's father, the Earl of Tamworth. It appears our girl belongs to a noble family! And as I was able to confirm her identity with the gown she wore when we took her in, they plan to reclaim her as their own, as they have every right to do."

Tears fell down his wife's face as she sat in a state of mute shock. After perhaps a minute or two passed by, she haltingly replied, "But—but Lizzy is *our* daughter! They cannot take my child away from me."

"I am afraid she is Elizabeth Bennet no longer. She is Lady Elizabeth Grey, and she always has been, even if we did not know it."

As Mrs Bennet burst into sobs, her husband did something he had not done for a long, long time—he comforted his wife. Pulling her into his embrace, he rocked her back and forth as she cried onto his shoulder, allowing his own tears to fall as they grieved together over their loss. When she quieted, he pulled back and took her handkerchief, dabbing at her cheeks while noting the sorrow that settled over her.

"I know I did not always understand Lizzy, but that does not mean that I loved her any less! She was such a happy child! It was only when she grew older, and so like you, that I simply could not fathom her ways!"

"I never doubted your love for her for a moment, my dear. For I know you love all of your children."

"And she *is* my child! No matter what this new family of hers might say!"

"I am afraid we need to give them time. I have written to Elizabeth to explain why we took her into our keeping, but truly, her family has suffered in her absence."

"What could an earl's family know of suffering!"

"I believe we know better than most the trials that come with the loss of a child. If you had seen the look on the earl's face when I presented him with Elizabeth's infant gown, you would have recognised the pain on his countenance, I assure you."

"She is not gone from us forever, is she, Thomas?"

"Not forever, no. But I believe she will not come back to Longbourn for some time. As much of a change as this will bring to us, I believe Lizzy bears the greater burden in her new life. She will be moving in lofty society, and it will probably be some time before she fully adjusts to her new position."

To his surprise, Mrs Bennet fluttered her handkerchief with an indignant expression. "Oh nonsense! That girl has the courage of ten men put together! I may not always understand her, but even I can see that she is made of sterner stuff than the average lady. Just think! Our little Lizzy is now Lady Elizabeth! I almost feel the need to call Hill for my smelling salts!"

As Mr Bennet chuckled, his wife's expression sobered. "Do you think—do you think she would accept a letter from her dear Mama? I feel I must apologise to her."

"Apologise? Whatever are you talking about?"

"The whole business with that horrible Mr Collins! I did not mean to press her so strongly, and I could see that they were not well-suited, but I was afraid. If anyone had ever found out she was not ours, she never would have made an acceptable match."

"I am sure Lizzy would read anything you choose to send her."

A frightened expression overcame his wife's visage. "The girls! Whatever will we tell the girls?"

"We can tell them naught but the truth. Jane already knows the entire story. She is staying with Elizabeth for one more week to help her settle in her new home."

Sensing his wife's consternation at another reminder of Elizabeth's new family, Mr Bennet pressed on with the last piece of news he had to relay. "We need to decide together how to tell the younger girls, for your brother writes that an announcement will soon be released in the papers. We cannot have our girls find out through idle gossip in the village."

"An announcement? The news will be all over Meryton before we know it! How will we ever face our neighbours again?"

"I do admit to a fair amount of unease regarding our situation. I may have a solution that would spare you and our daughters from as much of local society's gawking as possible."

Pausing to grasp her hand once more, a new resolve came over Mr Bennet. He may not have been able to change the past, but he could try to mend his ways and see to his family's interests. Perhaps this was the Lord's way of giving him another chance, and he decided in that moment he would not let it go to waste.

"I have been thinking it might be a good idea to go away for a while as a family. I realise I have not had as large a role in our family's life as I ought, and I think it would be a good idea to spend some time with you and the girls. What say you to a trip to the seaside? It may not be Brighton, but I believe Margate would hold plenty of amusements for our daughters."

"Oh Mr Bennet! Just imagine! Sea-bathing! What a delightful thing for our girls! But why not Brighton?"

"I beg of you to cease promoting the officers as suitable matches for our girls. Most of them do not possess an adequate income to provide for a wife and family. Would you have our daughters living in reduced circumstances, always on the move from place to place, with nary a thought as to when they might see us again?"

"I-I suppose I did not think of such things. I admit I only thought of how happy they would be to find a husband, and the soldiers all look so dashing in their red coats!"

"Happy for a time, but I doubt such happiness would last. After losing Lizzy, I own I am not terribly keen to part with any of my daughters—at least not so soon. And I do hope you would wish for them to find honourable men who can provide for their welfare. Marrying a gentleman is not a requirement. Even a country solicitor, like your father, or a vicar would do, but above all, let it be a man they can respect and depend upon. Perhaps if we make some effort to economise, I can add to their portions over the next few years. I doubt it will make much difference in Jane's case, but Lydia is only fifteen. With another five years or so, we may be able to set something aside."

As she absorbed his words, Mrs Bennet's expression grew thoughtful, until ultimately, a smile spread across her still handsome features.

"I think this trip will be just the thing to help our girls! But what about Jane? Should we not wait until she returns from London?"

"I mentioned my plans as a possibility to Gardiner in my

last letter, and he said he and Madeline would be happy to return Jane to us in Margate if need be. He said they might even join us for a time. Would that not be fun to have all of the children at the seaside?"

"Of course! Then we shall leave soon?"

"Yes, I think I can have everything arranged in about five days or so. I already sent out enquiries regarding a few cottages for let, and I should have the replies before long." Pausing to take his wife's hand, Mr Bennet gently continued. "I should also mention that your brother is arranging for Elizabeth's belongings to be collected from here and delivered to her new home. Jane writes that Lizzy wishes to gift her dresses and bonnets to her sisters, so I believe they will simply be gathering her books and trinkets."

All at once the happy expression vanished from his wife's face. "That is as it should be, I suppose, and what a kind thing for Lizzy to think of her sisters! I-I will set about collecting her things myself. In fact, I believe the jasmine fragrance she so prefers is just about ready for bottling in the stillroom. I was planning to purchase a lovely new glass vial I saw in Meryton for Lizzy's next birthday. Perhaps I can send it with her things? She would like that, would she not? A gift from her dear mama."

"Of course she would! 'Tis a fine idea, Fanny! In fact, why do we not go together tomorrow to purchase it? And we should give Mary, Kitty, and Lydia the opportunity to buy their gifts as well, after we share our news."

"Yes! They will want to send something to their sister. You are good to think of it."

"The plan was yours, my dear. I merely added to it. You love our girls, Fanny. You always have."

After his wife took her leave, Thomas Bennet sat back in his chair to reflect upon the new course he had set for his family. While a fair amount of guilt still remained, he was pleased to find his efforts, on the whole, instilled within him a sense of hope. He may not ever get his Lizzy back, but perhaps he could become the father his other children needed while he still had the chance. For such was the fate of a father to daughters. Eventually, and probably much sooner than he would like, he would lose them all—preferably to only the most honourable of men.

CHAPTER TWENTY-FOUR

As she sat in the opulent, private dressing room at Madame Devy's, an exclusive modiste who catered to the ladies of the *ton*, Elizabeth already felt somewhat exhausted by the morning's exertions. How tiring it was to be a lady of fashion! The day had begun at Grafton's, a high-quality linen-draper, and at first, Elizabeth had been delighted by the variety of beautiful fabrics, only to be shortly overwhelmed by the sheer quantity her mother intended to acquire. She had looked to her father for some assistance, only to hear him chuckle and declare he had absolutely no inclination to rein in her mother's desire to spoil her. In fact, Elizabeth suspected he went out of his way to encourage her mother to make additional purchases when she was distracted by Nicholas.

Elizabeth had been pleasantly surprised when her father announced at dinner the previous evening that he had always intended to accompany his womenfolk during their first foray together on Bond Street. Nicholas was therefore obliged to join the party, providing yet another protector to their merry band, complete with several liveried footmen in attendance.

At first, Elizabeth had felt such a large retinue was unnecessary for a mere shopping trip; however, once she had ascertained how large her new wardrobe would be, she soon saw the sense in bringing so many retainers. She was also forced to acknowledge the footmen were not simply there to carry their purchases, but also to provide additional protection from the gawking crowds. With her family out in force, and her undeniable resemblance to her mother so readily apparent, Elizabeth had been the recipient of more curious ogling than she had ever thought to experience!

Her father and Nicholas had done their best to shield Elizabeth and the countess; nevertheless, such pointed attention could not fail to discompose them somewhat. Her mother's smiles had taken on a forced edge on more than one occasion when they were stopped by various, little-known acquaintances. Yet, despite the unsettling experience, Elizabeth felt warmed by the devotion and care of her father for his wife.

While she had not known them long, Elizabeth had observed her parents closely at Tamworth House and had seen many indications that theirs was a truly loving relationship. Nicholas had assured her that their parents were very much in love, but it was still a novelty to bear witness to so close a union. Even the Gardiners, whom Elizabeth had upheld as the ideal example of wedded bliss, could not compare with the gentleness and unparalleled regard so easily displayed by her parents. In fact, the way her father often gazed at her mother, as though she were the only woman in the room, brought to mind the image of a pair of deep blue eyes—eyes that had been trained upon her in a similar fashion.

While Lord Tamworth and Nicholas had stayed with them at Grafton's, once they arrived at the modiste's shop, they announced their desire to complete an errand on Sackville Street and so had left Elizabeth and her mother with several footmen posted outside. Elizabeth's curiosity was roused, for she had noticed the conspiring smiles shared between her family members before the men departed. Alas, before she could persuade her mother to reveal their destination, Elizabeth had been lost to the whirlwind preparations of Madame Devy and her assistants. She was measured and draped with a variety of their previous purchases, as the modiste decided upon colours and recommended various fashion plates for her consideration. Calling upon every ounce of fortitude she possessed, Elizabeth had managed to hide her anxiety once she discovered her new wardrobe would include such a staggering number of morning, walking, and evening dresses, ball gowns, riding habits, and all manner of coats and pelisses that existed in the fashionable world. After Elizabeth and her mother made a few decisions, Madame Devy left to inspect the bulk of their acquired fabrics, planning to return shortly with her final recommendations.

"Once we finish here, Elizabeth, I believe our next stop should be Harding Howell & Co., for there we can find a nice variety of fans, reticules, parasols and such. Madame Devy will take care of the millinery, so that will save us another trip, but we do have an appointment at two o'clock at Wood's which we must keep. He is the finest cobbler in London, and as I know how fond you are of walking, we simply must order new boots and slippers for you soon!"

Her mouth agape, Elizabeth replied, "Surely, I do not require all that! My half boots are quite serviceable, as are the items I brought with me from the Gardiners."

"Dear, please indulge your poor mother. I have waited a lifetime to enjoy a shopping trip with my daughter, and your father and I think nothing is too good for you! You must allow us to spoil you as much as we wish. I do not intend to make you uncomfortable, but a proper wardrobe will be expected by others in society. I will not give anyone the slightest reason to doubt your new place with us, and the appropriate clothing will go a long way in staying the waspish tongues of the ladies in our circle."

Remembering the cutting comments of Miss Bingley and Mrs Hurst regarding the local fashions in Meryton, Elizabeth was forced to acknowledge her mother was right. If she wished to belong in her new family's world, she needed to look the part, regardless of how little she cared for such fripperies.

"You are right, Mother, I apologise. I do not wish to sound ungrateful, but I have developed a habit of trying to rein in such expenses, and I doubt it will be easily broken."

"I understand, and the sentiment does you much credit. While my family did not come from such limited means as the Bennets, neither did they possess your father's wealth. It took some time to accustom myself to my role as a countess, and even now, I fear I practise more habits of economy than I ought. I, too, should look to purchase a few new gowns, especially now that we will be in London until the end of the Season."

"You always look so elegant I doubt anyone could find fault with your appearance!"

"Whilst I appreciate your kindness, dear," her mother replied with a smile and indulgent pat on her hand, "the fact remains that I have not shopped in London for some time. Most of my clothing has been created by the local dressmaker in Kinver, near Heatherton Hall. I will need to armour myself appropriately in order to face the coming inquests once our knocker is officially up at Tamworth House."

"You speak as though we go to battle!" Elizabeth laughed.

"Aye, and you will find 'tis a fitting description! Make no mistake, society will arrive *en masse*, and the ladies are not so obvious with their attacks as a soldier with a foil. Do not worry though, my dear, for I believe you possess sufficient wit to parry their thrusts quite admirably."

Elizabeth smiled brightly. "I shall do my best not to disappoint you. Nicholas has already promised to be by my side as much as he is able, so between him and Father, I shall not lack in gallant knights, should I require rescue!"

"You know, 'tis a shame we cannot present you at court this year and be done with the more conspicuous aspects of our station. Your Season next year will, I fear, be just as eventful as the remainder of this one."

"I have no desire for such pageantry, I assure you! I am perfectly content to wait for such an illustrious meeting until I have had more time to adjust."

"Of course! You are right, it is probably better this way."

After a moment of hesitation, Elizabeth decided to question her mother on something she had wondered about for some time. "Nicholas has given me the impression that you were not always as averse to society as you are now. Are you looking forward to the next few weeks, or would you prefer to return to the country? We need not stay if it discomfits you in any way."

"It is not about what I would prefer, Elizabeth, and just because I am uncomfortable does not make it a bad plan. You possess such fortitude and cheer, my dear girl, even though you above all have experienced the greatest change. I own I feel rather humbled by your bravery, for I have hidden from the world for far too long. Now that you have been restored to us, perhaps I might recover some of my former self. I know, of course, that I cannot simply go back to how things were before you disappeared, but I want so much to be what you need! You cannot escape your place in society, but you *can* have a mother to serve as an adequate guide, and I would not abandon you for the world!"

Before Elizabeth could reply, Madame Devy returned to

the room in a flurry of silks with her plans for Elizabeth's wardrobe. "Pardon my absence, Lady Tamworth, but I had a sudden inspiration regarding the evening gown you requested for Lady Elizabeth!"

When she had first been introduced, Elizabeth had questioned her mother regarding the wisdom of informing the modiste about her identity. As it would still be two days until the announcement appeared in the papers, it seemed unwise to trust such a secret to a relative stranger. The introduction also filled her with an overwhelming sense of loss, as it was the first time she met someone new without the familiar and comforting address of Miss Bennet. Her mother, however, had assured her that Madame Devy was well-known for her discretion and was equally well paid for her silence. It procured her an advantage of sorts, as she would possess the latest *on-dits* regarding the mysterious Lady Elizabeth Grey before the ladies of the *ton* came flocking.

"When you mentioned your need for an evening gown for tomorrow, I recalled a nearly finished gown that I had prepared for a client a month ago that I believe will complement your beautiful daughter quite well! The colouring will suit perfectly, and I believe the fit will only require minor adjustments."

With a flourish, Elizabeth was presented with a lovely gown in green and ivory. The bodice was made of a rich, deep green velvet, complete with puffed sleeves and delicate lace surrounding the back collar. The ivory silk skirts were covered with a sheer overlay that featured delicate embroidery work in matching colour thread. Elizabeth had never owned anything so fine, and even though it was more ornate than her usual preference, the dress was elegantly done.

"'Tis a beautiful gown. Might I enquire as to why it was not purchased?"

"Certainly, Lady Elizabeth. This gown was part of a large order for a long-standing client, and I believe she ultimately found it lacking in adornments. To be honest, I was not offended when she chose not to keep it, as I did not wish to add anything more to my creation, for I believe it would have ruined the look of it."

Surprised that anyone would have found the gown wanting, Elizabeth was nevertheless pleased that the dress had been passed over, as she would now have something suitable to wear to dinner with Mr Darcy's family. After trying on the gown and allowing Madame Devy to make small adjustments to the hem and waist, Elizabeth turned to her mother for approval.

Happy tears filled Lady Tamworth's eyes. "Oh Elizabeth! You look so beautiful, my dear! Your father and brother will wish to hide you away once they have seen you in this!"

Turning to the modiste, her mother continued. "We will take the gown, Madame Devy. Are you sure you can have it sent to our home by tomorrow afternoon?"

"But of course, your ladyship! I also have a beautiful wrap that will complement it perfectly. I will send the whole ensemble as soon as I can on the morrow."

Touched by her mother's response, Elizabeth was gratified to have made her happy, for she knew she was not the easiest person to shop with, nor the most patient. She had to admit she looked rather pretty in the gown, and perhaps in the future, she might learn to enjoy such expeditions. By the time their appointment had come to an end, Elizabeth was in slightly better spirits as they reunited with her father and brother.

"Was your journey successful, gentlemen? I do not suppose you would share the details of your secret quest with me?" Elizabeth asked, a mischievous grin upon her face.

"I fear you will have to wait to have your curiosity satisfied," her father warmly replied.

Looking at Nicholas, Elizabeth raised her brow in question.

"Do not look to me, Sister!"

"But Nicholas, are you not dying to hear of all my gowns and hats! I could delight you with tales of lace and ribbons to your heart's content!"

In a decidedly dry tone, Nicholas replied, "Yet, I remain unmoved."

"In that case, you will simply have to assist me as I select all of my new fans, parasols, and the like."

With an exaggerated groan, Nicholas looked to his mother as he assisted her into the carriage and enquired, "Exactly how much more shopping do you intend to accomplish today?"

"Oh, do stop complaining, Nicholas. 'Tis most unattractive. We have only two more stops to make, and I am quite sure you will survive."

"If you say I shall, then I suppose I must."

Elizabeth felt Nicholas had acquitted himself admirably for the remainder of their outing, and soon enough, the entire family had returned to their home on Curzon Street. It was not until after dinner that Elizabeth finally learned what had occupied Nicholas and her father earlier in the day. Upon joining the women in the drawing room, her father presented her with a gift in the form of a velvet-lined flat box.

"Another present? I cannot imagine what was spent upon my wardrobe today alone! I have no need to be so overindulged."

Taking a seat beside her on the settee, her father gently took her hand. "Elizabeth, my girl, I realise how odd this must be for you, but I have waited years to spoil you so. We are not trying to buy your love, for it is easy to see your tender heart cares not for such things. Over the years, I have often seen items in shop windows and wondered whether you would have liked them. I even admit to having purchased one or two, indulging in a fantasy that you might actually be at home to receive your present. But now—well now you *are* here, and there is no greater gift than that!" He paused to collect himself before continuing. "And you need not worry about money! We have more than enough in the funds, and no debts weighing us down. Pray let your family give you what is rightfully yours, my dear."

"Having listened to a similar speech from Mother at the modiste, I believe I must conclude I have inherited my stubborn nature from both of my parents." Sighing slightly she conceded, "Very well, then. I shall endeavour to set my qualms aside regarding money, I promise."

"You best open your present, Elizabeth, for I fear it will test your resolve," Nicholas said.

Lifting the small brass latch with ill-concealed curiosity, Elizabeth opened the slim box and gasped at the sight before her.

"Before you object," her father remarked, "you should know this set was always intended to come to you. You were meant to receive it upon your official come out in society. Your grandmother, the late dowager countess, set it aside for you upon your birth."

Elizabeth gazed in wonder at the jewels within the case. A delicate, diamond strand necklace shone brilliantly in the candlelight, surrounded by a remarkable set of diamond-tipped, decorative hair pins fashioned in the shape of flowers.

"I had to take it to the jewellers earlier this week for a thorough cleaning and to make sure the settings were secure. You were meant to wear this for your first ball, but I suppose your first dinner party will have to do."

"They are beautiful, Father, and I will feel honoured to wear a piece of our family's legacy."

"Oh Harry!" her mother exclaimed, "it will look simply

stunning with the gown we selected today. I daresay Elizabeth will dazzle the Fitzwilliam men tomorrow evening!"

"Must you make my task more challenging, Mother?" Nicholas moaned. "I have already resolved to deflect any male attention away from my sister when I have the chance. The Fates are conspiring against me."

With the subject of the dinner before her, Elizabeth reasoned that now was as good a time as any to begin her awkward revelation. "About the dinner…I fear I have a confession to make."

"Whatever do you mean, Elizabeth?" A puzzled expression wrinkled Nicholas's brow.

"I-I did not make the connexion until recently, but you should know that I am, in fact, already acquainted with several members of the Fitzwilliam family."

Elizabeth looked to her mother and father and saw their astonishment mirrored Nicholas's. Elizabeth pressed on with her story. "Yes, well, there is actually an odd connexion to the Bennet family. Mr Collins, the heir to Longbourn, is Lady Catherine de Bourgh's parson, and as I am good friends with Mrs Collins, I visited the parsonage at Hunsford this Easter."

"Yes, I believe I recall Mrs Gardiner mentioning you had recently stayed in Kent," Nicholas asserted.

"Aye, I did. During my stay, we visited Rosings many times, as Lady Catherine often invites the Collinses to tea and occasionally to dinner."

"So you have met the famous Kentish Dragon!"

"Nicholas!"

"Sorry, Father, but I know very well you cannot abide Lady Catherine's company either," Nicholas replied without the smallest appearance of contrition.

Elizabeth attempted to stifle her laughter at her brother's outburst, for indeed, such a nickname fit the imposing lady all too well. "As I was often the target of her many enquiries, I can only assume that you, Nicholas, must have endured her censure at some point."

"She was rather frightening when I was a lad, but she has no great love for our family." After directing a sly smile at their father, Nicholas continued. "Well, not anymore at least."

"'Tis rather cruel to tease your father," their mother replied, though Elizabeth noted that she, too, was holding back laughter.

"I am afraid I am lost," Elizabeth said, curious as to the source of their mirth and her father's reddening countenance.

"It seems Lady *Catherine* tried hard to become Lady *Tamworth* before our parents met," answered Nicholas, shuddering slightly at such a prospect.

"No!" Elizabeth cried. "What a frightening thought! I cannot imagine such a match."

"I could not either, which is why it did not come to pass. Nevertheless, the lady is sister to my friend, and I would appreciate it if both of my children showed a little more respect."

"Of course, Father," Elizabeth replied. "I did not mean to be so disrespectful."

Nicholas suddenly looked at Elizabeth. "Just a moment! If you were present at Rosings over Easter, then you have met Richard and Darcy!"

Elizabeth blushed briefly. "Yes, I met the colonel, Lady Catherine, and Miss de Bourgh during my stay, but-but I was already acquainted with Mr Darcy."

Cursing her inability to control the ruddiness of her cheeks, Elizabeth pressed on with the last part of her story she planned to share that evening. "You see, Mr Darcy's good friend, Mr Bingley, held the lease at Netherfield Park last autumn. Netherfield is the closest estate to Longbourn, and so I have spent many evenings in Mr Darcy's company."

"This is astonishing! So both Richard and Darcy have met you as Elizabeth Bennet?" Nicholas asked.

"Yes, they have. So I suppose I must be reintroduced to the colonel tomorrow evening with my real name."

"I fear I may quarrel with Richard over his negligence!" Nicholas declared. "How could he fail to recognise you?"

"Nicholas," their mother replied, "we have not seen Richard for some years. He travels so often with his troops, and I doubt he ever would have thought to question your sister's identity when she was already known to his cousin. I have not seen the Darcys since they were children, so there is no mystery there as to why Mr Darcy did not recognise Elizabeth."

Could this be the reason for Mr Darcy's anguish? Could he possibly feel guilty for not reuniting me with my family sooner? Elizabeth supposed it was possible that Mr Darcy was suffering from some foolish notions of misplaced responsibility, for he seemed rather adept at bearing the burdens of others upon his strong shoulders. Suddenly, Elizabeth was distracted from her thoughts by Nicholas's laughter.

"A wicked thought just occurred to me, Elizabeth! If you have met Mr Bingley, then you must have been introduced to his sister, *and* you have also kept company with Anne de Bourgh. Tell me, are Darcy's attempts to escape the marital noose as amusing as Lisle has described?"

"You are wicked, Brother," Elizabeth replied with a nervous grin.

Laughing heartily at the plight of poor Mr Darcy, her brother must have failed to notice the deepening blush and small trace of alarm that darted across Elizabeth's face. She looked anxiously about the room until she noted the worried aspect of her mother. The concern radiating from such familiar eyes caught Elizabeth by surprise, prompting her desire to retire early, claiming fatigue from the activities of the day.

As she entered her chambers, Elizabeth crossed to the

window seat and stared out upon the moonlit garden below, unable to dismiss the belief that her mother had seen more in her gaze than Elizabeth was ready to reveal. It was a distinctly unsettling notion—the idea that the private secrets of her heart might not be quite so private anymore.

CHAPTER TWENTY-FIVE

Taking a deep breath as she stared up at the elegant façade of Matlock House, Elizabeth sought to set aside her anxiety over the coming introductions. The preparations for the dinner party had been calm and orderly at Tamworth House, a contrast to the frenzied tumult Elizabeth was accustomed to at Longbourn. The difference was stark, and she sighed at the loss of the excited chatter and petty squabbling of her younger sisters.

Her new lady's maid, Harriet, had quite outdone herself with Elizabeth's toilette. As she stood before the mirror in her dressing room, the true understanding of her change in station had finally settled upon Elizabeth with formidable gravity, for there in the mirror before her was a woman she hardly recognised.

The beautiful gown, delivered as promptly as Madame Devy had promised, was tailored perfectly to Elizabeth's small frame, and the dark green bodice suited her colouring quite well. Her thick, chestnut curls were elegantly arrayed between bands of ivory ribbon, while the Grey diamonds sparkled about her neck, and the diamond flower pins shone from various points in her fashionable coiffure. Elizabeth had never felt more lovely than she did that evening, and judging by the reactions of her family, they agreed.

As she descended the steps to don her gloves and wrap, her mother lifted a handkerchief to dab away the tears that had gathered, while her father and Nicholas gazed upon her in an affectionate mix of wonder and pride. Though still slightly uncomfortable with her new family's obvious regard, Elizabeth was grateful for their unquestioned approbation as she made her first daunting foray into their sparkling world. After she had endured another round of Nicholas's overprotective posturing, Jane approached her with a beaming smile and heartfelt compliments. While she knew she would never equal Jane's beauty, Elizabeth felt for the first time in her life that she might actually fare reasonably well were they to be compared side by side, though she had worried over Jane's simple attire. Elizabeth's mother offered to loan Jane some jewels for the evening, but in her sweet way, Jane demurred. She did not wish for the Matlocks to mistake her as a lady of means.

Now, grasping her sister's hand, Elizabeth found her courage and began the ascent to the doors of Matlock House. After entering the vestibule where her wrap was passed to a waiting servant, Elizabeth took the arm offered to her by Nicholas before he extended his other arm to Jane, the three of them following her parents to the parlour where their hosts awaited them. As she took in the gilded furnishings and somewhat ostentatious décor, Elizabeth was reminded vaguely of Rosings, and her nerves began to rise at the thought of meeting more of Mr Darcy's august relations. As they were announced by the butler, Nicholas ushered Elizabeth into the room where she was introduced to a surprisingly teary-eyed Lady Matlock.

"Oh my dear! Just look at you! The very image of my dear Amelia when we were girls! You are so very beautiful, my dear Elizabeth! Is she not lovely, Hugh?"

Blushing to the roots of her hair, Elizabeth turned to greet Lord Matlock in whom she recognised a likeness to Colonel Fitzwilliam.

The earl's voice was warm and jovial as he replied, "She is indeed. You must be quite proud to have such a daughter!"

"Of course, I am!" her father declared as he shook hands with his friend. "We are blessed to have found her again."

"And of course, we must introduce these lovely ladies to my sons," Lady Matlock continued. "Lady Elizabeth, this is my son James, the Viscount Lisle."

A handsome, light-haired man stepped forward with an eager expression and offered Elizabeth a respectful bow. "Lady Elizabeth, I am delighted to meet you at last. Your mother, my godmother, is very dear to me, and I know how happy your return has surely made her, for there can be no doubt that you are, indeed, her daughter."

Elizabeth curtseyed to the gentleman. "I thank you, Lord Lisle. May I introduce my sister, Miss Jane Bennet."

While Lord Lisle acknowledged Jane with a courteous bow, Elizabeth was surprised that his attention remained fixed on her. Normally, men were distracted by Jane's beauty, but it appeared her brother's friend was quite unmoved.

The sound of footsteps drew Elizabeth's attention to a figure approaching from the other side of the room, as a familiar, merry voice called out, "Well, what do we have here? Lady Elizabeth, indeed!"

"'Tis good to see you again, Colonel!" Elizabeth replied with a smile, comforted by the mischievous twinkle in his eyes, for he seemed truly pleased to see her.

"You cannot imagine how surprised I was when I saw Grey at the club this afternoon and found out I had already met his mysterious sister! My family has beset me with questions for the last two hours, for you have caused quite a stir, my lady!"

While his statement sounded sincere, there was something in his expression that convinced Elizabeth that the colonel was dissembling. For some unidentifiable reason, Elizabeth was fairly sure his enlightenment regarding her true birth had not come from her brother.

"You must forgive me," the colonel continued, "if I forget myself and call you 'Miss Bennet' once more."

"Never fear, Colonel, for I have brought you a 'Miss Bennet' to take my place. Jane, allow me to present Colonel Fitzwilliam. Colonel, this is my sister, Miss Jane Bennet."

"Delighted to meet you, Miss Bennet," the colonel replied with a gallant bow. "I have heard only good things of you, and I am sure you will make a wonderful addition to our party tonight."

"I thank you, though I fear Lizzy has praised me more than she ought."

"My sister is quite right to praise you, Miss Bennet," Nicholas asserted. "I could not have hoped for my dear Elizabeth to have a more worthy confidant. And speaking of my sister, Richard, I ought to take you to task for failing to see what was right under your nose!"

As her brother and the colonel joked over the latter's failure to recognise her in Kent, Elizabeth's gaze was drawn to another approaching figure, one she recognised by the mere cadence of his long, even strides. She lifted her eyes to his warm, yet decidedly nervous gaze.

Taking her hand in his, he bowed in greeting and spoke in the calm, deep voice she had come to adore, "Lady Elizabeth, you look beautiful this evening. I hope—I hope you are pleased to see me."

Recognising the apology in his words, an apology he could not offer in a parlour filled by their family and friends, Elizabeth offered an encouraging grin. "I thank you, Mr

Darcy, and of course I am pleased. I cannot think of anything that could please me more."

DARCY HAD PLACED HIMSELF IN A CORNER OF THE PARLOUR that was not immediately discernible upon a person's entrance into the room. Richard had chided him for his propensity to skulk in the shadows, but Darcy had desperately desired to observe Elizabeth's arrival without notice, as he had doubted his ability to keep his emotions concealed. It had been a long, torturous two-day wait to see her again, as he had been plagued relentlessly by guilt for leaving her in the manner in which he did and his fear of losing her should the evening go ill. When his aunt and uncle's butler had finally announced Elizabeth's party to the room, Darcy was grateful for his foresight, as he was positive the overwhelming adoration he felt for the woman he loved would be plainly visible upon his usually reserved face.

Elizabeth, *his* Elizabeth, was a vision! He recalled how entranced he had been the night of the Netherfield Ball when she had arrived in her simple, elegant ball gown, with flowers weaved throughout her hair, but tonight—tonight she was simply stunning.

Delight in her radiant beauty quickly turned to concern as Darcy perceived her nervous smile, wishing fervently he had the privilege to alleviate her present worries and lend her strength to face her new circumstances with the fortitude he knew she possessed.

Standing by Darcy's side, his cousin let loose a low whistle. "My goodness! I feel like a fool for not having seen the likeness to Lady Tamworth before!"

Darcy nodded. "'Tis an exceptional resemblance, to be sure. I can see why Grey was so sure of Lady Elizabeth's identity upon meeting her."

"Aye, and I suppose the beautiful blonde on Grey's arm

is Bingley's angel?" Richard gazed at Jane Bennet approvingly.

"Yes, that is Miss Bennet, though do behave. I will not have her toyed with, for she is very dear to Elizabeth and an exceedingly admirable woman in her own right."

"You have nothing to fear on my account, though you may want to practise addressing your lady with her title. I imagine Grey, in particular, will not take kindly to your informal way of addressing his sister."

Annoyed by his cousin's taunting, Darcy proceeded to ignore Richard in favour of observing Elizabeth with her family. Though he knew he was being ridiculous, Darcy could not help the feelings of jealousy that arose from watching Elizabeth's easy affinity with her brother. Lord Grey had not released his hold on Elizabeth's arm throughout the entirety of her introductions to the Matlock family. Their features favoured one another, far more than his and Georgiana's, though Grey had apparently inherited his stature from his father, while Elizabeth took after her mother's more diminutive form.

Richard had been right when he had predicted Grey would be a devoted brother, for there was no mistaking the protective way in which he hovered over his sister. Darcy supposed he ought to feel some sympathy for the poor man since he would one day find himself in a similar situation, but in that moment, he could only contemplate the possible hurdles that Grey could add to his suit.

Of more interest, however, was the long-awaited introduction of Elizabeth to his cousin Lisle. Darcy had been pleased to note that despite Lisle's obvious eagerness, the smile Elizabeth displayed upon their greeting was no different than the one she had given to his aunt and uncle. What was more interesting, however, was the somewhat reserved expression on the face of Lisle's best friend. Lord Grey had looked rather unsettled as his sister was introduced, confirming in Darcy's mind that Elizabeth's brother was not wholly favourably disposed to the plan to marry her to the Matlock heir.

"Well, I suppose I ought to dazzle our company with my entertaining presence. Do try not to hide for the remainder of the evening. Our plans will all be for naught if you cannot manage to engage our guests in more than your usually limited conversation."

"We cannot all be jesters," Darcy dryly responded.

Fixing his cousin with a stern gaze, Richard admonished, "Courage! Remember what Sir Rowland says, 'faint heart never won fair lady!'"

"I really ought to attend more to your reading habits."

"Nonsense! There is nothing wrong with a good English novel, but that is beside the point. I will endeavour to occupy Grey for a time so you can approach your lady."

Darcy stopped Richard with a quick grasp on his forearm. "Thank you, Cousin. You know I value your assistance."

"Think nothing of it. After all, 'tis merely a skirmish. You can thank me when the war is won."

Darcy could only admire how effortlessly Richard had set Elizabeth at ease, and sure enough, he soon succeeded at drawing her brother away so Darcy could finally approach the evening's guest of honour. Her expressions of pleasure at seeing him again joined by the brilliant sparkle in her hopeful eyes nearly overset his capabilities for rational thought, that is, until the arrival of her brother brought him painfully back to the complicated underpinnings of their current situation.

"Darcy! Richard did not mention you would be present tonight."

Reaching to shake the man's offered hand, Darcy replied, "It is good to see you, Grey. It has been some time since we were last in company."

"Aye, but that would be your fault, I imagine, for you do prefer to hide away at that great estate of yours! Although my sister tells me you were recently trapped in Hertfordshire for a time."

"I do not believe those were the exact words I used, Nicholas," Elizabeth chided, sending an arch look at her brother.

To Darcy's great annoyance, Grey once again took Elizabeth's arm and held her firmly to his side.

"Elizabeth, 'tis far too early in the evening for such looks. Do not forget what I endured yesterday for your sake."

"I am quite sure Mr Darcy has survived at least one shopping trip, or did you forget that he, too, has a younger sister?"

"Lady Elizabeth is right," Darcy interjected, "though I admit I greatly prefer for Georgiana to complete her purchases with Lady Matlock, for I know little about women's fashions."

"You see! I am not alone in my aversion to linen-drapers, haberdashers, and all manner of purveyors of ladies' accoutrements."

With a bemused glance in Darcy's direction, Elizabeth sighed. "I feel betrayed, Mr Darcy! You were supposed to convince me that my brother's antics were merely another aspect of his somewhat vexing nature. Now I fear I must sympathise with poor Miss Darcy about elder brothers and their lack of consideration over what we ladies endure at the hands of the modiste."

Darcy's chuckle drew surprised looks from several occupants in the room. "So I take it a day on Bond Street was not to your liking, Lady Elizabeth?"

"No indeed! For aside from the overwhelming exhaustion inherent in selecting far too many new gowns, I must admit the ogling we were subjected to made me feel rather like an exhibit at Vauxhall."

"Their curiosity will eventually wane, I suspect, but it

disturbs me to hear you have been made to feel uncomfortable."

"Thank you for your sympathy, but I believe I shall survive the experience with my usual courage intact."

"My sister is quite fearless, or so I am learning," Grey quipped before changing the topic of conversation. "But what about you, Darcy? I was surprised to hear that you were remaining in town for the Season. Lisle had been wondering if perhaps you were succumbing to his mother's pleas to find a bride."

"Nicholas!" Elizabeth scolded, though Darcy noticed a creeping blush on her face.

He suspected his own countenance suffered from a similar affliction. Fortunately for them both, the butler arrived to announce dinner, and Grey turned to follow the earl and countess, and swept his beautiful Elizabeth out of Darcy's reach.

WHILE PARTAKING OF THE SOUP COURSE, RICHARD CASUALLY glanced about the table to observe his fellow diners. As familiar as he was with executing strategic manoeuvres, he could not help but be disappointed by his mother's abysmal seating arrangements, for they were decidedly at cross purposes with his own tactical plans for the evening.

Having witnessed Darcy and Elizabeth's interactions in the parlour, he was more determined than ever to see his cousin win her hand, for despite his own self-professed blundering in his attempts to woo the woman he loved, clearly Darcy had done something right. The way Elizabeth's smile brightened when she saw him, and the marked change in her manner towards him from what he had witnessed in Kent was enough to convince Richard that if the lady was not yet in love, she soon would be. Why Darcy should still be so unsure of her regard baffled him, yet Richard had to admire the way such a small slip of a woman had rattled his cousin's usually unshakeable confidence.

Although normally the seat to his father's right would have been occupied by Lady Tamworth, the highest-ranking female guest in attendance, tonight that seat was taken by Lady Elizabeth as a special acknowledgement of her return to her family. Lady Tamworth sat to his father's left, while Lord Tamworth and Grey sat on either side of his mother at the other end of the table. This left Richard sitting next to Darcy towards the middle of their party, and his poor cousin could barely refrain from staring across the serving platters at Lord Matlock's delightful dinner companion. Of further annoyance was Richard's mother's decision to place James on Elizabeth's other side, which merely exacerbated Darcy's already heightened nerves—as readily displayed by the increasingly stern expression his cousin wore as the dinner progressed.

Taking advantage of the change in courses, Richard turned to Darcy and spoke in a rushed whisper. "If you do not begin to relax your jaw, I fear your face may become permanently fixed in a frown. Need I remind you that you have others to impress beyond your lady tonight? Her father is sitting at your side, and if you desire for him to become even slightly inclined to accept your suit, I suggest you make at least some effort at conversation once the earl ceases to speak to my mother."

With a clipped nod that clearly communicated his irritation at Richard's interference, Darcy's expression became somewhat less severe.

"After dinner, I will try to distract Grey and my brother so that you will have another opportunity to speak to Lady Elizabeth, but until then, please do try to restrain yourself or else I may resort to kicking you under the table."

"Duly noted. Now quit your harping and pass the salt."

After directing an eye-roll heavenward, Richard completed the request and turned to Lady Tamworth on his right. "And how are you faring this evening, my lady? I regret my absence over the years, especially so now, as I might have assisted you in reuniting with your daughter."

"Do not think on it, Richard! You know full well that Nicholas was only teasing you earlier. 'Tis strange to consider that a mere walk in the park should change our lives in such a drastic way, is it not?"

"Aye, my lady. And how have you enjoyed coming to know your daughter? I was impressed by her when she was naught but a simple country girl, but now she seems positively formidable!"

Lady Tamworth's light laughter filled their corner of the table, drawing Elizabeth's attention from her discussion with his father.

"Formidable, indeed! I cannot tell you how much Elizabeth means to me, for these past days have become some of my happiest. I could not be prouder of my daughter, for she is truly a wonderful woman."

"I quite agree, Lady Tamworth," his father interjected. "In fact, your girl was just telling me the most enchanting story."

As the countess fell back into conversation with Elizabeth and his father, Richard's attention was drawn to his other side, where the earl had finished a discussion with his mother and had now turned to Darcy.

"You will have to forgive me, but I cannot remember when it was that I last saw you, for I fear it has been many years."

"Indeed, Lord Tamworth. I believe it was my final year at Eton, so it has been some time."

"I was sorry to hear of your father's passing. He was a good man, and from all reports, I am told you are a credit to his memory."

"Thank you, my lord," Darcy replied in a quiet tone. "He was an excellent man, and I have quite missed his counsel over the last five years."

"And how have you adjusted to the management of Pemberley? You were quite young when you took on such heavy responsibilities."

"I was fortunate to retain a most loyal staff, and my father had been teaching me to care for the estate since I entered Cambridge. Our correspondence during those years is still often a valuable source of wisdom when I encounter problems with tenants or the harvest."

Lord Tamworth gave a thoughtful nod. "A wise idea. My son would most likely benefit from similar training, but I fear I have already passed him a weighty burden with my duties in the House. Perhaps now that my daughter is home, Lady Tamworth will be more willing to endure the London crowds, and Nicholas can finally learn more about running Heatherton Hall."

"I do not envy your responsibilities, my lord. I am a gentleman farmer at heart. London has never been to my taste, and I confess I would stay at Pemberley for the better part of the year if it were possible."

"You have a sister, do you not? How old is Miss Darcy now? I do not believe I have seen her since she was a babe."

"Georgiana is sixteen, Lord Tamworth."

"Sixteen! My goodness, I did not expect that. I suppose you are preparing for her presentation in a few years' time?"

"A prospect I do not relish, I assure you."

"As a father to a beautiful daughter, I must agree with you there." The earl chuckled. "Tell me, does she take after your mother, Lady Anne? For that is what Matlock has told me."

"Georgiana does indeed, though the resemblance is not nearly so strong as that of your wife and daughter."

"Ah, yes! I have been truly blessed, have I not? I have always believed my dear wife to be the most handsome woman of my acquaintance. When I first met her, I was instantly drawn to those fine eyes, and I cannot tell you how thrilled I was to see those same eyes in my beautiful Elizabeth."

"I did not know that you possessed such fondness for my best feature, Father," Grey quipped from across the table.

Turning to Richard's mother, Lord Tamworth commented, "You see what I must endure these days, Lady Matlock! Not only do I have such a teasing son, but I can also now lay claim to an equally teasing daughter!"

To Richard's chagrin, he noticed Darcy was oblivious to the laughter that erupted between his companions, apparently having missed the last half of this exchange. For once the earl began to speak about fine eyes, his cousin's gaze was inevitably drawn to the other side of the table, where he continued to stare at the earl's daughter with ill-concealed regard.

Left with no alternative, as the footmen arrived to remove another course, Richard gave a swift kick to Darcy's shin, sighing in frustration over what was sure to be an exasperatingly long night.

As the last course was served, Lady Matlock felt confident her evening had been a success. Lady Elizabeth was a beautiful young woman, with such happy manners and good humour, that Eleanor was certain the girl would make an excellent wife for James. For if the lady could make her nephew Darcy laugh, she could surely charm anyone if she set her mind to it. If only her husband would cease to monopolise the poor girl's attention! She had no idea what Hugh was about, for she had specifically placed Elizabeth next to James so they could begin to further their acquaintance. Instead, her son was obliged to make conversation with the young lady seated to his right, Miss Bennet. While Elizabeth's adoptive sister was everything genteel and sweet, she was also inconveniently lovely, a true beauty who would turn many heads were she ever to be exposed to the *ton*.

Apparently the girl's beauty was not a threat at the moment, for Eleanor detected a similar level of exasperation upon her son's countenance, and though he was everything polite to Miss Bennet, his attention was consistently drawn to Lady Elizabeth.

Once the pudding was removed from the table, Lady Matlock resolved to contrive another reason for her son and Elizabeth to converse. As James was an avid lover of music, and Amelia had professed her delight in listening to Elizabeth play, perhaps she could persuade the young woman to perform for them later in the evening. Pleased with her new plan, Lady Matlock rose from her chair to lead the ladies into the drawing room, leaving the men to partake of their libations while she enjoyed the opportunity to become better acquainted with her dearest friend's charming child.

CHAPTER TWENTY-SIX

Once the ladies had departed and the footmen had set out the decanters of brandy and port, Grey sat back in his chair and reflected on the various interactions he had witnessed between the men at the table and his sister. While still uncomfortable with the idea of Elizabeth being pledged to his best friend, he was pleased Lisle had behaved like a perfect gentleman, though he detected some annoyance at being unable to engage Elizabeth's attention during dinner. Lord Matlock had seemed especially pleased with his dinner companion; however, this brought little comfort to Grey as he suspected his lordship's motives centred on the prospect of securing a daughter-in-law. While Lord Matlock's attentions were not surprising, Grey had been far more interested in observing his sister with the two men who had, shockingly, already made her acquaintance.

Upon learning Elizabeth had been introduced to Richard in Kent and to Darcy several months prior in Hertfordshire, Grey's curiosity had been roused as to how they would approach her significant change in station. It was easy to see from their first few moments of conversation that

Richard and Elizabeth had established some sort of friendship over Easter, which was not surprising, as their similar wit and lively spirits would naturally promote an effortless rapport. Grey was relieved Richard's speech, while still affable, did not cross into the realm of flirtation. Knowing the colonel as well as he did, Grey could detect no signs of partiality for his sister beyond simple friendliness. The same could not be said for Darcy.

Even though he had not been in company with their staid cousin for some time, from the accounts given by Lisle and Richard, Darcy was just as uncomfortable and restrained around young ladies as he had always been. Having been pursued by numerous women of the *ton* for his fortune, title, and connexions, Grey was usually disposed to be sympathetic towards Darcy's dilemma, more so even as Darcy clearly lacked the patience to tolerate such marked attention well. Therefore, what he had witnessed so far this evening left Grey feeling distinctly unsettled. For while some trace of discomfiture was present periodically upon Darcy's visage, around Elizabeth, Darcy seemed almost...*comfortable.* Their easy banter before dinner surprised Grey, and their conversation suggested they were far more knowledgeable about one another than a few evenings in similar society could justify. Even more disconcerting, however, was the way Darcy's eyes seemed to follow Elizabeth wherever she went, which only served to strengthen Grey's resolve to continue his observations as the evening progressed.

"I must say your daughter is a credit to the Grey name," Lord Matlock declared, carrying his glass of port to Lady Matlock's former chair as he settled in to converse with Grey's father.

"Thank you, Matlock," his father replied, "though I do not think we can take much credit for her beyond her beauty."

"Nonsense! She clearly possesses the Grey spirit."

"That she does, but I still cannot overlook the influence

of those who raised her. Mr Bennet, in particular, paid much attention to her education."

"That man kept your daughter from you, Tamworth." Lord Matlock nearly growled his remark.

All at once, Grey felt three sets of curious eyes turned upon him as his companions pondered Lord Matlock's statement.

"What on earth is my father insinuating, Grey?" Lisle asked, his puzzlement made plain upon his features.

Knowing he could trust those present, Grey believed he ought to explain some of his visit to Longbourn, if only to avoid confusion regarding the Bennets' role in Elizabeth's disappearance.

"Lisle, how much do you remember about the story of my sister's abduction? You were eleven at the time, after all."

"I believe I know what most do—that your sister was taken by her nursemaid who suffered from a damaged mind after the fevers that swept through Staffordshire that winter."

"Well, as I told your mother a few weeks ago, the Bennets found Elizabeth as they were travelling home from London. They encountered the nanny not far from the coaching inn at Meryton."

"Meryton?" Lisle questioned.

"'Tis the town closest to Longbourn, the Bennet estate," Darcy interjected.

Surprised by Darcy's comment, Grey decided to gauge Darcy's familiarity with Elizabeth's other family.

"I keep forgetting you have been there, Darcy. Tell me, what did you think of the Bennets? Did you spend much time with them while you were in Hertfordshire?"

The sight of Darcy squirming in his chair amused Grey, as he could only imagine what the taciturn man thought of such an exuberant and undignified family.

"I admit I did not see much of Mr Bennet, as he seemed to keep to himself rather than join his family in society. I know him to be a great reader, and it was often said your sister was considered to be the favourite amongst his daughters."

"He made a favourite of the daughter who was not his own?" Lisle asked in an incredulous tone.

"Yes, well, both parents seemed to harbour some degree of partiality towards the children with whom they shared the most in common. Mr Bennet values Lady Elizabeth's wit and intelligence, while Mrs Bennet appears to favour her eldest and her youngest daughters. Miss Bennet's beauty comes from her mother, and the youngest, Miss Lydia, seems to share Mrs Bennet's more…boisterous nature."

"And what did you think of Mrs Bennet?" Grey asked, unsettled yet again by the depth of Darcy's knowledge regarding his sister's circumstances.

"I—well, I suppose you could say I had not an appreciation for her when we first met; however, her behaviour is somewhat understandable when one considers the family's situation."

"You need not worry about offending me, for Elizabeth has told me that Mrs Bennet's behaviour often borders on improper, and I have witnessed her eye for matchmaking first hand. Although Elizabeth believes Mrs Bennet loves her children, I strongly doubt I will ever become fully reconciled to the belief that the woman is motherly, owing to the grief my own mother has endured for being denied that same right."

"Understandable, Grey. I have witnessed your mother's struggles over the years," Lisle added, "though I suppose this does bring us back to the point at hand. My father implied Mr Bennet was in some way responsible for your sister's absence. Is this true?"

"In a way, yes. Despite his suspicions of Miss Summers's tale, Mr Bennet yielded to his wife's pleas to keep my sister. Apparently, due to a recent miscarriage, his wife suffered from an acute melancholy that only lifted the moment Miss

Summers placed my sister in her arms. She begged her husband to allow her to keep the child, and so Elizabeth was introduced to all of their friends, family, and neighbours as their second daughter, and Mr Bennet never breathed a word of what he had learned from Miss Summers."

"Does Lady Elizabeth know of this?" Darcy hesitantly enquired, his concern readily apparent.

"Aye, she does. Mr Bennet wrote to her himself. Whilst she has not shared the letter with me, I can tell she is unsure what she ought to feel."

Taking a sip of his brandy, Grey continued to watch Darcy as he, too, partook of the libation in his hand. Though still possessed of his usual reserve, the man's gaze as he stared into the amber liquid was distinctly troubled. Due to the quiet that had descended over their end of the table, the conversation of the two older men suddenly intruded upon their awareness, and the topic was not at all to Grey's liking.

"Come, Tamworth! You know I still have the papers here in my study. I do not see what harm it can do to examine them and make sure all is in order before an official announcement is made!"

"My daughter is only just returned, Matlock! I beg of you, please set this issue aside for now," his father replied in a weary tone.

The subject of their discourse was clearly understood by Grey's companions, as he noted the discomfort present on Lisle's and Richard's faces at their father's request. It was Darcy's countenance, however, that once again caught Grey's eye. For instead of witnessing a display of mere embarrassment, Darcy looked ill, a feeling Grey was beginning to share as the ideas forming in his mind filled him with increasing dread.

Settled quietly at her daughter's side on the settee, Lady Tamworth watched with pleasure as her oldest friend chatted with Elizabeth and Miss Bennet. Whilst she had always imagined her daughter and Lady Matlock would form an easy friendship, other more decidedly delicate concerns had clouded the countess's mind throughout the evening. When Elizabeth had owned to a previous acquaintance with certain members of the Fitzwilliam family, Lady Tamworth had not failed to notice how some of Nicholas's more jocular statements had unsettled her daughter—particularly those related to the tall, handsome, and rather reserved young gentleman currently sitting in the dining hall.

Lady Tamworth had lacked the proper moment to discuss her suspicions with Elizabeth, unsure also as to whether or not her daughter would be prepared to share her feelings, if she possessed any particular *tendre* at all. It seemed, at first, an odd match in her mind, as by all reports and observations, Darcy possessed a solemn disposition that was quite the opposite of her daughter's more cheerful nature. She had never heard anything against the young man, as he was known to be honourable and dutiful in administering his responsibilities to both his estate and his family. Nevertheless, the notion that they had formed an attachment prior to her daughter's recovery was difficult to fathom. Knowing Darcy's reputation, it seemed highly unlikely he would show an interest, let alone offer for an unknown country gentleman's daughter of little significance and no fortune, not to mention that Lord and Lady Matlock would have been highly reluctant to accept such a match for their wealthy nephew.

Initially, Lady Tamworth had feared her daughter was suffering from unrequited affections; however, their brief time spent in the parlour before dinner had dispelled any such misgivings. Lady Matlock had not mentioned she had invited her nephew to dinner that evening, and so the appearance of Mr Darcy had caught Lady Tamworth by surprise. Her astonishment at his presence was soon eclipsed by the way in which he gazed upon her daughter.

Having the great privilege of being so cherished by her own husband, Lady Tamworth knew well the look of a man in love, for in her mind there was no doubt young Mr Darcy loved her daughter, and she was also fairly certain Elizabeth returned his regard. Even if she did not receive confirmation of such feelings from Elizabeth, Lady Tamworth resolved to speak to her husband before they retired that night, as it was highly probable that some difficult and rather awkward decisions needed to be made in the near future.

"So, Miss Bennet, how long do you plan to stay with Lady Elizabeth in London?" Lady Matlock enquired.

"Only for another week, your ladyship. My family has plans to spend the summer in Margate, and my aunt and uncle, who reside in London, will be travelling with me to the cottage my father has let."

"How wonderful! A summer at the seaside is always pleasant."

Elizabeth agreed. "Jane is such a dear for postponing those delights for my sake. You see, I have made the rather heartless request that she stay in town for the first day the knocker is up at Tamworth House."

"Positively heartless!" Lady Tamworth laughed.

"Now see here, Amelia, have you been filling your daughter's head with stories of high society?" Lady Matlock asked in mock offence.

"Of course! I cannot leave my daughter completely defenceless!"

A puzzled expression covered Miss Bennet's face. "Are the ladies of the *ton* truly so frightening? I confess I am somewhat curious to see how different manners are here in town to those I have witnessed in Hertfordshire, but I cannot imagine the women who visit will be as dreadful as Lizzy anticipates."

"I would expect nothing less of you, angelic creature that you are!" Elizabeth responded with a smile. "Though you must admit that even amongst our limited acquaintances in town we have been exposed to some rather disingenuous characters."

"I am well aware of that fact, and I believe I am better equipped to guard myself against such false declarations of friendship now. Still, I believe it best to look for what is good and honourable in all people, especially when one considers that first impressions can be misleading," Miss Bennet replied with a pointed look at Elizabeth.

Surprised by the chastened expression on her daughter's face, Lady Tamworth responded, "You are perfectly right. I daresay Elizabeth will make many valuable acquaintances over the next few weeks, but it will still serve her well to proceed cautiously. There are many who will flock to our door simply out of curiosity. In fact, many young ladies may try to befriend Elizabeth merely to gain an introduction to Nicholas, as he is normally unable to entertain ladies at Tamworth House without a hostess present."

"Do you think so?" Elizabeth asked with a spark of mischief in her voice.

"Yes, my dear, but I expect you to guard his interests just as he would yours."

"Of course, Mother. I believe I will quite enjoy protecting my brother's honour, but that does not mean I will forgo the right to tease him about it!"

"As well you should!" Lady Matlock laughed. "My godson could use a little sisterly teasing if you ask me. Lord knows Richard, James, and Darcy have rarely held back their barbs over the years. If only I was able to spark some similar courage in my niece Georgiana! But then again, I suppose it would be intimidating to consider teasing the brother she practically worships."

"Your family does appear to be quite close, Lady Matlock," Miss Bennet commented. "It has greatly relieved my mind to discover Elizabeth has such a loving family, and I am sure her association with you will only be to her benefit."

"That is very kind of you, my dear," the countess replied, "and it is a great hope of mine that Lady Elizabeth will come to know my family better."

Turning to Elizabeth, Lady Matlock continued. "In fact, I was quite delighted to see you already consider my son Richard to be a friend. Undoubtedly, as you visit during the remainder of your stay in town, you will find many interests you share in common with both of my sons. Amelia has already told me that you play the pianoforte, and my family shares a great passion for music. My husband's younger sister, Lady Anne Darcy, was an excellent musician, and she passed along her considerable talents to her children, but my son James is also an avid enthusiast! Perhaps you might delight us all with a performance this evening?"

A flush of embarrassment flooded Elizabeth's cheeks. "I assure you my talents have been exaggerated. I have no wish to offend, of course, but I have not prepared anything for tonight."

"Nonsense, my dear! I am sure we have some music on hand with which you are familiar. Feel free to consult the selections available at the instrument, for I am sure your performance would be a delightful addition to our party!"

Lady Tamworth gave Elizabeth an encouraging smile as her daughter took her sister's hand and the pair walked to the pianoforte.

"I am not sure this is necessary, Eleanor. 'Tis her first dinner. You must give Elizabeth more time to become accustomed to such different surroundings."

"I know you want to shield her from prying eyes, but you must admit this is an excellent opportunity to practice in front of a highly forgiving audience. Besides, your daughter is not a timid little thing, and I believe she will survive the experience with her composure intact."

There must have been some familiar pieces, for soon Elizabeth was playing a light melody with Miss Bennet sitting at her side to turn the pages. Not long after she began, the men entered the room and settled in to enjoy the performance. As her husband sat beside her, Lady Tamworth turned and smiled at him as he held her hand and proceeded to watch their daughter with obvious admiration.

Sitting on the other side of the room next to his cousin Richard, Darcy's gaze was resolutely fixed on the beautiful performer, his adoration plainly evident on his handsome features. Indeed, such looks of blatant affection could hardly go unnoticed, for Lady Tamworth quickly observed her son was also watching Mr Darcy with interest.

However, her son did not seem terribly pleased with what he saw.

As Elizabeth began the final movement, grateful that her knowledge of the piece had saved her from considerable embarrassment, she could not help but reflect on some of the more confusing aspects of her experience that evening. Lord and Lady Matlock had both engaged her in rather detailed conversation. She supposed their interest in her was only natural, but something about their enquiries aroused her curiosity. Perhaps they knew of their nephew's interest in her, for it was almost as though they were assessing her suitability as a prospective bride. Knowing of the colonel's probable knowledge of Mr Darcy's visits at Gracechurch Street, Elizabeth supposed it was possible the Matlocks had some knowledge of their nephew's intentions, and mayhap that was the reason for his presence that evening. Yet, to Elizabeth, something seemed decidedly out of place.

Glancing in Mr Darcy's direction, Elizabeth was

warmed to see his true appreciation for her playing, as he seemed far more relaxed now than when he initially entered the room. His presence tonight had originally delighted her, though she noticed at times he appeared almost distressed, and she could not account for the reason.

Elizabeth had observed his frequent glances in her direction across the table, which were often followed by increasingly severe expressions that easily displayed his discomfort. While she was happy to see him speak to her father, she knew it was foolish to hope he had somehow managed to speak of their past and possible connexion. When the men had entered the drawing room, Elizabeth was almost alarmed by the pallor of Mr Darcy's countenance, for clearly something was said over port and brandy that had left him even more agitated than he had been before the ladies' departure.

She allowed her mind to wander as she continued her piece. Over the past two days, Elizabeth had frequently wondered whether perhaps Mr Darcy had planned to renew his addresses before she had told him her shocking news. She knew she would have readily accepted what she had so viciously spurned only a month before, and such thoughts brought about a pang of regret.

Whilst knowing it to be impossible, Elizabeth heartily wished that somehow she and Mr Darcy had been able to come to a better understanding before her life had been so thoroughly overturned—that their newly deepened friendship could have taken place before her brother had found her that day in the park.

Or better yet, if she had accepted him in Kent, would they have resolved their differences as an engaged couple and come to value one another as she believed they did now? Recognising the futility in such musings, Elizabeth attempted to set her worries aside as she finished the cheery tune she had selected, gratefully accepting the polite applause of her audience.

"I told you she would do well, Amelia!" Lady Matlock remarked.

"Aye, and you were right. That was delightful, my dear," her mother replied.

After thanking the ladies, Elizabeth rose from the pianoforte and looked to the corner of the room where Mr Darcy sat, hoping he would endeavour to speak to her. At first it seemed as though her wish would be granted, for he rose and began to walk in her direction, only to be waylaid by her brother who was then also joined by Colonel Fitzwilliam. Slightly annoyed by Nicholas's interruption, Elizabeth failed to notice another gentleman had made his way to her side.

"I was hoping we might become better acquainted, Lady Elizabeth. Would you care to sit with me?" Lisle asked.

"Certainly, my lord." After taking a seat on the nearest sofa, Elizabeth turned to the Matlock's eldest son. "I understand you spent most of your childhood in company with my brother. I must concede I am curious as to what tales you might be able to tell me."

The viscount laughed. "Is that so? And what sort of tales are you interested in?"

"The embarrassing sort, to be sure," Elizabeth said with a playful grin. "For you see, I am at a decided disadvantage. I am afraid Jane has provided Nicholas with far too many humiliating stories of my exploits, and so I desperately need your help to correct such a grievous inequity."

"I cannot believe Miss Bennet would be so cruel! She seems such a gentle creature!"

"Oh indeed, she is! 'Tis not her fault, for I realise many of my childish adventures display my rather stubborn and impertinent nature. She remembers such tales with fondness, as she can only see the good in her dear little sister, whilst completely overlooking my more troublesome ways."

"A doting sister, indeed!" he remarked before his expression grew thoughtful. "I must admit I find it strange that you share so many similarities with your brother. Even some of your expressions remind me of him, which is odd considering you were raised apart."

"I suppose you are right, Lord Lisle. Many aspects of my recent experience have led me to question the bonds of family—what connects us to one another."

Her companion looked upon her with a kind, sympathetic gaze, as the two of them sat in comfortable silence. As their conversation quieted, Elizabeth's interest was drawn to a rather irritated sigh that came from her father's direction. As she looked to him, she noticed he was engaged in a fierce debate with Lord Matlock, whose own voice had steadily risen in volume.

"See how well they get on together, Tamworth! I do not see why you should hesitate to make her betrothal to James official and save your daughter from fending off undesirable suitors!"

Suddenly alarmed, Elizabeth stood and faced the two earls. "Pardon me, my lord. Betrothal? What betrothal? Father, of what are you speaking?"

When both men stared at her in stunned silence, Elizabeth again beseeched her father. "Tell me, please! *My* betrothal? What can you mean?"

"Elizabeth," he haltingly began, "this is not the time to have this discussion. Please allow me to address this at home."

Willing her trembling voice to express her resolute determination, Elizabeth protested, "No! I would have you tell me now."

After staring at her for some time, a defeated expression overcame her father's countenance. "The week before your disappearance, Lord Matlock and I wrote a betrothal contract between you and Lord Lisle."

As the information penetrated her mind, Elizabeth faintly noticed the horrified gasp emitted by Jane. Still grasping for clarity, Elizabeth stuttered, "You-you wrote a contract? For an arranged marriage?"

With a pleading expression, her father begged, "Elizabeth, please allow me to explain."

Unwilling to hear his reasons, she held up her hand. Desperate for someone to deny such a horrifying development, Elizabeth turned to look about the room, noting the eager look upon Lord Lisle's face, the anger upon her brother's, and the steady tears that trailed down her mother's cheeks as she watched her daughter in distress.

Finally, her gaze rested upon a familiar pair of dark blue eyes—eyes that were filled with longing and anguish, but not shock. Enlightenment dawned, sharp and painful. *He knew.*

From the moment she had uttered her true name, Mr Darcy had known she was not free. So why was he here? Why did he still look at her in that way? Why could she see the adoration in his eyes and the torment in his features? Had he come to say goodbye, to leave her to this fate?

The air around her seemed to grow thicker, as though London's stifling fog had somehow invaded the opulent and fashionable drawing room of the Earl and Countess of Matlock. Desperately attempting not to give way to terror, Elizabeth focused on breathing in and out, as against her every inclination, traitorous tears clouded her sight. When she realised her efforts to recover any semblance of equanimity had completely and utterly failed, Elizabeth gave in to her true desire.

Escaping the room that appeared to be shrinking about her, Elizabeth turned and fled, uncaring of any offence she might cause or any censure her actions might bring, completely unaware that after only a moment's hesitation, a determined and even stride followed her steps.

CHAPTER TWENTY-SEVEN

The shocked silence that had settled over the drawing room after Elizabeth's departure, quickly followed by Darcy, was slowly broken by the quiet cries of Lady Tamworth and the efforts of Lady Matlock to calm her. Torn between his responsibility to provide comfort and reassurance to both his mother and sister, Grey had initially resolved to follow Elizabeth, if only to be absolutely certain she would not come to harm in her distress. His resolve, however, was tested once he turned to quit the room, as a firm hand gripped his shoulder to prevent his leaving. Turning back, Grey was caught by the colonel's serious gaze and the subtle shake of his head, and though it pained him greatly to cede Elizabeth's comfort to another man, even one as honourable as Darcy, Grey acknowledged that perhaps her well-being might be better served by addressing the confusion and disquietude that prevailed throughout the room.

Looking upon the baffled face of Lord Matlock, Grey easily recalled his earlier anger and abandoned all caution.

"What on earth possessed you to speak of the betrothal tonight? Let alone in Elizabeth's hearing!"

His indignation roused, Lord Matlock puffed out his chest. "Now see here, Grey! I cannot believe that I have done anything so objectionable! You act as though it were a great crime to want to secure the future of James and your sister!"

"Oh Hugh, stop your meddling!" Lady Matlock interjected. "Can you not see the distress you have caused poor Amelia!"

Grey's mother continued to cry into her handkerchief. His father had already crossed the room to her side and was attempting to soothe her.

"I cannot think on aught but the suffering upon her face, Harry!" she cried, as his father pulled her into an embrace. "I-I was going to speak to you later tonight about my fears, but now, what if we are too late? We have lost her! We have lost her all over again, for how can she possibly forgive us?"

Alarmed by the depth of her distress, his father attempted to reassure her. "Darling, we have not lost her. I promise we shall never lose her again! I will *not* allow that to happen, so please my dear, do calm down. Once she returns, I will explain everything."

"You see? Once Elizabeth knows all the particulars, I am sure she will not object to the match. I realise she is unaccustomed to how things are done in our circles, but I am sure she will adjust in time!" Lord Matlock declared, his posture gaining confidence as he blustered his inane assertions.

With his ire already considerably roused, Grey remarked in a scathing tone, "I believe you have already done enough damage tonight, my lord. Kindly refrain from subjecting my mother to further proof of your carelessness."

While the earl's expression darkened in considerable affront, Grey was spared his angry retorts by the intervention of his father.

"I agree with my son, Matlock! I asked you countless

times this evening to cease your talk of such matters. My daughter means far more to me than any alliance, and if the prospect of this marriage unsettles her so, then I shall do all I can to see to her happiness!"

"But you cannot mean to set the betrothal aside so easily!"

Responding to Lord Matlock's baffled expression and perhaps in an attempt to soothe the riled tempers of her guests, Lady Matlock intervened.

"I pray you will forgive my husband this evening, or at least pardon the blathering fool that has temporarily taken his place!"

"Eleanor!"

"No, Hugh! You have said enough!"

"But I do not understand," Lisle interjected. "Why would Lady Elizabeth object to the match? We have not been able to forward our acquaintance yet, so I do not see how she can be so strongly against the betrothal."

Looking to Lord Tamworth, Lord Matlock added, "James is a fine young man, and I am sure your daughter will admire him greatly once they are better acquainted. She seems a reasonable young woman, so surely she will not protest once she adjusts to her new situation!"

Wary of the vexation he saw on his father's face, Grey was surprised when the earl's proclamations were answered by none other than Miss Bennet.

"Begging your pardon, my lord, but you do not know my sister," she stated in a firm voice. "From the first moments we were old enough to contemplate such matters, Elizabeth has ever declared that only the deepest love will induce her into matrimony. My sister would never accept an arranged marriage, even to a man as respectable as your son."

"As noble as such intentions may be, Miss Bennet, I doubt Lady Elizabeth's resolve has been tested. Marrying for inclination alone is a fanciful notion amongst our set,"

Lord Matlock replied. "I am sure once her worries are assuaged, she will choose the sensible route for herself and her family."

"I am afraid you are quite wrong, my lord," Miss Bennet answered, stunning Grey with her bold words. "Elizabeth's determination has been tested in the past, and she has held firm to her principles."

"Do you mean to tell me that my sister has already refused an offer of marriage?" Grey asked.

After a quick glance at Richard, Miss Bennet calmly answered in a tone that easily conveyed the pride she felt for her sister's actions.

"Yes, Lord Grey. Last autumn my sister received a proposal from Mr Collins, my father's cousin and the heir to our family estate. Even though the match would have secured our family's future, Elizabeth refused his offer because she could not love him and was convinced they could never make one another happy."

"I can well believe that!" Richard declared with an awkwardly relieved chuckle. "The man is an imbecile."

In response to Grey's curious expression and raised brow, Richard elaborated. "Mr Collins is Lady Catherine's parson, and I believe everyone in this room is familiar with the calibre of man she typically prefers to have in her service."

After the collective recognition of the group had subsided, Miss Bennet continued. "Yes, well, ridiculous man or not, Elizabeth did not agree to marry him, despite the advantages the union would have brought, and my father, when presented with her objections, supported her wholeheartedly."

A new and surprising appreciation for Mr Bennet overcame Grey. Knowing the man had set little aside for his wife and daughters, the marriage of one of his daughters to the heir of Longbourn would have secured their futures. For the first time since meeting his sister's adoptive father, Grey was sincerely grateful for the love he clearly possessed for Elizabeth.

"You simply cannot imagine how the prospect of an arranged marriage would so wholly destroy my sister," Miss Bennet stated with fervour, adding in a quiet tone, "especially now of all times."

"Why now, Miss Bennet?" Grey asked, though he was fairly certain he knew the answer.

As her expression became somewhat guarded, Miss Bennet glanced about the room, clearly reluctant to further voice her thoughts in the present company. Determined to obtain the answers he sought, Grey made known his suspicions.

"My sister already has a suitor she admires, does she not, Miss Bennet?"

After a moment's hesitation, she responded quietly, "Yes. Yes, she does."

Turning to Lisle and Richard, Grey demanded, "I would like to know why I was prevented from following Darcy earlier."

"Do not look to me, Grey!" Lisle answered, clearly befuddled by the night's events. "I have no idea what Darcy is about."

"But I believe *you* do, Richard," Grey continued, "after all, you are Darcy's closest confidant."

Surprised by the turn in conversation, Lord Matlock interjected, "What on earth does this have to do with my nephew?"

"Darcy *has* been acting rather strangely this evening," Lady Matlock added from her seat beside Grey's mother.

Looking to his father, Grey saw the confusion on his face, and just when he thought he might voice his thoughts, Grey's mother placed a restraining hand upon her husband's arm and shook her head, turning to Richard with a pleading expression.

"Whilst I have my own suspicions, if you can shed light

on my daughter's distress, I would be most grateful, Richard."

Confronted with the troubled and heartsick look in his mother's eyes, Grey could see the moment Richard's resolve crumbled to dust.

"Though normally I would never betray the confidence of my cousin, I see little point in prevaricating now that all of my strategic plans have been blown to kingdom come."

"Plans, Richard?" Grey asked.

"Aye, for from the moment Darcy learned Miss Elizabeth Bennet was none other than Lady Elizabeth Grey, I have had the devil of a time keeping him from doing something drastic."

Grey interrupted. "I do not follow. Did you both not only learn *today* of her true lineage?"

"You will have to forgive my deception, but no. Your sister told Darcy herself at the Gardiners's home towards the end of last week."

An awkward silence settled over the room at Richard's declaration, while Lisle stared at his brother with a mixture of betrayal and shock.

Tamping down his anger over his own ignorance regarding the present situation, Grey pressed the colonel for further disclosures. "And why exactly was Darcy visiting my sister at the Gardiners' residence? How does he know of them? Precisely how long has he harboured an interest in my sister?"

"While I believe you will need to address the man himself for the particulars, I can assure you his attachment to Lady Elizabeth is of a considerably long duration, and his intentions have never been anything but honourable. From what I know, he was drawn to her not long after their original introduction in Hertfordshire, and his feelings only grew when they were thrown together again in Kent. After his return to London, he met your sister completely by chance and has since been calling on her with great regularity at the Gardiners' home."

Looking to Miss Bennet, Grey asked, "Is this true? Has Darcy been calling on Elizabeth this entire time?"

"Yes, he has. They met again the very night you were introduced to Lizzy. She was rather distraught after you left, as neither of us had any reason to suspect she was not truly our parents' child. In her distress, she ran outside and then—"

"And then she encountered Mr Darcy," his mother finished in an awed tone, a look of dawning clarity lightening her features.

Startled by his mother's interruption, Grey queried, "So, you knew of this?"

"No, Nicholas—that is, when Elizabeth told me of the night you met her, there was a portion of her tale that was missing. She mentioned fleeing the house and seeking refuge on a nearby bench until she regained her composure, yet she seemed almost worried at having revealed even that much to me at the time."

"Lizzy has not shared with me exactly what they discussed," Miss Bennet added, "but I do know Mr Darcy was very understanding of her anguish, even though she did not share the source of it, and she recovered far more quickly with his assistance than could be anticipated. In fact, I believe the only reason she has adjusted so well to all of the recent changes in her life is due to his unwavering devotion. Having witnessed their interactions myself, I can assure you they are very well-suited."

"Then why were we not told?" Grey pressed. "Why would your aunt and uncle fail to mention any of this to my family?"

With a slightly guilty expression, Miss Bennet confessed, "My uncle Gardiner wanted to tell you, but Lizzy begged him not to. You see, she and Mr Darcy had a few unfortunate misunderstandings at their last meeting in Kent, and she wanted—nay, needed—the opportunity to tell him the news herself."

"My cousin had no knowledge of her true circumstances until last week," Richard asserted. "He had no reason to suspect the woman he was courting was anyone other than Miss Elizabeth Bennet from a small estate in Hertfordshire. At least you can be assured his motives are far from mercenary."

"You mean Darcy was intending to offer for her?" Lisle asked in surprise.

"Of course, James!" Richard replied in a mildly vexed tone.

"I meant no offence!" Lisle grudgingly conceded. "'Tis only that it is surprising for someone like Darcy to choose to marry without any thought to fortune or position. He has always placed his duty to the Darcy name above all other considerations."

Richard chuckled. "I own I was rather shocked myself when he first told me of his interest; however, seeing them together, it does not astonish me in the least that he has so completely lost his heart to her."

"Then Darcy truly does love Elizabeth?" Grey asked.

Richard's countenance was graver than Grey had ever witnessed before. "It would completely devastate him to lose her now."

As Grey paused to comprehend all he had learned, he turned to Miss Bennet, and after a moment he asked, "And my sister?"

Glancing uncomfortably between Grey and his parents, Jane softly declared, "She loves him, too."

Grey's mother turned to her husband. "I was planning to speak to you tonight, Harry. For I have long suspected our daughter might harbour feelings for someone, though it was not until our conversation after dinner yesterday evening when I developed my suspicions regarding Mr Darcy. After witnessing the manner in which he looks at our daughter, I have no doubt he is very much in love."

"We will speak to Elizabeth, my dear," he assured her. "I cannot contemplate making her unhappy if it is in my power to prevent it."

"Well, this is certainly unexpected!" Lord Matlock grumbled.

Grey could see that his father was attempting to keep a tight rein on his frustration when faced with his friend's recalcitrance. Turning to Grey he asked, "Perhaps you might ask Elizabeth and Mr Darcy to return. Better yet, escort your sister inside, and I will meet the young gentleman in the study, if that is acceptable to you, Matlock."

"By all means. I suppose I should have a conversation with my nephew in any case."

"Please bear in mind, my dear, that you love Fitzwilliam, and your late sister would only want what is best for him."

"Of course, my lady," Lord Matlock avowed.

Crossing the room to kiss his mother's cheek and take her hand, Grey remarked, "I am confident Elizabeth will have calmed down by now, and she will be inclined to listen to you, Mother. She knows how much you love her. All will be well, I promise."

With a nod to his father, Grey turned and left the drawing room, his mind still reeling from all he had learned. Time seemed to be slipping from his grasp, as he realised with heart-breaking certainty, that he would be losing his sister far sooner than he had ever planned.

CHAPTER TWENTY-EIGHT

Nothing could have prepared Darcy for the look of acute anguish that had altered the brilliance of his beloved's fine eyes, as she once again had her world overturned in but a moment. He had watched with something akin to horror as his uncle had laid bare the knowledge of Elizabeth's betrothal with nary a thought to the delicate nature of such tidings. His alarm was certainly shared by many in the room, and for a moment, Darcy had worried Miss Bennet might collapse from shock as she looked between him and Elizabeth with grief-stricken astonishment. While Darcy was conscious of the crippling fear in Lord and Lady Tamworth's faces and the easily discernible anger in Grey's, he readily pushed them aside once Elizabeth turned her full gaze upon him alone.

In that moment, her heartbreak and confusion had rendered Darcy prostrate in trepidation, lost to the tears that had gathered as Elizabeth trembled in her struggle to contain such misery. When she turned and fled from the room, he could do naught but follow, restrained for only an instant by the rules of propriety that dictated he leave her comfort solely to her family. His heart, however, could only assert that his rightful position was at her side, and so without a thought to anyone else in the room, Darcy left. Richard had counselled him time and again to be bold in his pursuit of Elizabeth's love, and having felt as though he had failed her before, he could not possibly desert her now.

When he reached the entrance hall, Darcy was confronted with the concerned and agitated face of his uncle's ancient butler, Mr Hobbes.

"Mr Darcy, thank goodness! I did not know what to do. The lady was adamant that she be allowed to leave, but I simply could not condone any scheme that might possibly see her come to harm."

"Where is she now?"

"Just outside, sir. I have set a footman to watch over her."

Darcy was relieved by the butler's quick thinking. "Thank you, Hobbes. I will send your man back inside once I ascertain all is well. The lady has received something of a shock this evening, and I doubt she will wish for any of the servants to know."

"Very good, Mr Darcy."

Nodding in farewell to his uncle's faithful retainer, Darcy exited through the front door and descended the steps to Hill Street, comforted by the sight of a burly footman who had his gaze dutifully trained upon a petite and flustered figure furiously pacing back and forth only a few lengths away. Tapping Elizabeth's guardian lightly on the shoulder, Darcy motioned for him to return to the house, and after executing a swift bow, the man retreated up the stairs, leaving Darcy alone with the frantic young woman.

As she continued to walk to and fro, struggling to regain her composure, Darcy was struck by the way the diamonds that adorned her curls and her elegant neck were made sombre by the sight of her tears. Cautiously approaching her as she ceaselessly muttered to herself, Darcy quickly realised her tears of sorrow had been rapidly supplanted by those of anger.

Knowing well the heights of Elizabeth's ire when justly roused, he held back and allowed her to continue to expend as much frustration as her dainty, silk-covered feet could inflict upon the pavement. Since she had yet to discern his presence, Darcy called out to her quietly. Her head snapped in his direction, allowing Darcy to feel the full force of her furious gaze. Grateful he was not, in all likelihood, the principal subject of her outrage, he could not help but admire the way her eyes blazed when her temper was riled. A part of him had always found her irresistibly beautiful when presented with her stubborn fierceness.

"How?" she demanded. "How could they possibly have made such a choice?"

"Elizabeth—"

"No! You cannot understand, Fitzwilliam! My parents love each other. *They* married for love, so how could they think to deny me that same privilege?"

Startled and overcome by her use of his Christian name, Darcy failed to stall her ranting as her movements became increasingly agitated.

"Is this to be my life? Am I to resign myself to the common practices of high society without reference to my own happiness? Is Lady Elizabeth Grey to be nothing beyond one more dutiful, insipid ornament of the *ton* who merely exists to be traded like chattel? I tell you now, I will not, I cannot accept such a fate!"

"And I am not asking you to, Elizabeth," Darcy calmly replied, hoping his efforts would soothe her spirits.

Huffing in continued annoyance, Elizabeth ceased her pacing and wrapped her arms about her chest. "What else will I be asked to surrender?" she cried. "I do not even know your cousin! And while I do not doubt he is a good man, I cannot simply command my heart to feel affection where there is none!"

"No one admitted to the privilege of knowing you would think it possible," Darcy firmly stated. "You are the most genuine and artless woman of my acquaintance."

For a moment, his words seemed to penetrate her considerable fury, but then, all too soon, her countenance once again displayed a look of sheer defiance.

"Mayhap it might be best to leave, then."

"Leave? And where will you go?"

"Longbourn."

Silence stretched between them as their conversation came to a halt, interrupted by only the faintly discernible noise of the distant clattering of carriage wheels upon London's dark and filthy streets. Darcy's eyes filled with compassion as he stared into the heartbroken face of the woman he loved.

"They—they would never ask this of me," she began, her lower lip trembling. "I know you have no great love for the Bennet family, but at least with them I could be assured my life was my own, as much as any woman can claim it. And no one, not even Mama for all her complaints of my wild ways, would force me to be anything other than myself—would expect me to change to fit another world where I do not belong."

As fresh tears began to fall, Darcy could no longer restrain his instinct to comfort her. Taking a step towards Elizabeth, he slowly raised one hand to caress her cheek, his thumb carefully and slowly wiping away the evidence of her sorrow. Realising she had expressed the myriad of insecurities that had plagued her since the night he had found her alone all those weeks ago on Gracechurch Street, Darcy chose his words carefully.

"While I have every respect for the Bennets, you cannot simply run away, Elizabeth. I do not doubt in the least that they love you, and in coming to know you better, my estimation of their value has only risen as a result. They are not, however, your true family, and the woman I adore has far too much courage to abandon her rightful place, no matter what challenges may cross her path."

Releasing a slow, shuddering breath, Elizabeth nodded her acquiescence. "I must own you are right. 'Tis far more difficult to disappear once you have been found. And I know—I know my parents and my brother love me. Indeed, I doubt if I left them now that they would ever recover, and I could not bear the burden of my mother's further torment. I do care for them, but I simply cannot make sense of this."

Dropping his hand from her face, Darcy gently took her gloved palm in his, rubbing soothing strokes with his thumb across her knuckles. Gently, she raised her head and fixed him with an earnest expression.

"Why did you not tell me? You *knew*. The moment I said my real name you *knew* of the contract, yet you said nothing."

Closing his eyes, Darcy replied as gently as possible, "It was not my right to tell you. Even if I had been able to think clearly in that moment, I could never have dishonoured your father in such a way."

"Though I have ever admired your honourable nature, does your honour extend to leaving me in deference to your cousin? You left me so abruptly, and I have not heard from you since."

The pain etched across her features felt akin to a knife piercing Darcy's heart. To see the full effects of his hasty retreat, especially now that she was aware of the cause, was difficult to endure.

"I cannot lie. In the first moments, I fully admit to being lost to despair. I was not thinking rationally, and had I been left to my own contemplations, I do not know how long I would have succumbed to such a blow."

He fixed her with an intense gaze and continued. "Never, not for one single moment, did the news in any way change the way I feel about you! Fortunately, I possess a highly impertinent cousin whose stubbornness matches my own when I am at my most intractable. Richard reminded me that no one should ever dare direct the path of Miss Elizabeth Bennet, for I believe there are few who would succeed in conquering your indomitable will."

Taking a deep breath, Darcy pressed on, placing all of his hope in the delicate hand he continued to caress.

"Leaving—abandoning you is not an option. Only you, Elizabeth, have the power to send me away. One word from you and I will go if it is what you truly desire, but while I still have hope, I cannot depart. 'Tis as impossible to imagine as a life lived without you."

Looking up at him, her thoughts inscrutable, she quietly declared, "I cannot—I *will* not marry your cousin."

"Why? Why, Elizabeth? I need to hear your reason for myself."

As she bit her lower lip, Darcy could see her continued hesitation, and so he made one last admission, raising her hand to rest upon his chest and covering it with his own to lend him strength.

"You must know, you must see that my affections and wishes have not changed since we spoke in April. If anything, what I feel for you now fully eclipses any sentiments I so poorly expressed that day. I love you so dearly, so ardently, that at times I am still surprised by how fully you have claimed my heart. Only you, Elizabeth, could have forced me to see myself as I truly am. Only you could have convinced me of the error of my ways, and somehow, for reasons I still cannot fathom, you permitted me another chance. Your forgiveness has been one of the greatest blessings of my life, for it has allowed me to realise a measure of happiness I would never have thought possible.

"Whether your name is Elizabeth Bennet or Lady Elizabeth Grey, *you* are the only woman I could ever—*will* ever—love. Do you know how often I have berated myself for squandering the opportunities I had in Hertfordshire and again in Kent, how I have longed to thoroughly chastise myself for prolonging such agony as I have endured since that moment in your aunt's parlour when I believed my world was lost? I will ask you again, Elizabeth, why will you not marry my cousin?"

As he poured out his heart, Darcy noted the second a smile had first formed on his beloved's face, accompanied by a light in those dark eyes he so adored, filling him with hope unlike anything he had ever felt before.

"My reason is quite simple, I assure you. I cannot marry your cousin because I love *you*, Fitzwilliam Darcy. Truly, you are the *only* man I could ever be prevailed upon to marry."

Losing all restraint, Darcy reached out to tilt her chin upwards and gently pressed his lips to hers. All of the despair, all of the torment he had endured since he had first lost his heart to this incredible, incomparable woman was washed away in the sheer perfection of their first kiss. To be there, holding Elizabeth in his arms, filled Darcy with a peace and felicity he could scarcely have anticipated.

Recalled to their current location by the sound of a passing carriage, Darcy pulled back to rest his forehead against hers as they both sought to bring their breathing under regulation.

Still overcome by his good fortune, Darcy could not help but sigh. "Dearest, loveliest Elizabeth."

With a small murmur of contentment, Elizabeth gripped his hands. Noticing her slight trembling, Darcy was finally aware of how chilly the night had become. As he had no greatcoat to warm her, Darcy gathered her against his chest. As Elizabeth snaked her arms about his waist, holding on tightly to his strong frame, Darcy placed a small kiss to her soft, chestnut curls.

"I will speak to your father. You will not have to face him alone, I promise you. All will be well. I will not give you up, no matter what the cost."

In an obvious effort to lighten the mood, Elizabeth asked, "Will you always come to my rescue when I abandon all reason and run out into the streets of London in the dark of night?"

Laughing in delight at this wonderful woman who could brighten any moment no matter how difficult with her quick wit, Darcy replied, "Of course, my love. I can barely look away from you as it is, so you must resign yourself to my resolute determination to follow and protect you in all circumstances. In fact, you may tire of my relentless efforts at playing the gallant knight."

"I believe I shall endure your labours quite cheerfully, Fitzwilliam! Though for your sake, I do hope you possess the resilience of Hercules, as I am well aware that my own obstinacy rivals that of any supposedly elegant female."

"And I would not have it any other way, my dear, so long as you allow me the privilege of bestowing my protection whenever it is deemed necessary."

A pointed cough interrupted their exchange, drawing Darcy's gaze sharply in the direction of the Matlocks' door. If the look upon Grey's face was any indication, Darcy supposed *he* might require protection in the near future, as the baron's normally jovial features were pulled tight in clear displeasure.

"Kindly release my sister, Darcy. I should hate to be forced to threaten you with pistols at dawn. After all, given your legendary prowess with a sword, you can hardly expect I would be foolish enough to allow you to choose foils." His easy manner was undercut by the biting tone in his voice.

As though suddenly aware of the impropriety of their embrace, Elizabeth disentangled herself from Darcy's arms as a flush of embarrassment flooded her cheeks.

In a much gentler tone, Grey motioned to his sister. "Come, Elizabeth. You are wanted inside."

As she took her brother's arm, Elizabeth looked back at Darcy and graced him with a small smile of encouragement. Darcy's answering smile was interrupted by Grey's parting words, which had once again taken on a far less convivial intonation as he turned with Elizabeth to escort her indoors.

"You had better come along, Darcy. You are wanted in the study. My father has some questions regarding your interest in his daughter."

It appeared the day of reckoning was at hand, yet despite the sense of anticipation such an audience generated, Darcy could not help but experience a small measure of relief. For if all went well, marriage to Elizabeth—*his* Elizabeth—would finally be possible.

As he watched her elegantly ascend the steps to return to her family in the drawing room, Darcy drew upon the undeniable strength that came from knowing not only did he love her with every fibre of his being, but he also had the incomparable privilege of being loved in return.

Armed with this miraculous intelligence, Darcy confidently followed in her wake, determined to succeed in realising their every happiness.

CHAPTER TWENTY-NINE

With one arm resting upon the mantel, Lord Tamworth stared into the brightly lit fireplace in Lord Matlock's study as he awaited an interview he had hoped would not take place for some time. For what father could ever welcome the day that another man would lay claim to his daughter's heart?

This dinner party was meant to be a celebration of his precious Elizabeth's return, and now, if the colonel and Miss Bennet were correct in their assertions, the earl would be faced yet again with the prospect of losing his child. He did not possess the memories most fathers could boast to provide him solace. Instead, he had twenty years of pain and loss, years that should have seen him witness her first steps, hear her first words, and watch her grow from the four-month-old babe he had cherished into the beautiful woman she was now.

No recollections of watching her scamper about with her brother near the lake at Heatherton Hall, no images of her curled up by his side as they read her favourite book, and no memories filled with pride as he taught her to ride a horse. There was nothing but a void where a lifetime of treasured moments should have been stored.

Shaking away such dismal thoughts, the earl ran a trembling hand through his hair and straightened his waistcoat in an attempt to assume a calm and composed demeanour. For this meeting was not about him and what he would lose, but about Elizabeth and her happiness—something which his actions so many years ago had placed in jeopardy.

Lord Tamworth had allowed his own fear to dictate his daughter's future. When Miss Bennet had relayed the circumstances of Elizabeth's first marriage proposal and Mr Bennet's wholehearted approval of her rejection, he could feel naught but shame. Though he had not sought the alliance with Matlock for material gain, he had not considered his actions might prevent her ultimate contentment. He had thought only to protect Elizabeth, and the bitter irony that his deeds were the likely cause of her original disappearance only increased his self-reproach. From this point forward, the earl vowed to place his daughter's needs and desires first, and perhaps by doing so, he might even prove a worthy father to her in whatever limited time he was granted.

"You look as though you require extra fortification, my friend."

Distracted by his contemplations, the earl had failed to note the arrival of Lord Matlock who now held a glass of brandy before him.

"I felt that port might not be strong enough after what has taken place this evening," his friend continued with a shrug of his shoulders.

Accepting the tumbler with a nod of thanks, Tamworth took a quick drink before settling himself in one of the chairs before the fire.

Matlock gestured behind him. "You may have the use of my desk, if you like."

"I thank you, no. I hardly feel up to any pretence at

intimidation, though I must ask, is such a thing even possible with that stoic nephew of yours?"

Matlock chuckled grimly. "Darcy has always done well to project such confidence, though I must say, the boy has earned his stripes over the years. 'Twas no easy thing to take on such a vast estate at only two and twenty, despite all of George Darcy's preparations. I offered to assist the lad, and Eleanor even suggested that we take in Georgiana during the mourning period, but Darcy would not be separated from her. He has faltered a time or two, but he has learned and earned the respect of his household on his own merits. Any man could do far worse for a son-in-law."

"I thought you were not best pleased by our current predicament?"

"Come, Tamworth. I am not so unreasonable. I will admit after meeting your daughter, a betrothal seemed a perfect solution for my James, but I will not begrudge my nephew his choice if his heart is truly engaged. I would be a poor uncle if I thought to prevent his happiness. Lord knows the man has had little enough to rejoice about over the years, and if your lively daughter can coax smiles onto his face, then I am sure I will resign myself to the situation with reasonable grace."

Their conversation was interrupted as the door to the study opened and the subject of their discourse walked in, his face a mask of perfect, steady composure, save for the slight twitch about his eye that belied his nerves.

With a quickly executed bow, Darcy addressed the two earls. "I was informed you wished to speak to me. I gather some information was shared in the drawing room after my departure?"

"Yes, why not have a seat. I feel this may be a rather lengthy discussion," Tamworth began, gesturing to the chair opposite his own.

"Brandy, Darcy?" Matlock offered.

"No, thank you."

As the three men settled into their seats, Darcy chose to boldly address the topic at hand.

"Lord Tamworth, I want to start by apologising for my failure to approach you once Lady Elizabeth informed me of her true identity. Knowing of the agreement made between her and my cousin and of her probable ignorance regarding its existence, I was unsure how best to proceed. My despair was not easily set aside, and so Richard thought it prudent that I meet your family first to determine if anything might be done to alter such circumstances. I did not anticipate any mention of the betrothal this evening, nor your daughter's discovery of the contract in such a time and place," Darcy finished with a cool glance towards his uncle.

"Spare me that look, Darcy! I already expect further lectures from your aunt on my behaviour tonight, and I own I probably deserve it," Matlock grumbled. "In another light, you might even thank me, for it appears my inability to hold my tongue has brought about many surprising revelations!"

Darcy continued his silent, steady observation of his uncle without a trace of humour upon his features, and Lord Tamworth thought it best to intervene.

"Thank you, Matlock, but I believe the responsibility for this conversation lies with me."

Fixing the young gentleman seated opposite himself with a determined look, he continued. "I thank you for your explanation, Mr Darcy, however, I am far more interested in what you would have said had you acted upon your initial desire to speak to me about Elizabeth. I understand you have been calling upon her at the Gardiners' home, and your acquaintance with her spans many months, but I have yet to hear of your own feelings beyond the assurances provided by your cousin. I would rather hear your sentiments regarding my daughter first hand."

After looking down for a moment as though to gather his courage, Darcy looked up with an earnest expression. "Then I shall speak plainly, my lord. I love your daughter, and now that I am assured of her affections, I wish to marry her with your permission and your blessing. I can assure you my feelings are not the work of a moment, and my regard for her has endured many months and through many obstacles."

"Obstacles?"

"Yes, my lord. While I have admired Lady Elizabeth from almost the first moments of our acquaintance, my manners and behaviour did not impress her, and I was justly reprimanded. You should be very proud of her, as I have met few young women with such unwavering principles. She would never have been induced to accept me, even as Miss Elizabeth Bennet, if she found my character wanting. Thankfully, your daughter possesses a forgiving nature, and I have since worked tirelessly to earn her regard. I had hoped to ask for her hand before the revelation of her new circumstances. I care not for her title, nor for whatever dowry you have set aside. I simply need *Elizabeth* to make my life complete."

Convinced Darcy told the truth, Tamworth was forced to acknowledge he was a worthy young man indeed. He valued Elizabeth for herself and obviously loved her dearly. While recognising he owed this confession to his daughter, he felt compelled to share such knowledge with the gentleman before him in an effort to make amends for the distress the young couple had endured that night.

"I would have you know Elizabeth's mother and I have only ever wanted her happiness, but I have since come to acknowledge the decisions we made regarding her future were not made out of love, but fear."

Pausing to take another sip of his brandy, the earl turned his gaze towards the fire before he continued. "I have yet to speak of this to Elizabeth, and indeed there are many factors that had a hand in my decision with respect to the betrothal agreement that I have not even related to my son.

Most of my reasons are rooted in the experiences of Lady Tamworth's first Season in town."

He turned to look at Darcy. "Amelia was older than most of the debutantes that spring, as her mother had died shortly after her eighteenth birthday, and she was forced to wait another year for her presentation as she completed her time of mourning. Despite her age, she was no more knowledgeable about the dangers of our society than any of the other newly introduced ladies, and unfortunately, her father was not a careful guardian. Left with no mother to guide her, Amelia was quite adrift in the whirlwind of events that Season. The Mortons are a fine family, with very suitable connexions, and Amelia's dowry of fifteen thousand pounds was far from insignificant. She had no difficulty in attracting admirers, but unfortunately, not all of them were honourable men."

Staring into the contents of his glass, Lord Tamworth lost himself to the memory of that troubled time.

"My Amelia entered the London scene with such energy and good humour and those eyes, those enchanting eyes, only enhanced her natural beauty. The moment I saw her across the ballroom floor, I was lost. She captured my attention effortlessly, and to my deep disappointment, she captured the interest of other men just as quickly. I was hardly the only caller present in her aunt's drawing room the day after our introduction, and word soon spread of how lackadaisical her father was towards her care. I danced with her at every ball, I called on her every day I could, and still I could not protect her from the most determined of rakes. I made a point to follow her movements around every ballroom she attended. On one such evening, right before the supper set I had reserved on her card, her dance partner took advantage of the crush of the crowd and pulled her out of my sight. By the time I found her again, the rogue was attempting to force her into a closed room down a darkened hall to the side of the dance floor. I threatened him and he left, after which Amelia collapsed into my arms, sobbing, and I immediately proposed to her. You cannot know how much it has always pained me that I could not give her the romantic offer she deserved. In any case, our engagement provided the protection she needed, and she was able to enjoy the remaining social events she participated in during the Season's final months. We married that summer, shortly after her twentieth birthday."

"What became of the scoundrel?" Darcy asked.

"Oh, he never dared to approach my wife again. I discovered later he owed a large sum of gambling debts he was hoping to resolve before his father learned of his transgressions. He wanted to obtain Amelia's dowry in order to pay his creditors."

"And this is what led you to seek an arranged marriage for your daughter?" Darcy's gaze was filled with understanding.

"To be honest, I did not think on that event for some time. At the start of our marriage, I had no intention of directing the futures of my children in such a determined fashion. It was only after Elizabeth was born that I was plagued with such worries. You see, Darcy, as so many years had passed since Nicholas's birth, Amelia and I thought we would not be blessed with another child. Elizabeth was born ten years after our marriage, and we were completely overwhelmed with joy when she arrived. The moment I held her in my arms, I was enraptured. I know this will sound like boasting, but I doubt a more cheerful, enchanting little babe has ever been seen than my Elizabeth. It was clear from her earliest days that she favoured Amelia, and I had no doubt she would capture the hearts of many with her happy disposition and those beautiful, dark eyes. If you are ever blessed with a daughter of your own, Darcy, I believe you will experience similar feelings, along with the desire to deny her nothing."

Laughing lightly, the young man concurred. "I have no

doubt of that, my lord."

"It was not until I received a few letters after the announcement of her birth that my fears for her protection surfaced. I was dismayed to find that several of my peers were especially delighted that my wife had birthed a daughter and thought it an advantageous time to seek an alliance with my family. Much as your family's wealth is no secret, Darcy, neither is mine, and Elizabeth's portion is substantial. When confronted with the ambitions of others towards my little girl, I was immediately returned to all of the distress that followed Amelia before our engagement. For if my wife, with only fifteen thousand pounds to her name, had been so intensely pursued, then what could I expect for my dearest daughter? I do not possess a great admiration for many of the families in our circle, so how could I trust they would raise honourable gentlemen who would one day be worthy of my child?

"When Lord and Lady Matlock visited a few months after Elizabeth was born, I discussed my worries with your uncle, and together we decided to make the arrangement for Elizabeth and James's eventual marriage. It seemed the best possible solution at the time, as I could trust the Matlocks to raise their son well. The notion I was denying my daughter the same love match Amelia and I enjoyed never occurred to me, as I assumed she and James would grow to love one another as they interacted over the years."

"And then Elizabeth disappeared," Darcy stated.

"Yes, and all of my efforts to protect her came to naught. When Nicholas found my daughter again, I have to admit the betrothal contract was far from my mind. I was reluctant to discuss it with your uncle simply because I did not wish to lose her again, but now I see I cannot escape such a fate, contract or no."

Hope filled the young man's face. "Then you will grant your permission?"

"If Elizabeth accepts your offer, I will give you my

permission and my blessing to marry her. It is clear you love my daughter, and all I have ever wanted is for Elizabeth to be happy. I am sure that marriage to such an honourable gentleman as yourself will secure such a future for her. I only ask that you allow my family some time together before you take her away."

With the largest smile that Lord Tamworth had ever witnessed from the gentleman, Darcy responded, "Of course, my lord. I know how much family means to Elizabeth, and truly, I thank you. I promise to spend the rest of my life endeavouring to deserve such a precious gift."

Nodding in agreement, Tamworth turned to his old friend who seemed pleased by the obvious joy of his nephew.

"Well, Matlock, you said you still have the papers in this study? You have not spoken of this contract to anyone else, I hope. I would hate for either Lisle's or Elizabeth's reputations to suffer from a broken agreement."

"Give me some credit, Tamworth! Of course I did not say anything. Lady Elizabeth's recovery will not even appear in the papers until tomorrow, and it is not as though I boasted of the contract when it was created, for she disappeared only a week later."

Still grumbling, Matlock walked to his desk and proceeded to unlock a lower compartment. After he retrieved a set of folded documents, he gestured towards the fireplace and asked, "Would you like to do the honours, Tamworth?"

"I think your nephew might enjoy the privilege more," the earl replied, collecting the papers and handing them to his daughter's suitor. "Well, Darcy?"

"It would be my pleasure," he declared. Thrusting the faded files behind the grate, he watched as the contract caught fire, blackened, and crumpled to ash.

"You know, Darcy," Matlock began, "I am glad we can

avoid an argument over your choice of a penniless bride with no connexions."

"It is not a battle you would have won, Uncle."

Holding up his hands in surrender, Matlock declared, "I realise that, which is why I am glad I was unable to initiate it. Elizabeth is a delight, and I am sure she would have won me over eventually, even if she was a poor gentleman's daughter. At least this way we avoided a breach in the family, no matter how temporary, though I cannot see my sister approving of your choice, earl's daughter or no."

"Let us leave the issue of Lady Catherine for another day," Darcy dryly replied before turning back to Lord Tamworth. "When we return to the drawing room, I would like to request a private audience with your daughter."

"I thought you might," he acknowledged with a small smile. "Very well, then. You have my permission; however, I will request you remain cognisant of the time. After all, I need not remind you that Elizabeth has an extremely protective brother who will be more than eager to fulfil his duties as a chaperone. Best not give him any cause to increase his vigilance, or the next few months could be quite uncomfortable indeed."

Chuckling at the embarrassed look upon Darcy's face, Lord Tamworth turned to lead the gentlemen back to the rest of their party, satisfied he had made the right decision, but disheartened all the same.

CHAPTER THIRTY

"You are angry with me, Nicholas," Elizabeth remarked, noting the vexed look that remained upon her brother's face as they approached the drawing room.

"Angry with you? Why ever would you think such a thing?"

Elizabeth raised one eyebrow in challenge to Nicholas's persistently nettled demeanour which had not altered since he had discovered her outside with Mr Darcy. Stopping before the door to the drawing room, he turned to her.

"I will admit to some displeasure in finding you in Darcy's arms, but I can assure you my indignation was already fully kindled before I left the house. My anger concerning the events of the evening has not been easily set aside, for I have difficulty in pardoning those who would cause you such distress."

With a pat on her brother's arm, Elizabeth gently asked, "Did you know about the contract?"

"Yes, but I was only informed of it after the trip with

Father to Longbourn," Nicholas said in a defeated tone. "I do not agree with the decisions Father made, yet I do believe he only made them out of love and a desire to protect you. I am certain there is more I have not been told, for he has never once attempted to influence *my* decisions regarding a marriage partner. I hope you do realise he would never force his choice upon you. After all, he is meeting Darcy at present, is he not?"

"I take it our parents are now aware of Fitz—Mr Darcy's attentions towards me?"

"You could hardly expect that such a dramatic exit would have escaped our notice," he replied with a wry expression. "Besides, I watched your suitor throughout the evening, and I was not the only one who had their suspicions. Mother begged Richard to tell all, and Miss Bennet confirmed his claims."

Elizabeth watched as her brother shifted uncomfortably before taking her hand and continuing. "Mother feared if you knew of the betrothal, you might reject your place in our family. She has been considerably distraught since you fled the room, and while I know you have every reason to be angry, please—*please* do not hold this against her. I think she recognised your feelings sooner than anyone else, for she had already planned to speak to Father about you and Darcy."

Recognising the truth in Nicholas's words, Elizabeth nodded. "You know I would not wish to injure her, and I have had some time to calm down. I trust Mr Darcy to convince Father of the sincerity of our affections, and I have every confidence all will be well."

Her brother regarded her with a sad smile. "I believe you are right. All will be well."

Together they turned to enter the room, and almost immediately after crossing the threshold, Elizabeth was engulfed in Jane's embrace.

"I apologise for sharing your secrets," Jane whispered,

"especially as I know you have yet to reveal your feelings to Mr Darcy."

"You have no need to apologise," Elizabeth calmly replied as she held her sister. "My secrets have all been revealed. I have assured Mr Darcy of my regard, and he is speaking to my father."

Releasing her embrace, Elizabeth was pleased to see Jane's relieved smile. Looking beyond her sister, Elizabeth observed the uneasy faces of the other occupants in the room. Her mother, in particular, appeared to be incredibly anxious as she sat on the settee with Lady Matlock. Slowly approaching her side, Elizabeth quietly sat beside her mother.

"I cannot imagine what you must think of us!" her mother cried, reaching out to grip Elizabeth's hand, as though she feared that her daughter would flee once more.

"Mother, truly, I am well now," Elizabeth soothed, "though I must admit I am still confused why a marriage was arranged for me at all. You love Father. Why would I not be allowed a love match?"

With teary eyes, her mother disclosed, "Oh darling, I do believe it is my fault. Well, perhaps that is not quite true, but rather my experiences in society led your father to fear for your future. I was pursued by a rather unscrupulous man during my first Season, and it was only by your father's intervention that I was spared a pitiable fate. I was too young and naïve to suspect such villainy."

"I know too well how a charming countenance can hide a wicked soul, and how easily deceived one can be by the appearance of goodness when the person possesses none."

"Now, now," the colonel interrupted, "you cannot hold yourself accountable for falling victim to the lies of that cur! He is more practised and cunning than most."

"Of whom are you speaking?" Nicholas enquired in confusion.

Elizabeth noted the inquisitive expressions on the faces

of all but Jane and the colonel before he replied, his voice dripping with clear disdain, "Lady Elizabeth had the misfortune to meet Wickham in Hertfordshire."

"That horrid boy! I never understood why George Darcy favoured him," Lady Matlock commented, an expression of disgust covering her usually elegant features.

After sending a startled look to his brother that clearly indicated his displeasure at such news, Lord Lisle agreed with his mother. "Uncle Darcy was always particularly blind concerning the behaviour of his godson. I had the good sense to steer clear of Wickham when he arrived at Cambridge, for he certainly ran with a debauched set."

"Yes, well, no need to spoil our evening any further by dwelling upon the worm," Colonel Fitzwilliam grumbled.

"Indeed!" Elizabeth concurred before turning back to her mother. "I am sorry you had to experience such misfortune; however, I do not believe I would ever be happy with a fate not of my choosing. 'Twas no lie when I informed you of my stubborn nature. I doubt even had I been raised in your home, I would have wilfully submitted to such plans."

"That much is obvious," Nicholas said with a smirk.

After sending an exasperated glare at her brother, Elizabeth turned to her hostess. "I feel I must apologise for quitting the room so suddenly. I can only say I had not the ability to think rationally in that moment."

Lady Matlock waved away any need for such gestures. "'Twas entirely my husband's fault for burdening you with such startling news, and I must say, that even though I would have been delighted to welcome you as my daughter-in-law, I will be just as proud to claim you as my niece!"

With a mischievous expression her brother added, "I never would have imagined that a man like Darcy would have captured your interest. Your personalities are quite dissimilar. Who would have thought that you would be drawn to such a serious fellow!"

Her indignation riled, Elizabeth retorted, "Just because

he may not possess your ease in society does not mean that *I* find him in any way wanting. Mr Darcy is a very engaging conversationalist when he is comfortable, and I happen to appreciate his reserved nature. There are not many men of his consequence who would debate with a simple country gentlewoman as an equal, nor many who would accept the censure of an impertinent girl and address her ill-founded reproofs. He is kind, honourable, intelligent, and loyal. I do not see why anyone would question my regard for him."

After she had finished her fierce defence of Mr Darcy, Elizabeth observed the surprised but pleased looks on the faces of his relations and the somewhat flabbergasted expression on her brother's countenance.

"I believe there must be a story behind such an impassioned declaration. It sounds as though you have had quite an interesting courtship." With a placating look, he added, "I did not mean to offend, but I would like to understand how all of this came about."

Though hesitant at first, with the assistance of Jane and the colonel, Elizabeth recounted her many interactions with Mr Darcy since the previous autumn. Unwilling to share every detail, particularly the disastrous marriage proposal in Kent, Elizabeth simply related that she and her suitor had suffered from a grievous misunderstanding towards the end of her stay at Hunsford parsonage. Such deception prompted the colonel to roll his eyes, confirming for Elizabeth that he, at least, had known of his cousin's rejected suit and her intemperate response. When she related Mr Darcy's discovery of her the night Nicholas had visited the Gardiners' home for the first time, Elizabeth declared the shock she had received that evening had allowed them to be more direct with one another and resolve their earlier differences.

"So he began to court you at your uncle's home?" her mother enquired.

"Yes, he came almost every day close to the noon hour."

With a slightly amused expression, Nicholas remarked, "I knew I should have asked you why you always looked to the front window towards the end of my calls. To think I missed Darcy by mere minutes! I imagined I would have plenty of time to scare off your potential suitors, and I missed the opportunity altogether for want of being inquisitive!"

"Were you planning to intimidate me, Grey?" Lord Lisle queried, clearly diverted by Nicholas's disappointment.

Though uncomfortable at the mention of Lord Lisle's plan to forward his suit, Elizabeth was forced to hold back her laughter at her brother's look of ill humour.

"I cannot say I was thrilled by the prospect," Nicholas responded in a dry tone.

"You wound me," Lord Lisle replied with an appearance of exaggerated offence. Turning to Elizabeth with an awkward smile, he continued. "I hope you know, Lady Elizabeth, that despite the existence of the contract, I never would have agreed to go forward with the arrangement if you were not in favour of the match. Though I would have worked strenuously to earn your regard and change your mind, I would also never interfere with Darcy's happiness—though I do admit to a fair amount of jealousy that he had the privilege to make your acquaintance first. My cousin is a lucky man."

Elizabeth's words of gratitude were interrupted by the return of her father and Lord Matlock to the drawing room, followed closely by Mr Darcy. Anxious to hear the result of their meeting, Elizabeth's gaze was drawn to the man she loved, and upon seeing the exultant smile upon his face, relief, overwhelming and all-consuming, flooded her very being. Unable to look away, she followed his progress across the room until he came to stand before her.

Holding out his hand, Mr Darcy asked in a quiet, steady voice, "Lady Elizabeth, would you grant me the privilege of a private audience?"

Elizabeth took his hand and stood by his side. "Of course, Mr Darcy."

As he escorted her out of the room, Elizabeth looked to her father who had taken his place beside her mother. A tear trailed down his visage, but his smile at seeing Elizabeth's happy countenance was unfeigned. With a nod of thanks, Elizabeth grinned at her father before returning her gaze to her beloved, overjoyed to begin the next part of their journey with no more obstacles barring their path.

THOUGH HE FELT ASSURED OF HER ACCEPTANCE, DARCY still could not help the anxious fluttering that filled him as he escorted Elizabeth out onto the balcony overlooking the Matlocks' garden. Turning to face her, Darcy took both of Elizabeth's hands in his. After taking a deep breath, he uttered the words he hoped would confirm his dearest wishes.

"Elizabeth, you have my whole heart. Whatever else I have is yours, my love, if you would consent to make me the happiest man on earth by becoming my wife."

Elizabeth looked up at him through happy tears. "I love you, Fitzwilliam Darcy. You are, without doubt, the best man I have ever known. I cannot account for how I have been so privileged as to earn your love, but I promise to cherish you for the rest of my days and to love you as you deserve to be loved in return." Raising one hand to cup his cheek, she declared, "I would be honoured to be your wife."

Darcy quickly gathered her in his arms and clung to her in a fierce embrace, overwhelmed by the feelings of relief and joy that this delightful creature, this beautiful, witty, intelligent, and thoroughly maddening woman would finally be his. Pulling back slightly, Darcy lifted her chin and drew her in for a tender kiss. Before he lost himself completely, he placed a light peck on each of her cheeks and her forehead before finally resting his chin upon her chestnut curls and clutching her to his chest once more.

"I can scarcely believe I have won your love, Elizabeth. I will spend the rest of my days treasuring that gift, I promise you."

"How did you ever begin, Fitzwilliam? I was so contrary when we first met. I often tried to offend you whenever possible. Hardly the kind of behaviour to inspire tender devotion, for truly, what good did you know of my character?" she quipped with a small chuckle.

"What of your care of Miss Bennet at Netherfield? You may make light of such affection, but I can assure you that few gently bred young ladies would travel such a distance on foot to see to the care of a sister with a slight cold. You intrigued me from the start, my love. Most people never dared to challenge me. Yet, you never seemed intimidated in the slightest, despite my dourest mood. 'Twas not long before my admiration of your fine eyes proceeded into admiration for your intelligent mind and soon after into love for your generous heart."

"That was a fine speech, my love, though I still say I was a most troublesome female to woo. I am inordinately grateful for your stubbornness. You will definitely have need of it in the future, for I fear I will never be a very tractable wife."

Darcy laughed in earnest. "If I longed for a biddable spouse, I would not have pursued you so ardently. I desire a marriage of equals, but fortunately for me, God has granted me the love of a woman who is my superior in every way."

"More pretty words, my darling! 'Tis a promising start for our new understanding."

"Aye, and I will have plenty of time to practise, Elizabeth. Your father has requested a long engagement. Six months at the very least."

"Six months!"

"I could not deny his demand. It would be cruel for me to take you away so soon."

Leaning back to look upon her face, Darcy watched as Elizabeth's expression softened, and she slowly nodded in agreement.

"You are right, Fitzwilliam. I do want to know my family better, however much I dislike having to delay our wedding. I suppose this means we will marry in late autumn?"

"I believe so and from your father's estate, I would imagine. I doubt your parents would desire a town wedding."

"No, indeed!" With a slightly impish expression, she continued. "I suppose I should be relieved I need not endure the rigours of the marriage mart next Season! I can enjoy my time as a married lady rather than as a prize for all of London's eligible bachelors, though I must own, I have not the slightest idea what sort of prize I am!"

The corner of Darcy's mouth lifted. "Do you want to know, or will you wait until your father and I draft the settlement?"

"You know the size of my dowry?"

"Your father mentioned it in passing."

Elizabeth arched a brow. "I am endeavouring to set aside my qualms regarding my family's wealth. They are determined to spoil me, which I suppose will make your task easier if you harbour similar inclinations. I suppose I should be pleased I will bring *something* to the marriage," she teased.

"Elizabeth, you are *everything* to me. You must know that."

"Of course I do, silly man. After all, you did propose to me before my true heritage was discovered, did you not? Just tell me the amount of my dowry, Fitzwilliam."

With a resigned sigh, Darcy said, "Fifty thousand pounds."

She could only respond with a wide-eyed expression, clearly stunned by such a staggering figure.

Seeking a distraction, Darcy redirected the conversation.

"You know, the colder months in the north are not an ideal time for a wedding tour. Perhaps we could go travelling in the spring and avoid the Season altogether."

Elizabeth laughed. "I see what you are about! I am afraid I cannot indulge your reclusive tendencies, sir. I have promised my mother I will have my presentation next spring, so I am sorry to say we cannot avoid London entirely. Though I suppose this means I will make my curtsey as Lady Elizabeth Darcy, a happy thought indeed!" she added with a joyous smile.

Overcome with emotion at the thought of her carrying his name, Darcy leaned forward to kiss her again. After several passionate minutes, Darcy sought to regain his composure. He looked at Elizabeth, and her rosy cheeks and slightly swollen lips only served to challenge his resolve.

"I do believe we must venture inside before your father and brother can accuse me of taking liberties. I do not wish to incur their ire after having only so recently gained your father's consent."

"I suppose we must return, though I am loath to lose my time alone with you," she replied with a wistful expression. A moment later, her countenance took on a teasing aspect. "Speaking of taking liberties, what was my brother hinting at with his threat about a duel? Are you as fearsome an opponent as he implied?"

Darcy shrugged. "I may have won a few contests during my time at Cambridge."

"Only a few?"

"Well, all of them," he admitted. "Though that does not mean I have never lost a match."

The mischievous light in Elizabeth's expression grew. "Will you teach me? After all, now that I am a *lady* I am permitted a few eccentricities, am I not? I imagine that fencing with foils would be far more rewarding than batting about with muddy sticks as I did with Charlotte's brother."

Darcy barked out a sharp laugh. "Life will never be dull

with you, my love! But perhaps we should return inside now as I suggested." Shaking his head, Darcy took Elizabeth's arm in his and directed her towards the drawing room.

Upon their entrance, Darcy nodded to Lord Tamworth who stood to address the gathered assembly.

"It appears a celebration is in order," Lord Tamworth began, "for I am delighted to announce the engagement of my daughter, Elizabeth, to Mr Fitzwilliam Darcy! Matlock, I do believe we are in need of some wine to toast the happy couple!"

"It would be my pleasure." Crossing the room to summon a servant, Darcy's uncle briefly stopped to grip his shoulder in congratulations.

Seeing the happy grin Elizabeth directed at her parents, Darcy released her arm and watched her join them. As they embraced her, Elizabeth's brother approached Darcy and held out his hand. With a firm grip, Darcy accepted Grey's good wishes.

"I can rest easy knowing you may be one of the few men who might be deserving of Elizabeth."

"I know too well how fortunate I am to have been granted her hand. You will get no argument from me about whether or not I deserve her, for I fear I will never truly merit my good fortune."

With an appraising glance, Grey remarked, "You will do, Darcy. You will do."

As servants passed glasses for the toast, Elizabeth returned to his side as his cousins and Miss Bennet approached.

Jane laughed as she pulled her sister into an embrace before turning to face Darcy. "I am so happy for you and my sister, sir! I know you will cherish her as she deserves."

Darcy thanked her sincerely. "I hope you will look upon me as a brother, and I believe I speak for both Elizabeth and myself when I say you will always be welcome in our homes."

Elizabeth's brilliant smile showed how pleased she was at his invitation.

Darcy was startled as his cousin Lisle clapped him on his back. "Well, Darcy, it appears I was right when I thought you might finally be looking for a bride, though I do wish your choice had not been my best chance to escape the marriage mart. I will do my best to set my jealousy aside, I promise. You will be very happy together."

"Thank you, Lisle," Darcy stiffly responded, still uncomfortable with Lisle's obvious preference for Elizabeth.

"You have a right to every happiness, Cousin, and I daresay, Lady Elizabeth will keep you on your guard!"

"She will indeed. I must say I anticipate it with great pleasure!"

"According to Father, it seems you will have to wait a bit," Grey interrupted. "Though I suppose we should have the guest rooms readied at Heatherton Hall for the foreseeable future."

Darcy thanked him. "I intend to invite your family to Pemberley as well. 'Tis fortunate Staffordshire is not far from Derbyshire."

"Aye, it will aid me greatly in my quest to ensure that my sister remains happy for the rest of her days," Grey said with a teasing grin.

Smiling at the jest, Darcy looked from Grey to the joyful face of his lovely betrothed and felt a profound sense of gratitude.

"I promise you such a worthy mission will be my life's work, and with her smiles as my reward, I believe I will have no cause to repine."

CHAPTER THIRTY-ONE

Breathing in the salty, sea air as he sat in a chair on the veranda of their rented Margate cottage, Mr Bennet attempted to absorb the startling information that had been disclosed in the latest letters from London.

The last week had been a difficult one for the Bennet family. Only a day before the announcement had appeared in the papers, Mr Bennet and his wife had sat down with their younger daughters and relayed the story of Elizabeth's birth and abduction which had led to her instalment in their family. Mary, Kitty and Lydia had been understandably shocked and distressed at the thought of losing their older sister. Their genuine feelings of loss had moved Mr Bennet, for despite their silliness, he knew his daughters possessed good hearts.

Thomas Bennet could see that with more diligent instruction, his younger daughters could improve their manners. He had also confided in his wife that Elizabeth's family would probably discourage her association with her sisters if they thought the Bennets would bring embarrassment upon their daughter. Fearful at the thought of losing all connexion with Elizabeth, Mrs Bennet had been firmer with Lydia during her outbursts, and as a result, both Lydia and Kitty had become somewhat better behaved. They would always be boisterous by nature, but as long as they displayed the appropriate comportment in company, Mr Bennet would be satisfied. He had also taken pains to draw Mary into conversation and encourage her enjoyment of literature beyond the heavy tomes of Fordyce. While still prone to spouting moralistic admonishments, Mary seemed to be far more content and grateful for the increased attention from her parents.

The day the announcement had arrived, the Bennets had refused all callers at Longbourn, even the Lucas family. Mrs Bennet had spent most of the day in tears, and perhaps to spare the girls, Mrs Hill had kept the family matriarch in the comfort of her rooms. Mr Bennet had spent part of that day comforting his wife, and the other half in company with his daughters, who possessed no desire to socialise with anyone beyond Longbourn. Not wanting to be the subject of gossip, however unavoidable such a fate was, the entire family was relieved to depart the following day for Margate, leaving the four and twenty families surrounding Meryton to speculate amongst themselves about such momentous news. It appeared, however, that the intelligence of further significant events was unavoidable, even at their sun-bathed little cottage.

Glancing again at the two opened missives in his lap and the small stack of correspondence for Mrs Bennet and their daughters, Thomas Bennet could not decide whether to be more amused or pained by the recitation of Elizabeth's first dinner party in London. When the letter from Jane arrived, Mr Bennet had only expected that she would confirm her travel plans, and indeed, Jane and the Gardiners were set to leave London on the day previously arranged. He was shocked, therefore, when she described such a scene of chaos—at the home of an earl no less—

that had ultimately resulted in his dear Lizzy's engagement.

Arranged marriages, secret courtships, and at the end of it all, nothing was more astonishing than Elizabeth's choice of a husband. Mr Bennet never would have predicted that Mr Darcy, the proud, disagreeable young man who had slighted Elizabeth all those months ago, should not only fall in love with her but win her regard. Denial, however, was not an option, for the second letter on his lap, written in a very even hand, was from Mr Darcy himself.

Not only had the young gentleman felt it necessary to seek Mr Bennet's blessing and assure him of his ardent love for the woman the Bennets had raised, he felt it pertinent to disclose the unsavoury habits of a local militia officer so Mr Bennet would be able to protect his family. Grateful for such information and relieved the family had removed to Margate, Mr Bennet was encouraged by the honourable intentions of Elizabeth's betrothed, and with Jane's assurances, he was fairly certain Elizabeth would be happy with her chosen partner in life.

Interrupted in his musings by the happy sounds of laughter, Mr Bennet raised his gaze to see his wife and daughters ambling along the path towards their cottage. Kitty and Lydia were skipping arm in arm, their youthful exuberance on display, while Mrs Bennet and Mary followed at a far more sedate pace.

As they drew near, he called out, "While all of you have been gallivanting, the post was delivered with letters for each of you."

A chorus of excited cries surrounded Mr Bennet as the four women requested their letters. Raising his hands in a gesture for silence, he continued. "Before I pass out your correspondence, I believe you should all learn of the news that Jane has sent from London."

"Oh my sweet Jane! She is joining us soon, is she not?" Mrs Bennet asked.

"Yes, my dear. Jane writes that she will stay to experience the first day of callers at Lizzy's new home tomorrow, and then she and the Gardiners will leave London the following day. Her letter, however, contained far more momentous news, for it seems that our dear Lizzy has gotten herself engaged!"

"Engaged!"

"Aye, and to someone with whom we already hold an acquaintance! It seems *Mr Darcy* has been in love with Lizzy since he met her in Hertfordshire and has courted her over the last few weeks in London."

After a moment of stunned silence, Mrs Bennet and the girls erupted in unison with cries of astonishment and demands for further information. Reading aloud a portion of Jane's letter, in which she vouchsafed for the genuine affection between Mr Darcy and Elizabeth and her fervent belief in their future felicity, the surprised expressions on the ladies' faces gave way to smiles of delight.

"Oh, what a wonderful thing for our girl! Ten-thousand a year! And an estate and a home in town and all that is charming!" Mrs Bennet exclaimed.

"Yes, well, the most important factor is that our girl will be loved, my dear. I have had a letter from Mr Darcy as well, requesting our blessing on the match and assuring our family of his regard for Elizabeth."

Upon hearing of Mr Darcy's desire for their blessing, his wife's eyes filled with grateful tears. "How thoughtful of him, Mr Bennet! I believe Lizzy will be very happy, indeed!"

After agreeing with his wife, Mr Bennet distributed the letters from Elizabeth. She had written to Mrs Bennet and each of her sisters, and though he had not expected otherwise, Mr Bennet was still dismayed that the package came without a note for him. Knowing she was still struggling with the part he had played in altering her life, he resolved to be patient and accept whatever connexion Elizabeth was willing to entertain, hopeful that with enough time, she would be amenable to repairing their bond.

Satisfied by the happy faces of his daughters, Mr Bennet turned to his wife who was dabbing her cheeks with her handkerchief.

"Oh Mr Bennet! What a good girl Lizzy is! Here, read this for yourself."

Looking to the end of the letter where Fanny had directed his attention, a smile crept over Mr Bennet's face.

Please tell Papa that Mr Darcy and I plan to visit Longbourn after we are wed, if you would consent to hosting us for a time. We long to share our happiness with you all, as you will always be considered family.

All my love,
Lizzy

Exhausted and disgruntled, Caroline Bingley collapsed upon the settee in her private sitting room at the Hursts' residence. She had just spent another trying day taking advantage of her previous acquaintance with the newly discovered Lady Elizabeth Grey as she flitted from the various drawing rooms of her social betters in London. Miss Bingley had always desired a connexion with the more exalted members of high society, but that such an opportunity should come from the most unlikely and vexing of sources grated upon her very nerves. It had been galling to pretend to admire that impertinent, country chit, but she fully realised to do anything less would bring about her own social ruin.

Massaging her aching temples, Miss Bingley reflected upon the morning earlier that week when she had read the announcement in the papers. Her day had begun in the usual fashion, as she had broken her fast in the company of her siblings while perusing the gossip sheets before embarking upon her many social calls. Just as she was buttering her toast, her brother had dropped his cup of coffee, shattering the delicate china upon the floor and splattering the dark liquid upon the hem of Caroline's new morning gown.

"Charles, look at what you have done! My maid will never be able to remove these stains!"

After inspecting her dress, she looked up to berate her brother anew when he barked, "Hush, Caroline! I apologise about your new gown, but I think you will pardon me when you read this."

Glaring at him in disbelief, she accepted the paper he thrust under her nose and read the passage that Charles had indicated.

At first, astonishment was all she could feel until such sentiments were quickly supplanted by those of jealousy. It was not enough that the girl had distracted Mr Darcy with her *fine eyes* during their stay in Hertfordshire, but now she was an earl's daughter, one of the wealthiest in all of England! While Caroline could claim superiority over *Miss Eliza Bennet*, now that the brazen girl possessed wealth and a title, her place in the society of those whose approbation Caroline had long coveted was assured. After only a minute or two, her jealous ramblings were interrupted by her brother's voice as he took the paper from her hand and passed it to Louisa.

"Read there," he said while pointing to the passage before turning back to face her again. "So? What do you make of this, eh Caroline? I cannot believe that we never learned Miss Elizabeth, or *Lady Elizabeth*, I should say, was not the Bennets' daughter! Though I never saw any similarities between her and Miss Bennet, I still do not believe I would have guessed she was not of their family!"

Setting the paper aside, Mrs Hurst remarked, "I agree,

Charles! Not that I paid much attention to that family in any case—such dreadful manners! Though I suppose Miss Eliza behaved reasonably well." Turning to her sister, she continued. "I believe we should extend the hand of friendship to the new Lady Elizabeth! After all, she will need guidance in society, and she would probably appreciate advice from friends!"

Though she recognised the sense as well as the potential opportunities in Louisa's suggestion, the prospect of ingratiating herself to the woman nettled Caroline's sensibilities. Once she had agreed with her sister, the two of them resolved to make their association with the new Lady Elizabeth Grey common knowledge as they visited their London acquaintances.

For the next several days, Caroline had boasted to all and sundry of her intimacy with the newly recovered earl's daughter, a topic that had gripped the *ton* for the past week.

Several sightings had taken place already, for the Greys had been spotted on Bond Street as well as at the theatre, though they did not leave their private box at any point during the performance. Although Caroline had not seen the family herself, she had heard the rumours regarding the astonishing likeness between Lady Tamworth and her daughter. As Caroline gloated to others of a previous friendship with the mysterious young lady, she had been pressed to conceal her embarrassment when her friend, Alice Grantley, had informed her of the Greys' plans to accept callers the next day.

Rising from the sofa, Caroline left the room in search of her brother. As luck would have it, Charles had just returned from his club and happily joined her in the downstairs sitting room.

"Did you enjoy your time at the club, Brother? I hope you were able to visit with Mr Darcy, for we have not seen him at all since the day after we returned to London!"

"Darcy? No, no I did not see him today. His schedule

has been unusually busy of late, though I did see Colonel Fitzwilliam this afternoon. He mentioned Darcy has been occupied with a previous engagement, but he should be free to visit in the coming weeks. He was quite gleeful, now that I think on it, but you know the colonel, always jesting about something!"

"I was thinking that we should pay a call at Tamworth House tomorrow. I hear the knocker is going up, and we ought to show our support for our former neighbour."

"Surely, you do not mean to call at an earl's residence without an introduction?"

"But we have an acquaintance there!" Caroline scoffed. "I am sure it could only be viewed as a kindness that we would contact Lady Elizabeth when she is surrounded by so many strangers and in such unfamiliar settings. You would not want to slight her, would you?"

"Of course not! If you are sure it would not be an imposition, then I shall join you."

"Excellent!"

Pushing her jealous thoughts and feelings of scorn aside, Caroline resolved she would present her most congenial self to the former Eliza Bennet. Even if she must endure the trial of currying favour with one she had so fervently disliked, at least her efforts would serve to raise her in the estimation of London's first circles, and perhaps even improve her marital prospects. After all, Mr Darcy would surely be pleased by her desire to guide Eliza into more exalted company, and perhaps it would display her ability to do the same for meek little Georgiana.

Such musings soothed Caroline's wounded pride as she thought on the triumph she would experience should Mr Darcy decide to grant her the singular honour of becoming the next Mistress of Pemberley, a position that would satisfy her every hope and dream.

CHAPTER THIRTY-TWO

Returning from their morning walk, Elizabeth allowed her brother to assist her in removing her pelisse after he had doffed his hat and coat. Once she had passed her bonnet to the waiting servant, Nicholas took her arm again to lead her to the small, sunny room where the family usually enjoyed their morning's repast. When Elizabeth had first informed her family of her daily habits, her father and Nicholas had only permitted her morning constitutionals so long as she was accompanied by either her brother or the sturdy footman who had been charged with her protection. Though inclined to chafe under such restrictions, Elizabeth had resolved to accept their dictates with more forbearance, especially after Fitzwilliam had wholeheartedly agreed with their demands. As their home was situated in such close proximity to Hyde Park, Elizabeth looked forward to her daily stroll, and she found she enjoyed this time alone with her brother.

"Are you looking forward to the spectacles we shall witness today?" Nicholas asked as they sat down to break their fast, loading his plate with buttery eggs and ham.

Spreading jam onto a warm roll, Elizabeth replied with a teasing smile. "You do not sound terribly optimistic. Spectacles? Do you expect performances worthy of Covent Garden in our drawing room?"

"Indeed I do. They will line up in droves to meet you, though I suspect our home will already be quite full with your faithful supporters before anyone else has had the chance to arrive. Tell me, how early are we to expect Darcy today?"

It had become a source of amusement for her brother to comment on the unfailingly punctual nature of her betrothed. Over the past week, Fitzwilliam had taken to arriving ever earlier to spend as much time with her as he was allowed. This meant he typically appeared at Tamworth House in time to drink his morning coffee with the family.

At first Elizabeth had worried he was neglecting Georgiana, but Fitzwilliam had assured her that his sister was all but pushing him out the door. Miss Darcy had been ecstatic upon learning of her brother's engagement, and Elizabeth and her mother had spent several afternoons taking tea at Darcy House with the sweet young woman. Just as Elizabeth was about to reply to her brother's tease, the object of his jests walked through the door.

"Ah! A new record, eh, Darcy? Do not tell me that *you* are anxious about the circus that will soon arrive on our doorstep?"

"Good morning to you too, Grey." Turning towards Elizabeth with a small smile, Darcy walked to her side and kissed her hand in greeting.

"Good morning, Elizabeth. I trust you slept well?"

"Of course I did! You cannot think that I would let a silly day of social calls keep me from my rest!"

When her betrothed merely stared at her with a concerned expression, Elizabeth relented. "Oh, very well! I suppose I was a bit unsettled, but I assure you I am perfectly well. Besides, when I have so many valiant protectors ready to rush to my aid, how can I fail to be confident the day will end in success?"

With an amused shake of his head, Darcy poured himself a cup of coffee and sat in the chair next to her. "You will have some additional help today. Lisle and Richard plan to join us here while their mother holds court at Matlock House."

"I see my godmother has been making plans," Nicholas interjected. "I own I thought she would come by to support Mother, but I see the strategy in accepting callers at her own home. As our family association is well known, those who are not brave enough to call here today will no doubt flock to Lady Matlock for their desired dose of gossip."

"Gossip, Nicholas? Pray tell me it is too early in the day for such idle talk!"

The entrance of their mother and father interrupted the conversation at the table as all rose in greeting. Walking to her mother to place a quick kiss upon her cheek, Elizabeth then turned to her father.

"Did you truly expect aught akin to rational discourse today? I know I have been warned repeatedly about the supposed rigours of society for the past se'nnight. Do not tell me that you *too* possess no stomach for our trials this morning, or I fear we shall make a very sorry group!"

Laughing, her father replied, "I shall play my part well, but do not expect me to enjoy the experience!"

Elizabeth settled back into her chair. "'Tis rather unfair, you know. Men can say very little and merely sit and stare whilst looking suitably dignified, but if I were to do the same, I should be called very dull indeed."

"You say this as though you will fail to dazzle our callers! In any case, I cannot imagine you ever being content to sit quietly by," Nicholas said with a smirk.

"I do not know whether to feel emboldened or offended by such remarks, Brother."

"What I think Grey is trying to say, no matter how ineloquently," Darcy interjected, "is that you will be perfectly fine today, Elizabeth. Furthermore, your conjecture that men do not suffer for their lack of conversation is patently false, for I seem to remember a young lady who was not impressed by my reticence and admonished me to practise my woeful skills in company."

Thoroughly amused by the teasing look on her beloved's usually serious mien, Elizabeth joined in the laughter of her family as she acknowledged the truth in his words. "Indeed, I do not know how you will endure my impertinence for a lifetime!"

"Now, now. Do not make him rethink his decision! Not when the settlement papers are already signed!" Nicholas chuckled.

"Ignore your brother, Elizabeth," their mother intervened. "What was it you were saying about your aunt's plans, Mr Darcy?"

"She is sending Lisle and Richard to join us today, though I doubt they needed much persuasion, for I fear her drawing room will be as well occupied as your own. Richard already feels rather protective of your daughter, and at least at Tamworth House, Lisle can hide amongst other equally eligible bachelors." Darcy finished with a well-pleased look at Elizabeth's brother.

"You forget," Nicholas replied with an identically smug expression, "that no one is yet aware of your engagement."

"They will be tomorrow, Son."

Startled, Elizabeth turned to look at her father, and at her questioning glance he elaborated. "Your mother and I decided to send the notice to the papers. While we still intend for you to have a long engagement, I do not see the harm in announcing your news before the Season is out. At least this way you will not have to endure any speculation on potential matches, and hopefully, it will deter those from making your acquaintance who harboured any ambitions in that quarter. Besides, your mother pointed out it was highly unlikely that the pair of you could conceal your attachment for very long."

With a slightly reddened countenance, but a joyful smile nonetheless, Darcy quietly said, "Thank you, Lord Tamworth."

After dabbing the corners of her mouth with a napkin, Elizabeth rose from her chair. "Father, may Fitzwilliam and I walk in the gardens for a short time? I promise to stay in view of the windows."

"Of course, my dear. I will send your brother to fetch you when the others arrive."

Once they had left the room, Darcy took her hand in his as he led her to the back garden, not stopping until they were safely ensconced behind a wide tree. Without a moment's pause, he pulled Elizabeth into a searing kiss.

Pulling away with a shaky breath, Darcy declared, "I cannot wait until the day I have the privilege to greet you in such a fashion every morning."

"You will receive no argument from me when you do," Elizabeth replied with an airy chuckle, while still endeavouring to recover her own breathing after such an impassioned display.

Looking back towards the house, Darcy sighed and offered his arm, leading her along the flower beds as her blush slowly faded from her cheeks. Though he may have disliked the need for a chaperone, Elizabeth knew her betrothed was grateful for the amount of time her father permitted them to share whilst they were both still in town.

All too soon, Darcy would need to return to Pemberley, and Elizabeth and her family would retreat to Staffordshire for the summer months. As he had been away from his estate for a significant length of time, Darcy had confided in her that it would take at least a month or two before he would be able to visit at Heatherton Hall. Elizabeth's father had granted them permission to correspond during their coming separation, but neither of them could contemplate the possibility of such a long absence with any measure of satisfaction.

"I brought you another letter from Georgiana," he mentioned while pulling a folded note from his inner coat pocket. "Though I do not know what she has to write about, for she saw you not two days ago!"

"You will have to become accustomed to our frequent exchanges of sisterly confidences. Poor Georgiana has lacked such a balm for too long. I do not know how I could have coped with the trials of girlhood without my Jane."

"I am truly delighted at your easy friendship with my sister. I always knew you would be a good influence, though I do admit to my own surprise at how quickly you were able to overcome her reserve. Georgiana even mentioned her desire to join us today, although I believe she would have been utterly terrified at the prospect."

As she nodded her agreement, Elizabeth could only imagine how shy Georgiana would have fared in the chaos that awaited them that afternoon. Hopefully with time, they would be able to instil more confidence in Darcy's sister, as she would eventually need to be presented to society and would no longer be able to hide behind her brother's imposing presence.

"I thought Miss Bennet would be here when I arrived."

"Jane should be along soon, though I imagine the Gardiners' home is consumed in their preparations for their travels. I was able to visit them with Mother yesterday, and you would not believe how verbose dear little Meg was in her expectation of the delights to be had at the seaside!"

"I can well believe it! I must concede that, despite her resemblance to Miss Bennet, I have always imagined your young cousin greatly resembles your own behaviour as a child."

"You are probably right, my darling. You may well be doomed to confirm your own suspicions, should we have a daughter who takes after her mother, for my dear Mama

Bennet always said that one day I would have the dubious privilege of raising a child who possessed all of my relentless energy."

As they were still in clear view of the back parlour, where no doubt her brother kept watch, Darcy leaned down to whisper into her ear. "You think to tease me, my love, but were we truly alone, I would not hesitate to show you just how pleased I would be at such a possibility."

Elizabeth lightly swatted his arm before redirecting the conversation to safer topics. "I am grateful your cousins have agreed to join us today. It will be reassuring to have a few more familiar faces present."

Though still slightly uncomfortable around Lord Lisle, her brother's friend had taken pains to set her mind at ease about the abandoned betrothal. Elizabeth still felt he regarded her relationship with Darcy with some measure of envy, but he seemed determined to present himself as a friend above all else.

Ignorant of her musings, Darcy continued. "Aye, and I have asked them to attend Miss Bennet as well. Your sister's beauty combined with her gentle nature may attract more attention than she would like. I would not want her to be made uncomfortable."

Touched by his concern for her dearest Jane, Elizabeth replied, "You are truly the best of men."

As he looked down in mild embarrassment, their interlude was interrupted by Nicholas, who came to inform them that Miss Bennet and Mr Darcy's cousins had arrived. Together the trio re-entered the house and greeted the newly arrived guests in the drawing room.

"Ah! My besotted cousin emerges from his sanctum of love!" Colonel Fitzwilliam quipped with an exaggerated sigh before he turned to greet the others. "Lady Elizabeth, Grey, a pleasure as always. You know, Darcy, your absence at the club has already been noted. Bingley approached me just the other day, asking where on earth you have been hiding of late."

Darcy scoffed. "I have not been so completely preoccupied. I was just at Angelo's earlier this week, as Grey can attest."

"Truly, Grey!" Lord Lisle exclaimed as he rounded on Elizabeth's brother. "So? How did you fare against Darcy's blade?"

"My future brother is quite formidable. At least he will always possess the means to check my flippant tongue," Nicholas admitted, his amusement plain.

Elizabeth was pleased her brother had become resigned to his loss and could look upon the experience with more humour than when he had first arrived home. Darcy had been insufferably smug when he had called the following morning, and though she felt he deserved a little revenge for Nicholas's unflagging jests, it was all she could do not to scold the pair of them for their childishness.

"I tell you, Jane," she commented with a dramatic groan as she embraced her sister, "I do not think we could have survived a brother at Longbourn. Such pointless posturing! Such barbarity!"

"Let them have their fun!" Jane giggled, thoroughly diverted by both her sister's antics and the looks of mock offence on the gentlemen's faces.

"You think me barbaric, Elizabeth?" Darcy questioned with a sly grin. "Would you approve of my habits were I to carry your favour? After all, 'tis the least I can do as your devoted knight."

With an elegant flourish, Elizabeth pulled her handkerchief from her sleeve and presented it with a curtsey. "Very well. I suppose I must permit your exploits now, but do try to bring my brother home with all his limbs," she quipped with a wink at Nicholas, "for I am becoming rather fond of him."

"How generous of you," Nicholas replied with a roll of his eyes.

Elizabeth's parents entered the drawing room, and soon the entire party was seated in preparation for the day's activities. Though Elizabeth sat near her family, Darcy would not relinquish his place at her side, and although she joked he was making a very public claim through such a gesture, he had unrepentantly acknowledged it was precisely his intent. Now that their engagement would be announced upon the morrow, it appeared as though Darcy was not of a mind to hide their attachment in any way, and despite her independent nature, Elizabeth's heart swelled a bit at being so fiercely loved.

Once Tewes entered the room, the dreaded silver salver on his palm, Elizabeth took a deep breath and smiled up at her intended as her mother took the calling card from the plate.

"Oh! 'Tis our neighbour, Mr Townsend."

As they all rose to greet him, Elizabeth directed a beaming smile at the congenial older gentleman. A determined walker himself, Elizabeth and Nicholas had often encountered Mr Townsend on their morning rambles through the park, and his delightful, cheery nature had quickly endeared him to Elizabeth. He was also an avid ornithologist and his commentary on the bird life in Hyde Park made him a fascinating walking companion.

"What a pleasure to see you all! I simply had to call and wish you well on your endeavours today," the elderly gentleman enthused before making his introductions to the remaining members of their party.

Upon greeting Darcy, Mr Townsend exclaimed, "Ah, you are the young man I have seen so frequently of late! What brings you to the neighbourhood so often?"

Knowing his question to be well-meant rather than presumptuous, Elizabeth's father replied, "Mr Darcy is engaged to my daughter, Townsend. I trust you can keep such news to yourself. It will be announced in *The Times* tomorrow."

"Why certainly, my lord! Congratulations, young man! You are gaining an enchanting young lady, though I must say this all seems quite sudden!"

With a light laugh, Elizabeth confessed, "I have known Mr Darcy for above eight months, sir. We met before I was reunited with my family."

"My goodness! Well, a most hearty congratulations to you both!"

Just then, Tewes entered the drawing room to deliver another card, and judging by the look upon her mother's face, Elizabeth assumed their next caller was not simply another cheerful neighbour. Standing to bid farewell to Mr Townsend, her mother thanked him again for his visit as Tewes announced their next guest.

"Lady Castlereagh."

Steeling herself for her first meeting with one of the highly sought-after patronesses of Almack's, Elizabeth rose and curtseyed to the viscountess as the proper introductions were made.

After settling herself next to Elizabeth's mother, Lady Castlereagh remarked, "It is so good to see you in town, Lady Tamworth! I know dear Lady Matlock was most pleased by your arrival, and I must say, I cannot imagine a more significant reason than this! Why, the resemblance is astonishing! You are as great a beauty as your mother, Lady Elizabeth."

"Thank you, your ladyship," Elizabeth acknowledged with a small nod of gratitude.

"And I see Lady Matlock's family has eagerly welcomed your daughter," the viscountess continued with a shrewd glance at Mr Darcy and his place at Elizabeth's side.

"Indeed we have, Lady Castlereagh," Mr Darcy replied, "though my cousin Colonel Fitzwilliam and I were already known to Lady Elizabeth before she was discovered by Lord Grey."

"How intriguing!" she exclaimed, and upon seeing the return of the butler with another card, the viscountess turned to her hostess. "You must bring your daughter by later this week. I am sure I can provide you with vouchers for the remainder of the Season, though something tells me Lady Elizabeth will not lack for suitors!"

"You are too kind, Lady Castlereagh," Elizabeth's mother replied, as she stood once again to bid farewell to their guest.

After the lady's departure, Elizabeth gently laid a hand upon Darcy's arm, as his stern countenance displayed his discomfort at their guest's prediction of flocking admirers. With a slight shake of his head, her betrothed smiled at her in thanks as the pair prepared themselves for the next visitor.

After another hour of similar calls, Elizabeth began to feel fatigued by the monotony of it all, particularly the shocked expressions that most of their guests wore upon noting her likeness to her mother. The constant standing and sitting was tiring, and Elizabeth had witnessed Jane's displeasure at some of the more inane attempts at flattery they had endured. Fortunately, there were simply too many callers to accept them all, and so occasionally, when the proposed guest was not suitably acquainted with the family, they were able to turn them away with relative ease.

Not all of their guests were objectionable. Elizabeth had especially enjoyed making the acquaintance of Lady Penelope Talbot, a duke's daughter who had the reputation for being something of a bluestocking. After chatting for a few minutes on a newly released collection of poetry by Lord Byron, Elizabeth was determined to accept the hand of friendship she had been offered, and so the two made plans to meet at Gunter's for ices in two days.

When Elizabeth believed their afternoon was finally

drawing to a close, her mother turned to her with a puzzled expression on her face as she examined the most recent card the butler had delivered.

"I do not recognise this name. Elizabeth, my dear, are you acquainted with anyone by the name of Bingley?"

"The Bingleys have called?" Elizabeth exclaimed, turning to Darcy with a questioning gaze. "Did Mr Bingley mention this to you by any chance?"

"I have not seen Bingley in several weeks, though I cannot say I am surprised by Miss Bingley's desire to become reacquainted."

"Why ever for? You know as well as I that she did not care for my company."

"What is this?" Grey enquired before his mother passed him the calling card. "Ah! I do not believe you have had the dubious pleasure of meeting Miss Bingley, Mother. Forgive me, Darcy, I know Bingley is a friend of yours, and I have no quarrel with him, for he seems an affable enough chap, but his sister is truly dreadful."

With a nervous look at her betrothed, Elizabeth whispered, "What about Jane? Do you think it wise to admit them? I would not slight your friend, but I fear for my sister's well-being."

"It is your decision, Elizabeth, but you should know I have warned Lisle and Richard of this possibility, and they will be more than willing to defend your sister."

"I suppose we should allow their call," she conceded. "After all, it is not as though Jane wishes for Mr Bingley to renew his attentions, and he *did* host us for a time at Netherfield. It would only be proper to accept their well wishes now."

Elizabeth turned to her mother. "I believe we should let them pay their addresses. Mr Bingley and his sister are former neighbours of mine from Hertfordshire, and though I doubt I will encourage the acquaintance with the sister, Mr Bingley is a good friend of Fitzwilliam's, and I would not want to make him uncomfortable when I encounter him in the future."

"Very well, my dear, if you are sure," Lady Tamworth replied before turning to Tewes and informing him of their willingness to allow the call.

As Miss Bingley entered the drawing room with her brother, Elizabeth could not help but notice she seemed rather overdressed for a morning call. What was more disconcerting than her apparel was the forced smile that appeared upon her face. When her gaze rested upon Darcy, Elizabeth began to understand why the lady was less than pleased.

After they had risen in greeting, performed the introductions to Elizabeth's family, and exchanged banal pleasantries, Mr Bingley exclaimed, "Why, Darcy! I had no idea that you would be here today!"

"Indeed, sir!" Miss Bingley chimed in, her brow furrowing slightly at the close proximity between the gentleman and Elizabeth. "Are you here to congratulate Lady Elizabeth on finding her true family as well?"

"I have known of Lady Elizabeth's parentage for some time, Miss Bingley."

"Oh! Uh…how marvellous!" After a slightly pained expression left her face, she once again addressed Elizabeth with an air of false civility. "You must forgive my sister, Lady Elizabeth, for Mrs Hurst wished to call as well, but I am sorry to say she is suffering from a headache."

"Please express my sympathies, and I thank you for extending her well wishes," Elizabeth responded, purposely avoiding the suggestion of another invitation to her guest.

Miss Bingley then proceeded to compliment the countess on her arrangements and attire. As Elizabeth ignored her caller's insipid chatter, she was dismayed to discover Mr Bingley seemed yet again enthralled by Jane's beauty. Her annoyance, however, was soon replaced by amusement as she watched both Lord Lisle and Colonel

Fitzwilliam intercept all of his efforts to engage Jane in conversation. The mischievous twinkle in the colonel's eyes proved how diverting he found his current task, and it was all Elizabeth could do to rein in her laughter.

As her shoulders shook with barely suppressed mirth, Darcy looked to her in puzzlement. When she lightly touched his forearm and nodded her head in Jane's direction, he coughed slightly in his attempts to conceal his humour. Unfortunately, his actions alerted Miss Bingley to their merriment, and her eyes widened upon seeing Elizabeth's hand resting on Darcy's arm. Resuming a more proper distance from the gentleman at her side, Elizabeth smiled at Miss Bingley.

"My goodness, Lady Elizabeth! It appears your friendship with Mr Darcy must have improved greatly since we were last in company at Netherfield, for I seem to remember the two of you spent most of your time arguing!"

"As I have already told your brother, Miss Bingley, there is nothing wrong with lively debate. I happen to appreciate Lady Elizabeth's intelligence and her willingness to challenge me, particularly when I am in the wrong."

"Whatever could you mean by that?" Miss Bingley's voice had lost its pandering quality. "How could Miss Eliza —excuse me, *Lady Elizabeth*—possibly provide correction to an esteemed gentleman such as yourself?"

Clearly recognising the opportunity for a lark, Nicholas intervened in the conversation with a look of sheer devilry. "My word, Miss Bingley! You would make my future brother seem to be a man without fault! I hate to disappoint you, Darcy, but I cannot agree with such a depiction. I also doubt my dear sister would wish to live out her days with such a paragon!"

"Future—future brother, my lord?" Miss Bingley stuttered, her complexion taking on a mottled hue that clashed horribly with her chosen gown.

"Pardon, for I fear I have truly made a muddle of

things," Nicholas continued with a false look of chagrin at Elizabeth. "The announcement will appear in the papers tomorrow, but I suppose amongst Darcy's old acquaintances, such as you and your brother, I might be forgiven for such a transgression. My sister and Mr Darcy will marry later this year."

The silence that followed Grey's pronouncement caught the attention of their other caller, as Mr Bingley turned to Darcy and exclaimed with a jolly smile, "You are to be married? Congratulations, my friend, though I could not be more surprised!"

"I cannot regret my absence these past few weeks, Bingley. I have been more agreeably engaged," Darcy chuckled with a smile at Elizabeth.

"Indeed you have. You have spent your time well, my friend!"

Throughout this exchange, Elizabeth kept her gaze on Miss Bingley, fearful of the reaction that would occur once the lady's shock had passed. Fortunately, the allotted fifteen minutes of their call had elapsed, and so Elizabeth's mother rose gracefully from her seat to initiate their guests' departure.

"I thank you both for visiting my daughter, but I am afraid we have additional callers to entertain."

At this clear dismissal, Mr Bingley stood to collect his sister, all the while looking over his shoulder at Jane who was in fervent discussion with Lord Lisle and had only nodded slightly at his parting. With her brother's hand upon her arm, Miss Bingley rose reluctantly from her chair as she stuttered out a suitable response. It was fortunate she was reasonably cowed by the presence of an earl and countess, for Elizabeth was certain the young woman's displeasure and shock might have been voiced in a far less palatable manner had the news of her engagement to Darcy been shared in a less intimidating setting. Once the door closed behind the Bingley siblings, the gathered company breathed a collective sigh of relief.

"That was a risky ploy, dear brother."

"I will not apologise," Nicholas replied with a smug grin.

"You certainly possess a knack for drama," their father commented, his amusement clearly plain upon his features.

Turning from her family, Elizabeth looked to Darcy to gauge his reaction to the leave-taking of his friend. In a low voice she said, "I hope this did not make matters awkward for you and Mr Bingley in the future, Fitzwilliam, for I know how you value his friendship."

"You need not worry," he replied, speaking softly while taking her hand once more. "Bingley is an amiable fellow, and if this means I will rarely keep company with his sister, I could not be less bothered. *You* are my first priority, and anyone who dares to slight you will not be tolerated."

"I believe it will be no hardship to welcome such care, my darling." Elizabeth's brilliant smile lit up her dark brown eyes.

"Indeed, my love, for I have resolved that we will be the happiest of couples. I will spend the rest of my life endeavouring to inspire those beautiful smiles and your bewitching laughter. We shall be very happy indeed, dearest Elizabeth, very happy indeed!"

EPILOGUE

Pemberley
Summer 1817

Standing in front of the long windows in Pemberley's elegant parlour, Lady Elizabeth Darcy quietly sipped her cup of tea whilst keeping watch over the main drive to the house, intently looking for any signs of an approaching carriage. As the summer months drew to a close, she eagerly anticipated their annual house party that would culminate with the celebration of her twenty-sixth year. Whilst enjoying a rare moment of calm in one of her favourite rooms before their guests arrived, Elizabeth took the time to peruse her latest letter from Jane.

In the early autumn before her marriage to Mr Darcy, Elizabeth had hosted Jane at Heatherton Hall, and it was there she had met her husband, Mr Daniel Winters. The somewhat shy but rather handsome parson fell in love quite quickly with the angelic Miss Bennet, and Elizabeth was pleased to see Jane settled so happily in the parish adjoining her father's estate.

With enthusiasm leaping from the page, her sister described every detail of their newest niece, for Jane and her husband had journeyed to Meryton for the birth of Mary's first child. Only two years past, Mary had wed their uncle Philips's clerk, Mr Thaddeus Brown, and as they resided only a scant distance from Longbourn, Mary had requested the presence of the always serene Jane at her lying-in. Elizabeth well understood that Mary required additional aid to keep Mrs Bennet's nervous fluttering out of the confinement chamber, and so Jane had happily travelled from Staffordshire to be of assistance.

Delighted by Jane's effusions over the sweet infant, Elizabeth's smile only grew as the door to the parlour opened and in walked a most welcomed sight. Her husband strolled to her side and placed a gentle kiss to her temple, while shifting the precious bundle securely held in his arms.

"I happened to look in the nursery on my way down, and it seems *someone* could sense the imminent arrival of our guests."

Elizabeth's eyes met those of her sleepy daughter, still clearly struggling to throw off the last vestiges of her shortened nap. Her little hands were clutched securely around her papa's neck, and her riotous dark curls, a perfect match in colour to her father's, spilled across his shoulder.

"Which means that this little one was gazing up at you with those big brown eyes of hers and you simply could not resist. Do not try to fool me, Fitzwilliam. You can admit to dreading how much you will have to share Amelia Jane over the next few weeks."

With an adorable pout, Darcy ran a light hand through their daughter's curls. "'Tis not fair. While I do not begrudge the amount of time your parents spend with our children, considering the additions of my aunt and uncle, Richard, and your brother, I shall never be able to steal her away."

"Does Lisle not count in this list of meddling relatives?" Elizabeth giggled.

"He will be too occupied with his own daughter to try and take away mine, and I must admit, I believe I will thoroughly enjoy his efforts to chase after little Eleanor through Pemberley's halls."

Pressing a kiss to their daughter's head, he looked to Elizabeth and the letter in her hand. "What news from Mrs Winters?"

"Mary has given birth to a daughter, so we shall have to visit Meryton and Longbourn on our way into town."

"Of course, my love. I know the children will wish to visit their new cousin, as well as their aunts and Grandmother and Grandfather Bennet."

Distracted by the sight of dust clouds and an approaching carriage in the distance, Elizabeth made a small murmur of agreement before directing her husband towards the door to begin the long walk towards the entrance hall. Upon exiting the parlour, Elizabeth spotted Mrs Reynolds in conversation with a maid, clearly seeing to some final preparations, and motioned to her.

"Yes, my lady?" the housekeeper enquired.

"The carriages are approaching. Would you please be so kind as to inform Miss Darcy in the music room?"

"Certainly, madam," she responded as she turned towards the east wing, but not before directing a wide smile at the image of the master of the house speaking quietly with his little daughter, her small, chubby hands framing his face as she giggled at her papa.

Warmed by the sight herself, Elizabeth took a moment to once again reflect upon how blessed she was, not only in regards to her family, but also for those who cared for them so diligently.

When she first visited Pemberley, Elizabeth had been understandably overwhelmed at the thought of becoming its mistress, even after spending several months at her family's seat. Though Darcy had been thoroughly confident in Elizabeth's capabilities, it had been the calm and steady reassurance of Mrs Reynolds that had allowed Elizabeth to assume her new position with relative ease.

After the Darcys descended the grand staircase, Amelia Jane, who was now fully roused from her earlier slumber, began reaching towards her mother.

Elizabeth held out her arms as her husband transferred their youngest child. "Come to Mama, darling!" she cooed.

As Amelia Jane started to babble, the sound of pattering footsteps reached Elizabeth's ears just as her husband's deep voice called out in a warning tone.

"Alexander!"

Turning back towards the staircase, Elizabeth took in the sight of her son, a near perfect miniature of his father at only three and a half years of age, who wore a guilty expression as he clung to the banister. Despite his prominent Darcy features, their little scamp shared his mother's more precocious temperament, something her husband both delighted in and feared, as his son possessed little akin to caution. After promptly dismissing the nursemaid who had hurried after her wayward charge, Darcy addressed the sheepish boy at his feet.

"What have I told you about running down the staircase, Alexander?"

Looking down at his feet, Elizabeth could barely hear her son mumble, "To not to."

"Alexander?" his father queried, his quiet, but stern voice demanding a more thorough response.

Dropping his arms to his sides, Alexander gazed upon his father with a matching serious expression and responded in an earnest tone, "'Tis not proper or safe. Sorry, Papa."

"I know you are excited for our guests, but you must not disregard the rules, for they exist to keep you from harm. Also, I expect you to set a good example for Cousin Ellie."

"I will, Papa. I promise."

After another brief moment's pause, Darcy lifted Alexander into his arms, twirling him around to their son's great delight. Observing these precious, unguarded moments with their children, Elizabeth thought on how fatherhood had softened her husband's more fastidious edges. The same, unfortunately, could not be said for his valet, who Elizabeth feared was only one more ruined cravat away from giving his notice.

As soon as Georgiana had joined their party, the Darcy family descended the front steps as the first carriage came to a halt. After catching only a brief glimpse of the Matlock crest, the carriage door swung open to reveal a clearly exasperated Richard, who nearly bounded towards his awaiting hosts.

"I require rescue, Darcy! My mother has spent the last two hours taking full advantage of my captivity to enumerate the many qualities of the latest candidate she has procured as her next daughter-in-law."

"What is this foolishness, Richard?"

At the sound of Lady Matlock's voice, the welcoming party turned to the guests just stepping down from the carriage. After embracing Georgiana and sending a reproving look to her youngest child, Lady Matlock approached on the arm of her husband to greet Elizabeth with a kiss to her cheek.

"My dear, she is simply beautiful! Look at how Amelia Jane has grown since we last saw her, Hugh!"

Possessed of her father's more reserved nature, the child buried her head into Elizabeth's neck as her great-aunt stroked her dark mass of curls.

"Pray do not take offence," Elizabeth implored. "She will be far more relaxed in company once she adjusts to the presence of so many guests."

The opening of a second carriage door drew Elizabeth's attention as Lord Lisle stepped out, lifted his fair-haired daughter onto one arm, and held out the other to assist his wife. It was during Elizabeth's first full Season that she met the beautiful and rather bold Lady Rosalind Montgomery.

Despite the recommendation of her mother and Lady Matlock, Elizabeth had faced considerable hostility from the other young ladies of the *ton*, much of it owed to her good fortune in winning the love and affection of Mr Darcy, who had been quite sought-after for several years.

Lady Rosalind had come to her rescue during a dinner party when the gentlemen were still lingering over their brandies, and had valiantly delivered some rather cutting remarks to a chorus of spiteful women busily speculating over how the newly discovered Lady Elizabeth had ensnared one of England's wealthiest bachelors. Thereafter, the two women developed a firm friendship, and during an evening's entertainment at Darcy House, Elizabeth had introduced Lady Rosalind to Lord Lisle, leading to a whirlwind courtship and happy marriage.

"Rosalind!" Elizabeth cried as she walked in her direction. "'Tis so good to see you! Was the journey comfortable enough?"

"Of course, Elizabeth! It is not far from Matlock, you know, though I must grant that little Ellie severely tried her papa's patience."

With a rueful chuckle, Lord Lisle set Eleanor down and anxiously watched her scramble over to Alexander to join in whatever amusements Uncle Richard seemed apt to provide.

Just when her arms began to grow heavy under the weight of her daughter, Elizabeth was relieved of her precious burden by Darcy, who had once again come to her side.

Looking to his cousin, her husband remarked with a smirk, "I fear Richard is already organising some mischief with our children, Lisle. You may want to see that he does not get carried away before reinforcements arrive."

"Too late, Darcy, for it seems the final carriage is here."

As the last equipage came to a halt upon Pemberley's long front drive, Elizabeth watched her brother and parents disembark and make their way to the gathered crowd. A moment before he could open his mouth in greeting, Elizabeth's brother was ambushed by his excited nephew.

"Uncle Nicholas! Uncle Nicholas!"

"Alex, my boy!" Elizabeth's brother picked up the tiny lad and ruffled his dark curls before setting him down again so he could greet his grandparents.

After extracting a promise from his favourite uncle to join whatever scheme Richard had devised, Elizabeth watched her happy son run back towards the front lawn as she turned to hug and kiss her parents.

"My word, Elizabeth, he looks more like his father every day!"

Elizabeth directed a brilliant smile at her husband. "I do believe Fitzwilliam will tire of such comments as quickly as you and I did during my first Season. Though I must own, I think it absolutely wonderful that he takes after his handsome papa."

"At least my Amelia Jane was given her mother's beautiful eyes," Darcy added before reluctantly passing his daughter to her grandfather's waiting arms.

Elizabeth observed the now familiar look of contentment that spread across the earl's face as he smiled down at his granddaughter. As long as he was holding Amelia Jane, Elizabeth believed he could never be anything less than completely satisfied. While she did not doubt he loved both of his grandchildren equally, there was something about her little girl that had healed her father's heart from the pain of her disappearance all those years ago.

"Well, Elizabeth, shall I escort this little lady to the lawn so she can see what her brother and Ellie are doing?"

"Just be mindful to find some shade. I confess, I have quite given up on keeping her cap upon her head with all those curls!"

With an amused smile and a swift kiss to her cheek, her father strolled off to assist the major general in his attempts to corral the troops, and her mother followed alongside. Elizabeth linked arms with her husband and her brother, and the trio began to walk towards one of the towering Spanish chestnut trees under which the children and adults had assembled. With a parting kiss to Elizabeth's hand, Darcy jogged forward to sweep up a giggling Alexander, who was trying to coax his poor Uncle Richard into yet another race.

Sighing as she leaned against her brother's arm, Elizabeth remarked, "I am glad you have all come. Never shall I take for granted how blessed I am to have such a family."

"We are the ones who are blessed. Our first meeting in Hyde Park was nothing short of miraculous, for look what joy your recovery has brought to all of our lives! I never imagined I could be this content, and I look forward to watching such happiness grow."

To all this, Lady Elizabeth Darcy could only nod her fervent agreement, convinced that despite the difficulties they had endured to reach such bliss, every moment had been worth the undoubtedly priceless and charming picture before her.

The End

Subscribers to the Quills & Quartos mailing list receive advance notice of new releases and sales, and exclusive bonus content and short stories. To join, visit us at www.QuillsandQuartos.com

ACKNOWLEDGMENTS

Only through the constant support and encouragement of my parents, sister, aunts, grandparents, and friends was the writing of this book made possible. I have been blessed with a devoted group of readers who pored over each chapter and motivated me to continue my efforts until the final word was typed upon the page. Special thanks are given to both my mom and dad, my mom being the book's most devoted fan and reviewer, and my dad for his assertion many years ago that I would one day be an author.

I also would like to sincerely thank the team at Quills & Quartos—Jan Ashton, Amy D'Orazio, and Debbie Styne—for their hard work and encouragement which made this book a reality. To Jan, I will always be grateful for her early support and thoughtful guidance in helping me fine-tune the direction of this novel, and to Debbie, I could not have been blessed with a more constructive editor to kindly lead me through this process. Also, my heartfelt gratitude to Susan Adriani for designing a beautiful cover for this book!

ABOUT THE AUTHOR

L. M. Romano is, as Miss Bingley would say, 'a great reader', though she still owns to taking delight in many things. As an inveterate bookworm and a longtime lover of historical fiction, she is delighted to present her debut novel, *Forgotten Betrothal*, as a tribute to her love for the works and characters created by Jane Austen. As a history professor, she eagerly embraced the opportunity to delve into Regency England and the many facets of London's high society, which provided endless evenings of entertainment for both herself and any unfortunate family members who happened to be nearby.

A Northern California native, L. M. Romano currently lives with her husband in Ontario, Calif. She plans to continue writing, teaching, and reading countless books to her heart's content.